DEVILS AND DETAILS

ORDINARY MAGIC - BOOK TWO

ALSO BY DEVON MONK

Ordinary Magic:
Death and Relaxation
Devils and Details
Gods and Ends

Shame and Terric:
Backlash

House Immortal:
House Immortal
Infinity Bell
Crucible Zero

Broken Magic:
Hell Bent
Stone Cold

Allie Beckstrom:
Magic to the Bone
Magic in the Blood
Magic in the Shadows
Magic on the Storm
Magic at the Gate
Magic on the Hunt
Magic on the Line
Magic without Mercy
Magic for a Price

Age of Steam:
Dead Iron
Tin Swift
Cold Copper

Short Fiction:
A Cup of Normal (collection)
Yarrow, Sturdy and Bright (Once Upon a Curse anthology)

DEVILS AND DETAILS

ORDINARY MAGIC - BOOK TWO

DEVON MONK

Devils and Details Copyright © 2016 by Devon Monk

eBook ISBN: 978-1-939853-03-5
Paperback ISBN: 978-1-939853-04-2

Published by: Odd House Press
Art by: Lou Harper
Interior Design by: Indigo Chick Designs

DEDICATION

To the dreamers and mischief makers.
And to my family, who are often both.

CHAPTER 1

OLD ROAD out in the middle of nowhere?

Check.

All by myself with no cell signal?

Check.

Chainsaw-wielding maniac glaring at me through his one good eye?

Check.

Hello, Monday morning.

Chainsaw maniac was also dripping wet in the middle of a truly violent thunder storm and pointing the growling three-foot bar of rotating teeth toward me threateningly.

I rolled my eyes.

Gods could be such drama queens.

"Shut it down," I yelled over the buzz of the machine in Odin's gnarled hands. "Now." Just for good measure, I dragged fingers across my throat in a "kill it" gesture.

He yelled something which I couldn't hear over the blast of thunder that knuckled across the clouds. I was pretty good at reading lips, especially when the lips were using four-letter words.

I put one hand on my hip, the other dug the citation book out of my light jacket. It was August and the little town of Ordinary, Oregon, should have been sunny and dry. Instead, it'd been raining pretty much non-stop since July.

Our daily thunder storm sieges were courtesy of Thor, who was upset he wasn't on vacation here with the other gods.

"I will write you up." Odin couldn't hear me, but it turned out he was pretty good at guessing at a message too. Didn't hurt that I clicked the pen and poised it over the citation pad, giving him one last warning look.

He killed the motor on the saw.

Good choice.

"I'm busy, Delaney." He waved one beefy hand at the

stacks of timber—maple, oak, cedar, and a smaller pile of myrtle—surrounding him. Most of the logs were covered in bark, moss, and various fungi, but a few were cut down into butter-brown lengths and chunks. Wet piles of sawdust humped across the area to the side of his little house in the forest. More wood debris pillowed up against the poles of the tarp he'd been working under, and a thin coating of dust sprayed over the round of oak he'd been cutting through.

"This can't wait," I said. "If you need me to pull out my badge and drag you into town, I will. Or you can get out of the rain and get this meeting over with."

"Meeting," he scoffed.

"You think it's a joke?"

"Crow called for it, didn't he? Of course it's a joke. Waste of time."

"Crow has your power—has all the gods' powers," I reminded him. "He said it's important."

"Never trust a trickster, Chief Reed."

"It won't take long. Your soggy logs will be here. Sooner we leave, the sooner you'll get back."

I eyed the massive chainsaw that he held as if it were no more than a steak knife. "Crow's allowed to call an emergency meeting of deities."

"Pranks and parties," Odin growled. "What does he know about emergencies?"

"Well, since I'm sure he's caused quite a few in his time, I expect he can identify one correctly."

Odin grumbled and snarled. The thunderstorm grumbled and snarled back, flashes of lightning blinking away the mid-day gloom.

"I have a lot of work to do." He waved again at the pile of wood behind him. "It's been a slow year. This art isn't going to make itself."

Odin made his living selling chainsaw art. He was great with the chainsaw part of chainsaw art, but he wasn't all that good with the art part.

"Odin." I waited out a crack of thunder. "Come with me. We'll deal with Crow's emergency, then I'll go home and get dry, and you'll come back and make bigger piles of sawdust.

Deal?"

He curled his lip.

"I have a thermos of hot coffee in the Jeep. All yours."

His snarl disappeared as the reality of a nice hot cup of coffee soaked into his chainsaw-rattled brain.

The rain, which had been steady and cold, turned hard and freezing. It was like some god up there was pelting us with frozen marbles.

"Fine," he said. "Fine. This better not take all day."

He stowed the saw under the tarp, took one lazy swipe at the sawdust and wood chips covering his face and short beard, then stomped over to the Jeep. The Jeep bent under his weight as he crammed his huge shoulders, muscles, and girth into the front seat. He didn't bother with the seatbelt.

Thunder cracked again, rain going liquid and gloopy, drenching me even beneath my rainproof jacket.

Thanks a lot, Thor.

As if in answer to my thought, thunder chuckled across the hills.

ORDINARY STRETCHED along the Oregon coast, a small vacation town where gods kicked off their powers like a pair of old shoes and went about living a normal life among the creatures and mortals who lived here year round.

A Reed such as myself had always been in Ordinary. I'd grown up here with my two younger sisters, Myra and Jean. After our dad's death a year ago, I had taken over his place as Chief of Police. Myra and Jean worked with me, keeping the peace in the sleepy little tourist town.

We Reeds were mortal, with a twist. Our family line had been chosen by the gods for one important thing: to uphold the rules and laws of Ordinary by making sure god powers were guarded and the secrets of gods and creatures who resided in Ordinary remained just that.

I loved my job, loved taking care of Ordinary and all the creatures, deities, and mortals within its boundaries. Even with all the trouble that came with those responsibilities, I still managed to live a pretty normal life.

Why just a couple months ago, my heart had been broken by Ryder Bailey, the man I'd been infatuated with for most of my life. I pushed the thoughts of Ryder way, way to the back of my brain where there were so many pushed-away thoughts of him it was standing room only.

Still, it was better to keep my mind on my job instead of on things I couldn't change.

When gods vacationed in Ordinary, they became mortal. That meant they could get sick, hurt, or killed just like any other mortal. Like the fisherman Heim, who was also the Norse god, Heimdall, who had washed ashore dead. I'd not only tracked down the killer, I had also found a mortal to take on his god power before it tore apart the town.

That mortal was my ex-boyfriend, Cooper Clark.

Like that hadn't been awkward. *Hey, I know you and I used to date, and you dumped me at my father's funeral, but would you like to be a god?*

Okay, maybe my life wasn't exactly normal.

"What?" Odin snapped. His beefy arms strained to cross over his chest like twisted tree trunks.

"What?" I flicked the windshield wipers up a notch and slowed for the puddle that spread across one-and-a-half lanes of the main road through town. If Thor didn't get over his temper tantrum and give us a break, we were going to have to close roads and issue flood warnings.

"You look worried." He shrugged as if uncomfortable admitting he was paying that much attention to me.

"It hasn't stopped raining for five weeks, tourist dollars are way down, we've got a fundraiser coming up this week, one month of summer left, and our resident trickster is calling an emergency meeting. A little concern isn't out of place here."

"Think he's leaving?"

"Crow?" He'd been in town all my life. I'd grown up thinking of him as an uncle. It would be a different town without him. "I don't know."

"It'd be better without him."

"Right. Because unleashing the trickster god upon the living world would make our lives any easier. Gods leave here and the first thing they do is remind us that they have their full powers back."

Thunder broke the sky in half and set off several car alarms. "Point proven," I said.

"You like him."

"Crow? The annoying not-my-uncle?"

Odin wore an eyepatch over his left eye. So he had to lean forward and twist to make eye contact with me. "He's one of your favorites."

"And you think of Thor as a son."

"I know Thor," he said as if that answered everything. "So should you."

"I know the mortal Thorne Jameson." I slowed for the light, then turned into the parking lot outside Crow's glassblowing shop. "Decent voice, good taste in vinyls. Collects rubber duckies. But once he picked up that power and went full god of thunder? I don't know that guy hardly at all."

"You know the god power doesn't completely swallow our personality, nor does the lack erase it."

"Meaning?"

"Crow is a trickster whether he's carrying the power of Raven or just blowing balls for tourists."

I put the Jeep in park, biting back my smile. "You know how that sounds, right?"

He plucked at the dusty sleeve of his flannel shirt. "I meant it how it sounds. Crow isn't your uncle. He is just very patient."

"Patient?"

"He knows what he wants, Delaney Reed. And, like a spider, he will wait for his moment to strike."

I studied his face. No bluff and bluster there. Odin was very serious.

But Odin didn't exactly get along with the other gods in Ordinary. The rivalry between Zeus and him was on a constant simmer. The petty shots they took at each other's businesses and life choices kept Aaron, who was Ares the god of war, in a constant state of entertainment.

Other than Thor, who had picked up his power and was therefore unable to return to Ordinary for a year, Odin wasn't really buddies with the other deities.

"You think Crow's pulling a long con?"

Odin's deep blue eye shadowed down darker. A chill washed up my wet, cold skin. Just because gods put down their power didn't mean there wasn't an echo, a coal of it caught somewhere deep within them. They were mortal, but they were still the vessels of god power. It made them uncannily charismatic. It made them the flame mortal moths were all too tempted to fly into. And even that tiny spark was enough to make a regular gal like me sit up and take notice.

"Only Crow would know. But he has spent many years becoming your friend, Delaney. Your lifetime. Have you ever asked yourself why?"

"Because he likes me?" I gave him an innocent blink.

He grunted.

"Because I'm likable?" I fluttered my eyelashes. "Possibly even adorable?"

"You are not in the least." He tried to scowl, but the smile won out.

"Because Crow and all the rest of the gods in town are happy that the family job of keeping this town safe fell into my adorable, capable, likable hands?"

"We've had better police chiefs."

"Since when?"

He shrugged one mountainous shoulder. "I'm sure you weren't born yet."

"Well, then I'm the best you've had in ages."

He grunted. "I promised your father I'd keep my eye on you. Since I only have the one, I trust you won't make me strain it."

Oh. This was what he was getting at.

My dad had driven off a cliff. Crashed down and died right off a road he'd driven all his life. It had come as a shock to everyone in town: gods, mortals, creatures, and most of all, his daughters.

But I guess sometime before that, he had asked the gods to look after me, to help me as I took on his position as not only the police chief but also as the only person who could transfer god powers to a new mortal if a god died.

I might not be a friend to all the gods in town, but my

father...my father had been respected by them. As far as I could tell, the gods had promised to help me if I needed it.

It was annoying. And kind of nice.

"If I need help, I'll ask."

He studied me, and I was caught again by that magnetic pull of power echoing in him. Good thing my Reed blood was immune to such things. We Reeds were fire-proof little moths.

"Good." He nodded once. "Your father was too stubborn. He should have asked for help much sooner. Maybe things would have gone better for him."

"What does that mean? What things? What better?"

But he was already barging out of the Jeep, the door swinging wide so rain and wind could flip through the paper clipboard in the backseat and rattle the sack of groceries on the floor. The door slammed shut.

I took a deep breath to calm myself. Odin might not have meant anything by that comment except that my dad was stubborn and didn't know when to ask for help.

Another family trait.

Still, it had seemed like there was something Odin regretted. Some decision my father had made that Odin thought should have been vetted through the gods.

And while it was interesting that Odin was hinting about it, more interesting was that he was telling me about it now.

I wondered if it had something to do with Crow's emergency.

I flipped up the collar on my coat and stepped out of the Jeep. A fistful of rain slapped at my face and more trickled down the back of my neck as I crossed the parking lot to the shop's door.

Not even a little bit funny, Thor.

Lightning cracked like a wink. Thunder *ho-ho*'d on the horizon.

Jackass.

The parking lot was full of cars and the shop windows glowed a soft yellow. The neon CLOSED sign burned blue, keeping away waterlogged tourists who were probably disappointed they'd packed bug spray instead of waterproofing.

13

"How about you lay off the water works for the rest of summer?" I muttered to the sky, knowing Thor wouldn't listen to me. "We got nothing but wet to look forward to until next June. Can't you give us a break before you drown us?"

My phone rang. I curled my hand around it but didn't pull it out of my coat pocket yet. Odin stood in the doorway, bracing the door open with one big arm. He wasn't looking at me. He was scowling at the interior of the shop.

"Thanks." I checked the number on my phone. Ryder.

My heart stuttered into tiny beats and the world did that fade-away thing. All the Ryder thoughts I'd pushed off spilled out of my brain closet and started a party, front and center.

Ryder Bailey had been my childhood obsession, my pre-teen dream, my teen angst. I'd been in love with the man before I even understood that love might add up to something more than holding hands and swapping sandwiches at lunch.

After an eight-year absence, he'd come back to Ordinary, set up his own architecture business and, wonder of wonders, dated me.

Once.

Apparently, me taking a bullet was the deal-breaker for our relationship. He'd had his fun, we'd tumbled into bed for exactly one night, then just slightly slower-than-a-speeding-bullet, he was over me.

I still wasn't over him being over me.

Stupid heart.

"Hey," I answered, out of breath, even though it wasn't physical exertion that made my lungs malfunction.

Three months. We'd been working together off and on, me the Police Chief him our only Reserve Officer, for three months. I'd done my best not to be anywhere near him.

My sisters had wanted to kick him off the force completely, but we needed the manpower. Since they couldn't kick him out, they'd resorted to giving him the crap jobs, scheduling him opposite me, and occasionally making him ride along with them and their silent disapproval.

"Are you naked?" His voice was low, warm, teasing. If I didn't know better, I'd think he'd been drinking.

Whoa. Not what I'd expected. I pulled the phone away

from my ear to glance at the screen, then pulled it back so I could talk.

"Are you drunk? This is Delaney," I said. "Police Chief Delaney."

"I know."

Nothing but the soft sound of his breathing and a background noise I couldn't quite place. Cars? Voices?

"I'm at work," I said, happy that the words came out steady. "I don't know where you are, or what you think you're doing, but don't call me like this, Ryder."

"Wait. Delaney." His phone moved and a whoosh of wind gurgled down the line. "I thought you'd be in bed..."

A horn honked, and then another. A bus or something bigger...subway maybe, clogged up the background.

Where ever he was, it wasn't Ordinary. And from the slight softening at the end of his words, I'd say he was either exhausted or under the influence.

"Are you all right?" It was the best I could give him. Just because he broke my heart didn't mean I shouldn't worry about his well-being.

That was sort of the job description of being police chief. I'd be just as concerned for anyone else's well-being in Ordinary.

Liar, my heart whispered.

"Hell, I didn't think. What time is it?" he said. "I'm sorry."

"Ryder? You need back up?"

He chuckled a little at that, then the sound behind him grew louder, like maybe a lot of cars had all roared to life inside a parking garage.

"No, thanks. I'm good. I just. I wasn't thinking. Sorry about that, Chief. Should have listened and had the extra orange and cookie. Dizzy. What time is it? Oh. Morning."

"Ryder?" That slightly defeated tone in his voice kicked spikes through my heart. He sounded like he was saying good-bye. Like he was making a last call before being shipped off into something dangerous.

But Ryder was an architect. He didn't lead a dangerous life.

"I'm good. And Delaney? It's really nice to hear your voice. Sorry I...just sorry."

He hung up.

He hung up on me.

My heart rattled back into place like a dropped dinner dish, swirling, swirling to a ragged clatter.

Why had he called me? Why had I heard fear in his voice, or if not fear, worry, tension?

Why had he sounded like a man who'd been given his last phone call and had decided to waste it on a woman he'd dumped?

Why was I still staring at the disconnected screen on my phone?

I was dimly aware of Odin dragging his arm away, the door shutting, the room quieting. I looked up.

Dozens of gods were staring at me.

Neat.

More than half of them looked like they could read my mind and knew exactly all the things I was thinking about Ryder. How much I still cared for him even though he dumped me. How much I wanted to be his friend–no, how much I wanted to be more than that. How much my heart would jump at the chance to have him again, even though my mind knew that could never happen.

He had dumped me while I was lying in a hospital bed, shot. There was no chance for us, he'd made that clear. And I wouldn't let him hurt me again. I was done being burned by the men I thought loved me. I was fine being alone and didn't need to share my crazy life with anyone.

Then why did the sound of Ryder's voice make me so lonely?

I pocketed my cell and tipped my chin up, the drip of rain slithering from my long braid down my back. "All right. Where's the emergency?"

I did a quick head count. Twenty-five deities in the room. I knew them all, from Athena to Zeus. As per the rules of vacationing in Ordinary, they all had regular mortal jobs and gave back to the community in some way.

Death, who went by the name, Than, was the newest god

to give this vacation thing a whirl and had been in Ordinary for the last three months. He stood off to the right of the room, close to the glass blowing furnaces Crow used to make his glass art, and where Crow taught tourists how to make their own fragile, molten treasures.

Than was tall, thin to the point of gauntness, and austere in his manners. Today's outfit was a bright pink shirt with the outline of Bigfoot centered above words that said: UNBELIEVABLY ORDINARY. Over that, he wore a black Hawaiian shirt with what I hoped were oddly phallic geoducks. If not, then he needed an X-rating on that shirt.

His black hair was shaved close to his skull, and his eyes missed nothing as he silently considered each and every deity in the room. When he met my gaze, his expression was quiet and intense, studying me. He blinked once, a slow closing of that invasive gaze, and I found it suddenly easier to breathe.

He didn't smile—he never smiled—but there was the glimmer of wry humor in the angle of his eyebrow. He was enjoying this turn of events, this new, ordinary life he was living.

The gods could live, work, and even fall in love in Ordinary. However, procreating while in Ordinary was not allowed.

So far, none of the gods had wanted to have kids during their vacation time which meant, so far, I hadn't had to ban any of them from Ordinary.

The other deities shuffled and shoved Crow forward into the center of the room. They formed a half ring around him. None of them seemed happy to have been dragged away from their jobs and lives for the man who now stood in the middle of the room.

"Crow," I said.

"Delaney Reed." He gave me a smile that looked like he'd just swallowed needles. "Good of you to come."

"You called. We're here. What's the emergency?"

He wore a white T-shirt under a flannel hoodie. The white shirt brought out the coppery darkness of his skin and made his brown eyes glow beneath artistically messy black hair. He stuck his hands in the front pockets of his jeans.

"There's a...situation."

I waited for him to continue. We all waited. It was uncomfortable.

"Get on with it!" Odin yelled.

So much for order. A crack of thunder rattled windows and made the blown glass items shelved around the room shiver.

"The...uh...there's a problem." Crow's gaze fixed on me. He was sweating, a sheen across his forehead and upper lip. His eyes held an emotion I was pretty sure was fear.

I'd never seen him look this way before.

Never.

"It's okay." My instincts went red alert. "We'll figure it out. What's the problem?"

"The...uh...the...powers?"

I didn't know why he was asking me something about the powers. He had them. Locked up in the old furnace in the back corner of his shop. Once a year, all the god powers got moved to a new keeper. That person was always a god, and since the stored powers moved around, even the strongest rivals couldn't complain about some god unfairly having say over where their power was, and how it was being guarded.

"I know of them," I said dryly.

"They're sort of..." he shrugged.

"What does that mean? Use your words."

Twin droplets of sweat traced downward from his temples. His clenched smile looked like it would crack a molar.

"How about you show me?" I suggested.

He nodded, stiff as a shadow puppet, before he walked off to the furnace.

"It's...not as bad as it looks." His hand hesitated on the latch.

"Just open the oven, Crow."

"I called you." As if making that point was important. "I called *everyone* as soon as I realized."

"Realized what?"

He pulled the old metal door open, hinges grinding.

The furnace was empty. Cold. No god powers flickered there like flames made of crushed stars. No god powers sang there in the voices and orchestras only I seemed to be able to hear.

The furnace that should be filled to roaring with the power of each and every deity in this room was empty.

"Where are they?" I said into the hush. "Where are all the powers?"

Crow shook his head. "I have no idea."

LITTLE KNOWN fact: a room full of angry gods sounds a lot like a bingo hall fight. There was a lot of finger-pointing, insults, charges of cheating, grudges, moral lapses, and bad fashion choices. None of it had anything to do with the matter at hand.

"Enough!" I yelled from near the empty furnace. Crow was hiding behind me.

Coward.

Not that I was much of a shield against a couple dozen pissed off deities, but frankly, I was probably the only one in the room who didn't want him dead.

"Let's take this one step at a time. First, can any of you sense where your power is?"

A few of them shook their heads. A couple got far-off looks in their eyes as if they were trying to unsuccessfully pull up an old memory.

"No one?" I asked.

Zeus, who was dark-haired, tan-skinned, and kept his goatee trimmed and gelled, lifted one hand, long fingers spread. He was dressed in an elegant charcoal suit that probably cost more than I could get for my Jeep. He ran a high fashion and fancy decor shop for clientele who liked that sort of thing. Even here in this little beachside vacation town on the edge of Oregon, he did brisk business.

"Let me explain," he began, and I braced for a lecture. "Each of us knows that our powers are here. Within the boundaries of Ordinary." He didn't stop and look around the room, but I did.

No one nodded, but they weren't arguing either.

Progress.

I gave Odin the eye. He always argued with Zeus. But even he was silent, thick lips pressed in a tight, thin line.

His silence sent a roll of dread through my stomach. When Zeus and Odin weren't arguing, things were really going to the dogs.

"We know the powers are still together," Zeus continued. He took a breath, considering what to say next. "But without breaking the contract we have all signed to become citizens in Ordinary, there is no more we can do to find our powers."

The only deity who seemed minutely surprised by that was Death, who simply made a small, curious sound in the back of his throat.

Yeah, I had the contract memorized too. There was no drawing upon god power for any reason, for any emergency, life, death, or otherwise while the deity remained within the confines of Ordinary. When a god wanted his or her power back, that transfer was handled by a member of the Reed family. Specifically, me.

And once that power was picked up, the deity was required to leave Ordinary for a full year, no backsies.

That's when it clicked. Someone in this room had broken that rule and remained in town even though he'd pulled on his power.

I glared at Crow. "How did you do it?"

"Do what?" His eyes darted everywhere but my face. "I didn't steal the powers. Why would I steal them when I already *had* them? My power is gone too. I don't know where they are. I didn't do anything!"

His voice went up and up. I'd never seen him this freaked out.

"You have to believe me, Delaney." He wiped his hand over his mouth and finally, his gaze met mine. "I didn't mean for this to happen."

I could feel the anger, the frustration of all the people in the room like a dozen palms flat against my back, pressing me forward, pressing in to crush Crow.

I squared my shoulders and took a breath to calm down. Being angry wasn't going to solve anything. What I needed were facts, options, and action.

And maybe some back up. I considered calling in Myra and Jean. Between the three of us we should be able to keep this gathering from turning into a bloodbath.

Or maybe I should hide Crow somewhere like in a holding cell before the gods put two-and-two together and realized that just because Crow was a trickster and his power had certain flexibility when it came to rule-following, his actions had started these dominos tumbling.

"Raven," Odin grumbled, using Crow's god name, "Answer her."

"I thought I did." Crow's wide eyes asked for my forgiveness. For my mercy.

It was hard to see him like this, my friend. My almost-uncle. Even though he was technically more related to the gods in the room than he was to me, I was the only shield between him and the casually—*creatively*—vengeful deities at my back.

"Facts," I said in my calmest police chief voice. "Let's start there, okay?"

Crow nodded.

"Three months ago, you picked up your power to help me find Cooper Clark so that I could give him Heimdall's power."

"Yes."

"The other gods who picked up their power to help me find Cooper were Hera and Thor."

"Yes."

"Hera and Thor left town for a year, according to the contract." As if to punctuate that statement, thunder thumped across the sky, rattling windows and shelves.

"Yes," Crow whispered.

"You came back to town. You gave your power back into hiding. You broke the rules."

For the first time that day, I saw something other than fear on his handsome face. His eyebrows dipped and his mouth twisted a sideways smile. "Broke is kind of strong...bent, maybe?"

"Broke is exactly strong enough. Because it's the truth. That's the thing that is the opposite of what you usually do."

"Rude." His eyes flicked over my shoulder at the room

full of angry.

"Okay. Okay." He stepped out to stand beside me, though still back far enough I was between him and most of the room. He raised both hands, pleading for his brethren to stay calm.

"I broke the rule. I wasn't thinking clearly. I had my power back and that high, that invincibility of being filled with power..." He bit his bottom lip and shook his head a little. "You all know what it's like. I hadn't picked up my power in years. Decades."

Lightning strobe-lighted the room. Thunder cracked and growled.

"I let it get away from me. The temptation. The possibilities of what I could do with my power, and what my power could do...if I let it."

Someone, I thought maybe Ares, swore.

"This isn't my fault. Not really. Not me, Crow. It's my power, *Raven's* power's fault. Three months with no backlash? It tricked us. I'm as much a victim as you are."

The room dissolved into the bingo-hall shout-down again.

I let them all get it out of their systems.

Crow sidled sideways to get more of me between them and him.

"Nope." I pressed my hand on his upper arm and felt the damp heat of his fear radiating through his thin shirt. "They're not going to kill you. That would get them kicked out of Ordinary for good. They, apparently unlike you, follow the rules in the contract."

I turned. "None of you will kill Crow, because if you do, I will haul you in for murder and then banish you from town for the rest of your existence.

"Since you all know he's complicit in the misplacement of your powers, I will consider each and every one of you a suspect if Crow shows up dead, injured, or sporting so much as a new hangnail. The law is here for a reason, and I'm here to enforce it."

A few feet shuffled. A few voices swore. Finally, Frigg spoke up. She was just under six feet tall, yellow hair pulled back in a single ponytail that fell against her heavy flannel jacket. Her jeans were frayed near the knees, and a smudge of grease streaked one thigh. Her shirt had her towing company's logo over her heart: Frigg's Rigs.

"All right, Delaney," she said calmly. "We know how to follow the rules. And the rules say since Crow picked up his power, he gets kicked out for the next year."

"I agree." Crow made an offended noise. I ignored him. "But first we'll have to find his power so that he and it are out of Ordinary. Was your power in that oven too, Crow?"

He nodded.

"Then we have to find the powers before we can kick him out."

Frigg inhaled, exhaled. "Well, crap."

My thoughts exactly.

"So what we all need to do now is stay calm and start looking. Where could the powers be? Who might have taken them or," I held up my hand to cut off speculation, "could the powers have moved on their own accord, or been drawn away by some other natural or supernatural force?"

The silence was worse than the grumbling. Thunder rumbled, quieter this time. Maybe Thor was done drowning us with his displeasure of having to stay out of town for a year.

Zeus sighed. "Where do you suggest we begin searching, Delaney?"

A few of the gods threw deadly glares toward Crow, but I was pretty sure they wouldn't fire up the murder wagon.

Yet.

"We start with Crow staying with me."

"What?" he protested.

"Under protective custody, if you come with me willingly. Under arrest if you don't."

"Well, seeing as I have *so* many choices…"

"No choices," I said. "You have no choices."

"And then what?" Frigg asked.

"I'd like all of you to let the police handle this. No tearing this town apart on your own."

The room exploded into complaints and groans, and a few outright strings of curses in languages I didn't know.

Was someone swearing in Pig Latin?

I spread my stance, hands tucked on the front edges of my belt.

"We'll look for the powers. We'll question any creatures who might know where the powers could be. We have the resources of the entire town, mortal and creature at our call. You all have businesses to attend. As long as the powers remain in Ordinary, you continue your vacations just as if we knew where the powers were."

"You expect us to do nothing?" Hades spoke from near the back of the room. Hades was built like an ex-football player, wide at shoulders, thick through the chest. Even in slacks and sweater vest pulled over a pale orange button down shirt, he looked like he could break someone in half with a pat on the back.

He ran the frilly little beachside bed and breakfast where each room was decorated in literary themes: romance, mystery, western, historical, fantasy. For a god who ruled the cool, impersonal underworld, he was a happy, I'd dare say even soft-hearted man.

The contrast between what his god power represented, and what he preferred to do on vacation made me wonder once again just how much the gods held on to their mortal personalities even after millennia as deities. Or maybe just how much the gods delighted in doing the exact opposite of their normal god-power duties while on vacation.

"If you think of anything, tell me. If you see anything that could lead to your powers, tell me. If you have a vision or hunch or dream, I want to know. Ordinary is a small town. It shouldn't take us very long to cover it."

Of course I was massively simplifying the problem. It wasn't just finding the powers that was the problem. Whoever or whatever had taken them would need to be dealt with too, even if it was only Raven's own power that had hidden the rest of them away.

I had no idea what sort of creature or person in existence could not only sense god powers, but could also handle them and physically move them.

I made a note to look back over the list of current and

past creatures who had called Ordinary their home. Who in town could touch a god power and not be destroyed by it?

There was another possibility, of course. That the powers had been drawn away by some kind of supernatural force instead of some kind of supernatural being. It was a long shot, since I'd think any number of creatures and deities would feel something hinky going down in town, but it wasn't completely impossible.

But then almost nothing was completely impossible in Ordinary.

We'd need to check in with anyone sensitive enough to the forces, magics, and powers in the town who might have felt a shift.

Which pretty much meant I'd be going door-to-door asking people if they'd felt a disturbance in the Force.

Terrific.

"Well then," Ares, who looked like a twenty-something computer geek and owned the nursery and garden center, clapped his hands together to break the silence. "We have our battle plan. Crow stays with the Chief, the rest of us go back to our daily lives and wait for our powers to show up in the local lost-and-found. Easy."

But of course, the way Ares said it made everyone grumble again.

Just because he wasn't currently the god of war didn't mean he could resist stirring up trouble amongst his neighbors.

I glared at him, and he gave me an angelic smile.

Jerk.

"I know it won't be that easy," I said. "And I know you all are uncomfortable standing on the sidelines of a crime. But it *is* a crime. According to the contract of Ordinary, all crimes are handled by the police. Me. That doesn't mean I don't want your help. If any of you suspect where your powers might be, or who they might be with, call the station. We'll be the point on this investigation, but input on the search is welcome."

There was a general rumble of annoyance and agreement, and then Frigg opened the door.

"We trust you, Delaney," she said. "You've always done right by us." She walked out the door, then jogged through the rain.

The rest of the deities followed her example. Hades, Thanatos, Zeus, Ares, Athena, Brigid, Nortia, Momus, Poseidon, Bast, and many more, gave me a nod or a glare, then stepped out into the rain.

Only Odin and Crow remained behind.

Crow stood with his back against the cold furnace, his eyes closed as he pinched the bridge of his nose. His shoulders were slumped. He looked like a man who had just escaped being mauled by a room full of lions, tigers, and bears.

Close enough.

"Get your coat," I said.

He tipped his head and opened his eyes, but his fingers remained between his eyebrows.

"What?"

"Lock up the shop. We're going now."

"But...what?"

Okay, maybe he was still coming to grips with his near-death experience.

"You're riding with me today. Protective custody. I need to take Odin back to his place. Let's go."

"But my shop. My...my work. I can't just shut everything down."

"Yes, you can. As a matter of fact, you need to make some long-term plans about shutting it down or giving it to someone else to run. Because as soon as we find the powers, you will pick yours back up and leave Ordinary like you should have three months ago. You broke the rules. That's not going to fly."

Crow dropped his hand, his arms loose at his side, his head thunked back against the kiln. If defeat had an avatar, Crow could model for it.

"All right." His voice had gone very soft. "I got it. Let me shut things down. Give me a minute."

He pushed off the furnace and headed to the back of the shop to his small office and outside door.

"Do you believe him?"

I looked over at Odin who stood near the front windows. His back was toward me, his hands planted against his hips so that his elbows jutted out. He looked broad and strong as a granite outcropping standing there while the storm whipped against the glass.

"Crow?" I asked.

He grunted in agreement.

"Do I believe he doesn't have the powers anymore? That's pretty obvious."

Odin shifted his weight and turned toward me, backlit now by the gray day. "Do you believe he doesn't know where the powers are?"

My first response was to say yes, of course I believed he didn't know. He was obviously freaked out over the loss and afraid of what the other deities would do to him because of his lapse. I didn't think there had ever been a god who had failed to keep the powers safe and hidden while they were in Ordinary.

Crow had just put himself in the history books, and not in a good way.

But he had admitted the power tricked him. Maybe somehow, even in a subconscious way, he might know where the powers were. "If he knows, I'll make him tell me."

Odin shook his head slightly. "You heard me before, didn't you, Delaney?" His voice had an even timbre I wasn't used to from him. He sounded almost...fatherly. Odin had never been fatherly. Cranky, egotistical, and self-centered, yes. But not fatherly. Not to me.

"Heard what?"

"Crow is not your uncle. Not family. Really, none of us are. Your father understood that. There is a division between gifted mortals, like you and your bloodline, and gods who are temporarily mortal. Even though we don't carry our powers, we don't...see the world in the same way as a mortal. We can't. We have been changed too much by the power we bear."

I nodded. I didn't think I'd ever heard this many words out of him in all my years of knowing him. It was surprising enough that I didn't want to interrupt.

"We don't see the world in the same manner as mortals. We don't experience time as a mortal would." He gestured with one meaty hand as if he were trying to drag words out of the air, then planted his palm back on his hip. "We do not love as a mortal loves. Not even if we try."

Thunder rumbled slow and low outside and the rain picked up.

The entire conversation made me feel sad, though I couldn't say why. Maybe it was because it was so unexpected. I would never have guessed Odin had this kind of insight to share. Never would have thought he'd given any time to consider what a mortal might think and feel as compared to a god.

But then, he was known as a wandering god, as a wise man. Maybe the accident-prone, grumpy chainsaw artist I knew was just an act he put on. A part he played to fit in this ordinary town in this ordinary world.

"So if Crow has found a way to make you think he loves you, that he cares for you as a mortal cares for another mortal, think twice, Delaney, before you believe him."

Thunder rolled again, a soft rumble to the north, nearly out of town now.

"If I believe Crow doesn't care for me, for my well-being, because no god is capable of that kind of caring, then how exactly am I to take your advice, Odin? It's very *kind* of you to warn me like this."

He shook his shaggy head, his grin a slice of white in the dark shadows over his face. "I'm not saying this out of kindness. I'm just telling an officer of the law to be wary of me and my kind, especially when we're trying to be helpful."

"Or when you're worried about me?"

He scowled, but I wasn't buying it. It had only been a couple months ago, right after Heimdall's murder that Odin and several other gods had told me they had promised my dad they'd help me if I needed it.

There was plenty at stake for the gods to want to make sure I did my job and did it well.

But it wasn't just for their own survival that the gods had offered to help me. My father had forged a friendship with the gods of our town that hinged on mutual respect. He hadn't spoken much about how the Reeds before him had interacted with gods, other than to say they had always carried out their duties. But I'd gotten the impression that past Reeds hadn't seen the use in socializing much with the gods.

Back in those days, generations ago, the town was really nothing more than a small collection of buildings along the dirt road that followed the coastline dotted with fishing boats and cabins built into the hills. There wasn't much for a Reed to do but to occasionally hike out to a god's place and make sure they weren't using their powers while inside the town's boundaries.

Dad had changed that. He had been not just the police chief, he had also been a man the gods could turn to with questions, troubles, and opinions.

He had become their friend, no matter what Odin wanted to call it.

"Yes," Odin agreed, bringing me back into the conversation. "Especially when we seem to be worried about you."

"Are you?"

"Worried?"

I waited.

"You are more than your ability, Delaney. I understand that. Many of the gods do. But just as many gods and creatures and mortals in town see you as your job. As the law. As the police chief. That is a dangerous position to hold. One of extreme expectations. One that could put you in the line of fire when those expectations are not met."

A chill washed over my skin. Hera, who had gone by the mortal name Herri and run a bar here in town, had picked up her power to help me find Cooper too. Unlike Crow, she had left town for one year as required by the contract.

She had told me that there was a war coming. She had told me it was headed toward Ordinary. I'd been looking over my shoulder for three months. Other than the constant rain, Ordinary had seemed normal enough.

Until all the god powers had been stolen.

"What line of fire? If you know something about the war headed our way, I want to know."

"War?" his eyebrows shot down. "Is that what you think?"

Hera had also told me to choose my allies carefully. That people might not be who I thought they were. I studied Odin and went with my gut. I trusted him.

"Hera mentioned a war headed our way. Do you know anything about that?"

He rubbed one calloused thumb over the corner of his mouth, his gaze on the floor. "Through the ages there have always been wars among gods. Just because we vacation doesn't mean we give up our basic instincts. But war. Here." He was silent for several minutes.

I listened to the cars hushing by the shop, wet pavement making tires louder than engines.

"What does your blood tell you, Delaney?"

His words flashed like fire across my skin, then sank deep into my bones where they pulsed. My blood. Reed blood. Protectors of Ordinary.

We were connected to this land, connected to all the forces and creatures and gods who walked upon it. Our roots ran deep, into the soil, the sand, the salt. And I knew, in that quick instant that something was coming for Ordinary. A storm. War.

But all I said was, "I don't know."

"You had better. And soon. Your father didn't listen to the blood." He shook his head. "You understand that, don't you?"

I swallowed. What did our blood have to do with Dad, with a possible war? "What happened?"

"He chose sides. Too late."

Crow stomped into the room. "All right. I'm ready."

He wore a quilted canvas jacket and had shoved a gray beanie over his dark hair.

He was also wearing an umbrella on his head.

Neither Odin nor I moved. A hundred questions were spinning through my mind. Too late for what? Choose what sides? I wanted to ask Odin what he knew. It should have been second nature for me to grill him. I was a cop. I knew how to ask questions and get answers.

Also: umbrella hat?

As soon as Crow had walked back into the room, Odin

had shut down. That warmth—no, heat—that had been in his gaze, in his words, was once again stowed behind the man I'd known for so many years.

A grumpy, accident-prone chainsaw artist.

The quick change must mean he didn't want to talk in front of Crow.

Or he was just as baffled by the hat as I was.

Choose sides. Between the gods? Or was Odin just angry at Crow for losing his power and trying to make me turn against a man I considered my uncle?

"Everything okay?" Crow asked looking between us. "Delaney?"

"What is on your head?"

"My hair."

"Over that."

"My beanie."

Really?

"Why are you wearing an umbrella hat on your head?"

"Where else should I wear a hat? Really, Delaney, you're ridiculous."

Odin *hrumphed* and headed toward the door. "I've wasted enough of my time today on you, Crow. If Delaney weren't here I'd show you just how much I've enjoyed wasting my time on someone who couldn't do one simple job right."

Crow licked his lips and glanced at me for reassurance. I'd never seen him so nervous around another god before. No, strike that. I'd never seen him nervous around anyone before.

Either he was afraid of Odin, or he was playing me so I would take his side.

Okay, that kind of double-guessing everything was going to have to stop right now. I was not paranoid. I refused to become paranoid. Unless maybe I should be paranoid.

"Let's go, bumbershoot head." I waved at the door, telling them both to walk out in front of me so I could keep an eye on them.

Okay, maybe I was a little paranoid.

Crow stared at Odin's retreating form, then trudged along after him, waiting at the door for me to walk through so he could set the alarm and locks. He patted the doorframe gently, like he was saying good-bye to an old friend.

Well, he wasn't saying good-bye yet, but he would be. Losing the powers meant not only putting himself in jeopardy with the other gods, it meant putting the rules of Ordinary in jeopardy.

When the rules were broken, I was the one who had to answer for it. And I would.

As soon as we found his powers.

I gave him his moment at the door and dashed over to the Jeep.

I opened the Jeep and slid in, Odin taking the passenger side. He didn't buckle the seat belt or look at me. He just scowled at the rain, lost in his own thoughts.

"Just so you know," I said, as rain rattled against the metal roof and Crow jogged across the parking lot toward us, the umbrella hat a bright crazy blob in the gray light, "I appreciate what you said in there. I'll be careful."

"And will you call on me?" He still didn't look my way, didn't take his gaze off the gray and wet.

"Yes," I said, not knowing exactly what I was agreeing to. I wasn't close to Odin, not in a familial way, but the man here in my Jeep was steady, serious, and seemed to know things I wanted to understand.

"We need to talk. About Dad."

Odin grunted, but the line of his massive shoulders relax minutely.

"You know where I'll be."

Then the back door opened and Crow bulleted into the seat, slamming the door behind him. "Can we stop for food? I'm starving."

"No," Odin and I said at the same time.

Crow gave an offended sound, and caught my gaze in the rearview mirror.

"I haven't eaten since lunch yesterday."

"If you behave yourself, I'll stop for coffee before we head in to the station."

"Fine." He crossed his arms over his chest and frowned out the window like a petulant child. With a parasol on his head. Those things were never going to catch on.

"Suck it up, Crow," Odin growled.

One grouchy god.

Check.

One pouty god.

Check.

Silver lining? Starting a Monday out this bad meant it couldn't get worse.

IT GOT worse.

I'd dropped Odin off at his property, and Crow had claimed the passenger seat. He spent the next twenty minutes complaining about the rain, the gods accusing him of losing their powers on purpose, and having skipped dinner and breakfast.

"You're going to complain about how hard things are for you today, when you are the one who has made every god in town angry, lost their powers—*lost*, Crow—which is something no one has ever done in the history of Ordinary, and doubled my workload? Not to mention that you broke the contract with Ordinary by picking your power back up and then not leaving town for a year. I can not start to explain just how angry I am at you for that."

And even more, for making me think that his trickster power should be allowed to do that. I should not have trusted him.

He chewed on his bottom lip while I navigated the rain and traffic. "Buy you an Egg McMuffin with extra cheese?" he said quietly.

I sighed, trying to rein in my anger and worry. It had taken three months before anything bad had happened from him breaking the rules. Maybe we could fix it before anything else bad happened.

"Why didn't you eat dinner?"

"I was busy."

"Doing what?"

"I...was out of town. Picking up some things for my shop."

"You going to come up with a receipt for these things

33

with a date stamp on them?"

He rubbed at the bridge of his nose again. "I was out of town at a movie. I have the ticket for that."

That seemed a little more likely. We had a three-plex here in town, but it didn't always get the newest blockbusters. Driving into the valley to Salem or even Dallas, where they had bigger movie theaters, was pretty common. So was taking an extra hour to drive up to Portland and catch a show at the Imax big screens.

A mortal god leaving town wasn't outside the rules, though it was expected that the trips would be short, and that the majority of a god's vacation time was spent firmly inside Ordinary's boundaries.

"Why didn't you just tell me that?"

"I don't...I don't know." He groaned, his hand falling away from his face. When I glanced over, I could see the tremble in his hands. "I lost the powers, Delaney. I'm not an idiot. I'm not forgetful. I'm not careless. But I lost them. How does that even happen?"

"That's what I want you to tell me. Was there any sign of a break in?"

"No. I went to the movie, got home late. I didn't know they were gone until this morning."

"And how could you tell they were gone?"

"Just...something didn't feel right about the shop. I thought I smelled something, like cinnamon? I have some potpourri in the shop, but don't really like the smell of cinnamon. So I thought maybe a customer had left something behind—a coat, a hat. You know how some people go heavy with the perfume. I'd had some people in to watch me make orbs the previous morning.

"So I walked around, checked the shelves and displays. Checked the work benches, under them. And when I walked in front of the old furnace—the one holding the powers—all I felt was cold."

"The furnace door was closed?"

"Yes. I grabbed it and opened it, so if there were fingerprints, I ruined them." He winced. "I guess I should have called you. But I didn't think they were gone. Not really. Hell,

I stood in front of that cold furnace for fifteen minutes before it really sank in."

"What time was this?"

"Early. I went in early to catch up with stuff left over from leaving early the afternoon before."

"Rough estimate?"

"Six-thirty?"

"Did you see any signs of break in?"

"The back door was open. I went in through the front, which was locked. My security alarm has been acting weird the last couple weeks, so I didn't have it activated on the back door—only on the front. But there was still a lock and a deadbolt."

"Broken?"

"No. Opened."

"Someone had the keys."

"No one has keys to the shop. Not back door keys."

"What about Apocalypse Pablo?" Okay, that wasn't really his name. His real name was Pablo Fernandez, but everyone in town called him Apocalypse Pablo. Since he liked it, the nickname had stuck. "He comes in to clean for you, right?"

"Yeah. Works the rest of the time at the gas station on the north end of town. He's...well, you know how he is. Nice enough for a mortal, even if he's a little...intense. Good with glass, though. Not bad with customers—he's covered a couple times. I had to tell him to lay off the apocalypse thing after he made a little kid cry. But he only has the front door key. Back door is mine."

"Do you have copies of the key?"

"No."

"Would you have left your keys out where someone could make copies of them?"

He frowned and bit on his lip a little longer. "I don't know. Maybe? I've never worried that much about it. Who would go through the trouble to steal my keys, copy only the back door set, then break into my shop? Sure, I carry a lot of inventory, but the glass pieces won't sell for that much on the open market, and most of them have artist marks and serial numbers."

"Well, it wasn't the glass our thief was interested in, was it?"

"No," he said dejectedly. "It wasn't. But there aren't that many in town who even know about god powers, much less where they're being stored."

"More than you think. All of the creatures know about you gods. A few mortals. Who did you have in the shop for that last class?"

"Mortals. Tourists."

"Are you sure they were mortal?"

He frowned and shifted to look at me. "We don't have a lot of visiting immortals."

"Sure we do," I said. "Vamps, shifters, dryads, trolls, you name it, they've strolled through Ordinary."

"I would have noticed a troll in my shop."

"Even without your power?"

"Yes."

"Even if your power was angry with you?"

"What?"

"You picked it up, then you put it down a couple hours later instead of keeping it for a year as is required. Ever think maybe your power didn't like that?"

"The power isn't alive, Delaney. It doesn't think. It doesn't feel."

I flicked on the blinker and turned into the only McDonald's in town. There were four cars in front of us, so I put the car in park while we waited our turn in the drive-thru.

"I've never been a god. Never will be." The windshield wiper scraped across the window and I turned it off, letting the patter of rain take up all extra sound beyond the engine. "So I don't know what it's like to really be connected to a power. But I've held god power. And I can hear it, hear everything that it's made of. It might not be alive, but it has sentience, it has...needs."

Crow thought that over, finally nodded. "I suppose, yeah. I don't like to think of it as something that's separate. More like a costume I put on to play a part. A very powerful part. Fun too. When I carry my power, my full power, there is no beginning of it and ending of me. I am. Raven is."

"Do you think your power could pull a trick on you? Steal the other powers away on its own?"

"Not really. I think if powers could steal other powers we'd have seen that, we'd have heard about it in our histories. Gods can steal powers. Mortals, creatures can steal powers. We've heard all those stories. But I think power, if it has any awareness at all, isn't aware enough to actually think outside itself. Chaos only thinks of Chaos. Maybe it thinks of Order, because it is there to destroy it. But I just don't think Chaos would be aware enough of another force, like time, that it would be able to decide to steal it. Devour it, maybe. But own it? I don't think so."

"I asked Death if he could kill a power once."

Crow jerked. When he turned my way, his eyes were as wide as an open umbrella hat. Trust me on this. I had a ready comparison. "When?"

"When he first came to town. When I was carrying Heimdall's power."

"And what did he say?"

"He said he didn't know."

Crow whistled. "Do you think he'd ever thought about it?"

"No." I put the Jeep in gear and moved forward two places. "He did think it was interesting in theory."

"Terrifying, in theory." Crow wiped his palms on the tops of his thighs. "I'd never even thought of that. Tricking a god, yes. Tricking a power? Wouldn't happen."

"So who wants all the god powers? It isn't just one power that's been taken, like the power to be young, or to control time, or to rule over nature. This is a big pile of power. Who could touch that? Who could move that? Who could hide that?"

The car ahead of us pulled forward and I rolled up to the menu and speaker.

"I have no idea." Crow's stomach growled. "Good thing we have the best police force in the country to figure it out."

"Flattery won't get you out of this."

"Did I say country? I meant world."

"Knock it off, Crow. You're stuck with me, and you're

staying stuck. I've only begun to grill you for details. What do you want to eat?"

"Two ham, egg, and cheese biscuits, side of hash browns, OJ and a coffee, double sugar, double cream."

I repeated his order and got myself a plain biscuit, side of bacon, and a large black coffee.

It wasn't until we pulled away from the pick-up window and he was digging through his bag, heavy with grease and salt, that he finally spoke again. "God power only fits one person at a time, right? Only one vessel per god power?"

I sipped coffee and nodded.

"Then why would a god want all those powers?"

"Ransom? Revenge? So no one else could have them?"

"Maybe," he said around a mouthful of egg and cheese. "But most of us are here to get away from those things. Especially when it has something to do with our powers—our real jobs. Maybe we'll want ransom and revenge years from now when we're done vacationing, but most of us like the time off. From everything."

"You seemed to be taking this awfully gracefully for someone who has screwed up in such an epic manner. You do realize this is an emergency, right?"

"Well." He swallowed down a mouthful of orange juice. "Since only the god who belongs to the power can use the power—one vessel per power—I'm not even sure this rates as an emergency. I mean, only those of us who belong to the powers can use them. So what's the worst that can happen?"

CHAPTER 2

"HE'S DEAD," Myra said.

I still stood half out of the Jeep, my fast food bag in one hand. My heart thumped hard and thick in my chest draining blood from my brain.

Ryder?

"Who?"

Thunder walloped the air, rolling across the edges of the horizon as if upset to be leaving some part of town undrowned.

"Sven Rossi."

I blinked, rain running down my face. It took me a second or two to remember how to breathe while I processed what she'd just said. Another second to swallow and pull my fear in tight.

Ryder was fine. Ryder wasn't dead.

Why had I automatically assumed he was hurt?

Why had everything in my body gone cold when I thought that was true?

Love, my heart whispered. *You love him.*

I couldn't love a guy who'd dumped me after our first date. That was pretty much the hint of all hints that he really wasn't all that into me.

"Delaney?" Myra put her hand on my arm. Ever since I'd been shot, she hovered more, touched me more. As if I wouldn't be there when she reached out. As if she were afraid to lose me.

The bullet hadn't just changed *my* life. I wasn't the only one who had nightmares. Even our youngest sister, Jean, hadn't been able to joke away the bullet I'd taken at point blank.

I think both of my sisters seeing me get shot had only made it worse.

For all of us.

"I'm fine. Sven?" I asked. "When? How?" Sven was the newest vampire to Ordinary. He had been brought into Old Rossi's fold to become the latest cousin/distant relative/in-law/half-nephew of the rag-tag vampire clan. He worked—used to work—as a bouncer over at Hera's bar: Mom's Bar and Grill.

"Just got the call. Jean answered since I was tied up with Mrs. Yates' penguin."

"Where was it this time?"

"Attached to the church tower weather vane."

"We couldn't leave it up there?"

"Not with the thorny crown and cross they tied it to."

Mrs. Yate's penguin was a concrete yard ornament the local high school kids took all sorts of pleasure in harassing. We got a call almost weekly about it being found in some odd or compromising situation.

It was petty mischief that could have been stopped if Mrs. Yates relocated the penguin to her back yard, or better yet her garage, but she stubbornly plunked it down in the exact same place in her front yard every single time we brought it back to her.

Within a week or so, the penguin would be absconded with and taken on an adventure. It was getting to be so well known around town that someone outside of Ordinary had started a blog about it, asking for pictures of the penguin in strange locations. The pictures had flooded in, and so had the page views.

The penguin was quickly becoming Ordinary's most famous citizen.

"What happened? Where was Sven?" My brain had finally shaken off my initial shock. I strode to the station, Crow already ahead of me, umbrella hat flared over his shoulders.

Myra frowned, just as confused at his fashion choice as I was.

"We found his body about an hour ago."

"Who called it in?"

"Apocalypse Pablo. Said he thought someone was breaking into the shed on the back of the gas station property. Thought it might be zombies and wanted to sell them a window washer? Not sure how that makes sense, but it's what he said. I told him to keep an eye on the shed and stay away from it until I could get there. I didn't...I didn't think it would be anything more than maybe a nest of raccoons."

Crow opened the door and held it as we walked in past him.

"Did you go out there alone?"

"Yes. Ryder's been out of town for a couple days."

"I didn't know that."

She shrugged off her coat and hung it on the hook where it could drip. Doing so made her sleeves ruck up to reveal dark bruises on her forearms.

Huh.

"He had a job to check on up in Washington. Said he'd be back later this week."

I frowned. He had just called me this morning. "Did he say where, exactly?"

"No. Why?"

"No reason." I pulled off my coat and hung it beside hers. I flicked my gaze toward her arm, then raised an eyebrow, silently asking what those bruises were about. She hurriedly pulled her sleeve down and ignored me.

Weird.

"Tell me about Sven. Crow, stay here in the lobby and don't break any more of Ordinary's rules. And take off that ridiculous hat."

He popped a hash brown in his mouth. "This hat is going to catch on. I promise you that."

"Don't promise me that."

"Umbrella hats are going to be all the rage."

"Oh, I'm already feeling the rage." I flipped my fingers in what I hoped was mime for "kill it with fire."

Myra walked with me over to my desk. It was out of the way, but I still had a view of the lobby.

"Why is Crow here?" she asked.

"I'll tell you after you fill me in on Sven. You found him in the shed?"

I sat at my desk, the take-out coffee cooling between my palms. She pulled a chair over so we could both keep an eye on the lobby and Crow, yet still lean in close enough we could keep our voices down.

"I went out there because Apocalypse Pablo said the door was open and he'd kept it locked. When I got there, the lock was broken off the shed door. Too much rain to see any footsteps—

it's practically a swamp back there behind the gas station. I didn't see blood, no scuffs. Plenty of mud but it's been raining non-stop."

I took a gulp of coffee, nodded.

"The shed has an old tractor in it, some tools, but I could finally see a streak of mud through the dust on the floor that led to the back corner. I found him under a blanket. Shot."

"Still bleeding?" Cut a vampire and chances were he wouldn't bleed. Kill a vampire, and chances were the thick, slow blood that moved sluggishly through his veins was going to make an appearance.

"Shot through the middle of his forehead."

The horror of what she was saying clamored there in the back of my brain, but I didn't have time for it right now.

I liked—had liked Sven. He seemed to fit into the town and the vampires here with ease, and had made friends with pretty much anyone he met.

I didn't know anyone who would have wanted him dead. But he had come here after living a full, and probably overly-long, life outside this town. I didn't know what had happened in his past, what he had done, what had been done to him in the years before he decided to move to Ordinary.

It was agreed that Old Rossi took care of vetting the fangers who became a part of Ordinary. I knew he was very thorough in checking their backgrounds.

I trusted Old Rossi as my father had before me and my grandfather had before him. Old Rossi knew which vampires to bring into Ordinary, and which to keep far, far away.

But I'd never had a vampire show up dead inside the town's boundaries. Outside the town's boundaries either for that matter.

"One bullet is not enough to take down a vampire."

She rubbed her thumb over her middle finger, a nervous habit I hadn't seen her do for a while. "It wasn't just the bullet."

"Okay?"

"There were symbols drawn on his chest and both palms."

"What kind of symbols?"

"I've never seen them before."

That wasn't a good sign. Myra was the daughter Dad had

bequeathed all of his books and journals to. She had been steadily reading her way through them for over a year.

"What were they drawn with?"

"Blood."

"Excuse me?"

This was a vacation town. A sleepy beach town where little kids built sand castles and our highest repeat crime was expired parking meters. We didn't do corpses covered in weird symbols drawn in blood.

"Blood," I said.

"Blood. Looked like it to me. If it isn't, we'll know soon. I had the body delivered to Old Rossi."

"Not the morgue?"

"You think someone other than Old Rossi would know more about this? How to kill a vampire with only a bullet and some squiggly lines?"

She was right. Old Rossi had been in town for several hundred years. Back when it was just a spot where gods had chosen to vacation and creatures had decided to settle. As I understood it, he had been born mortal and done a stint as a soldier. I didn't know which war.

The story of how Rossi had been turned had only been pried out of him once, by some great-grand so far in my past I'd lost count of how many generations back. That story had been passed down in oral tradition, details lost over the years. By the time my father heard it, then passed it on to me, the names and dates had all been blurred by voices long dead.

The Old Rossi I knew was the same man my father and grandfather knew. To all outward appearances, he was a middle-aged, easy-going hippy sort of guy who ran naked meditation sessions and crystal-powered yoga raves.

He had, as far as I knew, left his long-ago-past life in his long ago past.

Rossi would know every way a vampire could be killed. Myra was right to have sent Sven's body to him.

"Have you heard from him yet?"

"He wants to see you."

I took another drink of coffee. "At his place?"

"You're not going alone."

"I won't. But we have something else we need to deal with."

"Crow?"

Thunder rumbled and a hard flash of yellow sunlight broke the clouds before being swallowed down.

Crow crumpled the paper bag and tossed it in the lobby garbage can. He walked a slow circle inside the small lobby, umbrella hat tucked under his arm, then stopped in front of the windows so he could stare out at the storm. His hands were shoved in his coat pockets, the beanie still tight on his head. I didn't think he'd run off, but I wasn't sure what he'd do now that he was officially on all the gods' shit lists.

"He lost the powers."

Myra blinked. Her eyes were wider than mine, a lighter blue beneath the straight dark bangs of her pin-up style. Whereas I had more of a runner's build like our dad, she had inherited all of Mom's curves. Even our unflattering uniforms couldn't hide her figure.

I tended to tan under my freckles, but she had pale skin. Right now she went down another shade.

"He lost what powers?"

Crow, in the waiting area, snorted. I threw him a glare, but he was still staring out the window. He rocked up on the toes of his feet then down, up and down, in a nervous movement that looked like he wished he could run out of here.

Not on my watch.

"The gods' powers."

"All of them?"

"All of them."

She stared at the lobby, lines pulling between her eyebrows. "How the hell did you do that, Crow?"

"Not on purpose. Not consciously either, which pisses me off, you know? What a great trick this would be...well, is, I suppose. But I didn't think of it. It's irritating to be out tricked."

"How did you even...how does *anyone* lose all the powers? That's never happened. That shouldn't even be something that *can* happen."

"We know," I said.

"So that's the emergency meeting of deities?" she asked.

"Yeah, he was smart enough to get everyone on board as soon as he found out they were gone."

"Well..." he hedged.

"You did call us as soon as you knew they were gone?" I asked.

"Almost as soon as I knew."

"How long did you wait?"

His gaze drifted up to the ceiling. "Maybe an hour, tops? I called a few gods first. Thought they were screwing with me. Asked them if they'd taken them."

"Who did you ask?" Myra moved over to her desk, pulling out a pad and pen.

"Death, first."

"Why Death?" she asked.

"He's new here. I've tricked him out of more than one soul over the years. I mean...a lot. He might look refined and restrained and smart, but he's fallen for the same bait and switches for centuries. I thought he might want to get back at me for some of that."

"And?" I asked, trying to connect the image I had of Thanatos—humorless and infinitely more interested in the little details of living a mortal life—with the idea of pulling a prank.

Could not brain my way through that.

"He said he'd never break contract with Ordinary in such a way."

"You believed him?"

He nodded. "Death has a thing about contracts. Then I called Eris, Ares, Bishamon, Apep."

Goddess of discord, God of war, God of warriors and punisher of evil-doers, and God of chaos. Looked like he'd covered most of the obvious bases.

"Nopes all around. So I called Poseidon."

"What?" Myra asked. "Why Poseidon?"

"Because when doesn't he screw up? Do you know how many times Poseidon has died? Not just died, but died stupidly and accidentally?"

Not that most people made it a point to die purposely, but he had a point. Poseidon's power had changed hands five times in recent history because the mortal—both males and females—

who tended to pick up that power, were always too confident about their ability not to drown.

Then they always drowned.

Just three months ago during the Rhubarb Rally, Poseidon had almost drowned when drinking a toast to the blessing of the Rhubarb Regatta.

But dying a lot didn't mean Poseidon was after the god powers. Nor that he had the ability to pick up all of them, move them, and find a place to hide them.

"Seems a little out of Poseidon's M.O.," I said.

Crow rolled his eyes. "Ask any of the gods. Most of our biggest disasters have happened because of Poseidon."

"He's the god of the sea," Myra said. "I'm not convinced he'd want anything to do with stealing god powers."

"Yes, well you haven't been alive for several thousand years. God of the sea is klutz of the universe. He probably tripped and somehow fell on the oven latch and let all the powers loose and doesn't want to get blamed for it. Trust me, he's a suspect."

"Trust you?" I put down my coffee. "Because you've given us so many reasons to do so?"

"Hey, I helped you find your ex-exboyfriend so you could give him Heimdall's power."

"He's still an ex-boyfriend, and you picking up your power to help me find him is what got you into this mess. You should have just left Ordinary for a year. Like the rules say. Like Hera and Thor did. Like *everyone* does."

"But I like it here," he whined.

"Of course you like it here—it's a vacation."

"What kind of consequences are we going to have to deal with from him not picking up his power?" Myra asked.

"Good question," I said. "If we're lucky—and we never are—maybe all that will happen is the powers will have been stolen."

She was still frowning. "It's in our job description to mete out punishment to the god who breaks the rules of Ordinary."

"Is there precedence for this sort of thing?"

"No," Crow said.

"I'm sure there is," Myra said. "But I'd have to look it up."

"Do that."

"What?" Crow said. "I thought you were my friends."

I raised my eyebrows at his fake outrage. "We are. But like it or not, once we find the powers, you're going to have to deal with the consequences. We have a job to do—look after Ordinary and make sure everyone plays by the rules. And you do have a job to do, Crow. A power to wield. You can't ignore it for eternity."

"You're not going to kick me out of Ordinary are you, Delaney? Throw me off of my Native land."

Yes, the mortal Crow had been born full-blood Siletz. Technically, well, and literally, this was his Native land. But the rules of Ordinary applied to all our citizens, no matter their race.

"I'm going to follow the rules laid down by our ancestors. Just like you should have." I was getting tired of telling him this. I started toward the door. "Myra, stay here until Roy comes in. Keep an eye on Crow. I'm headed out to talk to Rossi."

"I thought I was supposed to stay with you," Crow said.

"No, you're supposed to stay under our custody. Make yourself useful around here and handle some of our filing or something."

"Filing? You do know I'm an artist, right? I've won awards. I hire people to handle my paperwork."

"I'm sorry. I assumed you wanted to be useful. How about you spend the day in the holding cell." I glanced at Myra. "That position's open for important artists, right?"

"Always."

"Fine." He gave a dramatic sigh. "I'll do your menial labor. But don't think I won't talk to the tribe about this. Using a Native boy to do your grunt work. I'm feeling oppressed."

Myra gave him a bland look. "Please. Wanna talk oppressed? Woman in a man's world here." She pointed to the badge on her chest. "I'll be happy to put my three-quarter pay and glass ceiling against your cut of the casino profit, successful business ownership, and *godhood*."

He grinned. "Gotta love that Reed spirit. Marry me? I'm a successful business man, you know. We can be oppressed together."

Myra rolled her eyes. Then, to me: "Call when you get to

47

Rossi's. Call when you leave. I'll get hold of Jean so she knows what's going on."

"Okay. You got Apocalypse Pablo's statement?"

"Yep. It'll be on your desk by the time you get back.

"Good."

I gathered up my coat and a beanie, shivering a little as I slid into the cool and damp of them.

"I could loan you my hat," Crow offered.

"No."

"It will keep you dry. C'mon. You know you want it."

"I don't want it. No one wants it. It's stupid and isn't even a funny joke."

"Fine. You obviously don't understand fashion. Have fun being wet and so last year, beanie head."

I resisted the urge to stick my tongue out at him. "Bye, Myra. Don't shoot him anywhere he'd sue us for."

"Got it," she said.

I ducked out into the rain and trudged to the Jeep.

CHAPTER 3

THE VAMPIRE at the door wore a tuxedo and a scowl. It'd been awhile since I'd seen short, dark, suspicious Leon Rossi. Last time was at the July beach "clothing optional" bonfire Old Rossi had thrown. Leon worked night shift lead at the cannery and had been living in Ordinary for over a century.

"Chief." He stepped aside so I could enter. Rossi's home could at best be described as eclectic and at worst Winchester Mansion crazy.

"Didn't know you were pulling butler duty, Leon. Tux looks good." I unzipped my coat and he took it, holding it at arm's length so it didn't drip on his fancy shoes.

"Was out of town at a midnight wedding. Got the call about Sven. Didn't take time to change."

"Everybody here?" I asked.

"Yes. This isn't something that Old Rossi will take lightly."

"He shouldn't. Someone in his family is dead."

His eyes flashed that odd blue unique to angry fangers. "It's rare to happen. Not death, but the manner of it."

"Gunshot and blood symbols?"

His lips pressed together and I could see the slight indentation of his fangs pressing into his bottom lip. Leon was angry, and more than that, uncomfortable.

"Gunshot," he said.

All right. I don't know why he didn't want to acknowledge the blood symbols. Maybe it was a vampire thing.

"Were you close to him?" I asked.

"Never saw him outside of family gatherings. Didn't talk to him much then. He was nice. Followed the family rules."

The Rossis weren't related. The clan was made up of individual vampires Rossi had approved and given his family name. They passed themselves off as cousins, in-laws, and distant relations. They didn't make a big deal about it, and the mortals in town didn't question it. Since Old Rossi presented himself as a man who would rather make love than war, people expected him to help out his family members, take them in, line up employment, and help get them on their feet.

What most mortals in town didn't know was that Rossi carefully vetted every vampire who came into Ordinary and upheld a strict set of rules for vampire behavior. If a vampire stepped outside those bounds, Rossi took them down, quietly, and with no trace left behind.

That was another of Ordinary's agreements: Rossi took care of vampire behavior and violence, and Granny Wolfe took care of werewolf behavior and violence. As the police in town, we could arrest either type of creature if they were breaking the law, but if they dissolved into gang war or racial violence, Rossi and Granny put an end to it by putting an end to them.

Leon gestured me toward the interior of the house, and I followed.

"Where was the wedding?"

"Spokane. One of my coworkers needed a date. It was her sister's wedding. Since it was at night, it worked for me."

One of the reasons so many vampires came to Ordinary was because of the living conditions. Not only was it a quiet little town, it was also one of the few places in the world where daylight didn't harm vamps.

Vampires in town could go out in daylight, though they usually kept most of their skin covered and wore sunblock. I'd asked Old Rossi why daylight in Ordinary didn't hurt vampires and had gotten a vague lecture on geology, meteorology, and I'm pretty sure the Bermuda Triangle.

It didn't make sense then, and I hadn't asked again.

Outside of Ordinary, vampires accepted by Rossi could also move in daylight for limited times. That had something to do with his claim as their prime, the connection between them and him, and him and Ordinary.

If not for that, vampires would be night creatures only just like in the legends and movies.

"Her sister was furious she had a date."

"Sibling rivalry?"

He grinned wide enough to show fangs. "Had to break up a fight. Between the bridesmaids."

"Sounds like fun."

"Open bar and a show. I enjoyed it."

"By open bar you are talking alcohol, not jugular, right?"

"Sure, Chief."

Vampire activity outside of Ordinary was beyond my jurisdiction. Over state lines it was definitely outside my jurisdiction.

"You tell me anymore, I'll have to take you in, Leon."

"I suppose you would."

Well, now I was worried. Not that there was a lot I could do about it. If I found a dead body and told the cops a vampire drank them dry, I'd be laughed out of the station. Plus, there would be the problem of proof.

As in I had none.

Old Rossi kept some cutthroat lawyers on call for family members with legal problems. Lawyers who also happened to be vampires and would make sure I'd lose that sort of case.

Still, I'd do a quick check to make sure no one from Spokane had turned up dead after a wedding.

"I'm joking," he said. "I drank alcohol, not blood."

I tried not to let him see how glad I was to hear that. But he was a vampire. I'm sure he could tell my mood by my heart rate.

Voices grew louder as we neared a family room toward the back of the house that was the size of a hotel ballroom.

Leon wasn't kidding all the Rossis were here. At last count, we had sixty-four vampires in town. Many of them were hermits on the outskirts of Ordinary whom I never saw. But I knew Rossi kept tabs on them, and their comings and goings. I scanned faces of the vamps I'd rarely seen, reacquainting myself with them. They, of course, hadn't changed since I'd last seen them.

Long life had some advantages.

"He's in his study." Leon pointed to the door at my right.

"Who?"

"Old Rossi."

"Did you tell him I was here?"

He smiled again. His eyes focused on my neck and did not budge. I knew he was messing with me. "He knows you are here.

51

We all do."

Right. If it wasn't the scent of my blood that tipped them off, it was probably the whole vampire telepathy thing they all shared. I'm sure Leon had told Old Rossi I was at the door before I'd even rung the doorbell.

"Thanks." Still, manners were manners. I knocked softly.

"Come in."

I opened the dark wooden door and stepped into the room.

For a creature of the night, Old Rossi sure liked his pastels. The room was painted a soothing misty gray, the accents a soft white, the wood floor honey blond. Although this was his study, there were no books in this room and no desk. There was, instead, a curve of lush shell-blue couches, slender tables that seemed to have grown out of the honey flooring, and wall-to-wall white open-fronted cabinets with backlit glass shelves. All filled with carved eggshells.

Hundreds of eggshells, from huge ostrich eggs to tiny hummingbird eggs, all of them carved into impossible swirls, hollows and designs, perched on delicate glass pedestals that seemed too thin to for them to balance upon.

A few of the eggs were brushed with gilding or showed glints of diamonds and other precious gems and metals. A few were dyed so that the contrast in carved layers created landscapes and portraits. But most of them were simply soft shades of shell, carved into impossible twists and cages.

There was no carpeting on the floor. Every vibration of every movement in the house was telegraphed to the fragile sculptures. It said something about vampires that there could be dozens of them in this house and the shells weren't even trembling.

I took in a breath and let it out slowly, hoping my heartbeat didn't send anything tumbling.

Rossi sat on the couch, his back toward me so that I only saw his dark hair and wide shoulders.

"I need to speak with you," I said.

"I know."

I walked over to him, my feet falling as quietly as I could manage, the slightest rattle of glass and shell brushing the air with each step. When I rounded the couch, I could see what

Rossi was looking at.

Sven Rossi lay upon a glass table in front of the couch. The glass table beneath him was low to the ground but both long and wide enough to hold him. It seemed to be the only sturdy thing in the room.

Sven was naked, a white satin sheet draped over his hips. The designs drawn in blood across his pale chest seemed too loud in the room, a gory shout against the silence of the artistic carved shells that surrounded us.

"What is on your mind, Delaney?" Old Rossi's voice was toneless and soft, as if his words were sifting down from a long distance.

I tore my gaze away from Sven's still form, shoving aside my sorrow. I hadn't known Sven for long, but I'd liked him. To see him here, dead—totally dead and not just sort of undead—made me realize I'd miss him.

"Do you know how this happened?" I asked.

"Bullet to the head."

"That doesn't kill a vampire."

"No, it doesn't."

"So how did he die?"

"Ichor techne."

"Is that a kind of poison?"

For the first time since I'd entered the room, Old Rossi's eyes flicked up to meet mine. I gasped, then felt stupid for letting him see my reaction.

His eyes were red, deep heart-blood irises swimming in eyes gone black. A vampire hunting might have red eyes. A vampire starving might have black. But a vampire with red and black eyes was either a breath away from hellish, vengeful violence, or insanity.

I had never seen red and black eyes. Never seen the devil so near.

"It is an art." His voice was barely more than a hiss, a whisper of breath across tongue. "A very old blood art."

"Art kills vampires?" My heart pumped so fast and strong, I felt like my entire body was shaking. Instinct told me to run, hide, flee, but I knew that would be the fastest way to feel fangs sinking into my throat.

Old Rossi's gaze fixed on my throat, where I knew my heartbeat fluttered.

I didn't know if it was the fear, or just a brain glitch, but I couldn't stop the next words from falling from my mouth. "That would explain your interior decorating choices."

His gaze snapped up to lock on mine. Then his eyebrow slowly rose.

"Are you insulting my interior decorating tastes?"

"On purpose?"

He waited

"Yes?" I said.

Oh, dear gods. Why had I been honest? I didn't usually insult people when they were about to kill me. There was no denying that Mr. Devil and Darkness over there was a breath away from killing something. Probably a nervous police chief who was dripping rain on his wooden floor.

He blinked, and a wash of black faded to gray, the red to a ruddy amber. "I have impeccable taste."

He sounded offended.

He looked offended.

Offended was better than deadly.

"Says the man with a room full of eggs in boxes."

I resisted the urge to slap my hand over my mouth. His look of offense shifted to surprise.

"They are rare and valuable and *beautiful* and represent the fragility of life in balance with the universe."

He was right. They were beautiful. I opened my mouth to tell him I agreed with him, but he was on a roll.

"And furthermore, I went to great time and expense to wring as much ambient light and good vibes as possible out of this room and the entire house. The flow of chi in this place would register as a Category 5 hurricane. I not only have taste, it's *good* taste. For the eye and the soul."

This is where I didn't ask if vampires had souls. Certain creatures and deities in town would probably have an answer for that, and every one of them would be different.

So instead I said, "You know who else keeps eggs in boxes? Chickens." I held his gaze and hoped I got a smile out of him.

Old Rossi inhaled a breath and sort of choked on it as he

laughed. "Reeds. Un-fucking-flappable." He finished half-laughing half-coughing, then eased back into the cushions of the couch. "I thought your father was droll."

It was nice to see him relax out of his pounce and devour stance. Did wonders for my blood pressure.

"I'm sorry for your loss," I said, gesturing toward Sven.

Black washed over his eyes, was gone in a blink. "No more so than I." He waved one long, sturdy-fingered hand toward the loveseat to his left.

I walked around the dead body and took a seat. Not because I relished sitting down with a dead guy spread out in front of me like some macabre table cloth, but because my knees were threatening to buckle.

Adrenalin and seeing my own imminent death did that to a girl.

"Tell me what you see." He was back to staring at Sven.

I reluctantly studied the body again. "He's been shot in the head. I don't see any other visible wounds. No other sign of struggle or bruising."

"Is that all you see?"

"Other than the weird symbols in blood on his chest, yes."

Rossi shifted his head. "You see that."

"Who could miss it?" Red symbols on Sven's pale skin was like blood on snow.

There was a soft knock on the door.

"Come in, Ben."

Ben Rossi was one of Ordinary's firefighters. He was a nice guy, currently dating Jame Wolfe who was also a firefighter and a werewolf. They'd moved in together a couple months back, and had thrown a big housewarming party where they invited all their relatives.

They wisely had invited me and my sisters to help maintain the peace at the party.

Vampires and werewolves did not get along, but here in Ordinary, Old Rossi and Granny Wolfe worked to keep the animosity to as low a level as possible.

The smile on Ben's handsome face twisted into a grimace. His eyes scanned the room, looking anywhere but at Sven. "You wanted to see me?" His voice sounded strained, thin.

"Step into the room, please."

Ben did as he was told, but I could tell he didn't like it. He stopped as far away from the coffee table with the corpse as he could and faced Rossi.

"I'm sorry to ask this of you, Ben, but I need you to tell me what you see on my coffee table." There was a hint of power in Old Rossi's words, a weight that exerted pressure on Ben.

Ben's eyes met mine briefly—a shadow of fear, of revulsion—before he turned to Sven.

Ben blinked hard several times, and squinted as if he was trying to stare into the sun.

"Sven is lying there." Ben's words were clipped, breathless. "He is dead."

"Yes. Good." The weight of Rossi's words increased. "Tell me how he was killed."

Ben was panting. A trickle of sweat glistened at his temple, another at the curve of his throat. He swallowed, blinked hard again, as if trying to bring an impossible thing into focus.

"Silver bullet. One. Through the brain."

"What else?" Two words that made my ears feel like they needed to pop.

"I don't know." Ben whispered.

"His chest. Look at his chest."

Ben blinked and blinked, his gaze scanning over Sven's body, flitting across his face, neck, chest, unable to rest.

"I don't see, can't see anything else. A bullet. Just a bullet."

Ben was so distressed I was about to tell Rossi to let him go. I didn't understand what was going on, exactly, but I liked Ben and I didn't like seeing him looking so cornered and panicked.

"Do you see blood?"

Ben was visibly trembling now, his thin T-shirt soaked with sweat. Still, he stayed where he was, his gaze searching the dead vampire.

"No. No blood."

Holy crap. I could see the blood clear as day. Obviously Old Rossi could see the blood too. But Ben was not lying. Even I could see that.

"Thank you, Ben." Rossi's words were gentle, light and

laced with the vampiric tone that both hypnotized and soothed. "That is all I need. I'm sorry to distress you. Get a drink of water and rest. I'll talk to you soon."

Ben nodded woodenly, swallowed again several times and then all but fled the room, closing the door so quietly not an egg rattled.

"Okay, so Ben can't see the blood," I said.

Old Rossi had pushed up to sit on the edge of the couch, elbows propped on his thighs, fingers linked together, thumbs pressed against his mouth. He nodded.

"And that blood plus that bullet killed Sven."

Again, he nodded.

"So there's a way to kill your kind that isn't stakes, garlic, or solar power."

"Garlic is a myth. Although severing our heads works quite well. And so do the blood arts."

"Technical ichor?"

"Ichor techne. An art many centuries old. An art I thought burned, hidden, buried with the devils who first developed it."

Two ways I could take this conversation: ask about the devils who had developed a way to kill vampires I had never heard of, or find out who might have found that art to use now. And why on Sven. So I guess that was three ways.

"Did you know them?"

"The devils? Yes."

I waited. "Could they still be alive?"

"One of them is."

"Who?"

"Me."

Not what I expected. I wiped some of the sweat and rain off of my face and rubbed my palms on my jeans.

"Okay." I took a second to process that. "Okay. I've never asked about your past, and Dad didn't tell me anything more than we have noted in the family records. I'm going to assume you think this," I spread fingers toward poor Sven, "is tangled up with your past life? Lives?"

"It is."

"I'm going to need more than that if I'm going to solve this problem."

"Is that what you're going to do, Delaney? Solve this problem?" The fangs were starting to show, his usual hippy-chill attitude peeling away to give me a peek at the animal inside.

"I understand you take care of your own and the threats against them. But this is murder and I am the law in this town. Even if we buried Sven's death under a convenient story of him leaving for brighter horizons, we know someone killed him.

"They left him like that so we could find him. So we would know what they did to a citizen of our town. That won't stand with me. And it shouldn't stand with you."

He watched me with that damned steady gaze, the look that made me wonder how many of my fears he was cataloguing to use against me later.

"It wasn't a threat." Rossi said.

"Really? Because it looks like a threat to me."

"It was an invitation."

The biscuit and bacon I'd eaten earlier turned in my stomach. "Is that what the symbols mean? Some kind of invite?"

"No. The symbols are Sven's plucking apart, his undoing, his final death. His body is the invitation."

"To what?"

"War."

I let that sit between us for a couple seconds. Someone must have closed a door too hard somewhere in the house because the egg shells on their glass pedestals shivered and chimed.

"All right. What war? With whom? Over what? And if other vampires can't see this ichor techne, then was it an invite to you or to someone else, someone non-vampiric?"

"I was a mortal man many years ago, Delaney. When Rome seemed to rule the world." A shadow crossed his eyes, but it was not the black of killing. I thought it might be memory or regret.

I couldn't imagine looking back at memories from so long ago. Rossi had to be over two thousand years old.

Holy crap.

"This has something to do with Sven's death?"

"I was a soldier," he continued. "No different than the men beside me. Until we faced an army from the east. We were slaughtered, left broken and bleeding. Their soldiers defeated us.

Overwhelmed by numbers, we fell.

"But it was that night, as the wounded got on with the business of becoming the dead that the true enemy arrived. Devils, demons with fangs and a hunger for blood. There were only two of them. Impossibly tall and pale.

"They moved through the wounded, searching, sniffing. I had fallen near another soldier. Near my brother-in-arms. My *friend.*"

He practically spat that last word.

"I don't know which of us made a noise. Maybe it was me. That's..." He shook his head. "Too long ago. But they heard and they came sniffing our way. We were both drawn up and feasted upon. They drank our blood. It was horrifying. Painful. Until it wasn't. Until we begged for it."

"Vampires," I said to break the silence.

"Our makers. My maker."

"Are they still alive? Do you think they're behind this?"

"They are not behind this."

"What about your friend? The other soldier."

"Lavius is dead."

"Are you sure?"

He just gave me a long look.

"Then what does this have to do with Sven?"

"Only Lavius and I knew of the ichor techne."

"You must have learned it from someone. Knowledge gets written down, passed down. Who taught you about it?"

"No one. I created it."

"Before you were a vampire?"

"No. Many years after."

Which meant he must have used it to kill vampires. I didn't know why a vampire would need some fancy way to kill one of his own, and really, that was beside the point.

"Did you have records of it here? Or anywhere else in the world?"

"No. I've made sure the art was wiped clean from history, and not even mentioned in the myths."

Well, he'd done at least part of that. I'd never heard of it before, and I was in the know about the creatures in the world.

"So Sven being left with this drawn across his chest is

someone telling you, specifically, they've found your old weapon? Other vampires can't see the markings...how does that work?"

"I don't know."

"But you created this blood art thing."

"Yes. I created it. And it has always been visible to me, to mortals, to creatures including other vampires. I do not know how it has been changed to hide it from vampire sight. I do not know why."

"Totally ruins your reputation."

"What reputation?"

"Of being a know-it-all."

That got a fleeting smile out of him. "Focus, Delaney. This is a crime. You're supposed to be good at this sort of thing."

"All right. Tell me how this is a declaration of war."

"Sven was one of mine." The heat behind those words carried the strength of a thousand years. When Old Rossi brought a vampire under his wing, he became more than just their friend, he became their defender.

"Who wants to start a war with you? Someone you kicked out? Who hates you enough to want a war?"

Just because he accepted new vampires into Ordinary didn't mean they always stayed here. Rossi had more rules about bringing in vampires than I did about bringing in gods. If vampires couldn't live up to those rules, Rossi kicked them out.

Sometimes those partings were amicable, but not always.

"Do you have any enemies who would want you to suffer?"

He snorted. "Countless."

"I'll need a list."

He smiled, and it was almost his normal smile—no teeth. Except for the glitter of red in his eyes, he was very nearly the love-not-war guy I'd known all my life. He leaned away, lounging into the couch, both arms spread wide across the back of it.

"I am not in the habit of measuring how many people hate me, only how many love me, baby."

"Nice try, hippy. That's not a love letter." I pointed at Sven. Then a terrible thought crossed my mind. "Is it?"

"No. It is not."

"So give me names. Who have you made angry who might also have access to the ichor techne?"

Old Rossi sighed, and rubbed one hand over his hair, the most human gesture I'd seen out of him since I had walked into the room. He stared at Sven as if unable to look anywhere else. "I don't know. There is no one who comes to mind."

"Really?"

"Despite what you must think of me, I am a fan of peace and non-violent conflict resolution."

"Okay. So what do we do next?"

"We'll bury him. Hold a memorial service."

"I meant about his killer. About the invitation. The war."

"I don't know yet."

"We need a plan. Is there anything here we can go on? Anything that could be a lead? This town has resources we can call on, both mundane and godly."

"Let's keep the gods out of it. The only ones who might do me any good would be carrying their power, and when they carry power they do not listen to the needs of the undead."

"The gods in town could help even without their powers."

"I'd rather snip my left nut off than owe any of them a favor."

I could see he felt strongly about this.

"You might not have a choice in that. But I'll start with police records. See if there have been any unusual deaths in the area, things involving blood markings or shots between the eyes."

He was still staring at Sven, but grunted. I took that as an agreement and stood. I still hadn't dried out from the rain and the back of my thighs and butt felt cold.

"We're collecting information from the folks at the gas station and the people in the area who might have seen or heard something. I'll let you know if I find anything. If there's anything else you need, let me know."

Just before I opened the door, he spoke.

"How much do you know about Ryder?"

That sent chills over my chills. "Ryder Bailey?" At least I hadn't said: the guy I still can't stop loving even though he dumped me?

"Ryder Bailey."

"Um...well, we grew up together. His Dad retired to Florida and left him the cabin on Easy Lake that they remodeled together from the floor up. High school athlete, popular guy."

Handsome, funny. Kind. Always helping anyone who needs a hand.

"Came back to town just over a year ago with a fancy degree and clients and set up his own architecture business."

Folds origami, hangs his own art in his living room. Sexy as hell in bed. Gentle. Tastes like something deeper than caramel, something all his own. Something I wake up in the middle of the night craving.

"Hates rhubarb. Why?"

"That is Ryder's blood."

My stomach knotted and I glanced down at Sven. "Are you sure?"

"Of course I'm sure."

"Just his?"

"No. It is mixed with Sven's. That is an important part of the art."

"Mortal blood and vampire blood?"

"Yes. Killer and victim."

I shuddered. "You're telling me Ryder killed Sven."

"I'm telling you that's his blood. We won't know he's the killer until I question him."

I let go of the door knob. "You won't be questioning him."

Rossi shifted, his eyebrow lifted, eyes steady on mine. "Won't I?"

"No. Ryder is a mortal. That means he falls under mortal law. I will question him and you'll keep your hands off him."

"No."

"I'm not leaving this room until you agree to keep your hands—and everything else—off Ryder."

"Why should I do that?"

I could lie. I could try to strong arm him with legal threats. He wasn't the only one who could hire vampire lawyers. Just because Rossi ruled the vampires didn't mean he ruled Ordinary. But I figured the truth would work best.

"You understand that I am the law over you, over the mortals, and over the gods of this town. If you do anything illegal, I will throw you out of town. Permanently."

"You would never do that."

"Test me."

He glared at me. I glared right back.

"Do you love him?" he finally asked.

I don't know what he saw in my eyes. Probably something I wished I knew how to hide.

Rossi blinked. Opened his mouth, shut it, blinked again. "Oh, Delaney," he breathed, "are you sure?"

"No. Yes. Sometimes?"

"Is this recent? Since he's returned to town?"

"Yes and not really. I've loved him for years, but never said anything. We finally tried it a couple months ago."

"It? Sex?"

"Dating. And sex. But I got shot and we decided to take it slow."

Red flashed across his eyes, a flame moving fast. "Did he *dump* you?"

"That doesn't matter. I'm still sorting through the whole thing, which is personal and not a part of this case. You will stay away from him. I will find out if he is involved in Sven's death. If he is, if I find anything to tie him to Sven—"

"Such as his blood?"

"Which could have been stolen, or taken without his agreement. If I have any solid proof he was actually involved, I will let you question him while I am in the room with both of you. Got that?"

"Yes."

"I'll also take your word that the other vampires in town will stay away from him."

"I'll let them know Ryder Bailey is untouchable. But Delaney, if he is involved, I will not stand aside. Not even for you."

No pressure.

"If he's involved you will talk to me. We'll decide what's best. Unlike the vampires in town, Ryder Bailey has family who would wonder what happened to him if he went missing. He has college friends, business colleagues. He can't simply disappear without turning a lot of unwanted attention to our town.

"Remember, I am the police. I won't allow the murder of

any creature, deity, or mortal to go unpunished. Do you understand me, Travail?"

Very few people knew Old Rossi's first name. Even fewer ever spoke it. Something like anger hardened his features and I could see in him the soldier, the warrior, he had once been.

"More than you would think, Delaney Reed."

In those words were my dismissal. So I moved quietly through the door and closed it behind me, careful not to rattle a single, fragile shell.

CHAPTER 4

THE REST of the day dragged by with a few actual incidents to deal with—mostly fender benders from cars not stopping quickly enough on the wet street, or cars that were stalled while trying to navigate the puddles that swallowed the wet streets, or the car that got swamped because some tourist didn't realize driving on the beach in the waves wasn't as safe as it looked in a car commercial.

It wasn't until almost ten that night that I finally had a chance to talk to Myra and Jean.

We had the calls from the station forwarded, and met up at the all-night Blue Owl diner that had opened up on the north end of town last month. Terrible weather meant tourist traffic was cut to almost nothing. The diner had been struggling when it should have been doing its best business of the year.

The owner, Joe Boy, also owned the gas station where Sven had been found. I figured the diner could float for a year or so on the gas station profits. The diner had enough room in the parking lot and the back gravel lot for truckers to catch some sleep before taking the highway east toward the capitol of Salem, north to Portland, or further on to Seattle.

Other than one burly guy in a trucker's hat skyping on his tablet in the corner booth on the far side of the restaurant, it was us, the cook, and a single waitress.

We sat in one of the retro-style 1950s booths, each of us with a cup of coffee. The waitress, Piper, a mortal who had just moved into the area, had poured our coffee without asking, somehow knowing Myra would want decaf.

"What can I get you ladies? We have pie that would make your granny jealous."

Piper was in her early thirties, had long blonde hair that fell in soft curls. Her ears were pierced with tiny jeweled studs all the way from her lobes to the inward curl of the helix, and her face was squared at the chin, which somehow made her wide, sea-gray eyes softer.

I hadn't heard where she'd come from originally, but figured one of the town gossips would eventually fill me in.

"Let's make granny jealous," I said, realizing she had nailed exactly what I wanted. "Pecan if you have it and only if it's amazing."

"Best in the state."

"I'll have..."Myra started.

"Apple ala mode?" Piper suggested.

Myra looked a little startled and studied Piper's face. "Yes. That's perfect."

"And give me anything banana with lots of whipped cream," Jean said.

"We've got a banana-bourbon caramel cream that will knock your socks off."

"Good. I'm tired of these socks."

"Great." She jotted our orders down. "Sisters, right? Reeds?"

Looking between the three of us, most people might guess friends instead of sisters. I was built taller and more athletic like our father, had my long brown hair pulled back in a scrunchie and hadn't bothered changing out of my tan, button-down uniform over which I'd thrown a plaid flannel.

Myra was shorter than me and curvy in a soft blue sweater, rocking a noir pageboy hair cut and deep red lipstick. Jean, the youngest, currently had her long pigtails in several shades of turquoise tucked behind her ears and, even though she was the one who was actually still on duty, wore jeans. Her T-shirt had a head shot of the cartoon spy Archer on it, under which was written: I'D DO ME.

Despite our differences, it was something about our eyes that tagged us as sisters, all shades of blue from deepest to lightest. But it wasn't just the shape and color of our eyes that made it obvious we were from the same blood. It was the light. It sounded weird when I thought of it that way, but it was true. There was something about the Reeds in Ordinary, our bloodline having been chosen to uphold the laws of the town, that gave us a certain kind of light.

"I'm Police Chief Delaney Reed, and these are my sisters,

Myra and Jean."

"Oh. I thought Robert Reed was the police chief." She paused and must have already figured out the expression on my face because her eyes instantly filled with regret.

"He was," Jean said before I even had time to think of an answer. "He passed more than a year ago and Delaney took his position. All of us are on the force actually."

Piper's face fell and it was clear she was embarrassed. "I'm so sorry to bring it up. And I'm sorry for your loss. My condolences to you all."

"Thank you," Myra said. "He was a wonderful chief and dad."

"I'm sure he was."

"Well, if you need anything," I said, trying to lighten the mood. "Just give us a call. Welcome to Ordinary, by the way."

"Thank you. It feels like coming home."

I smiled. The little town had that effect on people sometimes. Someone would stop in on a vacation and then never go home.

"We're glad to have you. Where are you from?"

"Oh, we moved around a lot, my mother and I. Most recently, Utah."

"Pretty out there," I said.

"Pretty, but nothing like the seashore. I just hate living anywhere away from the ocean. Miss it too much. Now let me get you that pie. On the house."

"Thank you, but that's not necessary," Myra said.

"I'd like to. In thanks for all your work to keep this town— my home—safe."

"Sounds great," Jean said. "Thank you."

Piper nodded and headed back to the kitchen.

We all took a moment to ourselves and sipped coffee. Even though it had been over a year since Dad died, it was still hard to think that he was gone for good. There was a Dad-shaped emptiness in all of our lives, and I didn't think any of us knew how to fill it yet.

Music played softly in the background, a sort of melancholy blues and rock station that seemed to fit the rainy night, the diner, and our mood perfectly.

Jean pulled out her phone and fiddled with it a bit, Myra sort of gazed into the middle distance, and I rested my head against the booth, staring through the window beside us out at the night and the rain.

Piper was back before a new song started, just before things would have gotten really sad, pies balanced on a tray and a full, fresh pot of coffee in hand.

"Here you go, ladies. Pecan, apple, and banana bourbon caramel cream. Enjoy." She set the plates down, topped off our coffee, and sashayed off to check on the trucker in the corner.

"So what did Old Rossi say?" Myra ate the crust off her pie with bites of vanilla ice cream first before working her way toward the apple center.

I picked at the pecan, which was actually very good, then sat back and drank coffee. My appetite wasn't the best right now.

"Trouffle?" Jean mumbled through a mouthful of whipped cream.

"Yeah, trouble," I said. "Sven's been murdered. Bullet through the head wasn't enough to kill him but the blood symbols on his body were. Apparently Rossi came up with the blood-kill thing over a thousand years ago. He calls it ichor techne. He didn't explain how it's done, but he did say it's only used to kill vampires."

I wrapped both my hands around my cup and stared down into the liquid blackness.

"And?" Myra asked. "What aren't you telling us?"

"He said it was Ryder's blood on Sven."

They both stopped moving. Stopped chewing, stopped everything. Well, except for staring at me.

"You think he's telling the truth?"

I sniffed, and rubbed at my eyes. Suddenly I wished I could just curl up in the booth and ignore this day had ever happened.

"I don't know why he would lie about it. He was angry. He has every right to be angry. I'm angry."

Jean reached across the table and patted my hand. "Ryder doesn't have anything to do with this. He might be stupid sometimes, but he's not a killer."

The image came back to me of Ryder bursting into the station a few months ago when I was held at gunpoint by a woman. Ryder had handled his gun, and the high-charged situation, like a natural.

Maybe not like a killer, but like someone who knew how to deal with one.

Jean had always sort of idealized Ryder. She'd always thought he should be my handsome prince who would sweep me off my feet.

I didn't think she'd gotten over him dumping me yet.

"Rossi says it's his blood. We have to assume he has some tie to Sven's death. Did we get labs back on that bullet hole?"

Myra speared an apple chunk and used it to wipe up some of the melted ice cream. "It's a clean shot. 9mm bullet. There were no other bullets at the scene."

"Any prints?"

"Nothing clear enough. No boot prints, even though it was muddy out by that shed. Any tire tracks would have been run over by other vehicles using the gas station and washed out by the rain."

"So we've got nada," Jean said.

"We've got a dead vampire and a pissed off vampire," I said. "Rossi was holding a meeting. I told him to let his people know Ryder isn't to be messed with."

"What if he's trying to throw you off?" Myra asked.

"Rossi?"

She nodded. "What if he just wants you to think Ryder was involved?"

"Why would he do that? Ryder and I aren't dating. We're barely working together. What would Rossi get out of casting suspicion on him?"

Although, now that I thought of it, Old Rossi had warned me about trusting Ryder before. And Ryder had made a point to tell me that Old Rossi wasn't who he seemed to be.

Maybe something had happened when Ryder was younger and he still held it against Old Rossi. Or maybe Ryder had done some stupid kid thing that irritated the vampire.

Could it just be an old grudge?

"Do you two know if Rossi and Ryder get along okay?" I asked. "Are there any hard feelings between them?"

Jean licked banana cream off the tines of her fork. "Don't

think they really run in the same circles. Clean-cut Ryder and free-loving Rossi? There aren't a lot of social situations that would have put them in close contact over the years. Except the festivals and things like that."

We had four festivals a year in Ordinary. If you asked me, it was four too many.

"There's one more weird thing about this," I said.

They didn't seem at all surprised there would be more weird things. This was Ordinary, after all.

"The other vampires can't see the blood markings on Sven."

"Are you sure?" Myra asked. "Can they smell them?"

"Yes, I'm sure. He brought Ben in to prove it to me. I'd never seen Ben so close to a panic attack. He told Rossi all he could see was the bullet hole—he said it was a silver bullet by the way."

"Silver bullets kill werewolves, not vampires," Jean said.

I nodded. "Still, any kind of bullet is still a bullet."

"Okay," Myra said, compiling all that data into organized subsections in that methodical mind of hers. "Ryder should be back in town tomorrow. We can talk to him then, see if there's anything that points to him being involved with Sven's death. Maybe I'll drive by his place tonight, see if he got in early."

"No, I'll do it," I said.

"Delaney," Myra started.

"Let me. I know you and Jean have been trying to keep him out of my way, and I appreciate that. But I'm the chief here, and I'm the one who talked to Rossi and promised him I would check into Ryder."

"I'll come with you," Jean said.

"No, you'll go back to the station, or home with the calls forwarded, okay? Let's just keep everything about this as normal as possible."

"Dead vampire is not normal," Myra muttered before sipping her coffee.

"I know."

"How about the god power?" Jean asked. "Did you hear anything else about that?"

I shook my head. "Which reminds me, where's Crow?"

"I took him home," Jean said.

I groaned. "Really?"

"There wasn't any real legal reason to lock him up, and it's not like he's going to leave town without his power."

"He could," I said.

"Sure. But the gods in town would stop him before he even got one foot outside city limits. So I took him home—well, not *his* home."

She looked far too pleased with herself.

"Jean," Myra said. "What home? If I find him at my place, in my kitchen—or in my bed— I'm going to throttle you."

"Shit. Why didn't I think of dropping him off at your place? I have a key and everything."

"Jean," I said.

"Oh, take it easy. He's staying with Bertie."

Bertie was the town's only Valkyrie. She appeared to be a slight, bird-like woman in her eighties. While she was that, she was also the creature who made it her job to drag warriors off battlefields to their final resting places whether they liked it or not.

No one had ever put up a fight against Bertie and won.

It was no surprise Bertie was also the head of the community center, and pretty much ran all the behind-the-scenes events and gatherings that were hosted in Ordinary.

Those four festivals? All Bertie's doing. Honestly, I couldn't think of better hands, well, talons, in which to leave Crow.

"Okay," I said. "I give. That's brilliant. How did you get Bertie to agree?"

"I told her we'd each volunteer our time—no more than eight hours—at the next event she needed hands for."

Myra groaned and thunked her head on the table.

Dramatic? No. Not at all. The last time I'd gotten roped into owing Bertie a favor she'd forced me to judge a rhubarb contest.

Rhubarb.

Tastes like a demon's butt, no matter how much chocolate or alcohol is added to try to hide it. I thought giving ourselves over to Bertie deserved a little, no, maybe a *lot* of head thumping.

Jean, however, looked like she was enjoying torturing us. "Doesn't matter how much brain damage you give yourself," she said to Myra. "She'll still find you something to do for eight hours."

"I hate you," Myra mumbled.

Jean laughed and patted Myra on the head.

"When's the next thing?" Myra sighed.

"It's a fundraiser," Jean sing-songed. "Want to guess what it is?"

"No."

"Canoe jousting?" I said.

"Not this time. C'mon Myra. Guess. It involves pancakes."

She shifted her head to the side and cast a suspicious gaze at Jean's grin. "Is it a cook-off? A pancake breakfast? That wouldn't be terrible."

"Boring." Jean practically glittered with excitement. "Cakes on Skates!"

I heard the words, but couldn't make them fit together in my head.

"Skates?" Myra said. Was that actual interest I heard in her voice?

"Breakfast delivered to your door by people on skates. Costumes encouraged. She's got Hogan on board, so there will be cake donuts and cake cupcakes and cake cake, but he's got four kinds of pancakes he's going to whip up too." From the smile on her face, you'd think the man had invented breakfast pastries.

"Why skates?" Myra asked.

"It's also a contest."

We waited.

"How many deliveries a skating team can make. How many times a skater drops their delivery. How many tips they can get out of the delivery. Who gets back to the finish line first. That kind of stuff."

"Tell me Bertie already has judges."

Jean shrugged. "Who knows. You still have your old skates?"

"No."

"I do," Myra said.

"Good job, pack rat." Jean patted her shoulder. "You might want to loan them to Bertie so she can find some chump to sign up for deliveries. Unless you'd like to do the skating? Rebecca Carver will be doing it."

At the name of her old high school rival, Myra's face shut down into a scowl. "What's she doing back in town?"

"Slumming? Walking around in her Jimmy Choos, despairing about our lack of diamond-coated puppy baths and pills that make you poop gold? What? That's a real thing. Look it up."

Myra, who was still head-down on the table, rocked her head back and forth, having given up on the conversation.

"I got nothing," I said. "I'm out. It's been a long day and I want some sleep. See you two tomorrow." I threw a five on the table because even though Piper wanted to comp us our pie and coffee, she deserved a tip.

Myra said something that almost sounded like, "Gold poop pills. Brings a whole new meaning to gold digger." Jean laughed again.

I left them to it and pushed out into the cool, wet night.

I liked summer. I liked the ever-shifting coastal weather that brought us days of lukewarm fog, or nearly gale-force winds, or crystal clear sunshine stunners that made everything feel right in the world.

And sure, I liked the cool wet of autumn, winter, and spring in Oregon too.

But Thor giving us the middle finger for three months was really getting on my nerves.

"You couldn't give us one week of sunshine?" I asked as I tromped to the Jeep. "Come on, Thor. You know I'm grateful for your help in finding Cooper. I'm sorry you have to stay away from Ordinary for a year, but think of it this way. At least your power isn't lost."

I got in the Jeep and clicked on my seatbelt.

The rain seemed to lighten a little, the drops shrinking from nickel-sized to dime.

Maybe he was listening.

"You lay off the rain for the rest of August and most of September, and I promise we will throw you the biggest welcome home party Ordinary has ever seen when you come back."

I started the engine and guided the Jeep south toward town. By the time I turned east, navigating the quiet neighborhoods toward the lake, the rain was down to a soft drizzle that finally, finally, stopped.

I let out a long breath. "Thank you. Thank you so much, Thor."

I drove past the front of Ryder's cabin, then parked across the street. Moonlight filtered silver down through the clouds. Wow, Thor was going to give us a little break. I hoped he didn't change his mind in the morning.

Ryder's truck was in his driveway. Next to it was a sleek sedan with an in-state license plate, but not one I recognized.

Ryder was not only back in town, he also had company.

The memory of his phone call this morning rolled through my head. He had sounded tired, worried, and maybe drunk. He had sounded like he was leaving to do something he might regret.

Kill a vampire?

No. Ryder didn't know about the creatures who lived, or un-lived, among us.

Had he called because he was worried about returning to Ordinary? That didn't really make much sense. He lived here.

I studied the low glow coming through the window beside the door, probably light from the living room.

Maybe he had a date.

That thought hit me like a two-ton sledgehammer. Not that there would be anything wrong with him dating. He'd dumped me. We weren't together. So if he wanted to have a woman over, if he wanted someone else in his life, I should be happy for him.

Okay, not happy, but there were no legal grounds for me to slash his tires.

Maybe the chick's sedan had expired tags. Maybe it had been used in a bank robbery. Maybe I should go over there and check that out. Because it was my job, not because I was jealous.

I was moments away from running the plates when the porch light flicked on, bathing the front of the house in light.

I killed the engine and ducked down, hoping the night

would hide the Jeep. Why hadn't I parked out of sight of the front door?

Stake out 101, Delaney.

The door opened and two people stepped out onto the porch: Ryder and another man.

Yes! He was with a man, not a woman.

My heart did a leap of joy, which was totally unprofessional.

Ryder stood in the doorway scowling, his arms crossed over his chest. His dog, Spud, sat attentively at his feet.

Just watching Ryder, lit by the light of the porch and shadowed by night, made my heart thump harder. His wide shoulders were muscled from the hands-on approach he took to his business. He might design buildings, but that didn't keep him from going on-site and swinging a hammer. Those shoulders stretched the tailored lines of his dress shirt so that it was tight at the chest and biceps, but it skimmed his flat stomach.

Even at this distance, his dress slacks drew my eyes to narrow hips and long legs.

Ryder could model those business clothes, and more than one fashion magazine would take him on.

Since I'd seen him naked, I knew more than one underwear designer would take him on too. Those images were not helping me pay attention to what was happening at the porch.

They were talking. Maybe arguing? The man moved, his hand cutting a sharp line between them as if refusing something Ryder had said. He looked angry.

Okay, Delaney, pay attention.

Ryder's expression had gone flat and unreadable. He waited until the guy was done gesturing, then nodded, a clear invitation for the guy to leave.

The man leaned in a little, his finger pointed at Ryder's face, then off to the side at nothing in particular, or maybe indicating the neighborhood or town.

Hard to know. With the moonlight shaded by clouds, I couldn't even get a good look at his face.

Ryder didn't say anything. I could see his face thanks to the angle of the porch light and the fact that he was facing the street where I was hidden. He looked controlled, but the clenching of his jaw and something about the angle of his oh-so-relaxed body told me he was furious.

The man turned and I finally got a look at him. Light hair cut high and tight, square face. He was several inches shorter than Ryder, and wore a business suit tailored to his stocky build. I'd put him somewhere in his late forties, maybe early fifties.

From that single wash of light across his face I could tell he was angry too.

I didn't like him. I don't know why, but my split-second read on the guy told me he was a jerk.

I'd have guessed he was Ryder's boss, except Ryder was in business for himself. So maybe this was a big-wig client or an investor? Whoever it was, he got into his fancy sedan and left.

Even though I'd told Myra and Jean that I would stop by and talk to Ryder, now that I was here, I decided it would be better to talk to him tomorrow.

Good thing it was dark and cloudy. He hadn't noticed me sitting here in the Jeep.

I waited as he watched the man drive away. Then Ryder half turned toward the house.

Just as I was sure he hadn't spotted me, the cloud cover cleared and shot a beam of neon silver moonlight smack dab down on the Jeep, lighting it up. Lighting me up too.

"Thanks a lot, Thor," I grumbled.

Ryder noticed the light. Noticed the Jeep. Noticed me.

He paused, his hands clenching into loose fists, as if he were the one who had been spotted instead of the other way around.

I kind of hoped he'd ignore me. I kind of hoped he would just go inside.

He shut the door and jogged down the path to me.

I thought about starting the engine and gunning it out of there.

But that would be unprofessional.

Plus, I hadn't thought about it until it was too late.

Ryder knocked on the driver's side window. "Delaney?"

I rolled down the window. "Hey, Ryder."

"What are you doing out here so late? Something wrong? Need me at the station? Are Myra and Jean okay?"

See, this was the trouble with Ryder. Even though he was

the sort of guy who would date 'em and dump 'em, he was also the kind of guy who would reach out to people in need and help his neighbors and coworkers without hesitation.

"They're fine. We don't need you at the station."

He made a little "huh" sound then bent a bit lower, his arm draped across the door frame as he inspected the interior of the car. "So what are you doing out here watching my house, Delaney? Are you watching me?"

Yes.

"No."

"No?"

"No. I came here to talk to you, but I saw you had someone over and didn't want to bother you."

I wanted to look anywhere than at him, but if I looked away he would see the lie on me. Maybe he saw the lie on me now. Maybe he heard my heart beating for him, wanting him.

The wind ruffled his dark hair softly, the shifting gray and blue of moonlight casting him in velvet-edged marble. He was undeniably handsome, eyebrows thickest at the arch over mossy green eyes, nose straight and upper lip delectably heavier than his lower lip.

He looked tired. Lines at the edges of his eyes, across his forehead seemed deeper, and a full day's stubble spread dark along his jaw.

I wanted to kiss him. To press against his body and be surrounded by his scent, be filled with his warmth. My mouth went dry thinking about it, and other parts of me didn't care that he'd dumped me.

Would he take me back? Would he want me if I asked him to?

Maybe some of those questions showed on my face. Maybe my need, or my struggle to push my need away, lock it all up with the hope my traitorous heart would not give up, showed through.

Ryder didn't want me.

He had tried to apologize for how he handled the break up, or maybe for the break up.

Maybe he wanted me a little. But a little couldn't be enough. Could it?

His eyes were soft, and his lips curved in a smile that oddly looked sad. "Come inside," he said, all warmth and need and home. "I'd like...I need to talk to you too. Please come inside with me."

I shouldn't. Well, I *should* talk to him. Ask him if he murdered Sven. Ask him where he had been in the last forty-eight hours. But I knew if I followed him into his house, I wouldn't want to talk about murder. I wouldn't want to know if he was involved with Sven's death or anything else.

I'd just want him.

"We can do this tomorrow," I said in a thin voice I barely recognized.

His expression fell and I realized there had been something more than sorrow in his eyes. There had been hope.

This didn't have to be so hard. We had been friends growing up, friends all our lives before our one date and one night together that had not only ended before it had practically begun, but had also almost ended our friendship.

All those years of friendship deserved something didn't they? A chance?

"Okay," I said. "Let's go in. It's freezing out here."

He stepped back, looking relieved, but only far enough away to let me open the Jeep door.

"Not exactly the warmest summer we've had," he said.

Weather. We were talking about the weather.

I took it back. Our dating hadn't destroyed our friendship, it had blown it to smithereens and left behind the dust of conversations suitable for strangers over tea.

"Global warming," I agreed.

He didn't know Thor was behind our unseasonable storms, because he not only didn't know Thor was a god, he didn't know gods really and truly existed.

But I refused to chat about the weather, because really? We were better than that, even at our worst.

"Everything go okay today?" I asked as we walked up the path. "You sounded kind of...off."

"It went well enough. Sorry about the call, I was...I don't know."

I paused at the door, waited. "You were what, Ryder?"

He winced and gave me a look pleading for something. Maybe forgiveness. Maybe patience.

"I was missing you." That, said so low and soft, it was like a feather against my spine. "And I thought...and I thought maybe hearing your voice..." He shrugged one shoulder, whatever words he'd been about to say gone.

My heart gathered up those words like a bee did nectar. But my mind was still giving that clear thinking thing a try.

"You asked me if I was naked."

"You thought I was drunk."

"Well?"

"It was eight o'clock in the morning." He reached over and shoved the door, springing it open. "I was not drunk."

"You could have been."

"In what time zone?"

"The drunk one."

He snorted and shut the door behind us. I was standing in Ryder's house, with Ryder.

Last time we'd been here, one of us had been naked.

That one of us had been him.

My mind wandered over the memory of his body, his hard muscles, the sepia Leonardo da Vinci hand proportion sketch tattooed on his shoulder, the stars and artist's compass on his hip.

"I had just finished a meeting. Investors on a project in Seattle. Coffee?"

"It's a little late for coffee."

He took three quick steps forward. "Who are you and what have you done to Delaney?" He pressed the back of his hand on my forehead as if checking for a fever.

The warmth and pressure of that contact pulled a small gasp from me.

He was smiling, gazing down at me, so close I could smell his cologne worn and thickened by a long day against his skin, but made all the better by his unique scent mixed into it.

His eyes crinkled at the corners, laughter dancing in their depth.

"I'm right here," I breathed.

The glint of humor shifted, grew into something else. Heat.

Desire. Need.

His hand hovered, drawing fingers that gentled across my forehead, down my temple, then dragged along my jaw and slipped around to the base of my head. Fingers stroked my hair which was falling free from the hasty pony tail I'd put it in hours ago.

His gaze searched mine, asking.

I didn't know what I answered, but he tipped his head, angling his mouth nearer, nearer mine. I kept my eyes open for as long as I could.

"Delaney," he whispered, his breath warm across my lips.

I leaned, lifted, reached, just that fraction of an inch so that our mouths met.

Distantly, I felt his free hand slide around my waist. Distantly, I felt my hands skim across his ribs, my palms flattening on the wide, smooth planes of his back.

What I felt, what my whole world seemed to center on, where I began, where I ended, was that kiss.

Gentle at first, the kiss was warm, sweet. An embrace that sent a shiver across my skin.

Wild thoughts that this one, spare, aching touch would be all Ryder wanted to give trampled through me. And right on the heels of that was my logical mind yelling that this wasn't what I wanted. Wasn't what I'd said I wanted.

I wanted space. I wanted time.

Away from Ryder.

Didn't I?

He'd dumped me. No, that wasn't the worst part.

He'd *left* me. Walked away when I was bleeding, hurting, and vulnerable in a hospital room.

But even then, even when he had been telling me that he didn't want to be with me, hadn't he looked sad? Maybe even conflicted and torn up about his choice? Maybe that wasn't what his heart wanted, it was what his mind wanted.

And he'd listened to his mind.

Just like I should be listening to mine.

Or not, my traitorous heart said.

Feel, my heart urged. *Feel him.*

Ryder shifted the angle of his mouth against mine, the tip

of his tongue skimming gently at one corner of my mouth, then up, zinging warmth through me, dragging along the crease of my lips, asking for entrance, asking for me, asking for me to feel again.

I opened to him, a small sound slipping from my throat as his tongue plunged into my mouth, licking and tangling with my tongue, sucking, drawing me closer to him as he sank into me with promises of what we could be. What we could do.

Promises of us.

I lost myself to the sensations, a burring warmth building as his tongue, his mouth reminded me of what we had been together, how well our bodies had fit, how one touch from him struck a fire so deep within me, it burned my soul down to ashes, and somehow made it whole again.

I could lie to myself all I wanted. The real reason I didn't want to be around Ryder wasn't because I was angry at him for breaking up with me. Well, okay, yes, I was angry, but there was more.

I didn't want to be around Ryder because when I was near him, I didn't want to be anywhere *except* with him. When he was close to me, it felt as if a piece of my life snicked into place.

We might have only gone out on one date, but I'd known him my entire life. And he had known me. All the places where our years of friendship had planted roots had grown into something more. Something that friendship wasn't enough to contain.

He shifted again, his hand dropping lower to my hip, then his palm pressing against my butt, pulling us hip-to-hip. My hands followed his lead, and I rubbed one palm over the smooth material of his slacks. I could feel his very physical reaction to that, to me.

He wanted me. He wanted us. His words might say one thing, but his body couldn't lie.

And it was at that moment that my brain finally wrestled my heart to silence.

Ryder's blood was on Sven. Ryder might be a murderer or an accomplice to murder.

I might be kissing a murderer.

Crap.

I stepped back, stepped away, my hands lifting from the heat of him, from the strength of him as I put several paces between us.

He stayed where he was, for a long, long pause, breathing. We were both busy just breathing. Then he slowly lifted his head and straightened his back and shoulders. I kept my gaze on his eyes, no, that was no good. His eyes were glassy with need, his pupils wide. Lips were no better, they were wet and slightly swollen from the kiss.

I didn't dare look any lower. Ear. Ear should be safe.

So I stared at his ear. "We need to talk. You need to talk. This isn't talking."

He inhaled, held that breath. "Okay. We need to talk. Do you want to sit?"

Since my heart wanted me to do more than sit: specifically run into the bedroom and strip off all my clothes, and my mind also wanted me to run, out the door and as far away from Ryder as I could get, I thought sitting in the living room was a nice compromise.

I turned, blindly picked one of the chairs, sat there on the edge, hands gripping my thighs.

I stared at my knees, at my hands that were white-knuckled. Because I couldn't touch him. Because I shouldn't touch him.

Just breathe.

I had a job to do. There was no time for my private life, not here, not with a murder suspect. And if he was innocent, then I needed to know how his blood ended up on Sven. I needed to know what he knew.

If he hadn't been the one to pull the trigger, he might know who had. I needed a clear head so I could watch his reactions to my questions and read if he was telling the truth or a lie. With my heart pounding loud as a freight train, I wouldn't be able to hear his answers unless he shouted them.

Pull it together, Delaney. Do the job.

The clink of ice in a glass brought my head up. Ryder stood in front of the couch to one side of me, holding a glass of water. There was another glass in his hand. Looked like, smelled like whisky.

"Thought we could both use a drink."

Great. He'd left the room long enough to pour drinks and I hadn't even noticed. Losing my concentration in front of a possible murderer was every kind of stupid.

He smiled softly. "If you'd rather, I have some rhubarb juice in the fridge."

Just like that, he was my friend again. Ryder Bailey. The man I'd never stopped loving.

"Liar." I took the water. Sipped. It was good, cold, and helped clear my head. "You hate rhubarb."

He settled down on the couch, one arm spread across the back, the other propping the tumbler on his thigh. "No, really, it was given to me after the festival. Haven't opened it, but the expiration date is something like two years from now. The juice that never dies. Vampire juice."

I felt all the blood drain out of my face. "Why are you talking about vampires?" Even though my pulse was running too quickly, I was assessing his body language, and possible aggression levels.

Ryder and I were friends. But that didn't mean I wouldn't take him down, cuff him, hell, tase him, if he made the wrong move.

"It was a joke? Apparently a bad joke. What do you have against vampires? Read too many teen books?"

He was smiling, but there was something false about it. Something about his smile that wasn't my friend. Ryder had been gone for eight years. It was moments like this when I remembered there were parts of him I did not know. "Or maybe you've seen someone suspiciously vampire-like lately?"

He lifted his glass, swallowed the amber liquid, his gaze never leaving mine.

It was that motion, the bend of his arm to bring the glass to his lips that caught my eye. His long shirt sleeve was tailored, a little tight on his muscular arms. It was buttoned at the cuff, but there was a bulkiness under the material, at the bend of his elbow.

A bandage?

"I need you to unbutton your sleeve for me," I said.

His head tipped to the side, as if he hadn't quite heard me correctly. "What?"

"I need you to unbutton your sleeve."

"You want me to get undressed?"

"No. Just the sleeve. The left sleeve."

"Why?"

"There's been some trouble in town. I need to see your left arm."

He leaned forward and placed the glass on the coffee table in front of him. "What if I say no?"

"Are you going to?"

"I don't know. I thought we were going to talk."

"This is talking. We're talking."

"No." He leaned back against the couch, but did not look relaxed. "Were you outside watching my house because of whatever's happened in town?"

"Yes."

"Okay. So this is police business, and even though I am a reserve officer, you're not going to tell me what's going on before you ask me to strip?"

"I didn't ask you to strip. It's just an arm, Ryder."

"From the look on your face and your tone of voice, it's a lot more than just an arm. What happened?"

"Someone was killed."

"What?" He shot straight off the back of the couch, a look of complete surprise on his face. "Who? When? Here? In Ordinary? Have you caught the killer? No, of course you haven't, you're here. Wait. You think I'm the killer? Me?"

The cascade of emotions and reactions he rolled through seemed genuine. If anyone else but my childhood friend were acting the way he was, I'd believe them.

But there was something about the tightness at the edge of his eyes, something about the hard line of his mouth that belied his actions.

Oh, Ryder. This is one time in your life you're going to regret that you and I were such good friends.

Cop instincts told me to play along, to act like I believed him. To act like he didn't know anything about Sven's death. Even though my heart was sinking, and a part of me wanted to find a small room, shut the door and just scream and scream, I instead took a drink of water.

"I need to see your arm. You don't show it to me, I'll put you in cuffs, take you into the station and cut the shirt off of you."

He blinked a couple times as if my words confused him.

"You're angry."

"I'm not kidding."

He opened his mouth and inhaled, then let the breath out in a huff. "I can't believe you think I'm lying."

"I didn't say that."

He unbuttoned his left cuff but lifted his hand and sort of waved his finger at me. "That face says otherwise."

"What face?"

"The I-think-you're-lying face."

"And you're not?"

He shook his head and then rolled up the sleeve. "I don't have anything to hide. Why would I lie?"

His sleeve was rolled up to just below the bend in his elbow. "Happy?" He turned his arm so I could see it. It was a nice forearm. Muscled, tan from whatever spring sun we'd gotten months ago. There were a couple of scars that had healed white beneath the dusting of hair.

But that wasn't the part of his arm I needed to see.

"The whole thing," I said.

"My sleeve doesn't roll up any farther."

"Then take off your shirt."

He smiled and there was a hard edge to the grin. "So you *are* trying to get me naked."

"Just your arm."

"All right." The word had a bit of a drawl to it. Ryder leaned forward and unbuttoned his shirt. My gaze flicked away from his face long enough to see he was wearing a T-shirt beneath the button down.

He tugged at the rolled up sleeve, then pushed his shirt off both shoulders, letting it pool around his low back.

His elbow was wrapped with a light gauze which was holding down a pad at the inside of his elbow.

"So what happened to your arm?"

"I gave blood."

"To whom?"

"The Girls Scouts." His eyebrows dipped down tight and he looked really confused. "Red Cross. Who else?"

"Do you donate often?"

"When I can."

"Here in town?"

"No. I was in Seattle at a meeting. But there was a blood drive going on outside the restaurant next to the hotel."

"So you decided to stop in and do your civic duty. How very Boy Scout of you, Bailey."

"You're not a fan of saving lives?"

I held his gaze. I couldn't accuse him of giving blood to be used as a vampire murder weapon. But I could get my hands on the Red Cross record base. Unsurprisingly, there were a lot of vamps who worked for the agency, and I was sure Rossi knew a few who would be able to tell us if Ryder had actually donated.

"I'm a police officer," I said after another sip of water. "I'm all about saving lives."

"Then why are you staring at me like I'm keeping secrets?"

"Because you're keeping secrets."

His expression stayed closed off, flat. And then a little grin—a very Ryder grin—curved his mouth. "Why would you think that?"

"I don't think it, I know it."

He nodded. "So are you."

I lifted one eyebrow, so he continued. "Keeping secrets. What aren't you telling me, Delaney? Is there something about the death that I should know about?"

"Nothing I'm at liberty to share."

He pulled the remainder of his shirt tails out of his slacks and tossed the shirt casually over the arm of the couch. Then he leaned forward, arms resting across his thighs, hands clasped. He looked like a man who was about to make a deal.

"I want to make a deal."

Called it.

"No."

"You wouldn't say no if you heard the deal."

"Still no."

"I'll tell you what you want to know."

"Anything?"

"Yes."

"And why would you do that?"

"There are some rules."

"Rules."

"My deal. My rules."He held out one finger even though they were still linked. "One: I can refuse three questions."

"Okay." Despite myself, I was warming up to this game.

"Two: you can only ask me ten questions."

"Okay." No deal breakers yet.

"Three: you have to agree to the same for me. Answer seven of the ten questions I ask you. Honestly."

"Honestly."

"You want me to tell the truth. I want the same in return."

"And how long does this deal last?"

"Until the questions run out."

I didn't see how this could go wrong. I could answer anything he asked honestly. He might not like the answers but I could give them to him.

"All right. Deal."

He smiled and leaned back. "So ask."

"Did you really donate your blood to the Red Cross?"

His eyebrows plunged. It was not the question he expected. "You sure you want to ask me that? I already gave you the answer."

"I want an honest answer."

"Yes, I donated my blood to the Red Cross. You're not very good at this game, Delaney."

"You think it's a game?"

He lifted a palm in a shrug sort of gesture.

I searched his eyes. The problem with our little truth or truth game was that we had to trust that neither of us would lie. He didn't look like he was lying, but he might be. Vampire murderers weren't the most reliable sort, one would suppose.

"My turn," he said.

"That's not how it works."

"It's how it works. One question for one question."

"You didn't say that in the rules."

"It's in the small print."

"What small print?"

87

"Right here on the tip of my tongue." He stuck his tongue out at me and I couldn't believe how stupid and sexy it made him look.

I tried not to smile. From the bull-hockey totally sincere look on his face, he was trying not to smile too.

"All right, slugger. Ask your question."

"Have you forgiven me for breaking up with you?"

Man went right for the gut. Had I? He had given up on me. On us. And yet he was right here, in front of me, still a part of my life. Maybe a friend. Maybe more.

Maybe a murderer.

I put that possibility aside for the moment.

"Yes."

He nodded slowly, and bit at his bottom lip then released it. "Thank you."

"Did you kill Sven Rossi?"

His shoulders jerked. "No."

I searched his eyes, his face, his body for the truth behind that single word.

He held up a hand. "I'd like this to be outside the question game."

"All right."

"Holy, shit, Delaney. Sven's dead?"

"Yes."

"How? Since you're asking me if I did it, I assume you don't think it was an accident."

"He was shot."

Ryder rubbed his palm over his face, fingers lifting to tug his wind-mussed hair. "Jesus. Okay. And you think this has something to do with me?"

"Are we back on the question game?" I asked.

It was his turn to study my face. I could guess at what he saw. I had a good mask of indifference when I needed it. My eyes met his steadily. Waiting.

"Sure. Do you think I have something to do with Sven's death?"

This might be my childhood friend in front of me, but there was something about those words, about how carefully he said them, as if he were using the question as a means to an end.

Ryder wanted something from me, or expected me to be or do something.

He was digging for information just as hard as I was. I knew my motivation. What was his?

"Yes."

Slight tightening of his eyes was the only response I got from that. Now it was my turn.

"Do you know who killed Sven?"

"Pass."

"What? No."

"I said I won't answer three questions. That's one."

"If you don't answer it, I'll assume the answer is yes."

"Assumptions are not the truth."

I finished off the water and set the glass down. "I think we're done here."

He watched me stand, watched me walk toward the door. Just as my hand wrapped around the handle, he asked. "Do you trust me, Delaney?"

I swallowed hard. Wondered if I did trust him. Wondered if I was just trusting a man I'd known years ago, instead of the man I didn't know now.

"Pass."

I opened the door and walked out into the night.

CHAPTER 5

SOMEONE WAS staring at me. Since I was sleeping, in my bed, in my house, the sudden knowledge that I was not alone was more than a little disconcerting.

My gun rested on the wooden stepladder I used as a night stand. I could grab for it, but whoever was staring at me would see that move coming from a mile away.

Unless they had already found the gun and were pointing it at me.

That thought pushed me right over into instantly awake, eyes open, adrenalin pumping, sitting up.

"Delaney, dear. It's about time. I've been waiting."

I blinked at the voice, and also at the face of Bertie, our town's one and only Valkyrie who was sitting in the corner of my room, in a chair, sipping something that smelled like tea.

Bertie's white hair was cut short and a little spiky, making her sharp green eyes too large in her heart-shaped face. She wore a pantsuit in a lovely red that might make other people think of roses, but made me think of blood, and a scarf with little red cherries printed on it tied at her neck.

The tea was in a china cup that must have come from her kitchen because I didn't own anything that delicate. Her fingernails were sharp and painted gold.

I should really start locking my front door.

"Why are you in my bedroom?" I glanced at the clock. "At six-thirty in the morning?"

"Because I need to be at work by seven, of course."

"Of course." I echoed like that made any sense. "Bertie? Seriously?"

"I'm delivering your package."

"Package?"

"The one your sister left with me yesterday."

I pressed at my eyes with my fingertips and tried to get my brain working. "Crow. You brought Crow here."

"Exactly. Now, since you're awake, I'll get my day started. The fundraiser is taking quite a lot of time to coordinate. I'm always so short on volunteers. I'm going to have to reach out into the community more vigorously if people don't start stepping forward."

Subtle, she was not. But then Bertie didn't so much recruit volunteers as conscript people into service. "Coffee before blackmail," I said.

"If you want breakfast alone, you should really start locking your front door."

I shoved the heavy quilt off my legs and swung my feet down to the floor. I was wearing what I usually wore to bed: T-shirt and boy shorts. "Not a lot of people bother to climb the million steps to my house, and those who do aren't usually criminals."

"Yes. Still. Most people don't have to be murderers to have ulterior motives."

"Did you hear about Sven?" I asked.

"Yes."

I wouldn't have expected another answer. She was, after all, a creature who pulled fallen warriors off the battlefield and escorted them to the party pub in the sky. It made sense she would be in the know about the newly departed.

"Do you know anything about his death that might help me find his killer?"

She paused with the graceful curve of the cup poised right at her mouth. Her eyes went hawk-sharp at that question. "Are you accusing me of something, Delaney?"

"No." I rubbed at my forehead, stared at the floor a second, then back at her. "I'm not accusing you. I've just never dealt with something this...big before. Vampires don't just show up murdered in this town. I'm not sure that it's ever happened before."

"It hasn't."

"The whole thing has me on edge. I'm new to this position." I pointed at my chest, just over my heart. "Bridging power for the gods is one thing. Police chief is another. And this death is going to bring too much attention to our little town."

"No one has to know about it. He was a vampire, dear. He

91

didn't have family outside Ordinary."

"Apocalypse Pablo already knows about the body."

"One mortal can be easily convinced not to remember what he saw. Old Rossi should have already taken care of that by now, actually."

Vampires and their mind-suggestion power. It should be against the law.

"Ryder knows too."

She raised one eyebrow and sipped tea. Apparently, her previous suggestion stood for Ryder too.

Yes, I understood that Ryder was just as mortal as Apocalypse Pablo or me...well, maybe a little more than me, but I hated the thought of stealing away his memories just because we could.

"That won't really solve the problem."

"The problem of the outside world finding out about Sven?"

"The problem of who killed him."

"You are sure it was murder?"

"Yes."

"None of the Wolfes have been brought in to question?"

The Wolfes were a big extended family of werewolves that owned the rock quarry in town, among other things. Granny Wolfe had made a truce with the Rossis years ago. The terms of the truce were that they'd both keep the murdering of respective family members to a minimum.

"I haven't checked in with them yet. But I will. Have you heard anything concrete that would make you think they took out Sven?"

"No. Nothing at all." She frowned a little. "How was he killed and where was he found?"

I figured she already knew this information. "Bullet through the head. The shed outside Joe Boy's gas station."

She sipped, her eyes focused somewhere else as she thought that over.

"What kind of bullet?"

"Silver."

She blinked, then shook her head slightly. "I was asking about the caliber, but silver is also interesting. Several of the

Wolfes carry guns."

"Several of everyone in town carries guns."

"What did Rossi say?"

I stood, winced a little at my stiff back and scowled at my bed. I hadn't been asleep long enough to get a crick in my back. "Rossi is not pleased."

"But he's taking care of it, is that correct?"

"It's not something he can take care of, Bertie." At her look, I continued. "Not something that he alone can take care of. Someone killed Sven. Murder is against the law. Mortal law, which is the law we follow in this town, the law I enforce. Someone in town committed murder. I'm going to find them, arrest them, and lock them away for life."

"What if it's not a mortal?"

"I'm worried at how much you're insisting it might be a werewolf. Did the Wolfes do something to bother you? Forget to fill out their volunteer forms for the next festival? Laugh at your Cakes on Skates idea? Overcharge you for gravel in your driveway?"

"Don't be silly," she said primly. "My driveway is clay pavers."

"If it is someone in the Wolfe family, then that's up to Rossi to deal with, since they have laws in place between their kind," I said. "If it's a mortal, or any other creature in town, then that's on me and the law."

"And if it's a god?" She watched me over her cup, golden fingernails gleaming in the low light coming through the windows.

"If it's a god, then I'll deal with that too. Just like my fathers and mothers before me."

"You think you can handle a rogue god?"

"I think there isn't anyone else around here who could handle it better than me."

She sipped tea, the last of it, from how deeply she tipped the cup.

"Well, then. Since you have god powers to track down and a killer to find, I'll be on my way and let you do your work." She stood and started toward my bedroom door. "I don't know who killed him, Delaney. That is beyond my knowing. I do know he wasn't killed in Ordinary."

"What? Wait. How?"

"Because *that* is within my knowing. Every death that happens on this soil, I will know." She shrugged. "Mostly the gods, but I am old enough and have been here long enough that I've developed a sense of when mortals and creatures die too."

"And Sven wasn't murdered here?"

"No."

"Do you know where he was killed?"

"No."

"Does Rossi know Sven wasn't killed in town?"

"Do you think anyone could be quick enough to kill one of his before he was there to stop them?"

Vampires were not slow.

"No."

I chewed on that information. If Sven hadn't been killed in town, I'd need to find out when he left and where he went. Unlike the vacationing deities who were on a pretty tight leash went it came to walkabouts, creatures could and did wander the world at their leisure and pleasure.

If Bertie was right, and Sven had been killed outside of Ordinary, then why had he been found in the shed inside town? Yes, it was on the outermost northern edge of town, and a person wouldn't have to drive more than half a mile to be officially out of town, but either someone had brought him back or he had somehow gotten that far on his own.

Rossi said the ichor techne was an invitation, which would mean someone had dropped off Sven's dead body. Dead before he was even inside of Ordinary again.

Another reason Rossi was so angry. Since all the vampires seemed to be able to speak with each other thought-to-thought, he would have known where Sven was, might even have heard his last thoughts.

I'd need to talk to him to find out exactly how the telepathy worked, and what rules and restrictions he enforced. There might be other details that he or another vampire could give me, clues that could lead to the killer.

"Yes, then," Bertie said into what I realized was a long span of silence. "I'll leave you to your busy day."

"Thank you, Bertie."

"Thank you for giving ten hours of volunteer time for the Cake and Skate."

"Eight hours."

"Excuse me?"

"We agreed to eight hours each. Jean told me."

"Oh," she said with a playful glint in her eyes. "I must have remembered incorrectly. Thank you for *eight* hours." She gave me a quick smile and I knew the next time we spoke she'd accidentally forget again.

"When is it, again?"

"Saturday. Starts at eight in the morning. I'll expect to see you at the Puffin Muffin bright and early."

Bertie was nothing if not persistent.

"Coffee's free for volunteers, right?"

"So is the cocoa and marshmallows."

Like I was a child.

"Fine." I padded across the floor to the bathroom. "I'll be there. But I'm not skating."

"Oh, I'm sure we'll find a better way to use your talents."

She said it so sweetly, it shouldn't have sounded like a threat. But it totally was.

A shower was definitely in order. After a good hot soak in the nice strong spray, and as much vanilla body wash as I could spread over every inch of my skin, I stepped out of the shower and got dressed.

A quick glance out the window told me we were looking at rain with a chance of downpour today—no surprise there—so I gave my summer shorts one longing look and, instead, pulled on a pair of jeans and tank top.

Over the tank top I layered a thin T-shirt and over that I buttoned up my work uniform. I attached my badge over my heart, just below my name tag, and checked my reflection in the standing mirror propped against one wall.

Well, my tan wasn't getting any traction this year, but my wash of freckles still spackled my nose, cheeks and forehead. Eyes with that in-between blue and green color looked a lot like my dad's. I brushed my hair even though it was still wet and wrapped it back in a quick pony tail at the base of my neck.

95

I thought I had the kind of face and build that most people would say was average or maybe just on the athletic side of average. Jogging, which I'd missed out on yesterday, kept me lean, and my job kept my fashion choices practical.

I wondered what Ryder saw when he looked at me. Was I more police chief now than the girl he'd grown up with? Was I still the woman following doggedly in her father's footsteps? Was I the small town girl he was just humoring?

Was I someone he could love?

Or was I the person who was going to lock him away?

And not in an adult-fun-time kind of way.

I pulled on socks and my boots—boots, in August—and walked through the small living room to the smaller kitchen.

"You're out of cocoa mix." Crow hunched at my table, elbows planted and palms spread on both sides of his face like he was trying to keep his head on where it belonged.

"Drink a little too much last night, did we?" I strolled over to my coffee pot, measured out grounds and hit the go button.

"That Valkyrie could out-drink a sailor. Or a fish. Or a sailor fish that's been stranded in the desert with nothing to eat but salt for a week."

He hadn't moved so his words were coming out a little smooshed from how his mouth was also a little smooshed between his palms. His eyes were closed and he wore the same clothes I'd seen him in yesterday.

There was no umbrella hat in sight.

Thank goodness.

"She didn't even let you get a change of clothes?"

"Said you'd handle that. Wouldn't let me go home. Evil babysitter. I would have just slept."

From the way his words sort of faded off there near the end, I wasn't sure he hadn't been sleeping at the table.

"Any ideas about the powers?"

"They're still lost?"

He didn't add to that, so I poured coffee in my big travel mug, threw in some sugar and cream and grabbed a granola bar out of the drawer.

"Let's get to it." I patted the top of his head.

"Don' wanna."

"Don't care. You're in my custody and I need to get to work."

I walked out into the living room and pulled on my jacket. Maybe the rain would lighten up today.

Yeah, I might as well wish that the god powers would show up in a basket on my doorstep with a note on them.

"C'mon, Crow. Move it." I opened the door. There was not a basket of god powers on my doorstep. There was a god.

Death, to be exact.

"Good morning, Delaney."

"Hey, Than. What brings you by? Want to see me bleed again?"

He raised an eyebrow as if he had no idea what I was talking about.

"The last time you showed up on my doorstep? I got shot. I'm thinking you might be bad luck."

"I am very good luck. You were lucky I was here, vacationing when you were shot, as your wounds did not prove fatal."

I smiled. "Nice try. Just because you don't have your power doesn't mean someone can't die, I recall you telling me that before you signed the contract to vacation in Ordinary. Although if someone does die, they're gonna miss out on your delightful sense of fashion as their soul goes to the great beyond."

He glanced down at his neon green shirt that said LEAGUE OF EXTRAORDINARY GENTLEMEN across the chest. I wasn't sure if it was a bowling team, or a comic book club, or maybe part of that croquet team Odin and Thor had pulled together.

"Are you insinuating that this attire is unsuitable to a vacationing man?"

"No. Not at all. Join the bowling team?" I pointed at his chest. "Shirt?"

"Polo."

I wasn't sure if he was telling me what kind of team he was on or shirt he was wearing.

"Come again?"

"I've joined the polo team."

"We have one of those? With long handled mallets and

horses?"

"We use croquet mallets."

"So either you're playing with a team of long-armed Sasquatch, or you're riding really short ponies."

He sniffed. "I take it you find this hobby of mine amusing?"

"No. I'm glad you've found a hobby. How goes the kite shop?"

Crow shuffled up behind me, zipping his coat and shoving a beanie over his head. He still looked hungover as hell, but at least he was moving. He produced the umbrella hat from out of nowhere and gingerly fastened it over his head.

Great.

Than's obsidian eyes flicked to Crow, keen with interest in this new fashion statement, then away, as if ignoring a worm among the fruit.

"The shop is adequate. The sales are not. Weather," he added as if I hadn't noticed the non-stop rain. "But I did not come to discuss the weather."

I stepped aside so Crow could exit my house, then followed him and Than off my tiny covered porch since there wasn't enough room for three people to stand on it. Of course, now we were all getting wet—well, Than and I were. Crow looked smugly dry under his stupid hat. I started down the stairs.

"What did you come to discuss?"

"The contract of Ordinary. A contract you are currently in breach of."

Right. Death. Had a steely eye for rules and dotted lines being signed.

"I thought only Mithra would take me to the mat for that." Mithra was among other things, a god of contract. He had never been to Ordinary, as far as I knew.

"I assume you're talking about the missing powers?" I went on. "Technically they are still inside Ordinary, still together in one place, and therefore still within the contract guidelines."

"Do you know for certain that those things are true?"

We'd reached the bottom of the hill and I continued on to my Jeep. "No. But I don't know they *aren't* true."

Crow sniggered and got into the passenger side of my Jeep.

Than didn't even crack a smile. But then, Than never smiled.

"One day," I said. "One day I'm going to get you to smile, and it is going to be one of the proudest moments of my life."

The eyebrow twitched again, but his face stayed the kind of bland that would make oatmeal jealous.

"I am not the only god who will not tolerate a breach of contract."

"Understood. But since we haven't broken the contract yet, well, only Crow has broken it, I say the rest of you are still in the green."

"Green."

"Maybe yellow. But we aren't in the red yet. Trust me."

I opened the Jeep door, waited to see if that brush off and false confidence would be enough to hold him. I knew he wasn't the only god who was a stickler for contracts. I knew he wasn't the only god who was angry about the missing powers.

Heck, if I were a god, I'd be angry about it and would certainly do a lot more than politely remind the police chief that she had screwed up big time.

"I will, Reed Daughter. But even my trust must be earned."

And now my little goose bumps shivered to full quack. "I'm doing everything I can. We'll find the powers. We'll get them safely back under lock and key and if you want to reclaim your power and leave town, I'll be more than happy to help with that too."

He nodded, just a fraction of a movement. Rain spattered down on his head, soaking his dark hair and tracing rivulets through the creases of his face.

I wondered what he'd look like in an umbrella hat.

"I do not doubt you, Reed Daughter, but I do not trust in your choice of guardians for the power."

"Yeah, maybe Crow wasn't the best idea."

"Hey!" he said from inside the Jeep.

"But it was his turn. I won't make that mistake again."

That seemed to ease some of the darkness in his gaze. "Excellent. If I can be of assistance, please do call upon me."

I nodded. "Thanks, Than, I will. Two things: you might want to wear a jacket in the rain, or at least a hat. An umbrella is another popular wet-weather choice."

His eyes glittered. I wasn't sure if it was with humor or annoyance.

"And please call me Delaney."

His mouth twitched, but didn't quite pull into a curve.

Darn it.

I slid into the front seat of the car.

"Delaney?"

Death held a white envelope between his fingers. He must have pulled it out from beneath that crime-against-nature green shirt of his because it was mostly still dry.

"This is for you."

"What is it?"

"An envelope, I presume."

Ha-ha. Funny guy.

"From you?"

"I found it on your doorstep."

My stomach clenched at those words. I mean, it wasn't like people left me unmarked envelopes every day. I had every right to assume it contained trouble, bad news, or both.

"Thank you." I took it, glanced at the front, which was plain white, unmarked, then the back, which was the same, and also sealed. "Would you like a ride?" I tucked the envelope into my inside pocket.

"Yes, thank you." Than settled into the back seat of the Jeep. "If I may inquire, Crow," he said primly. "Just where could one purchase such fetching head wear?"

Before Crow could answer, I started the engine and flipped on the windshield wipers hoping to drown out Crow's laughter.

No luck.

CHAPTER 6

"CAN I shoot him yet?" Jean sat on the edge of my desk, her foot swinging, her bubble gum pink hair pulled up into two tight buns above her ears.

"Who?"

She widened her eyes like she couldn't believe I'd ask her that. "Our new, annoying mascot."

"I heard that!" Crow slumped in a chair in the lobby. He'd somehow gotten hold of a stapler and a wastebasket and was shooting staples at the wastebasket from about five feet away.

"One more staple, and you're paying for a year's supply."

I heard the quiet *snick-click* of the stapler shooting. "Bill him," I said to Jean.

She grinned. "Bill him and make him take over our volunteer shifts for Bertie?"

Crow snapped out of his slouch and approached the empty front desk. "I object. That's cruel and unusual punishment. I thought you needed my help to find the powers."

I took a sip of coffee and studied him. He looked worried, which wasn't an emotion I'd ever seen last with him. But then, I didn't think he'd ever screwed up on this massive of a scale before.

"I brought you into custody to try and keep you out of trouble and also to try to keep you alive. You made a lot of enemies among the deities."

He made a derogatory sound. "None of them like me anyway. I'm not afraid of them. They don't even have their powers." He waggled his eyebrows.

I rolled my eyes. "You know they don't need their powers to kill you, right? Mortals have been offing mortals since the dawn of mortals."

He didn't look concerned. "What's with the secret envelope you haven't opened?"

"Secret envelope?" Jean asked.

I narrowed my eyes. He'd done that on purpose to divert the conversation. Brat.

I hadn't opened it yet because I didn't want to deal with whatever was inside it in front of Jean. I wasn't sure if it was instinct or just because I was sometimes an over-protective big sister, but I wanted a look at the contents before I got her or Myra or anyone else involved.

"It's not a secret."

Crow raised his eyebrows. "So open it."

I glared at him extra hard, which only made him smile extra wide.

"What envelope?" Jean asked again. "Where did you get it? Where is it?"

I sat back and put my cup down. "Death gave it to me. He found it on my doorstep this morning."

"Death was on your doorstep?"

"He wanted to make sure I was making the finding of the powers a priority."

"Okay, so why haven't you opened the envelope?"

"It slipped my mind."

She sat there and gave me a look that was so much like our mother that I almost laughed. "Fine, it didn't slip my mind. I wanted to deal with it in private."

"Why?"

"It was left on my doorstep, unmarked." I tugged at my coat on the back of my chair and pulled the envelope out. "I wanted to make sure it was something we could handle before I shared it with you and Myra—and yes, I would have shared it with you."

To demonstrate, I handed her the envelope. She took it at the edges, just like I did, and after a moment glancing at the front and back, held it up to the light. "A letter?"

"I think so."

"Open it," Crow said. "Seriously, I've never seen anyone take this long to open their mail."

Jean pointed a finger at him. "You don't get a vote." She handed the envelope back to me. "Open it."

I pulled out my pocket knife and used the sharp blade along the seam. There seemed to be just a piece of paper inside. In case I was wrong, I made a shooing motion to get Jean off my desk, then stood and tapped the open end of the envelope onto the desk. No powder or other substance fell out.

Paranoid? Maybe. We were a little town several decades behind bigger, more modern towns, and hadn't had anything deadly mailed to any of the inhabitants. Still, we hadn't had a vampire killed in town before either.

Progress wasn't always a good thing.

I tugged at the paper inside, and unfolded it.

It was plain, white, unlined. The handwriting in black ink was neat, sharp, and slanted hard to the right.

Police Chief,

Do not let anyone read this letter. Not your sisters, not the gods, nor any creature. Meet me behind the Blue Owl diner at midnight. I know who took the power.

The letter wasn't signed, dated, or otherwise marked.

"Well?" Jean leaned toward me. I folded the letter and tucked it back in the envelope.

"I'm not going to lie to you, but I can't tell you what the letter says."

"Like hell you can't."

"Tell me instead," Crow suggested.

"No."

The silence in the room would have been comical if I didn't know just how annoyed I had made Jean.

"Is it about the murder?" she asked, no more humor in her voice.

"I'm not going to do twenty questions with you too."

"Is it?"

"No. And that's all I'll say."

"Is it from your boyfriend?" Crow asked.

"I don't have a boyfriend."

That, apparently, was top-quality comedy right there and Crow laughed himself silly. When he finally got done and focused on me again, his mirth turned to surprise. "Oh, come on. Have you forgotten Ryder Bailey? Your boyfriend?"

"We're not dating and we're not going to date." That

103

sounded firm. Sounded sure. It didn't matter if I secretly wasn't so sure it was the truth.

"You two have been dating since eighth grade." He held up one hand to stop me from arguing. "Walking each other to class, showing up at the same birthday parties, helping each other with school projects, and let's not forget those long looks when you didn't think the other was looking." He made a kissy face while batting his eyes.

"We weren't dating. We were kids."

"You joined the volley ball team just so you could see him outside the locker room when he was warming up for baseball practice."

My eyes went wide. I'd never told anyone that. There was no chance that I'd been that obvious about Ryder. "I joined volleyball because I liked the game."

"Because the games gave you a chance to see Ryder sweaty without his shirt on."

"Who told you that?"

Jean snorted.

"Like anyone had to tell me?" Crow smiled again, but this time it was more the smile of an uncle who had known me since I was born. "Delaney, you've always loved him. Maybe as a friend for a while. But as you got older, it was a different kind of love."

I gave him what I hoped was a piercing glare. "What do you know about love?"

"So very many things," he said in a way that carried the years of his life that were far from mortal. "Enough to know he loves you too."

"If you think he loves me, why haven't you ever told me that before?"

"Hello? Trickster god. It's a lot more fun to watch you two crazy kids bumble around and try to figure it out on your own."

This time Jean laughed. "Just when I thought I couldn't stand you for a second longer, umbrella head, I change my mind."

"So is the note from Ryder?" Crow asked.

"No. And before you ask: it's not dangerous, it's not signed, it's not anything that will be a problem."

Jean shook her head. "Not good enough for me. Let me see it."

"No."

"Delaney, you're going to let me see it."

"Do you have a bad feeling about this thing? A doom-twinge?" Jean could usually feel when something bad was about to happen. It was her special skill.

I held up the envelope. Her expressive blue eyes ticked to the envelope. I could almost feel her trying to see what was on the paper inside.

"No," she finally said after a full minute.

"Then you know this isn't something that will endanger my life."

She didn't really know that. None of us had that power. But if it were truly dangerous, Jean would at least have a bad feeling about it.

"I have a bad feeling about it," she said.

"Really?"

She dropped her eyes. "No. But I don't like that you're not telling me what's in that letter."

"I'll tell you tonight," I promised. "You're working graveyard, right?"

She nodded, and stifled a yawn. "Should have been out of here an hour ago. Have you seen Myra?"

Just then, Myra walked through the door. Showing up exactly when she was needed was Myra's special skill.

"Morning." She looked a little tired, but had a bag of pastries in her hand that smelled like apples and cinnamon.

"Morning," I said as she hung up her coat that was wet, but not dripping. Looked like we might be finally getting a break in Thor's temper tantrum. Her shirt was untucked, and lifted a bit. Just enough to show me a little bit of skin that was bruised green.

"You're in late. Something come up this morning? Fall in the shower?"

She shook her head, but wasn't making eye contact. If I knew her, and I did, I'd suspect she was keeping something from me. Which meant she was.

I didn't like the idea that whatever it was, it involved bruises.

Maybe for once it was something good? Myra deserved some happiness. She had always been the most serious of us Reed girls, but since Dad had died, that subtle joy inside of her had seemed to falter and fade.

Maybe she had a boyfriend. She hadn't dated since Tristan left for Europe. It had been a quiet sort of love affair—which is the only kind of love affair Myra had ever had—and Myra never really spoke of him except to say that they had parted as friends.

Or it was possible I was just projecting my hopes and issues on my sister. Just because I wished I had figured out where I really stood with Ryder and had done something about it, didn't mean all of my sisters wanted to be dating.

"You still seeing Hogan?" I asked Jean.

She gave me a look that told me just how random that question seemed.

I waited. It might have come out of the blue, but I was still curious.

"It's complicated?" she finally said. Well, sort of asked.

"Is he bothering you?" Myra used that protective tone she'd had ever since I'd been shot. "Do I need to go talk to him?"

"Delaney got an anonymous letter on her doorstep this morning!" Jean blurted.

Total diversionary tactic, the rat.

It worked. Myra's cool blue gaze shifted to me with laser-like focus. "Show me the letter."

I held up the envelope, flipped it so she could see front and back and then shoved it into the pocket of my coat.

"Not funny." Myra advanced. I noticed Crow made himself busy staring at the uninteresting notices and tsunami evacuation routes that covered one of the lobby walls. "Give it to me."

She wasn't usually this bossy. Well, no, that's not true. She was always a bit firm about the things she wanted to happen. But the last year and a half had put a grimness in her I wanted to take away.

So I stood up and gave her a hug. "I'm fine. It's a letter. Nothing dangerous, Jean isn't getting any vibes off of it, and it's a private note—but not from Ryder. I'm going to tell you what it says tomorrow morning because the person who wrote it wants it to be private for a little bit. But I won't do anything dangerous, and I won't let anyone hurt me, and I'll be smart and careful, Mymy."

I hadn't meant to say so much, but it all came pouring out of me in the quiet seconds while our cheeks were pressed into each other's hair.

She finally switched her stiff one-palm-only hug to something with a more familiar squeeze, then stepped away. "You aren't supposed to be more annoying than Jean." Her words were light, but the fear in her eyes that she quickly tucked away wasn't.

"We decided to put annoying on rotation. I pulled the short straw today."

She nodded, her eyes asking me not to do anything stupid that would make her regret her decision to not read the letter.

I hoped my eyes were asking her to tell me why she was hiding bruises.

"I will be *safe*."

She still didn't believe me, but knew I wasn't going to back down.

"Donuts?" I glanced down at the bag in her hand.

"Um...yes. New health food bakery is finally open. They're giving away free samples today. I picked some up to...try."

Jean snatched the bag out of her hand and opened it, peeking inside. "They smell okay."

They smelled wonderful. And she would have said so if she weren't in a "complicated" relationship with Hogan, who owned the best bakery in town.

She pulled out a little glazed apple fritter with a dab of what looked like vanilla cream in the center.

"Apple fritter ala mode," Myra said. "All organic ingredients."

Jean raised one eyebrow, took a bite and chewed. "Damn it," she said.

I held out a hand and she gave me a fritter, then passed one on to Myra. We both took a bite. That little confection was full-on delicious, flaky, rich, and the vanilla must have used sour cream for just the right amount of tart to balance the sweetness of the apple.

107

It was the best apple fritter I'd ever tasted.

Jean was frowning at her fritter.

"Too sweet," I said.

"Terrible texture," Myra added.

Jean flashed us both a smile. Hey, if she was dating Hogan, then that was the only baker who got the Reed sister support.

She handed a fritter to Crow, who wonder of wonders didn't tell her it was the most delicious thing he'd ever eaten.

"So, I'm outs," Jean snuck another fritter and tucked it into her cheek as she walked over to the coffee table. She held the bag of pastries over the trash can. "Should probably just toss these out, right?"

"Or," Myra said quickly, "we could put them on the counter in case anyone else comes by today."

"Like Roy," I said. "He'll be in to work the front soon. He should probably try one just to keep in the know on the new businesses in town. It's community support and all that."

The scowl she gave us might have been more convincing if she weren't busy swallowing her second fritter. "But just this once, right? We allow these in the station for the good of the town. After that, if we eat donuts, we get them from the Puffin Muffin. Because we want to support our long-term businesses too."

"Yes," I said.

"Of course," Myra agreed. "We will love all donuts equally, but the Puffin Muffin's most of all."

Jean rolled her eyes and placed the bag next to the coffee pot. "Don't get into trouble." She pointed at me. Then she pointed at Crow. "If you do anything, or don't do anything to make her get into trouble, I will handcuff you to Odin. Without your silly hat."

"Clever hat, you mean? The umbrella hat that keeps me dry? The hat that is a fashion statement that is totally trending? That hat?"

Jean pulled on her coat, flipped up the hood and pointed at it, like she was reminding him there were, indeed non-silly hats in the world. Then she strolled out into the light drizzle.

As soon as the door clicked shut, Myra and I were elbowing each other in a race to the bag of fritters.

She threw some sweet elbow blocking moves I'd never seen her use before and got there before me. She held the bag in her fist like a war prize. "Tell me what's in the letter."

"Not happening. Not even for those donuts."

"Plus," Crow said, "they are giving out free samples today. Delaney could just go get more for herself."

Myra shot him a death glare. Crow smiled. "See how helpful I am?"

Trickster. Always trying to stir up trouble. We Reed girls got into enough of it on our own.

I knew how to solve the donut dilemma. Blackmail. "I'll tell Jean you ate them all."

"Seriously? You'd tattle?"

"Or, we could split the remaining donuts and never speak of it again." I held out my hand. She looked at it for a moment, then took it in a firm handshake.

"Deal."

"What about me?" Crow whined.

"They're free. Get your own samples."

CHAPTER 7

I HAD a day to kill before I could go meet my anonymous pen pal behind the diner, so I decided to check in with Old Rossi. I had a couple questions about that vampire-only telepathy that connected the members of his clan.

Had he felt Sven die? Had any other vampire? Had they heard his final thoughts, or had they seen through his eyes?

Was there a chance someone in town had seen or heard Sven's killer?

Old Rossi held a number of classes each day. Usually things like yoga, meditation, and lately some kind of Zen scribbling. Calling ahead would have only gotten me his answering machine. I drove to his house.

Crow was in the passenger side of my Jeep. Since I'd lost the rock-paper-scissors to Myra, I was his default babysitter.

"You're telling me you're not dating Ryder?" Crow apparently didn't know when to let a subject die.

I listened to the intermittent shush of windshield wipers while we stopped at the red light. Vacationers of the hearty Oregon variety walked the sidewalks, making the best of their beach stay with window shopping, hot caramel corn, wine and beer tastings.

I caught a glimpse of Chris Lagon, our local gill-man and owner of Jump Off Jack Brewery, wearing a tank-top and shorts, walking toward a coffee shop and looking happy as a gill-man in the rain.

The town's three Furies—Al, Tisi, and Meg—laughed and shoved each other as they roller skated across the crosswalk. They wore roller derby shorts that showed off their dark legs and light jackets. They must be practicing for the Cake and Skate coming up. I wondered how Bertie had roped them into it.

Something bright and odd moved up ahead and I squinted at the man exiting a shop as I realized what the *it* was. An umbrella hat. The person beneath it was tall and lean, and walked with the perfect posture I'd only seen Death carry off.

Great. Now Death had an umbrella hat. I hoped Crow hadn't seen him.

"We're not dating. You can get off that subject now."

"Not dating doesn't mean you don't love him."

Crow stared out the side window and seemed peaceful. Like he wasn't trying to stir up trouble. Like he was a guy who had known me since I was born and who cared about the state of my heart.

Odin might think I should never trust a god, that no one who was a vessel for such great power could also have the capacity to care for a lowly mortal like me, but I didn't think that was true. Crow had always been fun to be around, kind to me, or certainly not cruel in his teasing. He and my father had gotten along well too.

That meant something to me.

"Do you love him, Delaney?" Crow turned to study my profile as I eased down the main road.

"If that made any difference at all, we would still be together, I think. He's not the same guy who left this little town eight years ago. I'm not the same girl, either."

"So you do still love him."

He tipped his head a bit, his eyes telling me I could lie, but he'd know it if I did.

"It's not that easy."

He chuckled. "No. Love isn't. There are the few—very few—who fall into love and never quite break the surface back into the real world, but for most people, for most beings, love is not an easy road."

When I didn't say anything, he brushed at a non-existent speck of dust on my dashboard. "I don't often offer advice."

I laughed, one short bark. "You're always telling people what to do."

"Sure, but I don't offer advice. Not real advice, not really. Understand?"

Wow, I was currently witnessing a miracle right here in the front seat of my Jeep. Crow was being serious.

"All right. I'm listening. Advice away."

"I've always thought you and Ryder would find a way in

this world. Together. I'd thought you'd tell him about the gods and creatures in Ordinary a long, long time ago, but you've kept that secret, haven't you?"

I nodded. That was part of being a Reed. You knew all the secrets of the town and didn't share them.

"Your father liked him, you know. He thought you and Ryder would have tried dating after high school."

"Ryder went to college out of state."

"I know. In the long run it's probably a good thing. Let him broaden his horizons, stretch his mind and conceptions of the world. But he came back here, Delaney."

"His house is here."

"He didn't come back for a house. He came back for you."

"Well, if that's true, he had a weird way of showing it. He dumped me, Crow. He was the one who called it off, not me."

"Because there are things he doesn't want you to know about his life."

"What?"

"You aren't the only one who has secrets, Delaney. Ryder's been gone from this town for eight years. He's lived a life you know nothing about—a life no one knows anything about because if you listen to him, you'll realize he never really goes into detail. He brushes away any pointed inquiries and changes the subject. That is the behavior of a man who has something to hide."

"Are you telling me I should love him and trust him or I should take him in for questioning?"

"I'm telling you love makes you vulnerable. It strips away all the shields and safety nets and leaves you open for great joy, and occasionally a lot of pain. Sometimes, when someone loves someone else with everything they are, they will do stupid things. Like not telling them something about their past. Like not telling them the secrets they are afraid will hurt the other person."

"What secret could he have that would hurt me? I'm a cop."

"What secrets do you have that could hurt him?"

I had a lot of secrets. Pretty much half of my life was something I didn't talk about to anyone in town except the deities, creatures, and my sisters. It had always been that way. It was better for the creatures and the deities that their existence not be discovered. It was better for the mortals too.

But it wasn't all that great on my love life.

I'd dated a few times in high school, but every boy I'd been with broke it off. They'd told me I was too into things they weren't interested in. Like following in my father's footsteps and becoming a cop.

They didn't know that I hadn't really had much of a choice. Well, maybe that wasn't completely true. Dad would never have forced me into police work if I'd hated it. But I idolized him, wanted to be just like him. And since he was also a bridge for transferring god power to those lucky few mortals who could become vessels for it, just like me, I felt the closer I fitted my footsteps into the path he'd chosen, the more likely my success would be.

Luckily, I loved being a cop. So did Myra and Jean. We loved taking care of Ordinary. Not just the creatures and vacationing gods, but all of our other neighbors.

"You know I'm in an unusual line of work, right?" I asked him. "Telling Ryder the secrets of the gods and creatures, and everything else isn't the same as something he might not want to tell me."

"You don't think a mortal could be hiding a dangerous secret?"

I flipped on the blinker and waited for a gap in traffic to take the turn up to Old Rossi's place on the hill.

A little girl, probably six, wore a mini-umbrella hat. I noted with surprise, that her mother did too.

"Lookee, lookee," Crow said. "Wouldn't catch on, you said. Stupid hat, you said."

I ignored him. "What kind of dangerous secrets do you think Ryder might be hiding?"

"You read the headlines. You get the police department chatter. Humans are capable of all sorts of terrible things."

I laughed. "So...what? You think Ryder's part of the mob? Or is dealing drugs or has suddenly decided to take up human trafficking as a side business?"

Crow was quiet a moment, as if trying to decide how he was going to answer me.

"Sorry," I said. "I'm listening. I'm trying to hear you and not judge what you're saying."

"That," he said. "Say that to Ryder. Tell him you'll listen."

"And find out he spent eight years in and out of jail?"

"And find out what he spent eight years doing. Really doing. With whom. *For* whom." He waved his hand dismissively. "Yes, he got his degree and says he worked for an architecture firm. Have you followed up on that?"

"His work history? We brought him in as a reserve officer. We checked his background."

"Everything on the record."

"What do you think there was to find off the record?"

Crow rubbed at his mouth and his eyes narrowed. "Delaney, this isn't...you're making it hard for me to decide what to say. So I'm not going to say anything. But I am going to ask you a couple questions. Okay?"

Seemed like a lot of people liked playing the Q&A game lately. "Fine."

"Does Ryder act more like an architect or a law enforcement officer?"

"A cop? You think he's a secret cop?"

"Just. Answer."

"He runs a building business. Of course he's an architect."

"That's not what I asked."

Okay, so the question was: Did Ryder act like he was in law enforcement? The image of him striding into the room when I'd been held at gunpoint, the easy way he not only checked over the situation, but also kept an eye on any other possible threats. His calm under pressure and that flash of hard light in his eyes that settled like a granite edge when he was talking about certain things and people.

Yeah, he acted like he'd had training. Myra had even said the same thing to me a few months ago after the Rhubarb Rally. Since my sisters had done a lot of work to keep Ryder's schedule and duties far away from my own shift, I couldn't say I'd seen him in cop-mode much these last few months.

But the feeling that I'd been shoving to the back of my heart for too long was more than just intuition. It was knowledge.

"Yes," I said, "he acts like a cop. What does that have to do with love?"

"Nothing. Everything. It has to do with secrets. The things people won't say because they want to keep someone they love safe."

"He doesn't want to tell me he's a cop?"

"He doesn't want to tell you a lot of things. Maybe he's not a cop. But what I know for sure, is he is not just an architect, and he did not move back into this tiny town because he thought it would be good for business."

"You think he lied?"

"I think he hasn't been forthcoming."

"And you know this how?"

His black eyebrows raised and so did the corners of his mouth. "Hello? Trickster. I know when someone is putting on."

"If he is hiding something, that's all the more reason why I shouldn't be in a relationship with him."

"Tell that to your heart."

"My heart isn't stupid enough to fall for a man who might be keeping dangerous secrets."Crow shook his head.

"What?"

"Now who's the liar?"

I didn't have time to answer because one: I didn't want to, and two: we had arrived at Old Rossi's place.

I parked the Jeep right next to Ryder's truck.

What was he doing here?

I tried to picture him doing Zen scribbles or hot yoga....

Hot yoga had its appeal. Ryder sweaty, shirt clinging to his chest, his flat stomach, muscles flexing as he moved, stretched, thrusted.

"Are we getting out today, or should I order us a pizza?" Crow asked.

Okay, so maybe my mind had been wandering a bit. "You can stay here."

"Nope. I'm very interested as to why our Mr. Bailey is here at big daddy vamp's house, aren't you, Delaney? Do you think it might be a *secret* meeting? Full of skullduggery?"

I ignored him and got out of the Jeep. Yes, it was odd that Ryder was at Old Rossi's house, especially since Rossi had warned me off of Ryder, and Ryder hadn't ever seemed all that friendly to Rossi. Not to mention I'd specifically told Rossi to leave Ryder alone.

There was little chance Rossi would want to give me time to answer questions about what he had felt, what any of the vampires might have felt, when Sven had been killed.

But I didn't want Rossi to do Ryder any damage. It had been Ryder's blood on Sven, it had been Ryder's blood used in the ichor techne. It was possible that Rossi had called Ryder up here so he could kill him.

Well, hell.

I resisted the urge to pull my gun. Instead, I walked quickly up to the front door.

Even though I had been here only a handful of hours ago, it felt like an entirely different house. Funny what sunlight can do to a place.

I knocked. I heard voices coming closer. Three, I thought. Two I recognized: Old Rossi and Ryder. The other I didn't.

Crow stood behind me now. Guess he didn't want to wait in the Jeep.

Old Rossi opened the door. For just a second, a heartbeat of a moment, his eyes narrowed. If I were anyone else in town, I might think that he was unhappy to see me. But since I knew Old Rossi, I knew he wasn't just unhappy, he was annoyed.

Interesting.

"Hi, Rossi. Can I have a couple of minutes of your time?"

"This isn't ideal, Delaney."

"It won't take long." I stepped into his house. I didn't have to be invited across a threshold—human had its advantages—and he stepped back, the annoyed rolling into a simmering frustration that was not quite anger.

Really, if he wanted, he could send one of his family members to take care of me. Vampires were at least three times as strong as a human. If he wanted me marched off his property, he could make that happen with a snap of his fingers.

But it would be really stupid of him to push this to a physical kind of confrontation. Better just to see me in and answer my questions rather than fight me and watch as I locked him and his entire clan up in a silver and garlic-lined prison cell.

Yes, I was human. I was also a Reed. That meant some things. It meant I didn't back down, I didn't break easily, and I had the kind of endurance that let me manhandle god powers if I had to.

"I see you have company." I waved vaguely over my shoulder toward Ryder's truck out front.

"So do you." He flicked a look at Crow, then crossed his arms over his chest. He might have looked intimidating if he wasn't wearing soft gray yoga pants and a worn out shirt with: LET'S GET DOWN, DOG written across the chest.

"Is Ryder taking up yoga?"

Old Rossi almost never smiled with his teeth, but would curve his lips. He had the kind of face that said "smolder," and his smile reached his eyes with a sort of diamond-hard glitter. If one didn't know he was a vampire and couple thousand years old, one might think he was a handsome cologne-ad model, even though his eyebrows were thick and low to his eyes and his nose was strong. His messy dark hair, a little too long, only accented those killer cheekbones of his.

So the unfulfilled smile carried a power. It made one want to see his teeth, see his smile, see what would make a creature like him laugh.

Sort of like a spiderweb looked incomplete—all those holes—and therefore safe for a fly to duck through.

"Delaney," Ryder's familiar voice called out.

I looked down the hallway past Old Rossi. Ryder walked my way.

My heart took a jump and went for a double-Dutch beat. I'd just seen him last night, but there was no denying the happy that flooded my senses when he was near. I practically thrummed with it.

Behind him was the man I'd seen arguing with Ryder on his doorstep the other night.

"What brings you by?" Ryder asked.

"Yes, Delaney," Old Rossi asked. "What brings you by?"

"I just wanted to check a few things with Rossi."

The vampire's eyebrows flicked up. Behind him, Ryder's did the same.

Okay, so maybe I wasn't sounding as casual as I thought I

117

was.

"Don't think we've met." Crow strode up past me and Rossi, aiming straight at the man I still hadn't been introduced to. "My name's Crow. I run the glassblowing shop here in town."

"Pleased to meet you." The man's voice was a low rumble with a bit of an accent from the other side of the continent. He shook Crow's hand. "Name's Jake Monroy."

"Friend of Mr. Rossi's?" Crow asked.

"No," Ryder said. "He's here with me. Mr. Monroy is looking at investing in land and businesses in town. I told him I'd show him around while he's here."

"Are you selling land?" I asked Rossi.

He finally realized he wasn't going to get rid of me or Crow and turned his body to open up the circle of conversation.

"I am not selling." Rossi motioned to the living room and we all made our way toward a more comfortable setting.

"I might be interested in hiring Mr. Bailey to remodel my studio."

Maybe that was the truth. Rossi used the second home on his property for his classes, and I didn't think he'd done much to update it in all the time I'd known him. But it was too much of a coincidence that he had a dead vampire covered in Ryder's blood show up yesterday and now was keenly interested in hiring Ryder today.

"An upgrade," I said. "Is business that good? I mean, with our weather being so wet this year, you can't be bringing in that many vacationers." I gave him an innocent look.

He gave his own look that said I was laying it on a little thick.

"Not at all. The weather has given me time to contemplate the changes I'd like to implement. I've been impressed by Mr. Bailey's concepts and creative vision. I'm excited to see what energy he can bring to this project."

All of that was pleasant enough. A pleasant pile of bologna. The only thing Old Rossi was excited about was keeping Ryder close at hand in case he felt like killing him.

I could just picture them going over the details: *Hey, Ryder? What do you think about re-doing the edge of the balcony?* Shove.

No. That wasn't going to happen. I might not be able to admit out loud that I loved him, but even if I hated Ryder, I wouldn't leave him in Old Rossi's hands when the vampire was literally out for blood.

"Could you and I speak privately?" I asked.

Old Rossi narrowed those ice blue eyes, but I squared off to him, my hands on my hips, letting him know it wasn't really a question.

"Maybe after I've given Ryder and Jake my time and attention," Old Rossi said. "I know you're a busy man, Ryder, with other appointments today."

"No, that's fine." Ryder had folded down on the couch and looked more relaxed than any of us except maybe Crow who was mooching around the edges of the room. "I'll jot down some notes about that studio. Go on ahead."

Of course, Ryder also caught my eye. He didn't think I was there on some kind of casual house call either. He knew I was investigating a murder—a murder that I wasn't giving him any details about. I was pretty sure he was leaping to all sorts of conclusions as to why I needed to talk to Old Rossi.

He wasn't right about me thinking Old Rossi was a suspect, but he wasn't wrong about my reason for being here. Or at least what my reason had been before I'd seen Ryder's truck in the driveway.

"How considerate," Old Rossi said, his voice tempered but his eyes hot. "And you, Mr. Monroy?"

The man I did not like even though I'd barely spoken to him, shoved both hands in his pockets, the right one stopping short as it caught on a squared-off ring on his finger. "No, it's fine. You go on and deal with the...*officer*. Our business can wait."

Wow. Could he have sounded any more resentful and condescending?

There is a thing vampires do right before they go for the throat. It's sort of a black heat that radiates from them. I knew this because my father had told me. He knew it because he'd seen vampires attack before.

In all my years in Ordinary—which was all my life—I'd never seen any real vampire violence. Bar fights? Sure. Yelling matches? Yes. Petty squabbles and some dirty underhanded revenge that involved rotted shrimp and old eggs? Of course.

But the pure distilled anger and violence Old Rossi radiated at being told what to do, like a child, was eye-opening.

A little heart-stopping too.

And just as quickly as it had happened, that dark violence was gone. Old Rossi wasn't radiating anything except a sort of vibe that advertised he was fond of sandalwood and long walks on the beach.

"Miss Reed." He extended his hand as a sign for me to follow him out of the room. He never called me Miss Reed. I suddenly felt like I was being called out of class to see the principal.

He was upset I'd interrupted him. Well, too bad. He wanted to know who killed Sven and so did I. And only one of us was a police officer.

"Drinks?" Crow asked, having found his way to the bar in the corner of the room. It wasn't even noon yet, I didn't think alcohol would make any of this easier.

I flicked him a look that I hoped said: *Behave yourself* over my shoulder as I walked out of the room. His look said: *La-la-la. I can't hear you,* as he studied the label on the vodka.

Rossi strode—well, with his grace it was more like glided— angrily into the eggshell room.

He opened the door with enough force to make the chicken shells tremble.

"*What*," he snarled, "do you want?"

I shut the door carefully behind him and refused to be intimidated.

"Why is Ryder here?"

"I told you."

"You told me a lie. Now tell me the truth."

"I don't like him. I don't trust him. I don't think he is innocent in the death of one of my own."

Well. He didn't mess around. Good. I liked it best when Rossi was being blunt.

"You don't have to like him or trust him. But you do not get to decide on any creature, deity or mortal's innocence in this town. That's *my* job, and I am good at it. So you want to try that again? Tell me that you didn't bring him out here to kill him?"

One eyebrow rose up toward the curl of black hair that brushed his forehead. "If I were going to kill him he'd already be dead, and buried so quickly, he'd still be steaming six feet under."

"Why don't you trust him?"

He paced over to his couch. He didn't sit, instead walking along the back of it, his hands gripped at the wrist behind his hips. "That is a question I would rather not answer. Are you sure it's the question you want to ask?"

"Yes." I could tell him I had ideas, theories as to why he had been trying to warn me off Ryder ever since he'd found out we were dating. But I didn't want to influence what he was going to say.

"That isn't the question you came here to ask me, is it Delaney?"

No. "Yes. One of them." See? I could be truthful.

He had reached the far side of the couch and studied the eggs in cases there for a moment before turning back toward me.

"He smells funny."

Okay, that was not what I expected him to say.

"Funny how? Like ha-ha? Or like weird? Is it a blood thing? A fanger thing?"

He looked mildly offended by the fanger remark, but continued as if I hadn't said anything.

"Throughout the years there have been those who hunt. Those who seek out the creatures of this world. Those who would eradicate anything that is different, misunderstood, alien."

"You think he's a vampire hunter? Like Buffy? Sam and Dean? Seriously?"

I had it on good authority that there were no vampire hunters in the world. Sure, there were people who were curious about cryptozoology. There was scripted monster hunting that might make for a good half-hour slot on some fake historical or nature channel. But there were no organization of hunters who really believed there were real vampires in the world.

"There is an organization of hunters," Old Rossi started, and I could only blink several times as my brain did some revisions and carried the dumbfounded. "It has not long been formed. Throughout the years, such organizations come...and go."

From the slide of his tongue over his upper lip, I could guess how exactly those organizations had disappeared.

"They often die from being ignored. If they are exposed, mockery is their bane. This is not a world that wishes to believe in the things that linger in the shadows." For that he gave me a lazy half-smile.

Okay. Maybe I liked it better when he didn't smile.

"So you think...there's a group of people hunting vampires? Killing vampires like Sven? You think Ryder is a part of that group?"

"It was his blood."

"He donated blood. To the Red Cross."

He snorted. "You believe that?"

"I checked the records. It's on the up-and-up. He donated blood. I think someone used his blood to kill Sven."

"You think there is someone who wants Ryder blamed for Sven's death? Who hates him that much?"

"You."

Old Rossi breathed out hard enough his nostrils flared. "How many times do I have to tell you that if I wanted him dead, I would take a very direct action toward that goal?"

"Would any of your clan want him dead because you don't trust him?"

"Possibly. But they would not act upon that desire without consulting me."

"Would you know if someone had done it?"

"What do you mean?"

"How connected are you to the other vampires in the town? Can you read their minds? Can you see through their eyes? Hear through their ears?"

"Didn't your father ever explain the blood bond of our kind?"

"Not in detail. I know you all have an...awareness of each other. You can read minds. Mortal minds and each other's minds."

He waited to see if I was going to add any details to that.

"Really? That's all?"

I shrugged. "We try to respect every creature's privacy. There's probably more in the books."

"Which you haven't read?" He shook his head.

"Yet. I'll get to it. It's been a slightly crappy year."

He unhooked his hands and rubbed at his temples. "All right." He hitched one hip on the back of the couch and leaned there. "Vampires mate."

"I know that."

He held up one finger for my silence. "Vampires mate. Mates can read each other's minds, see through each other's eyes, hear through each other's ears. Vampires born as blood relations also have this ability with their genetic relation—so sisters or brothers, fathers or mothers."

I didn't tell him I understood the meaning of the word "relation." He was talking. That's what I needed.

"In general, we can communicate thought-to-thought, but seeing and hearing via another of our kind is not easily done. Sometimes lovers can make that connection. As the prime vampire, I can force a connection to any I accept as my family."

"So you all have telepathy, but the sight and audio is more specific."

"Yes."

"Is it influenced by distance?"

"No. Although Ordinary has an amplification effect on those abilities."

Interesting. I'd have to go back to that little tidbit later.

"So you'd know where any of your clan is, even if they're outside Ordinary?"

"Of course."

"Did you know Sven wasn't in Ordinary when he was killed?"

He was silent. Still.

"No."

"He was killed, then dragged to the shed out by Joe Boy's."

"And how do you know this?"

"Bertie."

"And how does a Valkyrie know where he was killed?" As soon as the words were out of his mouth, he seemed to realize

123

what he had said.

"Exactly. Valkyrie. Good with time of death. Especially for the warrior type. So I'm guessing Sven didn't go down without a fight. Is there anyone who was connected to him? Anyone who could have felt his death? Seen or heard his attacker?"

He tipped his head and stared at the middle distance as if he were silently reciting a list. Maybe he had turned on the prime brain-to-brain phone line and was asking that question to the clan.

"Etta. They were close. She might have felt something. Do you want me to talk to her?"

"I'd like to talk to her."

"I'll call for her."

"Don't summon her on my account. I know where her house is."

He already had his cell phone out of his pocket, his thumbs tapping over the screen. "I'm not summoning. Vampires don't *summon*. We text."

He tucked the phone back in his pocket. "She'll be right over."

It was clear he didn't want me talking to her unless he was present. "What are you worried I'll do to her? You know I'll be nice."

"I'm not concerned about how well you'll behave, Delaney. But Etta is not taking Sven's death nearly as gracefully as I."

"I can handle myself."

"Good. Handle yourself here. Now, if you'll excuse me, I need to address the business I left in my living room."

He glided out the door and I followed behind him. "I thought you'd stay behind."

"I thought you knew me better."

He stopped so quickly, I almost ran into him.

"He dumped you, remember? There was a gun involved."

"He didn't shoot me and this isn't about dating. It's about you keeping your promise not to handle this murder investigation. It's about your promise not to grill Ryder for answers. It's about your promise to let me do my job, not lock me away in a room like I'm the fragile shell."

"You really should come to my meditation classes. You

carry all your stress in your..." he gave me a thorough up-down glance, "...everything."

"Say, Mr. Rossi." Ryder chose that moment to step out of the living room, meeting us in the hall. "I got a call and have a couple things I need to take care of. But I've...uh...drawn up the rough estimate for what we talked about. If you have any other questions, give me a ring. I always have my phone on me."

Rossi took the paperwork Ryder offered in the very smart binder that had his business logo embossed on the front. "I'll be sure to find you soon," Rossi threatened.

"I'll be by this afternoon." Mr. Monroy obviously was going for friendly, but something about his hard brown eyes almost made it sound like a warning. "I think your business is ready to take off, Mr. Rossi, and I can guarantee you I'm the man who can offer you a myriad of possible plans to go forward."

"This afternoon?" Rossi raised his eyebrow and gave him a sort of half-baked smile.

So he was playing the stoner hippy with the guy. Interesting.

"I'd love to. Sure man," he said. "I have some stuff to take care of and a couple classes to ease my way through."

That lazy attitude was like catnip to the other guy. His dark eyes got a little wider, pupils going big. "Tonight then?"

"I don't think you need to barge in on his free time, Jake. Tomorrow should be fine after Mr. Rossi and I have had time to go over the quote."

I heard the words Ryder was saying, but the tone was saying something different. It said that Jake had overstepped whatever deal they had between them and Ryder was pissed.

"Oh, I'm sure Mr. Rossi would let me know if I was being a bother. Plus, I have a feeling he's a night person. Am I right?"

Yeah, and Jake's tone was a big middle finger to whatever Ryder had been not-saying to him.

What I couldn't understand was why this guy was pushing so hard to talk business with Rossi. Unless that wasn't what was going on.

For probably the first time in my life I wished Rossi were listening in on my thoughts. But since I didn't have that skill, and in theory all vamps were instructed not to eavesdrop on mortal brains in town, I wanted to tell this guy to back off before he made himself a nuisance to the pissed off vampire who looked like he'd rather have the guy over for a midnight snack.

"Hey Jake," Crow said, "I'd like to take you up on your offer to talk over that property I own out by Road's End."

Crow owned property in Road's End? That was some of the most sought-after real estate in town.

"We'll catch up tomorrow," Old Rossi said. "Come by any time. My class schedule is on the web page. We're flexible about start and stop times."

I watched Jake try to tamp down his anger at being blown off. He clamped his back teeth and offered a stilted smile.

"Sure. That will be fine. I'll come out tomorrow."

"Thanks again for your time," Ryder said. "Rossi, Crow, Chief." He started toward the door. "Coming, Jake?"

Jake did not look like he wanted to go anywhere. He also looked like he didn't like Ryder telling him what to do.

"Actually, I'd love it if you sat in on the talk, Ryder." Crow flicked me a *You're welcome* look. "How about I buy you gentlemen coffee? There's a new bakery in town I've been wanting to try out."

Well, that was amazing. Crow offered to cover the bill. Pretty sure it was gonna start raining frogs soon.

I might even buy an umbrella hat if that happened.

"See you later, Delaney." He also started for the door. Jake had no choice but to walk down the hall too.

I wanted to thank Crow for getting Jake off my hands, and not giving Rossi a chance to agree to a late meeting with the man. I didn't know what Jake really wanted, but every instinct inside me said he wasn't just a real estate developer.

Ryder, at the door, glanced back at me and there was a look in his eyes and a rakish smile I couldn't ignore.

Then all three men were gone, leaving me and the vampire.

"I don't like him," I said.

"Crow?" Rossi asked.

"Jake."

"The Reeds have always had good instincts."

"Promise you won't kill him."

Rossi didn't say anything for a long moment. Finally: "I'll make us some tea while we wait for Etta to arrive."

"That wasn't a promise."

"The Reeds have always been perceptive too."

ETTA SHOWED up halfway through my first cup of tea. Old Rossi's kitchen was state-of-the- art stone and chrome with navy blue accents.

His tea collection covered an entire wall of the kitchen, loose leaves carefully displayed in small glass containers. There had to be a couple thousand dollars worth of tea on those shelves.

After being informed that some of the leaves were rarer than the town, he brewed me a small pot of something that gave off a surprising peach fragrance. His own cup smelled strongly of wood and a deep green that reminded me of rain in the forest.

Etta arrived silently, in that vampire way. "You needed me?"

She wore a hoodie and jeans and was leaner than the last time I'd seen her. Her wide brown eyes were red rimmed and her dark skin seemed pale, the tumbling curls of her hair pulled back in a tight band.

Old Rossi produced another cup that smelled softly of mint and green tea and handed it to her while ushering her over to the island to sit.

She settled across from me. Rossi somehow managed to make where he sat seem like the head of the table.

Etta wrapped long fingers around her cup and stared down at it. Rossi caught my gaze and nodded toward her.

I hated having to talk to the bereaved so close to a death. I usually made Jean come along

with me. She was good at giving comfort, good at somehow making it seem like there was hope when the world was wrapped in darkness.

"I'm sorry about Sven," I said gently. "And I'm doing everything I can to find out who is behind his death. I have a couple questions. Do you think you could answer them?"

She nodded, still staring at her cup.

"Were you dating?"

Nod.

"When was the last time you saw him?"

Pause, then her mouth curved into a watery sort of smile. "Four days ago."

"And where were you?"

"My bedroom." Her eyes flicked my way.

"Okay." I nodded and took a sip of tea, encouraging her to do the same.

She seemed to notice she had a cup in her hand, then glanced over at Rossi, who also nodded toward her cup. She raised it, took a sip and pulled the cup away for a moment while the tip of her tongue darted across her lower lip. Then she tilted the cup back for a longer drink.

Some of the tension I hadn't noticed in Old Rossi seemed to drain away. I wondered if anyone had been looking in on Etta or if I needed to make sure someone was taking care of her.

"Have you noticed anyone around him lately who didn't like him? Anyone who wanted to argue, fight? Anyone who had made threats?"

"He worked as a bouncer," she said. "He got threats every night."

"Anything different or unusual?"

She held very still, her cup pressed into her bottom lip as she inhaled steam through her nose. "He said there were men there...mortal men. At the bar."

I waited. Plenty of mortals lived in town and a world of them surrounded us. Didn't sound unusual to me.

"They were quiet. Watched him a lot. Went to the bar every night for a week, drank, but didn't say much. They weren't from town."

That still didn't seem unusual. Maybe they were in town for a business seminar, or were passing through for a number of other reasons.

"Why did he mention them?"

"He said they smelled funny."

I tried not to make a weird face. "Okay. How so?"

She shook her head. "He couldn't explain. But that's...that's the only unusual thing he mentioned."

"Etta," Old Rossi spoke in a low voice. "Tell us everything."

I didn't know if he put any vampire influence behind it, but her eyes flashed and she put her cup down.

"Ryder Bailey was there."

"Where?" My stomach parachuted to my knees.

"At the bar. He met those men. Sven said he looked surprised to see them, then sat with them. That was...that was the last time the men were at the bar. The last time Sven said anything about them, anyway."

Her voice faded away to a whisper, or maybe I just lost the ability to hear her clearly over the pounding of my blood. Ryder was there. Ryder was with the suspicious, funny-smelling men. Which meant Ryder was linked to Sven. Again.

I didn't have to look at Rossi to know what he thought about all this.

Ryder was there. Ryder's blood was on Sven. Ryder was guilty.

Ryder wasn't guilty unless proven so. That was my job. To prove or disprove his guilt. It occurred to me that maybe I wasn't the best person for this job. But who else would be?

Myra and Jean both had opinions on Ryder, on him dumping me. Would they be able to push that aside and treat the case fairly?

No, I could do this. If Ryder was guilty...everything in me tightened, like a deep string in my soul had been plucked. Still, if Ryder was guilty, I could keep a clear head about it. The law, my job came first, no matter what my heart wanted to believe.

"Did Sven mention if Ryder left the bar with them?"

She shook her head.

"Okay. One more question, Etta, and then this will be over. Did you see or hear Sven's death?"

Her pupils went wide until black nearly swallowed the thin ring of brown. Her nostrils went hard, her mouth tightened. "Yes," she hissed.

I ignored the ice encasing my nerves and the very real instinct that was screaming *danger, danger, run, run*. "What did you see?"

"Hands of death. Blood of death. Eyes of fire."

Old Rossi sipped in a quick breath. Those words didn't

mean a lot to me, but they meant something to him.

"Did you see who was there?"

"Yes."

"Did you see his killer?"

"Yes."

"Do you know who it was? Can you describe the killer?"

"Ryder Bailey. The last person Sven saw was Ryder Bailey."

Well, crap.

CHAPTER 8

KEEPING ICE cream cold at the bottom of an active volcano would be easier than trying to make Old Rossi agree not to end Ryder's life right then and there.

The only thing that made Rossi back off was the very real promise that I would throw him, and the entire Rossi clan, out of Ordinary if he killed Ryder before I had a chance to prove him guilty or innocent in the court of law.

Yes, I could throw all the vampires out.

No, some of the other creatures wouldn't like it.

Yes, certain creatures, such as the Wolfes, actually *would* like it.

Maybe I could get most of the gods on my side to back me up.

But the threat of being exiled from town didn't mean a lot to a furious vampire. A furious prime.

At least Rossi was old enough to know how to contain and control his fury.

Unfortunately he controlled it by making "deals" that were a lot more like "threats" and were just *this* close to being "preachy" and "condescending."

"You *do* understand the terms?" he asked for like the fifth time.

"I am not a child, Rossi."

He blinked. "Compared to me, everyone is a child, Delaney."

"Not Bertie. Not the gods and goddesses. Pretty sure we have a couple gnomes older than you."

"Delaney." His mouth pulled down against what looked suspiciously like a tolerant smile. Or frustrated grimace. Yeah, probably more that last thing.

I started counting on my fingers. "Don't let Ryder out of town. Don't let him out from beneath my supervision. Don't let him out from under the watch of one of your people who has sworn not to harm him in any way. Don't expect him to be innocent. Don't confront him on my own. Those terms?"

He pinched the bridge of his nose. Did vampires get headaches?

"And the last term to our agreement?" he asked behind his palm.

"I let you question him."

He nodded, but that condition of Ryder remaining unscathed was the one I was least comfortable with.

"I'll be there when you question him," I said.

"We didn't agree to that."

"We're going to agree to it now."

He dropped his hand, long fingers brushing over the soft cotton of his pants. Etta had already left. It had taken nearly an hour for me to wear Rossi down to this agreement. Who knew standing one's ground made one sweat so much?

His eyes were dark, no color left in them, but they were not insane rage-red either.

Good enough.

"You push me, Delaney."

"I won't get in your way when you question him. But I will be there or it doesn't happen."

"Fine." He gathered our cups off the counter and took them to the sink. "Good-bye, Delaney."

And that was my cue to get the heck out of there. I let myself out, moving determinedly to the door. I took a few deep and shaky breaths once I reached the cool, damp air of the afternoon, and resisted bending in half to keep the blood from rushing out of my head.

That had been exhausting and terrifying.

Etta had seen Ryder.

Sven had seen Ryder.

Rossi had hired Ryder for a remodeling job.

I didn't know how I was going to keep him safe. I didn't even know if I *should* keep him safe.

The only car in the driveway was my Jeep. A slightly soggy scrap of paper was tucked under the windshield wiper.

I pulled the paper out and got into the Jeep before reading it.

You're welcome was written in Crow's tight, strong script. Below that were a few brushes of ink that sketched a crow in flight.

Cute how he thought doing me a tiny favor like getting Ryder out of the vampire's kill zone was going to settle his dues with me. He was still the one who had lost the god powers, and we still had no clue as to where they could be.

I pulled my phone, texted him: *Better be at the station by the time I get there.*

Before I had time to start the car, a text pinged back: *Already there. Ryder didn't kill Sven. Stop listening to the vampires.*

After that he had attached emojis of an angel, a bat, some kissy lips, and a banana.

I didn't want to know why he included the banana.

I texted back: *I'm a cop. I listen to everyone.*

Good. Listen to me. Ryder's innocent.

Prove it.

I don't need to prove it, he texted back. *I'm not a cop.*

Typical. Just couldn't leave anything alone. Always had to get in the middle of it and stir it up. If I hadn't seen how genuinely ill he'd looked at losing the powers, I might even suspect he'd done that on purpose just to liven things up.

The phone rang. I started the engine and picked up the phone, thumbing on the hands-free. "What do you want, Crow?"

"It's me," Myra said. "Crow's not with you?"

"He took Ryder and Jake Monroy out for free donuts. Said he's at the station."

"Maybe. Roy's there. He'll keep an eye on him. How did it go?"

"Not great. Rossi hired Ryder and Monroy for some kind of remodeling project or business franchising thing."

"Uh-huh."

She knew just as well as I did that Rossi wanted to keep Ryder close enough to snap his neck without the added trouble of Rossi having to leave his own property.

"Anything else?"

"I talked to Etta. She was dating Sven."

"And?"

"She said Ryder was at the bar the last time Sven was seen alive. She also said she saw him when Sven died."

"Ryder?"

"Yes." I rubbed my forehead. "I don't have any solid proof, and she's grieving. Plus, her view was via telepathy. We can't submit that to court."

"Right." It was only one word, but it had a lot behind it. Like the sickening truth that if Ryder had killed Sven with blood and some kind of ancient ritual, it meant he knew what Sven was. That meant he knew there were creatures in Ordinary, maybe even knew there were gods here.

Which made Rossi's theory that there was a group of vampire hunters all the more likely.

Could this day get any worse?

"Have you thought...considered that it might be Ryder?"

My heart beat so loud I was surprised I could hear my voice over it. "Yes."

Then there was nothing but silence on her side and fear on mine.

"I'm headed over to talk to Apocalypse Pablo at the gas station," she said. "Meet you there?"

"Sure." I was relieved she hadn't pressed the Ryder thing. We had plenty enough circumstantial evidence to question him, to detain him, right now.

But I was determined to get the truth out of him without having to throw him in jail.

And yes, I could admit my personal feelings were in the way.

That wasn't going to be a problem.

I made it to the north side of town in a couple minutes. It was raining again, not too hard, but hard enough for Granny Wolfe, who was standing just outside the gas station and mini-mart doors, to have a bright rainbow-striped umbrella hat on her head.

Day, meet worse.

Myra pulled up right after I did and we both started over to the matriarch of the werewolf pack.

Unlike Rossi, Granny actually looked old. She was that sort of weathered in-between age that could be anywhere from seventy to ninety-nine, her long, heavy hair a shattering of silver and jet black with a streak of white that curved up from over her left eyebrow. Her face was square, her jaw strong, but it was her eyes behind her big-framed glasses that drew all the attention. So large and such a pale hazel that they were faded yellow.

Granny had on bright pink capris, and an eye-watering yellow vest with explosions of orange flowers over a long-sleeved red shirt. Sneakers and white socks finished off the outfit.

I was pretty sure fashion wanted her brought in on assault charges.

"And there they are," she said in a voice that was strong and cigar-rich. "Two of our town's sisters. I thought I'd find you out here today."

"At the gas station?"

"Oh yah, oh yah," she said. "And scene of murder. That too."

Werewolves had big noses. All the better to put them in your business, my dear.

Not that I'd ever say that to her.

"Do you know anything about the murder?" Myra asked.

"Well, now. I know there is one less unliving living amongst us. Rossi's get."

"It was Sven," I said. The rain tapped gently on her bright umbrella bonnet while Myra and I moved under the edge of the roof line to stay out of the drips.

"Don't I know that."

"I guess you do," I said. "Do you know anything else about it?"

"I know there weren't any of mine involved." Here she paused and her glasses slid down her nose as she gave us both a stern look over them. "We had nothing to do with our...delicate neighbors."

Delicate was not a word I'd use to describe vampires, but then, I wasn't a werewolf.

"You've just been standing outside the gas station waiting for us to show up at the scene?" Myra asked.

Granny chuckled. "No. Not like that. I was lunching at the Blue Owl and Piper over there says Apoca-blo is in rare form.

No way I want to miss a show. That boy just cracks me up." She laughed, showing long, strong teeth. "So I come on over, think I'll get a smoke and a show. Then I hear you coming down the road, and thought we could have a chit-chat."

Just then Apocalypse Pablo strolled out of the mini-mart.

Pablo was shorter than me, skinny, tan, and the most cheerful doomsday believer in the world. Idaho-born and bred, he had neatly combed dark brown hair and teeth that were slightly too narrow behind his wide lips.

"Well, hi there, Delaney, Myra, Ms. Wolfe. How nice to see you all. You ready for the end of the world? We have a terrific sale on squeegees today. If you haven't stocked up, now's your chance."

"Think there'll be a big run on squeegees after the apocalypse?" Granny Wolfe's eyes glittered.

"There sure might be. Lots of people just aren't thinking ahead. You know a squeegee is a multi-tool—it's so darn useful! Just because it's the end of the world doesn't mean it can't be a tidy world."

Granny hooted, enjoying that answer. "As you say, sonny. Just as you say. We like our disasters clean, don't doubt." She dug in the pocket of her baggy capris and fished out a cherry cigar.

"Hold on..." I started.

"Oh, Ms. Wolfe," Apocalypse Pablo interrupted. "You really can't smoke here. You're at a gas station." As if she weren't aware of exactly where she was, he waved his hands toward the pumps.

There were no cars, but the NO SMOKING signs on the posts between pumps and plastered across the wall Granny was leaning against were pretty obvious.

Myra and I gave her twin glares.

"So I am, I see." She rubbed the cigar out against the wall of the mini-mart, then pocketed it. A haze of cherry-scented smoke mixed with the freshness of rain.

"Are you ready?" Apocalypse Pablo swiveled toward Myra and me, a smile wide on his earnest face. "End is coming soon! Any day now. If you haven't secured a place in heaven for your soul, you're going to feel real awful about that. Real awful." That last he delivered in a conspiratorial whisper, his hand cupped around his mouth.

"I'm good," I said.

"All stocked up," Myra answered.

"You have a squeegee, then? Two?" He was as excited as a kid counting down to his birthday. "You'll want a back up 'cause it's going to get all kinds of messy. Blood and gore and fire. Brimstone. That's messy too, I'd expect."

Not for the first time I wondered if he were getting "apocalypse" confused with "Christmas".

"We got it covered," I said. "But we do want to ask you about the other night."

His grin faltered and fell apart, his sunshiny eyes suddenly dark. "Oh, that was an awful thing. That poor man. Now he's going to miss the apocalypse."

Granny coughed her way through a laugh, then reached over and patted him on the shoulder. "There, there now, sonny."

A truck pulled up and rumbled to a stop right beside Granny.

"Hey, Granny." Rudy, one of the many Wolfes in town waved at us through the rolled down window. "Ready to go, or do you need a few more minutes?"

"Oh yah. I'm ready." She strolled over to the truck, opened the door and bounced up inside with a nimbleness belying a woman of her age.

"Hey there, Rudy!" Apocalypse Pablo sang out. "You ready for the end of the world?"

"Sure am!" Rudy said.

"You might need some squeegees to keep things clean. You know. During the apocalypse."

"Naw," Rudy drawled, showing a lot of teeth in his grin. "We Wolfes like it messy."

He tipped a couple fingers at his forehead and eased back out toward the road.

"He's going to wish he had a squeegee," Pablo said sadly before he instantly brightened. "So you want to talk about poor Mr. Rossi being dead in the equipment shed?"

"Can we go inside?" I asked.

Myra was already opening the door for us.

Pablo pivoted on his heel and practically bounced into the building. "Hi Stan! I know you like me out there waiting for cars, but Ms. Reed and Ms. Reed need to talk about the dead guy."

Stan was middle-aged, heavy in the face and belly and one of the most cutthroat bowlers I'd ever met. He smelled of cigarette smoke and Old Spice. He gave Myra and I a seven-ten split nod.

"Help yourself to the office. Can I get you coffee?"

His coffee was number three on the ten most toxic substances in Ordinary.

"No thanks," Myra and I said at the same time.

Apocalypse Pablo took us past the snacks, toilet paper, and cold remedies, along the dimly lit wall of soda, beer, and energy drinks to the narrow door in the back.

Stan's office was also a storage room complete with a desk in the middle that was a relic from an age when aluminum was the exciting new material.

"So." Pablo glanced over at the chair behind the desk, where he should be sitting, then looked at us expectantly.

"Go ahead and have a seat," Myra said.

"Right. Sure." Instead of walking around the desk, he dropped down into one of the folding chairs next to the shelf of beach towels and sunglasses and cupped his knees with his palms.

Myra somehow managed not to roll her eyes and took the seat behind the desk.

That left me the other folding chair. I picked it up and placed it a little closer to Pablo.

"I know Myra already talked to you but we just wanted to go over a few questions."

"I understand."

Since Myra had already gone through this, I took point. "When did you start your shift that day?"

"Three o'clock. I work the swing shift." He enunciated like I had a microphone in my hand.

"Were you working alone?"

"No, Stan was here until five o'clock, and then Lulu came in."

138

Lulu was Stan's eldest daughter. "I thought she was going to community college."

"She is. She still pulls a shift now and then when she needs spending money."

"Was she here all night?"

"No. She left after being here only fifteen minutes."

That seemed weird.

"Why?"

He reached out and dragged one finger over the open top of a box near his knees. "Well, she got invited to a party at a friend's house. Netflix and beer. Since it was so slow, I told her to go."

"Does Stan know that?"

"Oh, sure. He's fine with me covering the till and the pumps if it's quiet enough." His finger had finished tracing the edge of the box and he dunked his hand in. His eyes were wide and innocent and locked on mine.

I glanced at his hand.

He was holding a squeegee.

"So why did you go to the shed if you were covering the till and the pumps?"

"That was after my shift. I closed up at midnight sharp, just like we always do." He punctuated that with a little poke of the squeegee. "Then I checked the shed to make sure it was locked. We don't get into it that often, but it's our property, and you never know when someone might decide to get up to some mischief. It was locked. But when I came in to open the next morning, I saw it was unlocked."

"Did you see anyone by the shed? During your shift or in the morning?"

"I did not. We have a camera on it."

"What?" Myra and I said at the same time.

"Oh, yes. Didn't you know? Stan has this crazy idea that he saw Bigfoot stealing our light bulbs the other day. Bigfoot." He waved the squeegee around like he was scrubbing that image out of the air. "I think he's just been to that quaint little local-color museum down in Newport one too many times."

Apocalypse Pablo had a real knack for being polite. "Quaint" was actually "cheesy" and "local-color" was "outdated snake skin oil and hokum" shop.

Not that it wasn't a fun place to visit for precisely those reasons.

Still, Stan was on to something. Bigfoot did have a light bulb fetish, and he was a bit of a klepto.

"Can we see the video?" Myra asked.

"Why sure!" He stood, but not before snagging three more squeegees out of the box. "I'll just ring up your squeegees, and then we can take a look at it on the computer out front."

There wasn't a computer in the office. They probably only had one tablet or laptop that they kept at the counter with them.

He jiggled two squeegees at me, waiting for me to take them from him. I didn't know if it was Stan's idea to have him push the squeegees, or if it was Apocalypse Pablo's idea. But it was an effective way to move stock.

I gave in and took the squeegees.

He lit up like we'd just executed the passing of the Olympic torch.

"Fantastic," he said. "We are going to be *so* ready for the end of the world."

He handed Myra the other two, and she didn't resist either.

"Follow me, Ms. Reed, and Ms. Reed." He practically glided out of the room, humming some pretty little tune under his breath.

"You buy, I'll check the tape." I handed her my squeegees. Or was it squeegi? Squeeguses?

"Give me your card," she said.

I pulled my cash card out of my wallet. "They're on sale."

"I'm not paying for them."

"They are all the rage in apocalypse accessories. Useful. Like umbrella hats, apparently."

"I don't need a squeegee. I already have two."

I threw a look over my shoulder as I walked out the door. "You hoard squeegees?"

"I have one for the car and one for the bathroom. It takes more than two of one thing to constitute hoarding."

"Like six?"

From the crinkle of her nose and corners of her eyes, I knew she would have slapped me upside the head if we weren't on duty. Being professional. Officers of the law.

"Two of these are yours, idiot."

Apoca-blo was already behind the counter making himself busy at the register. Stan, who was leaning one hip on a tall stool near the lottery tickets, raised an eyebrow at the cleaning utensils in Myra's hands.

Then he grinned. Yep. This had to be his idea.

She tipped her chin up and gave him the dare-you look I'd last seen on her face when she bought her first pack of tampons from Scott Holderman, the hunky senior running back who used to work the grocery store.

Stan, just like Scott, wisely averted his eyes and made no comment.

"We need to take a look at your video from the last couple days," I said. "Can you queue that up for us?"

"Sure. No guarantee we'll get a good shot. The rain has really been messing with my equipment."

If Thor kept up his pity party, Ordinary was going to rust clear through by next spring and leave nothing but a sinkhole behind.

Myra declined paper or plastic and came over to stand next to me. Stan positioned the laptop so that all three of us could see the screen.

A bell rang out and Apoca-blo dashed out from behind the till. "Got a customer. Do you officers need me to stay?"

"No, we've got your statement," I said. "Thank you, Apoc—ah, I mean Pablo."

"Sure, sure." He pushed out the door and before it closed, I heard his cheerful greeting: "Good afternoon! Such a nice day! Are you ready for the end of the world?"

Stan shook his head. "Something not right with that one. But he's a good worker. Heck of a salesman. Nice kid too. Just..." He shook his head like that explained it all.

And it did. Compared to the things that happened in Ordinary, and the citizens who made it their home, one happy-go-lucky apocalypse enthusiast wasn't even a blip on the town's weirdness radar.

"Here it is." Stan clicked on the link to the video feed. "I have it set to record from sundown to sunrise. As a security

141

measure for my employees."

And for catching Bigfoot in the act. He wouldn't mention that because everyone knew it was crazy to believe that Bigfoot was real. And yes, Bigfoot got a kick out of that.

Stan hit the button and the black and white video played. It was a still shot of the shed, and just a corner of the road beyond it. The only way I could tell the recording was playing was by the occasional car that zoomed down the road at a fast-forward speed.

We watched as the time stamp ticked down. Nothing changed at the shed. No one drove close to it, no one walked near it, no one touched it.

The sky was dark, raindrops a flurry of silver lancets.

Something flashed by the screen.

"Wait," I said.

Myra tensed beside me at the same moment.

"Back up slowly."

"I think it was just a bird." Stan backed up the recording, a little too quickly so that we got only the briefest glimpse of something moving in front of the camera again.

"Slow it down," I said.

He hit play and the recording rolled, rain falling at the right speed.

I held my breath, curled my fingers so that I could feel the press of my fingernails in my palm. Had we really caught a break? A clue as to who had dumped Sven's body in the shed?

Would it be Ryder?

Please don't let it be Ryder, I chanted silently. *Please don't let it be Ryder.*

Stan stabbed the button to stop the recording. "Sweet Mother Mary," he breathed.

And there, frozen on the screen clear enough to crawl through it, was a man.

My mind furiously cataloged hair, eyes, face, jaw.

Not Ryder. Oh, thank gods.

I broke out in a cold sweat and shivered in relief.

"That's Sven, isn't it?" Stan said. "His face...it's wrong. Animal..."

"It's the lighting," Myra said.

It wasn't the lighting. It was his fear, his pain, his death. Sven looked more vampiric in that image than I'd ever seen him in life. His eyes were wide, pupils blown out to cover any color, a hole centered in his forehead above them. His face was sharpened, and out of shape. At the paused moment of the video his three-quarter profile showed bloody, swollen lips hanging open enough to reveal the wickedly sharp point of an elongated fang.

He was dead.

"We'll need to take this file," Myra said. "To look over it more carefully." She smoothly killed the video, erasing Sven's face from the screen.

My heart was hammering and I had to take little gulps of air to get my breathing back to normal. The sheer horror of death on Sven's face triggered my *run now, run now* instincts.

I didn't know how Myra remained so calm.

"Sure, sure," he said. "Where do you want me to send it?"

"Here. Let me do it." She took over the keyboard and sent the file to our secure server, then erased the video from his hard drive. "Are there any back up copies?"

He shook his head. "Just the computer."

"Okay. Since this could be admitted as evidence, we'll hold the copy. We'll try to get it back to you if you want it after this investigation is over."

Stan looked a little pale. "That's okay. I don't need to see it again."

"Thank you for this," I said. "I know that was hard to see. If you need someone to talk to, I could refer you to a couple of good counselors who work with the police and other emergency responders in the area."

"No," he said, his voice a little thin. Then, stronger: "No, that's fine. I'm just sad for him. For his family. For the Rossis. You're going to catch whoever did that to him, aren't you?"

"Damn right we are."

"Good. Thank you. Both of you. I sure miss having your dad in town, but he'd be real proud of you girls."

We mumbled our good-byes and left with our squeegees, Myra crowding into the front of my Jeep with me.

Doors shut, rain pattering down. We both sat there just

trying to get sea legs on reality again.

"Okay," I said. "Pull it up. Let's see it."

She took a tablet out of the inside pocket of her coat—trust Myra to be prepared for anything—and pulled up the video.

We watched a super-slow motion Sven get dragged in front of the camera, face toward the lens like they knew he was being recorded. Like they knew we would find the tape.

An invitation, just like Rossi had said.

Neither of us spoke as we watched the rest of the scene scroll out.

A hand reached out of the darkness behind Sven. From the angle, the other person was shorter than Sven, supporting him under the arms, sleeves plain and dark. The hand wrapped around Sven's head and clamped down tight on his mouth.

It was a man's hand. Wide, thick. In the crappy light and downpour it was hard to make out any distinguishing features.

Even though the picture was blurred by rain, there was a sort of haze of light radiating from Sven's chest. From the ichor techne painted there.

The video feed cut, sputtered, picked back up. The time stamp was five minutes later. The screen showed nothing but darkness, rain, and the watery shape of the shed, door open, the darkness beyond it a gaping maw.

I couldn't tell if there were any footprints in the mud and gravel and grass that separated the shed from the mini-mart. Didn't see tire tracks.

"Well, hell," Myra said. "I'll get Jean on this. See if we can enhance the video. That looked like a man's hand to me."

I nodded. "Have her check the fingers. I thought I saw something, maybe a ring."

She rewound the video, then started it forward in tiny, slow skips.

We watched the hand arc up, forward and just before it curled toward Sven's mouth, Myra paused.

We stared at the fingers. "Maybe?" I asked.

"Maybe." She turned off the video and then touched my arm. "Who did you think was going to be on this video, Delaney?"

"No one."

"I saw you in there when Stan first played it. You thought it was going to be Ryder. Do you know something I don't know?" She waited, her patience endless.

"No."

"Maybe you should step down from this one," she said quietly. "Let Jean and me handle it."

"I can handle it."

"Even if Ryder is involved?"

No.

"Yes, even if Ryder is involved. I know how to do my job and keep my heart out of the equation."

That look in her eyes, the one that was probably pity, told me she didn't believe me, but was nice enough not to call me out on it.

"I've seen the bruises you think you're hiding," I said softly.

She frowned, then stared out the window at the rain. "I'm not hiding them."

"Yes, you are." I pressed my palm on her knee. "Myra. What's going on? Where are you getting those bruises?"

Her eyes narrowed a bit and spots of red flushed her face.

"It's okay," I said. "You can tell me. Is it a man? Are you dating someone? In secret? Did someone hit you?"

"What?"

I'd never heard her voice so high. "Oh, my gods, Delaney! You think? You think I would just let..." She shut her mouth, eyes flitting back and forth, trying to read the worry, and yes, confusion on my face.

"I'm a trained police officer. Nobody hits me and gets away with it."

"Then why are you bruised? On your arms. On your hip."

She exhaled and laughed. "You really think I'd hide something like that from you?"

"You *are* hiding that from me."

"But not for those reasons. Come on. We're sisters. You know I'd have you at my back the instant anyone tried to hurt me like that. We promised. We all promised each other when we were in middle school, and Jean took that head shot in dodgeball, remember?"

145

"I remember." Jean had still been in elementary school. Little Tommy Richard had been a headhunting jerk when playing dodgeball. He targeted the girls and hit them with the ball as hard as he could when the teacher wasn't looking. Usually in the face.

Myra and I stole our Dad's police department T-shirts, made fake brass knuckles, and cornered Tommy after school. I recited police codes at him while Myra explained what they meant.

"You touch our sister again and you'll be 12-16A."

"A fatal accident."

"You hit her in the head at dodgeball, or in PE, or the halls, or anywhere, and there's gonna be 12-49A."

"Possible homicide."

We were really selling it, slamming our fake brass knuckles into our palms and closing in on him.

Since we were older and taller than him and he was only ten, he went pale and sweaty and made a break for it.

"You better run. You 12-19!"

That was *request for tow truck*, but I'd been sort of in the moment and hadn't memorized all the really cool codes yet.

"I just thought." I sighed, and rubbed my hand over my face. "It's been a weird few days. I'm glad it's not what I thought it might be."

"Good," she said. "Good."

"But I still want to know why you're hiding bruises."

"I'm not hiding. I'm...uh, sort of joined a team."

"Wrestling?"

"No."

"Martial arts?"

"No."

"Circus performers? Dance troupe? Cheer Squad? Want to help me out here?"

"Roller Derby."

"Roller Derby. We have that?"

"No. Salem has it. Cherry City Derby Girls."

For all that my sisters and I are really close, it's not like we don't get days off. Salem, Oregon's capitol, was only an hour's drive east from Ordinary. There would be plenty of opportunities for her to drive there for practice and games.

Plus, Myra had seemed a lot more relaxed lately.

"You like it?"

A wicked little smile curved her mouth. "Love it."

"Did you think I wouldn't approve?"

"No. I just...I just needed something away from here, you know? Something my own. A place to clear my head and not have to deal with..."

"Everything?"

She nodded.

I patted her knee. "Good. Can I come to a bout sometime?"

From the look on her face, it was just what she needed to hear.

"I'd like that."

"All right. Back to the station?" I started the Jeep.

"Maybe you should take a long lunch and get some rest instead."

"Do I look that bad?"

"No," she lied. "But you haven't taken a break today have you?"

"Not since drinking tea with the vampires."

"Take an hour or two. We'll hold down the fort. Maybe you can get a nap." At the mention of it, it was suddenly exactly what I wanted.

She was good at that too.

CHAPTER 9

I FOUND myself standing in the middle of my living room, arms wrapped around my elbows, staring at nothing.

My coat was thrown on top of my couch and I only had one boot off. I inhaled, exhaled, digging up out of my funk.

Sven had seen Ryder when he died.

Unless that was a vampire trick—an implanted suggestion.

Ryder wasn't on the tape.

That wasn't Ryder's hand.

Was it?

My thoughts circled again, questions that just made more questions and answers that couldn't be proved.

What if he's guilty?

I'd stop loving him. Right? I'd have to. No one loved a murderer.

Liar, my heart whispered.

A knock at the door brought me fully conscious. I glanced at the throw blanket I'd been planning to crawl under, then pushed my shoulders back and walked to the door.

I opened it without glancing outside first.

I should never do that.

"Hey." Ryder held a bottle of wine in one hand and his heart in his gaze. "Got a minute?"

I should say no. I should tell him to leave. Tell him I didn't want to see him, couldn't see him alone like this.

Don't be sexy. Don't be a murderer. Don't be a sexy murderer.

He bit his lower lip and I was a goner.

"Sure." I stepped back, let him into the house and shut the door. "Wine?"

He glanced down at it like he wasn't sure it should be there. "Yeah. I feel like I owe you an apology."

"For?"

"Letting my business get in the way of a police investigation today. With Jake and Rossi and...everything."

Are you innocent? Did you kill Sven? Are you a murderer?

"It's fine. Everything worked out fine."

Liar.

I stared at his right hand holding the wine, trying to decide if it matched the blurry hand of the killer in the video. Maybe I stared a little too long.

He raised his hand, holding the wine out to me. "Uh...Delaney?"

Yep. Definitely a little too long. He moved to stand in front of me, close enough I could feel the heat from his body. I took the wine and set it on an end table.

Was it cold in my house or was I just a little too freaked out about my not-boyfriend being a maybe-murderer?

"Tell me you didn't kill Sven."

That startled both of us. He caught his breath, held it, his mossy eyes hurt at the accusation. Hurt and confused. "I already told you that last night."

"I know. I need to hear it again."

"I did not kill Sven Rossi."

It sounded like the truth. It felt like the truth.

But then, wishful thinking had a way of feeling like the truth sometimes.

"Why do you think I would kill him?"

He was whispering. I was whispering too, like somehow, if we didn't put our voices into the words, that would make this less real.

"Someone saw you. At the bar. With a group of men."

I almost thought I could hear his heart stop beating.

"Who saw me?"

No denial.

I shook my head. "Truth. I still have seven questions left."

"So do I."

"Were you at that bar?"

"Yes."

Six questions. Technically, by his rules, it was his turn to ask. I wasn't following his rules.

"Who were they?"

"People I work with."

"Killers?"

149

That left me with four questions.

"Delaney...just..." He stepped away, paced toward the kitchen, then back. He stopped and leaned his shoulder on the corner between kitchen and living room, right next to my little breakfast nook. He crossed his arms over his chest.

"How many times do I have to tell you I'm not involved in Sven's death? How many times do I have to tell you I don't know who was?"

I watched his eyes, watched the tension in his shoulders, his mouth. Part of what he said was a lie. Or maybe all of it.

"Only once if it's the truth."

He ground at his molars, watching me. I watched him back.

"I had nothing to do with Sven's death."

Your blood killed him. Those words locked right behind my teeth, but I couldn't get them past my lips. I wanted to tell him what I knew. Come clean. Not just about Sven's murder. About everything. About Ordinary, the creatures, the gods. His blood used as ichor techne.

Could he explain that?

I wanted to trust him. That was my problem. I wanted to tell him I knew he had to be involved, and I wanted him to have a reason, an irrefutable explanation that would clear him of this crime for good.

Maybe it was time to push this into the no-turning-back territory.

"Those men don't have anything to do with your architecture business, do they?"

"Delaney."

"They came here because they are a part of an agency. A group. Of hunters."

Yep. I was putting cards on the table. No turning back. Pressuring him to react.

"A group of hunters," he said. Was his voice a little tighter? "What are they going to hunt on the Oregon coast in August? Crabs?"

"Vampires."

He held his breath.

That. That was enough of a tell. He knew. He knew about the hunters. Or vampires. Or both.

His eyebrows lifted up, and he exhaled on what sounded like a forced laugh. "Vampires? Are you bingeing on Buffy again?"

Nope. Not believing him. Too flippant, too tight, his voice too thin.

"Is that one of your questions?"

"No."

"That group, and I'm assuming you by association, are here in town looking for vampires. I'm assuming you've either been hired by someone who trained you how to kill vampires, or you are working for an agency developed for the same reason."

"I'm an architect," he protested.

"And a shitty liar."

We stood there, silent again and it felt like if one of us blinked, we would be declaring a surrender.

"Truth," I said. "I know more about this town than you ever will, Ryder. And vampires amongst us is just scratching the surface of the weird here."

"I don't—"

I held up one finger. "Think very carefully about what you're about to say. I am the law here. Law of this city, county, state, country, and above all that, law of Ordinary. I have vowed to keep Ordinary's citizens safe. All of them. No matter their race, creed, or other circumstances. I failed Sven. But that doesn't mean I will fail to bring his killer to justice. I'm brutally efficient at keeping the peace. Do you understand what I'm telling you?"

"That you believe vampires are real, and you might actually be a mob boss?"

"That I believe I have enough evidence to haul you in on murder charges. Unless you start talking and trust me to do my job to prove you're innocent."

"I *am* innocent! You're the one telling me over and over that I'm guilty."

"I'm trying to trust you here, Ryder. Could you trust me back a little?"

"Is that one of your questions?"

"Yes."

"I'm trying."

His jaw tightened and flexed, and his eyes narrowed, creasing lines in the corners and between his eyebrows. Finally, he uncrossed his arms and stuck one hand in his back pocket. It was a stance he took when he was unsure or going out on a limb.

"We're going to take a second," he said, "and do some hypothesizing."

"This isn't a game."

"I'm very aware of that. If you're telling me the truth, you are admitting that there are vampires in Ordinary. Are you using the term vampire as a metaphor or slang?"

"No."

"How did Sven die? More than just a bullet through the head?"

Now he had five questions left. I nodded.

"He was a vampire?"

Again with the nod. Four.

"Who else in town is a vampire? Old Rossi? All the Rossis?"

"Is that one question or three?"

"One."

"Pass."

"Who were those men you met?" I asked. "Who do they work for? How do you work with them?"

"You only have one question left after this."

"I know."

He rolled one shoulder back and tipped his head so he was looking at me a little sideways. "I can't—I can't talk about that." He said it so quietly, I almost missed it.

"You don't want to make me doubt your level of involvement in this," I said. "It won't end well. You don't know the kind of pressure I can bring to bear on this situation. On those men. On you."

"Are you threatening me?"

Two. "I'm telling you the truth, Bailey. Deal with it."

"You're kind of hot when you're all bossy and in control."

"Flirting won't work on me."

It totally would.

"What will work on you?"

"You only have one question left after this."

He took a couple steps forward, closing the space between us. "I know."

What works on me? That sexy look. Your sexy eyes. That smile that makes my mouth go hot, and that purr you get in your voice when it drops an octave and teases across my spine.

"Honesty."

"Honesty?" He was so close to me I could loop my fingers in the tops of his jeans almost without moving. "Or a confession maybe."

"Honesty."

His eyes were faded jade, flecks of brown scattered within them. He had a couple freckles on the arcs of his cheeks, almost invisible beneath his tan. His nose was strong, and the laugh lines at the corners of his eyes were trails of pain and joy. He was familiar waters and uncharted shores. He was the boy I'd always known and the man I'd never met.

He was innocent words and guilty eyes.

And he was absolutely not someone I should kiss.

Should not lean toward.

Should not slip my fingers along his waist and stroke up his back.

He bent just slightly, easing down to me, the shape of him, the scent, the heat swallowing up all my space, all my world, all my air.

"I've done some things I regret," his words were warm puffs of air across my cheek, moving toward my mouth. "Breaking up with you before we really had a chance to see if we would work out is right up there on the top of my list. You want honesty? All right. I want this."

His blunt fingertips pressed across my waist, skimmed up my back, one palm warm and right between my shoulder blades, the other shifting lower, cupping heat onto my lower back.

"I want a second chance I don't deserve. I want to be with you, Delaney. And honestly?" His mouth drifted closer to mine, breath soft against my skin. "I didn't kill Sven. I haven't been near him since I went to the bar to meet those men who, yes, think the town is full of vampires."

A hot current raced down the core of me like a heating coil on fire. I wasn't sure if it was lust or victory. He had told me the truth. Admitted there was a group of vampire hunters in town.

That's what Rossi had suspected. All I had to do now was figure out which of them had killed Sven, who sent them to do so and why, and then see that justice was done.

Kiss me, my heart begged, over and over in rhythm to my ragged pulse. *Kiss me, kiss me, kiss me.*

But my mouth had other ideas. "You said you work with them."

He shifted away, inch by inch until he was standing above me looking down into my eyes.

"Not how you think."

A bucket of ice down my pants couldn't have chilled me quicker.

It was my turn to take a step back. "Then tell me how you know them, who they are, and how you're involved in this mess."

More than a hint of my official tone crept into my voice. From the flash of irritation in Ryder's gaze, he wasn't a fan of that kind of bossy.

"There are things you shouldn't know, Delaney. Things I can't talk about."

"I want names. I want to know who's behind the group of hunters. I want to know any information you have on who killed Sven. This is murder, Ryder. Someone lost his life. In my town—our town. A place that is supposed to be safe. So I don't give a damn what you think you can't talk about. You will talk about it to me. Or I will take you in and deal with you with the kind of thoroughness you might never recover from."

Something kindled in his expression—hunger—and I felt the snap of sexual tension spark between us. And right after that, I felt his anger.

"You've already decided what I am," he all but growled. "Already decided I am guilty and not owed the same kind of protection as any other person in town. Decided it the moment you got your hands on whatever evidence you think implicates me in this thing."

"Your blood. They used your blood to kill him."

I said it softly, but Ryder's head jerked back as if he'd been slapped and his mouth went thin. He stood there for a long moment, his eyes sharp and turned inward as if he weren't in this room, as if I weren't standing in front of him, as if this conversation weren't happening.

"That's why you were asking about the Red Cross."

"Did you really give blood to them?"

"It was a Red Cross mobile van. I thought it was a whim...but maybe..."

I waited as he sorted through things he didn't want to tell me. I could press to make him talk, but he'd push back. Better to give him a minute and see if he would come around.

"Who would have wanted your blood? Who would have taken it, and wanted to implicate you in Sven's death? Someone in your group?"

"My group?"

"You said you're a part of them. The hunters. Tell me how."

He was still tight, his fists clenched at his side, the fabric of his shirt straining against the bulge of muscle. He looked like he wanted to hit something.

I understood the feeling.

"How about I make us both some coffee?" I asked. "We can talk this out. Take our time." It was a peace offering. A cease-fire. He nodded, accepting both. "Sit down and get comfortable."

I walked into the kitchen, which was mostly hidden from the living room. I made myself busy at the sink, then the coffee pot, measuring out my favorite grounds, putting in extra. I needed either espresso-strength coffee or whisky, and my day was far from over yet.

By the time the coffee was done, and I had two cups poured and made the way we liked them, he was sitting on my couch.

"Just so you know," I handed him the cup, "I'm on your side here, Ryder. There are a lot of reasons why I shouldn't be, but I refuse to throw you under a bus because you make a convenient scapegoat. I really do want justice. I really do want to catch the killer. It won't do me or anyone any good if I pin the crime on someone who was stupid enough to get sucked into this insanity."

155

He swallowed coffee. "Thanks for your vote of confidence." Sarcasm. Yeah, well, I had just told him he was stupid.

"You're welcome." I took the chair across from him, blew across my coffee, then took a sip. "What are you caught up in?"

He drank, and for a long moment, I thought he wasn't going to talk. Then something changed in him, as if he had made a decision, and even though he wasn't comfortable with it, he wasn't going to shift course.

"I was approached by a man who wanted to know about Ordinary."

"When you were working for the firm in Chicago?"

"Sophomore year of college. His name was Frank Walsh." He lifted his eyebrow as if to say his name really wasn't Frank Walsh.

"Is that what we're calling him?"

"That's what he called himself. But it wasn't who he was. Eventually, when...things weren't adding up, I looked into him. Name and driver's license number belonged to a man who had been dead for fifty years."

"Vampire?"

"That wasn't the first thought that went through my mind, no. I confronted him about it. Thought it was identity theft. That's when I realized it was a test of sorts. That I questioned him. That I was observant."

"Is Frank one of those men you met in the bar?"

"No. Frank was my boss."

"Is he a vampire?"

"No. Though I still don't know what his real name is."

"I thought you worked for yourself."

He took a gulp of coffee. His fingers pressed into the mug, knuckles white. "I do."

How could two little words hold so much ambiguity?

"All right." I'd let it slide for now. "How is Frank involved with Sven's death?"

"Frank is a part of a research group."

I waited. He drank coffee. I rolled my eyes.

"Do not make me get the pliers to pull this out of you, word by word, Ryder, because I will."

The corner of his mouth twitched slightly. "Bossy."

"Stop enjoying this," I grumbled.

A full smile curved his lips and set a sparkle in his eyes I hadn't seen for far too long. "You just hate not knowing something. Have all your life. It makes it *so* easy to needle you. If I stop talking, if I do nothing, you'll lose your nuts. You do know you don't actually have to know everything about everyone everywhere all the damn time."

"And you do know I'm an officer of the law. It's my job to know things. A lot of things."

"You're nosy."

"It's a small town. I get paid for being nosy."

"Good career choice, by the way. High school counselor talk you into it?"

"Nope. My dad. My high school counselor thought I should teach P.E."

"I could see it. Whistle power. Brass knuckles. Bossing people around trying to make them play fair. Expecting the best of them, never giving up on them even when they disappoint you."

I was surprised to hear that he thought of me in that way. Was I like that? Did I expect people to be, if not good then maybe diligent, no matter what was proved otherwise to me? Did I want a fair playing field for people, did I want to enforce rules that would level the disparities in the world?

Yes.

It warmed me to realize he knew me that well.

"Don't make this about us." The words came out too thick with emotion.

"How can it not be? This is us. We're right here throwing these dice, dealing with our devils and taking huge risks on faith and trust."

"Devils I have plenty of. Give me details."

"Not sure that can happen."

"Trust me that I will do my best to keep you safe," I said.

"Trust me that I will do the same," he said.

So we were both hiding secrets, and navigating dangers that the other person wasn't aware of. Crow was right.

Cards, meet table.

"The vampires in town know you're involved in Sven's death."

His body language went hard even though his facial expression didn't change. He took it for what it was: confidential information given freely. I was trusting hard here. I just hoped he would return the favor.

"The men at the bar came to the notice of my boss. They are...known to the agency I work for."

Pretty sure he didn't mean housing agency.

"If I can't prove your innocence in the next couple days, you're not going to be alive long enough for it to matter."

Another piece of truth, freely given.

"Ordinary is being targeted. We don't know who is behind the sudden attention."

"Who do you work for?"

"Who is the prime vampire?"

We sat there, stared at each other. My heart was beating too fast—fear. If I confirmed what he suspected, if I outed Old Rossi, I would be taking him into a confidence that could not be undone.

It would leave both my town vulnerable to whatever he was really mixed up in, and it would leave him vulnerable to the forces in my town.

"Ask me something else," I said.

He didn't hesitate. "What really killed Sven?"

"An ancient blood spell. What is your agency's objective?"

"To contact the unknowns in this town."

"Contact as in kill?"

"We didn't kill Sven. Deadly force isn't forbidden, but isn't encouraged."

"Define contact."

"Just what it sounds like. You've told me there are vampires in the town. That Sven was one. We're here to meet them. To offer them certain protections. To ensure they have oversight."

"Oversight?" He obviously didn't know much about vampires if he thought they would allow an agency to keep tabs on them.

He tipped his head in agreement. "What is a blood spell?"

"What agency do you work for?"

He leaned forward and set his cup down on the short table between us. "That's..." He sighed as he leaned back, then rubbed his hand over his mouth.

"You want to know anything about vampires in this town, you want to find some way to facilitate that 'oversight' or make contact, you're going to have to go through me."

A wash of heat poured off him, his eyes went intense with a focus that had nothing to do with this town, these deals, or those words. That spark between us smoldered, kindled, and caught.

"Jesus, Delaney," he breathed. "I don't want to hurt you."

"Who said I'd let you?"

He stood up. I was standing too, even though I didn't remember getting off the couch. Then one of us moved. Or both of us moved. All I knew was that suddenly the space between us was gone.

I looked up into his eyes and knew the want there was echoed in me. I could feel it like a strumming beneath my breastbone, a rhythm as primal as time, as the sea, as a heartbeat.

Whatever we might have, whatever our past had made us, whatever our future might be, we could not deny this draw, this connection. We had walked away, but were walking back together as if there were no other state in which we could exist. As if we would always walk back together no matter what ripped us apart.

As if we'd been doing it our whole lives.

And maybe we had.

"Delaney," he whispered, his palms on either side of my face. In that one word, my name whispered and husky between his lips, lived layers of emotions. I thought I understood. He was trying to protect me, didn't want to see me hurt again, shot, or worse.

What I should do was step away. Take care of business. Take care of my vampires, my murdered friend, my town.

It would be selfish to do anything else. Reckless.

I grabbed hold of the front of his shirt and dragged his mouth down to mine.

At first, I thought I'd read this wrong, read the heat

between us as attraction when it was something else. Then his mouth softened, his body bent. His fingertips pressed against my jaw, cheekbones, back of my skull as he angled my mouth to better fit his own.

I lost myself to the warmth of him, the sensation of his lips, sliding against mine. His tongue darted across the corner of my mouth, and I opened in answer, licking across his lower lip, wanting him and finally, finally tasting him: coffee, mint, and something rich and unique that made my heart beat heavy and slow.

We kissed, until the world disappeared, until the doubts and questions were burned away. When I couldn't breathe any more, I pulled away.

"Don't..." Ryder reached for me again, to pull me near.

But I took another step back. And another.

I had kissed him. Kissed the man who had dumped me when I was lying in a hospital bed. Kissed the man who was still not proven innocent. Kissed the man who wouldn't tell me who he worked for.

All those things were just details.

No, they were the devils.

Was there a difference?

"Who do you work for?"

The warm, open lines of his body tightened. His eyes that had seemed glassy, soft, narrowed down to slits. His mouth hardened into a frown.

"Is that all this is? All you care about?" His voice was deep, angry.

"Why shouldn't I care about that? You won't tell me, and we can't build anything..."

...*between us*...

"...on this case until you do."

He wiped his hand over his jaw, and when he pulled it away, there was a sardonic grin where his frown had been. I knew him well enough to know that grin covered anger.

"The case. That's your priority. Your only priority. Fine. You shouldn't care who I work for because I'm not going to tell you. If you want answers out of me, then you're going to have to play by my rules, Delaney, not yours. You can't use...whatever this is between us to make me do what you want."

Hold on there. What? He thought I was what—throwing myself at him to get information? I didn't know if I should laugh or punch him.

My unreasonable heart didn't care about a case, a murder, or anyone's innocence. It wailed at me to argue with him, to tell him that I loved him, even though he was being a total idiot. Maybe I was too, but that was exactly the reason I was fighting so hard for him, whether he knew it or not.

But my heart didn't get to run my mouth. That was all brain territory, and right now my brain was one-hundred percent cop.

"Then we have a problem. You won't get your answers unless you tell me who you'll be sharing them with. I, however, have ways to find out what I need to know without you. I will find out who cuts your checks, Ryder. If you want any kind of damage control in your life, in your job, in your innocence or guilt, you'll talk to me now."

Silence stretched under the weight of words neither of us could speak. Our secrets locked away all sound, smothered trust. That attraction between us wasn't gone, but two tons of stubbornness had buried it deep.

"I'll see you at the station," he said like I had just asked him to have a nice day. As if this entire conversation had never happened.

"Fine."

Ryder made it a point to walk around the couch and around me, so we weren't even within each other's reach. I didn't know if that was to keep him or me from reaching out.

But just in case, I crossed my arms over my chest and hugged my ribs tight to keep from doing anything else I'd regret. The door opened, and I waited, back turned, until I heard it click closed again.

CHAPTER 10

I AM not ashamed to admit I spent the next hour under the blanket on my couch trying to sleep while the conversation with Ryder played on endless loop through my brain.

What I had gained from our talk had to be separated into two distinct piles in my head. The case-related stuff, and everything else.

Ryder insisted he was innocent. Told me he was working for an agency that suspected, and now knew, there were vampires in Ordinary. An agency that apparently could take that revelation not only in stride, but also had a plan in place for how they wanted to contact vampires. That suggested to me that they were already in contact with vampires outside of Ordinary.

I wasn't sure if that was a good or bad thing. What did he mean they wanted oversight? was that just a code word for nefarious experiments? Blackmail? Something worse? For all I knew that agency could be building an army of vampires, or be making sure that no one else could do so.

While I might trust Ryder, I was not dumb enough to blindly trust some secret agency.

Ryder all but told me those men he'd met in the bar were behind Sven's death. Maybe one of them had been the hand in the security camera. He'd told me those men were hunting vampires but weren't part of whoever he was working for.

So we possibly had two groups in town, at the same time, looking for fangers.

Why?

Rossi had said it was an invitation. That Sven's death was a calling card from his past. Someone who he or Lavius had taught the ichor techne.

Someone who wanted Ryder blamed for the death.

Which could be someone in the opposing group of hunters. Or some other vampire. Or, hell, Old Rossi himself if he had decided the double-double cross was in his best interest.

There simply wasn't enough hard information to go on at this point.

Maybe when Jean went through the video files she would come up with something solid we could pursue.

Until then, I had a meeting at midnight I didn't want to be late for.

BY THE time I was done checking in with Myra, and Jean who was poring over the video and still hadn't come up with anything more we could use, it was close to dinner time. So I drove to the diner to eat something while I waited for midnight to roll around.

Piper looked a little startled when I walked in, but quickly gave me a big smile. "Hey, Chief. One tonight?"

"Yep. Go ahead and stick me in a corner, if you have one. I've some paperwork to get through." That was the partial truth. I was going to go through the stack of notes on the case, but mostly I wanted to be somewhere unobtrusive. Whoever had sent me that letter might already be here in the diner. I wanted to people watch for a while.

"This okay?" She stopped at the table in the far corner from the door, next to a window, with a view of the door and most of the diner.

"Perfect. Like you read my mind."

Her smile faltered, eyes going wide for a half second before she recovered. "Well, I'll be right back with coffee and give you a minute to check out our diner menu."

I nodded and made a show of sorting out places for the file folder, my phone, and the wire condiment carrier in the middle of the table.

Something about Piper was tugging at my brain.

I hadn't told her I wanted dinner, though I did. She'd mentioned the dinner menu. This was exactly the table I'd been hoping to sit at when I'd first walked in and she'd taken me to it without my prompting even though there were a couple other corner tables available.

Coincidence? Skills of a long-time waitress?

Maybe.

But now that I thought about it, she had known Myra, Jean, and I all wanted pie the other night, had brought us coffee, then poured two regular and one decaf without us asking.

I wondered if Piper was a precognitive, or if she had the ability to read minds. I knew she wasn't vampire...her skin was the wrong tone, she wasn't vamp-thin. Besides, Rossi would have told me about her when she came to town. She could be a witch, or part fae, or any number of other things, and I wouldn't know it.

And while being a precog would make waitressing pretty easy, it seemed like there were other and better uses for that kind of talent.

But then, I'd watched gods and goddesses choose jobs for which they were wildly unqualified. Sometimes a person just had to take any gainful employment that was available to them.

And sometimes a person didn't want their job to have anything to do with anything else in their life.

I made a note to check into her background, and watched her chat with customers. She refilled coffee, ice tea, and sodas at the perfect moment. She checked to see if the meal was all right at exactly the second when no one's mouth was full so they could actually answer.

That right there was an unnatural talent.

She ducked down the hallway past me, grabbed a wooden highchair, set it next to a table that would seat four, then was at the door to greet a young couple followed by an older couple who were obviously their parents. The young woman was holding a baby on her hip.

The baby wore a tiny umbrella hat.

Sigh.

Still, Piper had known they were coming through that door before they came through that door. She hadn't even glanced out the window. Definitely some kind of ability.

Creatures and deities were required to check in with any one of us Reeds, and usually Bertie when they first came to town. But mortals with powers, such as witches, telepaths, empaths, mediums, were a little harder to keep track of. So many mortals with powers either didn't know they had powers, or spent their lives trying to hide them. Most of them probably didn't even know that Ordinary was a gathering place of the weirdly-abled.

I turned my gaze down to my menu and tried to decide between something moderately healthy, and something that I actually was hungry for.

I glanced back up when I sensed eyes on me.

Ben Rossi and Jame Wolfe had just come in. Jame waved a couple fingers and tipped his head in question.

They wanted to sit with me.

I realized that actually, I'd like some company.

I nodded, but they were already walking my way, either because Jame could tell I was going to say yes because I was giving off body language a werewolf could recognize, or because his boyfriend, Ben was reading my mind.

Wait. I was pretty sure Rossi had told me vampires couldn't really do that.

No...he'd just said they couldn't all read each other's minds.

"Hey-a Chief," Ben said with a smile that looked a little tight. "Mind?" He waved at the table.

"Have a seat. You off shift?"

Jame Wolfe and Ben Rossi were one of those couples who were testing the tensile strength of love. For one thing, they weren't even the same kind of creature, Jame being a werewolf, and Ben being a vampire. For another, their two families did not get along.

Add to that the fact they were gay in a small town, and worked together in the fire department. Any one of those would be the *coup de grâce* to a relationship, but they were making it work.

"Yep. Next two days off. Thought we'd catch a meal," Ben said.

I raised one eyebrow. Vampires could eat. Not much, and in my experience, they tended to pick a few favorite foods and nibble. Vampires could also drink, which seemed a little easier on them than solid food. Blood was needed to refresh and restore their strength, and most of the vamps got their supply through some Red Cross back channels, or held a blood drive here in Ordinary to sample the local flavors.

It was a nice way for the town to unknowingly support their

neighbors, knowingly feel like they'd done a good deed to save lives—and they had: undead lives—and it allowed the no-non-consensual-biting rule to remain in place.

Still, I didn't think Ben was hankering for diner food.

Jame, on the other hand, might be on for a full meal deal. Werewolves were carnivores with high metabolisms. According to some recent horrified gossip in the Wolfe camp, one of the younger girls had gone vegan. It was almost enough of a shock to take the Wolfe family attention off of Jame and Ben's illicit relationship.

"Eat here often?" I asked.

"Now and again," Jame said in his low, soft voice. Everything about him seemed thick and solid: shoulders, chest, arms, fingers. Even his dark hair and closely trimmed, slightly reddish beard were thick.

Ben, who was half Jame's body mass was just as strong as his partner, if not stronger. Vampires tended to be slender, but that did not make them weak.

"Why are you here tonight, Chief?" Ben asked with a knowing look.

Piper appeared at that moment, and handed Ben and Jame menus. As she reached, I noted she had written *#5 T-sour* on her pad.

"Hey there, gentlemen. Can I get you tomato juice? Lemonade?"

"Tomato juice," Ben said.

"Lemonade," Jame said.

That wasn't odd, right? Out of all the drink items on the menu she had chosen the two they wanted. Or had they just agreed to her suggestions because it was easy? Maybe she'd served them before and remembered what they liked to drink.

"Have you decided on dinner yet?" she asked me.

"I'll have the soup and half a turkey on sourdough," I said. "And keep the coffee coming."

"You know I will." She moved her pen like she was writing on the pad only it didn't look like the pen pressed to the paper.

She walked off to refill a coffee cup a few tables down.

"Can I see your menu?" I asked.

Ben handed me his. "I already know what I'm getting."

Jame laughed once, a sort of low chuffing sound. "They make better fries at Jump Off Jack."

"Please," Ben scoffed. "Any fry in a storm."

Jame was studying the menu, his eyes bright with laughter, but also very focused. I wasn't surprised to see him staring at the steak section like maybe he was going to order one of everything.

"I didn't like the ribs, right?"

"Too much sauce," Ben affirmed. "Do the porter steak. Extra pepper, extra rare."

It was cute how they'd been a couple long enough to know each other's preferences. It made something in the center of my chest sort of ache. I'd never really had someone in my life who knew me well enough to order off the menu for me.

Well, except my sisters.

But the connection between these two men wasn't at all on the same level as a sibling tie. They were part of each other's lives because they chose to be.

Despite all the outside pressure that seemed more than willing to keep them apart.

I scanned the menu. #5 was the soup and sandwich. Piper had already written that down on the pad before I ordered. The T-sour, I assumed was the turkey on sourdough bread that went with my soup.

So Piper definitely had an ability she wasn't talking about. I'd have to find a way to bring it up to her. Let her know she was safe here. Let her know she wasn't the only person who had some kind of skill, power, magic.

Ben pushed the condiment carrier against the wall, and leaned back, one arm draped behind Jame, hand dropping to his boyfriend's back pocket. "Have you made any progress on the case?"

"Which one?" I put the menu down and Jame set his on top of mine, lining up the corners.

"The murder."

I inhaled, nodded as I released the air slowly through my nose. "We still don't have the murderer pinned down, but we're getting closer. Do you know anything about his death?"

Ben narrowed his eyes as if fighting off a flash of a

headache. "Sven was...private."

Jame chuffed again and Ben grimaced. "Even more private than most of us Rossis. But he was the newest here in town. And I think...I think he came here to get away from something."

"And you think that something was what caught up to him?"

He frowned and dragged his fingertip in looping circles on the Linoleum table top. "He had scars. I saw him without his shirt once."

Jame raised an eyebrow, his nostrils going wide. Ben immediately responded to that slight shift in his partner's body language. "Please. He was so not my type. It was at the bar where he worked. Someone barfed nachos with extra cheese all over him while he was trying to get them into a cab. It was dark, but he took off his shirt to change into a clean one he had in the trunk of his car."

"What kind of scars? Where were they?"

"Across his back, shoulder-to-shoulder. It was writing. Carved into his flesh, and whip marks all the way down to his belt line."

I didn't know if vampires could heal scars they received before they were turned. "Were they uh...recent?"

"We don't scar," he said, answering my unasked question.

"So before he was turned. Okay. Do you know what the writing said?"

"It was a little hard to see, and I'm rusty on my Latin...but yeah. I'm pretty sure it said: Divide and Rule."

I let the words settle in my brain, trying to make a connection. "In Latin?"

"Yes." His eyes flicked up to mine, as if that should mean something more to me.

"Rossi was Roman," I finally said.

Ben nodded slowly. "Yes."

Okay, but that still didn't do me a lot of good. "Do you think those words have something to do with Rossi?"

Ben chewed on the corner of his lip, the razor tip of his incisor briefly denting the soft flesh of his mouth.

"Tell her or I will," Jame rumbled.

Before Ben could say anything, Piper was back. "What can

I get you gentlemen?" She set the lemonade and tomato juice down in front of them.

Jame ordered his steak and Ben asked for the fries with a side of Worcestershire sauce.

Piper didn't even bother writing down the orders, but she did refill my coffee before saying she'd be back in a blink. Then she sashayed off.

"Tell me what?" I asked.

"Rossi makes every family member strip before he allows them to stay in town."

He delivered it with the same kind of nonchalance one might expect to hear from someone saying shoes must be removed before one was allowed to board a plane. None of the vampires who came to Ordinary were young, either in mind or body, so it wasn't like he was creeping on minors. Still, it bothered me.

"Why?"

"He doesn't want to be surprised by anything."

"Such as?"

"Messages. Things from the past—his past—that might put Ordinary, and all the rest of us in danger."

"On bodies." I still wasn't sure why that was important.

"He..." Ben glanced over at Jame. Jame shifted so that his shoulder was pressed against Ben's in support. "This isn't something I'm really supposed to share outside the family." Ben laughed a little at himself. "But we all know I'm not one to follow the rules."

Jame's arm moved and I knew he squeezed Ben's leg under the table.

"Rossi doesn't accept every vampire who wants to live in Ordinary. We have to prove ourselves. That we will follow his rules, your rules, and mortal rules. We have to swear loyalty to him, his laws. Things like no hands-on feeding, no kills, no wars. All disagreements are taken to him, and him alone. In return, he swears to keep us fed via blood drives and to protect us from anyone, anything that would want to do us harm."

"Right," I said. This was all stuff I knew.

"Have you ever asked yourself who he's trying to protect us from?"

"Humans?"

His smile was wide and wicked. "Not a lot of humans think we exist."

"Gods? Werewolves?"

He shook his head. "Gods treat us like any other creature—which is to say we're basically below their notice. And yeah, there's tension between weres and vamps. But it's navigable."

"Vampire hunters?"

He stilled and his eyes, for a moment went black. "Did he tell you about that?"

"I know they exist."

"They do." He licked his lower lip, a little more fang showing. "They're...that's not much of a concern to us."

"All right. I give up. Who is Rossi trying to protect you from?"

"His past."

"You already said that. Can you be specific?"

"Rossi was turned at the same time as another mortal. They fought in wars together. More than one, through the centuries. They were close. Brothers. Then they had a parting of ways. Rossi thinks he was killed. But there's a reason Rossi is the prime of our clan. He is a jaded, suspicious old bastard. He never saw the body of his brother-in-arms. Won't believe he's dead, and therefore won't believe he's not a danger to him or us until he sees his rotting bones."

"Rossi thinks Lavius is alive?"

"He told you his name?" Ben said that with a sort of stunned reverence. "Holy hell, Delaney. Holy hell."

"He told me he knew he was dead."

Ben hummed a little sound of agreement. That must be the line Rossi told everyone. Except, apparently, Ben.

"And why did he tell *you* something different?"

Ben grinned again. "We're...uh...close."

I was trying to picture Ben and Rossi and Jame in a threesome and doing a terrible job at making that work in my head.

"What does that mean?"

"I'm one of his." At my look he smiled again, but this time

it was softer, and so very much older. "He turned me. It was...a long time ago. And it was a gift of sorts."

"So that makes you blood related?"

Jame chuffed again.

"I'm sort of his only son."

Wow. That was not in the history books or records that my family kept on Ordinary. I wondered if Dad had known about that. Wondered if Myra knew.

"Do most of the Rossis know this?"

He shrugged and it was the typically graceful, flowing vampire thing. "It's not a secret. But we don't exactly hang out in the front yard playing catch either. Our relationship isn't brought up often."

"Why?"

"He's very protective."

"So the fewer people who know you're related, the less of a target you are if Rossi's past comes looking for him?"

"Something like that."

It both surprised and impressed me. That kind of caution spoke of feelings, maybe even a caring relationship.

It was sweet. Who knew Rossi had it in him?

"Did the words on Sven's back have something to do with Lavius?"

His gaze dropped and he went back to drawing on the table top. "I don't know. Maybe. Sven wasn't as old as me, not nearly as old as Rossi. But I've seen those words, written in Latin before."

"Where?"

"In Rossi's letters and personal papers. It was used as a closing in several documents."

"Coincidence?"

Ben stared at me for an extended moment. "I hardly think so. Do you?"

That slightly imperious tone made me curious about which time in history Ben had been originally born into, and what his occupation or social status might have been. Right this moment I'd have said royalty, or maybe snooty school teacher.

"No," I said. "Coincidence is the one thing I don't believe in when it comes to Ordinary."

At that moment, Piper was back, a tray with all of our food balanced on her arm. She placed each order in front of the correct recipient.

"All right then. Is there anything else I can get any of you?"

"This looks great, thanks." Ben stared at his fries like they were a starving man's last meal, his fingertips pressed into the table top on either side of the mound of potatoes.

"Thank you," Jame added, having already cut a chunk from the steak and stuffed it into his mouth.

I gave her a smile. "This is perfect. Say, Piper. When do you get off tonight?"

A little color hit her cheeks, but I couldn't tell if she was surprised by my question or just overheated from the job. "I'm done at eleven-thirty. Pretty late, unless you're pulling graveyard shift?"

"No. But if I'm around by then, let's talk."

She held very still, studying me like I was a language she couldn't read. "Sure," she finally said with a false smile. "Let's talk. Need steak sauce?"

"No thanks," Jame said around another bite.

"Then I'll leave you to it." She hurried off to the next table.

No, I'm not really the one in the family who gets vibes. But something about her willingness to talk with me had the tin can rattle of fate.

One thing for sure, I was going to ask her exactly what abilities she had. I didn't want a repeat of suddenly finding out we had a shape-shifting mimic in town.

Talk about an awkward race for mayor.

"Why are you freaked out over Piper?" Jame asked as he stabbed steak, potato chunk, steak onto his fork shish kabob style.

"I'm not freaked."

He paused with the food halfway to his mouth, gave me a look. "She worries you." Statement. Long stare.

"Nice alpha glare. But that doesn't work on me."

He grinned and just like that was back in motion again. "Something about her," he said with his mouthful.

"Something," I agreed. "I'll let you know when I figure it out."

Ben was currently sucking on a French fry with the kind of ardor not usually allowed in a family restaurant. "She's not human."

"What?" He hadn't exactly mumbled around the fry, but I wanted to make sure I'd heard him right. Because other than the apparent ability to see into the future of menu orders, she seemed very human to me.

He must have gotten his fill of sucking out the oil and salt. He licked up the length of it one last time then gleefully bit the fry into tiny pieces as he pushed it tip-to-end between his teeth. "She isn't human." He shook Worcestershire sauce into his tomato juice, dipped a new fry into the juice and started with the sucking again.

"What is she?"

He paused. Exchanged a look with Jame.

Jame straightened from being bent over his plate, sat back, and took a long drink of lemonade, watching me over the rim. Okay, maybe the alpha thing was a little unsettling.

"We thought you'd know." He placed his lemonade exactly back on top of the ring of condensation it had left on the table.

"Why?"

"She smells like a god."

"You're kidding me."

That look was definitely not kidding.

"Gods smell?"

This time he gave me a slow blink. Yeah, okay. That was a dumb question. Every kind of thing probably had a specific smell to a werewolf.

Holy crap. She was a god.

"But not a god," Ben added. He nipped down another fry with tiny, vicious bites, and swirled a third in his glass like it was fancy shrimp in gourmet cocktail sauce.

"Explain?" I picked up my half sandwich and took a bite. Really decent combo of turkey, cranberry and cream cheese on lightly toasted, lightly buttered sourdough. Simple, handmade, and because of both: delicious.

"She's not *not* a god." Jame said this like it was a conversation they'd been having before they'd gotten here.

"And not *just* a god." Ben pointed his fry at Jame.

"Something else. Something more. Or less. Just...something." He held Jame's gaze and slowly slid the entire fry between his lips, sucking enough to hollow his cheeks as he devoured it whole.

From the look on Jame's face, the fry-play his boyfriend was engaged in was doing it for him. He gave Ben a look that might best be saved for the bedroom.

"Hey," I snapped my fingers. "Love birds. You're in a family restaurant. Don't make me be a cop on my dinner break."

They gave me twin unrepentant grins.

I ate soup and tried to look imposing. Soup was good too. Hearty vegetable with just the right amount of basil.

"So you're not sure she's a god?"

Ben inhaled, exhaled, and his eyes did that vampire-light flash thing as he considered the question. "We thought you would know. Reed family job and all that."

"I didn't think she was a deity. She didn't stow her powers, so if she is of the godly persuasion, she's found a way to smuggle herself into Ordinary without the regular alarms going off."

"You have alarms set up for god invasion?" Jame's steak was gone, but he was still working his way through the potatoes, the neglected pile of green beans pushed carefully off to one side.

"Not physical alarms, no. I'd know. It's...I guess it's a part of our agreement with the deities. I can spot one a mile away."

"So she isn't?" Ben was done with his fries and sipped the tomato juice pausing to lick his bottom lip every once in awhile.

I watched Piper wipe down a spot on a recently cleared table, then tuck her cloth in her apron pocket and walk back to the kitchen. Was there something godly about her?

I could hear god power, knew the song of it, even when it was stored away and the god was vacationing as a mortal. A little echo of that power resided within the deity. I had gotten used to hearing it with Odin, Crow, Than, and the others. But I knew they were gods. Maybe I was just tuned into it because of that knowledge.

"I don't hear power, don't...sense it in her." That worried me more than if I *had* sensed it.

Jame stole a few fries off Ben's plate and stuffed them in

his mouth, making a point to lick each of his fingertips as he gave Ben that alpha stare.

"Maybe whatever else she is covers it up," Ben suggested. "Maybe she doesn't know what she is."

I shook my head. "If she's a god, she knows. Power is never subtle, not even when it's contained. I'll talk to her. Do you think Lavius is alive?"

Ben didn't even blink at the subject change, but Jame tightened, all the muscles of his shoulders and arms bunching beneath his shirt.

"Rossi said he's dead," Ben said.

"I already heard that from Rossi. I want to hear what you think."

"I think he's alive. I think he had Sven killed."

"Do you have any proof? Anything I can use?"

If I thought Jame had been tense before, he was practically granite now. "No," Jame said.

"Maybe," Ben corrected. Another long-term argument? From the flare of annoyance on Jame's face, yes.

"When I get that proof, I will contact you," Ben continued as if his partner wasn't balling his hands into fists hard enough to make his knuckles pop.

I looked between the two of them. Settled on Jame. "Don't let him do anything stupid, all right? One Rossi was murdered. I don't want to see that happen again."

Now that I knew Ben was Rossi's actual vampire-related kind-of-son, I really didn't want to see what Rossi would do if Ben were hurt.

"I'll look after him," Jame rapped his knuckles on the table top. "No matter how stupid he's being."

Ben made a dismissive sound. "I'll have you know I'm older than both of you by a long shot. I know how to look after myself, thank you."

"Yeah," Jame said. "So did Sven."

"Sven was foolish," Ben said. "And trusting. I'm smart and suspicious. Besides." He flashed a winning smile. "I'll have you tight—very tight—at my back."

Okay, that was a bit over the line for subtle double-entendres.

Jame turned on the alpha-smolder and Ben laughed. Apparently, it didn't work on vampires either.

"I'm serious, Ben," I said. "If you have anything that will help me catch the killer, I want to see it. But not at a risk to your life, understand? And if you do anything—anything—to mess up this case or compromise my investigation, I'll bring you in on charges."

Ben tucked his smile away, though I still saw laughter in his eyes. "Understood. I promise not to jeopardize myself or the case."

He pushed the plate of fries away with a sort of regretful frown, then turned toward his boyfriend. "You done eating? Because I'm in the mood for a night cap. Something...hot and strong." He watched the smile pull the corner of Jame's mouth and there was a new hunger that passed between them.

I started calculating the melting point of Linoleum and vinyl.

"Good-night, Chief," the werewolf said without taking his eyes off Ben.

"Night, boys. Have a good couple of days off. Remember to stretch before and hydrate after."

Ben chuckled. They stood, Ben sliding his arm around Jame's wide back, long fingers plunging down into Jame's back pocket. They talked quietly to each other and grinned as they walked out of the diner, oblivious to the people around them, and oh, so obviously in love.

I sighed. They made it look easy, even though they had so many factors working against them.

Why couldn't I figure out my dating life? It wasn't like the questions were hard to solve. I either loved or didn't love Ryder, and would either give him a chance to prove he was innocent or not.

And I either forgave him for dumping me or I didn't.

Easy.

Why did it all seem so much harder than that?

My half-eaten turkey sandwich and quickly cooling soup didn't have any answers for me, so I finished my meal, and checked in with Myra and Jean one more time to see if they'd made any progress on the video.

It was easy to stay busy with work while I drank my way through a pot of coffee. The Blue Owl had that sort of outside-of-time effect. People came and went, first the families, then the late night diners, then the college kids and singles loading up on good, cheap food between hitting the bars.

Through it all, Piper was cheerful, friendly, and prompt. But I never once heard so much as a peep of power.

What I did hear was a text from Jean, who had gotten a clear view of the ring on the hand across Sven's mouth. She was looking into any identifying marks that would lead to its owner.

She sent me a picture of it. All I could see on my phone was the band, and that it was clearly a man's fingers, so I wasn't much help.

But at least it was something we could go on.

By the time eleven-thirty finally rolled around, I'd given up coffee and was sipping a cup of tea. The last bunch of twenty-somethings laughed their way out of the diner, waving at Piper and each other.

Three of them put umbrella hats over their beanies and made silly faces and high-fives.

Oh, for Pete's sake.

It had stopped raining. Even though clouds still crowded the edges of the moon, light shone through.

There were no other customers in the diner. No cars in the parking lot. I hadn't seen anyone walk around outside, didn't see anyone loitering now. But in a half hour, I was supposed to meet someone out there.

It was time to go.

I stood and Piper stopped by the table. She set down two slices of pie and an extra pot of tea. The plate in front of me had blueberry crumble, her plate was the chocolate mousse I'd seen so many diners rave about tonight.

"I know it's not midnight," she said, "but since you're here, and I'm here, and no one else is, how about if we just do the meeting now?"

"Meeting?" But then it hit me. She was the anonymous letter writer.

CHAPTER 11

"SURE." I gestured to the chair across the table.

Piper sat with a sigh, tired from her long shift at the diner. I moved some of the paperwork out of the way while she poured tea for herself and for me, and took a sniff or two to see if I could smell anything god-like about her.

She smelled like fried foods and something sweet like honey and cinnamon. She took a sip of her tea and I watched her, listening for the song of power within her.

There was no song. Maybe it was because she was off her shift and therefore wasn't keeping up the waitress face, but there was something sort of...glowy about her. Something that reminded me of the sea, or of a sunset on it.

"Why did you write the letter?" I asked. "You know you could have come to me or any of my sisters and we would have listened to you. Kept you safe."

"I don't know that. I don't know any of you. Didn't even really know your father." She picked up her fork and started on her pie, eating it from the wider back edge of the crust first.

I followed suit and took a bite of the blueberry crumble, starting tip first. "I can promise you, you can trust us. My sisters and I are here for every man, woman, god and creature in town."

Her lack of reaction to that made it clear that she knew about god powers, gods, and creatures in town.

"Why didn't you come to us?"

"You're the police. The law was broken. I didn't think you'd be happy with the things I had to say."

"If you know who took the god powers, I can assure you, I am very happy with what you have to say."

She paused, watching me with eyes much older than they had been just moments before.

"Powers?"

"Powers. And before you act like you don't know what I'm talking about, I know you are more than mortal. What are you,

Piper?"

"What do you think I am?"

"At first? Maybe a witch. Or a precog."

She laughed, a light, happy sound. "Really? You thought I could see the future?"

"You know every order before anyone tells you what they want to eat. You know how many people are coming through that door before they're out of their car. You know where people want to sit before they make up their mind."

"I'm—that's just being observant."

"You knew I wanted the number five with a half turkey on sourdough. I've never ordered that here and you had already written it down before I asked for it. Don't kid a kidder. Can you see the future?"

She exhaled and went back to eating pie, not looking at me. "Not really see it, no. I just get certain flashes of things. Like I saw that I had written the order on my pad, so I wrote it. Turned out it was right. And I saw a flash of showing you to the table, of getting the highchair for that family earlier, all those things. I've always thought of it as an overactive intuition. Lots of people have strong intuition."

"It's more than that. Trust me, Piper. Tell me."

She put her fork down even though there was only a small triangle of chocolate pie left just begging to be eaten.

"This isn't something I've ever shared." Her eyes darted up to me, then down to her pie again. "I need to know you will give me amnesty."

Well, well. That was unexpected.

"There are rules in Ordinary. Laws set by the gods and mortals who have been here long before me. I have to follow those rules, Piper, because those rules were set into place to keep everyone—all the mortals, all the gods, all the creatures of Ordinary—safe. Are you in danger?"

She glanced up at me, her eyes wide, two bright spots of color flaming her cheeks.

"I'll take that as a yes, you're in danger."

I pushed my pie to one side, which was a shame since I'd only gotten through half of it and it was really good pie. "Okay. I'm here to help you. Whatever it is, I will do my best to make sure the laws of Ordinary protect you. My sisters and I will do our best to protect you. I swear it on my family's name. Talk to me, Piper. I promise I'll make this better."

She bit the inside of her cheek, and from how stiff she held her shoulders this wasn't an easy decision for her.

"I'm...I'm not just human."

I thought we'd already established that. But I nodded encouragingly.

"My mother was human. And...um...my father wasn't."

So far so good. I nodded again and gave her a little smile.

"My father is a god."

Okay, I'd been ready for almost anything out of her mouth. And yes, Jame had said she smelled like a god. But for some reason I hadn't thought she could be the child of a god. A demigod. I'd never met a demigod. We didn't have any in town. I wasn't even sure what the rules were for a demigod to live in town. Were they half on vacation? Did they have to carry a part-time mortal job? Did they have power? Was that power great enough to need to be stored away? Half stored away?

I couldn't hear a god power in her. If she had a power, she wasn't currently carrying it.

"Terrific!" I said.

She startled.

That came out with a little more force than I'd expected. "Good. Good," I said a little more quietly. "You're a demigod. You do know you are wildly over-qualified for diner work."

She gave me a hesitant smile. "It pays the bills. And the free meals aren't so bad."

"You're really good at it, by the way."

"This isn't my first time on the floor. But I like this place." She looked around at the diner and I wondered what she saw in it. The Blue Owl had been remodeled several times over the years and had been several kinds of eateries. They had expanded their hours for the summer, and seemed to be doing brisk enough business with their 1950s decor and atmosphere.

But I thought maybe it wasn't just a diner Piper was looking at. It was a moment in time, an era that no longer existed. An era in which she had been young.

"Do you know who took the god powers?"

She nodded and turned her attention back to me. "About that." She twisted fingers together and placed both hands on the table, wrists close together as if she were already in handcuffs. "I know who. And I know why."

"Good," I said. "That's perfect. Can you tell me who first?"

"Yes. Me."

It was really good that I wasn't drinking tea at the moment because I would have spit it out. "Wow. Okay. So that's why you were looking for amnesty. Right. Can you tell me why you did that?"

"I'm not proud of what I did."

"But?"

"I...owed someone. And I didn't owe them money."

"Who?"

"A god."

"You're going to have to narrow that down a bit."

"Mithra."

God of contracts. Judiciary. All-seeing protector of truth. Not surprisingly, someone who had never vacationed in Ordinary.

"You owed Mithra the powers? All the god powers in town?"

"What? No! No. I owed him my life."

"He was blackmailing you? Was he blackmailing you? Why was he blackmailing you?"

She tipped her chin up and I saw the strength of her. Definitely demigod. I didn't know how I had missed it before.

"He negotiated the situation between my father and mother. For my life. He was the only one who cared. The only one who helped when my mother needed help."

I inhaled and a low, throbbing headache took up residence behind my eyes. Maybe I had a skewed perspective on gods—okay, certainly I had a skewed perspective. But sometimes getting a god involved in a mortal matter only made things worse.

Surprisingly, mortals were generally pretty good at getting out of messes on their own.

"Okay, I think you need to take it from the top. Which god is your father?"

"Poseidon."

I bit my teeth on a groan. Of course it was Poseidon. The god who couldn't even vacation without killing himself over it. Crow would be giving me a big fat told-you-so right now.

"How many years ago was that?"

"Seventy-six. He met my mother while he was vacationing here. She was the daughter of the grocer."

I did some math. Piper looked like she was in her early thirties, not well past retirement age. Poseidon had a habit of dying while vacationing in Ordinary, and the current Poseidon was only a few years into his godhood. So the Poseidon who was her father would have been in town when my grandpa was acting as the bridge for god powers.

I really wished Myra were here since she kept track of the history better than I did.

I glanced over at the door. And wouldn't you know it? Myra strolled up and knocked quietly on the glass.

Just when she was needed most. I really wish I had that gift.

Piper looked less impressed. "What is she doing here? Did you call her? Are you arresting me? Is she arresting me?"

"Settle down. No one's arresting you." I stood and walked over to the door. It wasn't locked because the diner was never closed, but it was easy to forget that in our closed-by-eight-o'clock town. I opened it for Myra and started back to the table. Piper had slid out of the chair and was standing with her arms wrapped around her ribs like she was trying to protect her vulnerable bits.

"Hey, Piper," Myra said. "Is everything okay?"

Myra didn't always give off the warmest vibes, especially when she was in cop mode. Even though she was wearing jeans and a sweat shirt, she was still giving off that stern cop body language.

But out of the three of us Reed girls, I had always thought she was the most nurturing. Her voice, when it softened like that, reminded me of Mom. Myra could soothe a kitten who'd been locked in a tumble drier if she had to.

And thanks to Jean, she'd had to.

Twice.

Maybe that's why that cat of ours was always getting stuck

in weird places: Jean. I made a mental note to grill her about it.

"You said you wouldn't tell anyone. You said you didn't." Piper's eyes were tight, her eyebrows dipped in a hard scowl.

Whatever trust I'd been building with her over pie was about to be blown to bits if I didn't say something soothing, something comforting and trustworthy right this minute.

"Piper is Poseidon's daughter and she's in a bit of a jam we're going to try to help her out of."

Myra blinked, rockabilly eyeliner winging at the edges of her wide blues making her eyes even more pale. But that was the extent of her reaction to me blurting out that we had a demigod in our midst.

"We can do that. Is there any more of that tea? It smells wonderful." She walked past Piper, snagged a cup off the counter, then took my seat and poured tea. "You two want a little more while you catch me up?"

She held the pot over Piper's cup.

"What do you say, Piper?" I asked. "Three heads are better than one?"

"Except for Cerberus," Myra said. "Just...dumbest dog ever."

"Oh, please. He's not dumb, he's just easily distracted."

"All three heads are easily distracted. And they all have a different idea of what the body should be doing. It's sad."

"It's kind of funny." I sat down next to Myra and made a grab for my pie, but she had already commandeered the plate, my unused spoon and the last half of my blueberry crumble.

Jerk.

"Going to have a seat?" I asked Piper.

She glanced at the door and the escape it offered.

"Come on. You'd know if we were a threat, wouldn't you? You could tell?"

She slowly unwound her arms from her rib cage and brushed at strands of hair that had gone a little wild around her head. "Yes. I can tell if I'm in danger. Although you Reeds aren't very easy to read."

"That makes me curious as to what kind of powers you have." Myra licked the last of the blueberry off the spoon. "I'd like to record them in our histories sometime if that's okay."

"She keeps the books on Ordinary." I pulled the plate away from her and pressed the tip of my finger into the remaining crumbs of crumble. "But we can do that later. What we really need is to hear the rest of your information about the god powers."

"Power," Piper said.

"You know something about the missing powers?" Myra asked.

"She gave them away."

"To whom?"

"Mithra."

Myra's eyebrow ticked upward, but she just sipped her tea. Then: "He's never liked us much. I take it we'll need to negotiate with him to get them back?"

"I figure. Think he'll go for an offering of goats this time? Cute goats?"

"Last time we had to get him tickets to the national 4-H Skill-A-Thon, didn't we?"

"Yes. And a subscription to a chocolatier magazine."

"He does like judging pralines and young people with livestock. If only there was a chocolate goat contest. He'd love that."

"You bribed him?" Piper looked like she couldn't decide on being shocked or amused as she finally took the seat across from us.

"Not a bribe," I said. "It's just that Mithra has a certain way of conducting business. He is big on action and reaction, cause and effect. And equality. If we want something from him—the god powers—he will expect something of the same value from us in return."

"Tickets to a livestock show is equal to god powers?"

"Maybe?" Myra shrugged. "It's hard to get a read on him sometimes. What did he give you in exchange for the powers?"

"Power. Singular. One. And it wasn't like that. I owed him for helping my mom."

"No, it's still an exchange. He gave you peace of mind. Stability. In return, he asked you for the god powers—very plural. How is it he thought you would be able to get them?"

"He didn't ask. Not exactly."

We waited.

"My mother passed away a few years ago. It was...hard to watch her age, to see her lose so much of her vitality, her mind. They said it was Alzheimer's there at the end, but...I don't know, maybe it was. She said she could see things. Angels.

"Three months after her diagnosis, she was gone. The last thing she said to me was that I had to go to Mithra. Pay him back. She said if he hadn't answered her prayers, I wouldn't be alive."

"Do you know if your mom got pregnant while here in Ordinary?" I asked.

"I think so."

"And Poseidon was on vacation at the time?"

She nodded.

"That's the problem then. The contract the gods sign when they first come to Ordinary states that they can't procreate while here. It's not usually a problem. Deities aren't really fertile while they take on a mortal life. So for your mother to get pregnant, Poseidon would have had to have been carrying his power. If he was carrying it while vacationing in Ordinary, that's against the rules."

"Mithra is all about following the rules," Myra said. "I'm sure he knew what happened."

"But...she said he hid her away to make sure she could have me. Isn't that breaking the rules? Isn't my life breaking the rules?"

"Technically," I said. "But it was Poseidon who broke the rules, not your mother. If you had been conceived outside of Ordinary, there would be no problem, no rules would have been broken. Honestly, the rule is there more to protect the mortals than the deities. The punishment for breaking that rule is the god has to leave Ordinary for ten years—not exactly a hard sentence on an all-powerful, immortal being."

"She thought I was going to be taken from her."

"That's not the way it works," I said, trying to use Myra's motherly tone. From the weird look on Myra's face, I didn't quite stick the landing on that.

"I promise you, if your mother had gone to the Reed in charge, the worst that would have happened is that she and

Poseidon would have had to settle down outside the city limits."

"Oh," she said. I watched as years of doubts, years of worry crossed her face and then faded away, leaving her more human, and a little tired. "I thought I'd be killed. Or she would."

"No." Both Myra and I said that at the same time.

"The laws of Ordinary are here to protect children. Even children of gods. Maybe especially children of gods."

She nodded and picked up her cup, her gaze turned inward as she took a drink.

I wanted to give her time to digest all this information, but I had a town full of anxious power-naked gods, and a murderer to catch.

"Did Mithra want all the god powers in payment for him keeping the secret of your parentage?"

"You keep saying all the powers. He only asked for Raven's power."

I pressed back against the vinyl of the booth. I had a good idea of why he wanted Crow's power.

Crow had broken the rules. But he'd said because he was a trickster, his power would allow that. I had foolishly thought that was true.

Mithra knew Crow had broken the contract with Ordinary. Had probably been watching and waiting for a chance like this. Mithra was a stickler for contracts.

Plus, Crow had somehow pissed off every god I'd ever met. I couldn't rule out a little bit of spite figuring into this.

"Mithra knew the power would be near Crow," she said. "I knew it was in his shop."

"Is that one of your abilities?" I asked.

"If I'm close enough, I can sense that god power is near. It's like feeling electricity in the air. It took me a little time to figure out it was in the old glass-blowing furnace. When I had that figured out, it took me some time to get to it."

"How did you get to it?" I asked.

"Pablo at the gas station has the key to Crow's shop. I went in the front door and out the back. But don't blame him. He didn't know what I was doing. I told him I was going to check Crow's shop for him while he was gone. I told him Crow said it was okay."

So that would be breaking and entering. Now on to the burglary. "How did you transport the powers?"

"What do you mean?"

"Most people—creatures or otherwise—can't touch the powers. How did you physically carry them?"

"An empty water bottle."

"What?"

"A water bottle? It's what I had handy."

"You put all the god powers in Ordinary in a water bottle?"

"No, I put Crow's power in a water bottle."

"All the powers are missing, Piper."

"All of them?" She blinked hard, and went a shade of green I hadn't seen since Jean was in kindergarten and licked the bottom of her shoe on a dare.

During the field trip. To the dairy farm.

I really shouldn't have been so proud of myself for making her fall for that.

"All of them?" she asked again.

"All of them."

"I was just trying to get Crow's."

"You did," Myra said. "And you also took the power of every other god in town."

"Oh, crap."

Oh crap, indeed.

"I didn't mean to. You have to believe me. I never meant to take all the powers. Just Crow's."

"We believe you," I said. She opened her mouth and I reached over and patted her hand. She waited, probably expecting words of wisdom or comfort.

"You done screwed up."

Myra sighed.

Hey, I never said I was good at this kind of thing.

"But," I said, "there were extenuating circumstances. You aren't the only one who screwed up. Technically, Crow broke one of Ordinary's rules. So technically Mithra could be considered correct for stepping in. Though technically, Ordinary is outside his influence and we'd rather he'd let us handle our own business just like all the other gods outside Ordinary do. We have rules for that too. Don't worry. This could be much worse."

"He wants to meet you," Piper blurted out.

"Who?"

"Mithra. I just gave him the powers on my afternoon break. He said he wants to talk to you, Delaney, tomorrow. About the rules. About power. And he wants you to bring Ryder Bailey with you."

I could not have been more shocked if a fish had suddenly ridden by on a bicycle. With an umbrella hat on its head.

"Ryder?" I finally said. Or thought I did. It came out more like a squeak.

"Did he say why he wanted to see Delaney and Ryder?" Good ol' Myra. Nothing knocked her off her footing.

"He said it was Delaney's job to make sure the rules of Ordinary aren't broken. And he said he has questions he wants Ryder to answer."

"Ryder doesn't even know about the gods," I said. "Or god power. He wouldn't believe Mithra is a god. He is so not coming with me. No. No way."

"I promised he would," Piper said.

I groaned. "Why?"

"I thought he knew! He's on the police force, and Myra and Jean and Roy know. Why wouldn't he know about the gods?"

"Because we don't share that kind of information easily," Myra said.

"This is officially worse," I muttered.

We were all silent.

"Has this ever happened before?" Piper asked in a small voice. "Has anyone ever screwed up as badly as this?"

"Oh, honey." I gave her a firm pat on her hand. "You have no idea."

"Right. Now. We'll need a few more details." Myra pulled out her tablet and tapped it to life. "About everything."

"Then what?" Piper asked.

"Then we fix this," I said with a lot more confidence than I felt.

CHAPTER 12

WE WENT over the details of the water-bottle power heist for two hours. When she did it, who she talked to, how long she carried the power around like the most dangerous energy drink in the universe.

Piper insisted she went to meet with Mithra at the casino this afternoon and handed over the powers. I believed her. Myra took notes. We asked her every question in different ways about a dozen times. Got the same answers.

So when Myra wanted to follow me to my house so we could go over "just a few more details," I told her no. I also suggested she go home, get some sleep, and that we'd worry about it in the morning.

I may have mentioned I spilled some of Ordinary's secrets to Ryder. Not the god secrets. Or the creature secrets. But definitely the vampire secrets. Well, some of them.

Myra may have read me the riot act about our duty as Reeds and how keeping secrets was a huge part of those duties. And reminded me of Ryder's possible involvement in murder, and my possible inability to think he was a suspect because of my heart's definite involvement with him.

It was almost four o'clock in the morning by the time she was done going through all the reasons I shouldn't have told Ryder there were vampires in town. She also wasn't happy that I'd told him he'd have to get through me if he and his vampire-hunter buddies, or his vampire-friendly buddies, wanted near any kind of creature in this town.

I'd told her I thought it was worth the risk for him to know if it got us closer to Sven's killer. She wasn't mollified.

She had ended the conversation with, "I wish you didn't love him, Delaney."

"Because it puts Ordinary in danger?" I asked, rubbing my fingertips over my scalp and yawning. I was too tired to argue over the "love" part of her statement. Maybe even too tired to kid myself about that any more.

I loved him.

Stupid heart.

"No, you idiot. Because it puts *you* in danger." Then she'd reached over and given me a quick, tight hug. "Sleep. I'll see you later. Let's think this over. Maybe we'll both make better decisions in the morning. Or afternoon."

Which was why I was surprised to be stumbling out of my bed and into my living room to answer the door at seven a.m.

The door wasn't locked—I still wasn't convinced I needed that kind of security in this town. I yanked it open. "This isn't later. This is still way too earlier."

"All right then," Ryder said as his eyes took a quick detour to check out what I was wearing. "Huffing the hand-sanitizer a little early, aren't we?"

I was suddenly very awake. And suddenly very aware I was wearing an over-sized T-shirt.

And nothing else.

"Ryder? You're...um...you're not Myra."

He leaned a little back on one hip, his hand in his front pocket and the devil in his eyes. "Nope."

"Why are you here? Is there an emergency?"

"I'm here to apologize, which, frankly, might be now a dozen times I've done that in the last few days. I'm thinking of asking for a cumulative discount on your forgiveness."

"Apologize? What for this time? No, wait. Don't answer." I dragged my fingers through my hair which, oops, made the shirt lift a little, then pressed fingertips against my eyes. "All right. I'm gonna need coffee for this. And pants. Come on in."

"Don't get dressed on my account."

I meandered over to the bedroom. "Start the coffee, would you? And make it strong." He shut the door behind him and I did the same. I gazed at my unmade bed, the soft blankets that looked so inviting, and sighed.

Clothing was a T-shirt and jeans. I brushed my teeth, hair, and put on deodorant. It gave me enough time to guess what Ryder was apologizing for.

For lying. For not telling me who his boss was. For not telling me more about the agency he was working for.

For dumping me?

No, he'd already apologized for that. Several times.

Or there was the possibility he was apologizing for something new. Some problem I'd have to deal with on about a minute and a half of sleep.

Great.

I needed boots for this conversation.

I strolled out to the sound of voices. Myra, Jean, Crow, and Ryder all lounged around my living room, drinking my coffee and chatting away like this was a book club.

Myra looked relaxed and well rested, when I knew she'd gotten the same amount of sleep as I had.

How did she do that?

"Okay. Who decided to throw a party at my house without telling me? And could you please un-invite me?"

Crow chuckled, but Jean stuck her hand straight up above her head, elbow locked. "I did. We did. Before you get all crabby about it, we're not going to let you do what you did last time."

"Do what which last time I did what?"

"Get shot while you were trying to solve a case."

I inhaled against the fist of frustration that clogged my throat. Jean and Myra still hadn't let that go. I really needed them to stop hovering like I was one brick shy of a Jenga collapse.

"I'm not going to get shot. Have I ever been shot before then? No. That was sort of a one-time deal. It's not going to happen again."

"We're not just worried about guns," Myra said in a now-now-calm-down voice I sort of hated. "There's a lot going on in town and I decided we need to talk about it. All of us."

"No." I glared at her. There were two people in this room I didn't want in the middle of the conversation about the missing god power or the ongoing murder investigation. Ryder and Crow.

"We agreed on this," she said.

"When?"

"Last night when we discussed it."

"Was I awake? Maybe I nodded off and you thought I was just nodding."

She gave me a look that said she didn't think I was funny.

Ryder pointed at the Chewbacca cup on the table. "Caffeinate. We'll figure it out."

It was so close to what I'd told Piper last night, I almost laughed. "Fine," I said, even though it was not at all fine. I sat and took a drink.

Lots of sugar, favorite cup, coffee strong enough to be used as an interrogation device.

Perfect.

I took a second gulp and glanced at Ryder.

He winked at me.

Winked.

My heart got all warm and gooey.

"I thought you were going to apologize for something."

"I am."

"Well?"

He made a circle with his fingers, indicating everyone in my house. "Pretty much this."

"This intervention was your idea?"

He tipped his head with an eyebrow raised. "Well, I've been recently reminded, at length, that I'm a part of the police force. Since I have taken vows to look after Ordinary, there was no getting out of this team-building exercise. Although I don't see Roy here."

"Team Go Away and Let Delaney Sleep?" I asked Myra. She ignored me.

"Roy's keeping an eye on the station. And because it needs to be said," she turned her attention to Ryder, "Delaney told me about the conversation you had with her, Ryder. That you know there are vampires in town."

Jean tensed up and Crow laughed. Crow tried to cover his glee with a cough that totally didn't work.

I muttered, "'Laugh it up...'"

"...'Fuzzball'," Ryder finished for me.

I lifted my Chewy cup in a toast. That was an old Star Wars reference. Not a lot of people got it these days.

"As we all know, we're dealing with a murder in town that involved a vampire," Myra went on like a kindergarten teacher who refused to give in to her students' antics. "We understand you have some information that could be useful to our case."

That teasing glimmer in Ryder's eyes faded. "I already made it clear to Delaney that I didn't have anything more to say on that unless she was willing to answer a few questions for me."

"No," I said.

"What questions?" Jean asked.

"Are there more vampires in town? Who are they? Who is their leader? How can I contact them?"

"That's easy," Crow said.

"No!" all us Reed girls chorused at once.

Crow sniffed. "Spoil sports."

"You are still on my shit list," I reminded him.

He made a raspberry sound. "You love me and you know it."

"We are not at liberty to share that information," Myra said. How was it that she was acting more like the police chief than I was? Could it be that I was still tired, possibly muddled because half of this conversation involved my not-ex, long-time-crush hotty of a boyfriend, and also that I hadn't had nearly enough coffee yet?

Yes. Yes, it could.

"You understand that the persons of interest trust us to act in their behalf," Myra said. "We've sworn to keep them safe and keep their confidence. We won't break that trust."

Ryder took his time studying her serene face, then shifted his gaze to Jean for a bit, then finally to me. "None of you are going to tell me anything I want to know?"

"If you would answer *our* questions, we might be able to facilitate a meeting with someone in town who could help you," I said.

It wasn't quite a bluff, wasn't quite a promise. I was however, certain that Rossi would be more than happy to let Ryder know he was the big bad vampire in town. Rossi enjoyed threatening people he didn't like, and he most certainly didn't like Ryder.

Plus, I was pretty sure I'd agreed to let him be around when we questioned Ryder.

Ryder's shoulders shifted as he leaned forward to put his empty coffee cup on the table. When he sat back, he looked like he'd made up his mind.

"Anyone want to tell me why the glassblower is here?" he asked.

"Maybe I'm a vampire," Crow said.

"Nope," I said.

Crow just shrugged and gave Ryder a wide grin. "Maybe I'm something else."

"This isn't about you." I finished off the last of my coffee and sighed. "Jean, did you bring the photos?"

She pulled a folder out of her messenger bag and handed it to me. I sorted through the video surveillance shots. She'd done a great job cleaning up the images. The snap of the hand with the ring was particularly clear.

It looked familiar to me. Where had I seen that ring before?

"These are the images we got off of the surveillance camera outside Joe Boy's." I passed the folder to Ryder.

He opened it and studied the images.

"You said you know it was a group of vampire hunters that killed Sven. We can trace that ring, and will find the man who had his hand around Sven's mouth. We'll bring him in. But you could save us a lot of time, and do some good in building a positive position with the vampires in town if you would just tell us everything you know about this."

Ryder held his breath a minute, deciding.

"His name is Rick Mortin. The man who is a part of the vampire hunters. He's the head of the hunters sent to Ordinary. I can't make out enough of that ring to recognize it."

"Vampire hunters."

"Yes. We didn't know they were doing anything more than reconnaissance. We'd been tipped off that they'd be heading this way earlier in the year. I was supposed to keep my eyes out for them. Intercept them before they contacted any of the targets."

"Targets?" Jean asked. "Holy shit, Ryder. Who the hell do you work for?"

The waves of disappointment and anger radiating off Jean was pretty hard to watch. She had always idolized Ryder as the perfect upstanding guy. The guy she wanted to see date her oldest sister, and make a happily ever after with me.

But that wasn't how it ever worked in real life.

"I work with an agency that reaches out to supernaturals

and creates lines of open communication for the continued peace and advantages to our respective races."

"Tell me that's not an acronym," she muttered. "No, wait. Just tell me the name of your agency."

"I work with the Department of Paranormal Protection."

"Thought they were unfunded back in Eisenhower's days," Crow said. "Some kind of internal nut jobs tried to take over?"

Ryder didn't quite cover his surprise at Crow's knowledge. "Not exactly. There was a...change of leadership and the agency was reenacted under the Homeland Security act. The department has been functioning in various capacities since 1910."

"Hunting vampires?" Jean asked.

"We don't hunt."

"Oh, are we back to lying already? That's no fun," Crow said.

"We don't hunt to kill or eradicate, though, yes, there is a history of that in the early days of the agency. There are splinter groups who cling to the idea of human superiority and purity. Groups like the vampire hunters who came to town."

"Splinter groups," Myra said. "Are they a part of the Department of Paranormal Protection?"

"No. They are unsanctioned. We take every action possible to shut them down."

"Every?" Crow asked and even though no one had brought it up yet, we were all wondering just how black ops his black ops agency was. Would they kill the members of the vampire hunter group?

"There are rules and orders we follow," Ryder said. "We try to respect our nation's laws."

"But you kill people." The way Crow said it, and the way Ryder didn't react to it, was answer enough.

"Okay," I said. "You are cleared to use deadly force if necessary. That's not that different than what we do on the police force. Those men who were in the bar before Sven was killed were part of a dangerous splinter group, right? Not just a group of friends who decided to become ghost busters?"

"We—I hadn't thought so. They are in good standing with the department, and weren't out of their rights to put eyes on the inhabitants here."

"You work for DoPP?" Jean asked. "Or with them?"

"Neither. I'm...freelance."

"What does that mean?" I asked.

"I'm the local boy, know the town, know the people in it. Educated. The agency is always on the lookout for people they can hire to be liaisons if a sighting is confirmed."

"Sven's death was a sighting?" Jean asked. "No, wait, those splinter group guys were here before Sven died. What made them think vampires were in town?"

That was a very good question.

We all waited silently for Ryder to answer it.

"There was a boat that capsized a couple years back."

I knew exactly where he was going with this. We'd tried to squash the story, spin it so the wider news stations didn't pick it up. We must have missed something. Or Ryder's group had good ears and caught the gossip and statements that the survivors shared with friends and family.

"Eight tourists on board," he continued, "all of them non-swimmers. They reported their rescuers dove to save them, eyes glowing in the dark water. Said they had incredible strength and agility, including one who dragged two unconscious people up from the deep at the same time."

That would have been Chris Lagon, our local gill-man, who was our go-to guy for water recovery. He was not a vampire, but yeah, the other rescuers were vamps.

"They said the rescuers didn't seem out of breath even though they weren't wearing any breathing gear. One kid said she could hear her rescuer talking to her in her head. Sang her a silly song as they headed for the surface."

That probably would have been Ben. He had a way with kids, and keeping people calm in tense situations.

"They said they walked on water."

Crow snorted.

Non-breathing, telepathic-singing, and eyes-glowing? Yes. Walk on water? No.

"Vampires aren't really known for their deep-sea-diving abilities," Myra noted.

"Sure," Ryder said. "But mortals aren't known for glowing

eyes and not having to hold their breath under water. That meant my organization took notice."

"So they sent you home to check it out?" I asked.

Something a lot like betrayal was uncoiling in my chest. Or maybe just disappointment. I really had hoped Ryder had come home because he wanted to be here. Be a part of the people, the events, the day-to-day living of a small beach town.

"I came home." He said it with emphasis. "That was my choice. They had the option to send me out to check on possible sightings throughout the state. But when your dad passed away, I knew I had to stay."

"What does our dad's death have to do with it?"

"Do you really think he drove himself off the road in broad daylight?"

All of us girls went still, tense. None of us believed that, but there had been no proof of any foul play.

Odin's words came back to me. He said Dad waited too long to choose sides. I really needed to figure out what sides were involved.

"No," I said quietly. "Do you know something about his death?"

He shook his head. "Nothing solid. But I'd known him for most of my life, Delaney. My dad was friends with him. He always told me Robert had more going on than just being police chief. I thought he meant he had kids to raise, or maybe relatives outside town to deal with, but Dad made it seem like it was something more. Something dark. Something your dad might have told him in confidence. He would never tell me what it was."

"You got vampires out of that?"

"I got that things don't add up in Ordinary. There is more here than is seen on the surface. You're the one who confirmed vampires."

"I only confirmed that because there are hunters in my town, probably killing them."

"I know." He didn't look happy, but I wasn't sure if it was because I was mad about hunters being in town, or he was mad about Sven's death.

"So your agency wants to contact vampires?" Jean asked.

"We're an outreach. Very few people believe in the supernatural, and some that do are pretty unreliable. But the DoPP has been making human-supernatural relationships stronger for over a hundred years."

"Why have we never heard of you?" Myra asked.

"Why should you have?"

It was a loaded question. It was an opportunity for us to tell him more about our extraordinary town, more about us and our extraordinary citizens. I glanced over at my sisters and could tell they were thinking about it. Pondering if we should tip our hand and let him know what we were.

"It's not like the DoPP is going away, isn't that right?" I asked Ryder. "Now that I've confirmed there are vampires in town, you're not going to send your boss a report saying everything is ordinary in Ordinary, are you?"

"I haven't submitted my report yet."

"Why?" Myra asked.

"Because I don't want to put someone I loh-v...care about in danger. I care about all three of you Reeds. If you tell me to, I'll lie to my boss. I'll tell him Sven was a one-and-done, and that there are no other vampires in town."

Yes, I'd caught that Ryder had almost said "love" when he was offering to keep our secrets secret. I shoved that way, way back in my brain so I could think about it later. But I could already tell my heart was drawing little swirls and flowers and smoochy faces around that faltering admission.

"What kind of trouble would you get into for that?" Jean asked. "For lying?"

He pursed his lips. "Dunno. Haven't had to do it yet."

"Do they kill freelancers who don't toe the company line?" Crow asked.

Ryder's gaze went steely even though his voice was light. "Maybe they'll let me off easy."

He didn't trust the agency. Not really. No wonder he was worried about hurting me. Hurting us.

"You don't know anything about the consequences to breaking the rules?" Myra asked.

"Well, they have a list of options. Not sure if I would fall under three-strikes-you're-out, or shiny-light-wipes-the-memories."

We were all silent a minute. I was trying to work out if he was joking or not.

"They don't really have a Men In Black light, do they?" Jean asked.

Ryder smiled. "I wouldn't know if they did or not, would I?"

"Okay," I said. "I can talk to the vampires in town. Find out if they want to meet with you. Find out if they want to negotiate with your department. Would that work for you?"

He nodded. "It would. We're offering our help in keeping them safe. I'd like you to tell them that. Tell them we were not a part of Sven's death and we'll do everything we can to bring his killer to justice."

Myra and Jean both nodded, so I took that as our agreement. I would contact Rossi, let him know he could talk to Ryder—while I was also in the room—and Rossi could decide if he wanted any contact with Ryder's agency. Easy.

"But first I want to know who is the head of the vampires."

"We're not going to tell you that," Myra said.

"Is it Crow?"

"Yep," Crow said. "I vhant to dreenk your blahd."

"Nope." Jean smacked Crow on the arm. Crow chuckled.

"It's not you, is it, Delaney?" Ryder said this with such a flat expression and neutral voice I knew he was working hard not to let any emotion seep through.

"We slept together," I said. "You know I breathe. You know my heart beats."

The blank look on his face lifted, and it was clearly relief that was left behind. "That's what I remembered, but I know vampires can alter memories if they want. Make a person think they saw something they didn't."

"Wait," Jean said. "Is that why you broke up with her? You thought she was a vampire? Talk about intolerance."

"Racist," Crow muttered.

"I'm not racist." Ryder picked up his coffee mug, realized there was nothing in it, and put it back down again. "I just didn't want to mix business with personal life."

"You're a cop," Myra said. "She's a cop. You dated her

when you were both working for the same department."

"I'm a reserve officer. I figured I could quit that if things got too complicated in our relationship."

"Who's your boss? Is it really some guy named Frank?" I finally asked. This was the question I kept coming back around to. It felt important.

He smiled, just a faint curve of his lips. He liked this part of it, when I tried to get the information out of him. Liked to make me work for it.

Jerk.

"Who's the head vampire in town?"

"I am."

I startled and was on my feet, hands reaching for a gun that was not on my hip.

Old Rossi stood in my living room, just inside the door, a killing look in his eyes.

CHAPTER 13

VAMPIRES ARE silent when they want to be. I had no idea how long he'd been in my house. He could have been there all night which was frankly a little pervy.

I wasn't the only one who had jumped at his voice. Ryder was on his feet, his hands very carefully away from his sides as if proving he was not trying to go for a gun.

Myra, Jean, and Crow were all still seated. Myra quirked an eyebrow at me. "Lock. The. Door. Seriously, Delaney, when are you going to act like an adult and take your own security seriously?"

"You couldn't knock?" I asked Rossi.

"Every once in a while I prefer a dramatic entrance." He strolled into my living room, which now felt like a shoe box. My house was small. Hosting six adults in one room was where it really started feeling like it.

"Rossi," Ryder said. "I can't say I didn't suspect it might be you."

"Oh?" Rossi peered down his nose at Ryder, his expression flickering between amused and angry. "Why are you in my town, Agent?"

That vampire tone could be used to influence people, to hypnotize, or to alter memories. I'd seen it make people say more than they wanted, and force the truth out of them.

It didn't really work on me or my sisters. Our Reed blood was pretty immune to most of the creature and deity tricks in town.

Still, I could feel it, like knuckles pressing at my temples.

I knew Ryder must feel it too, since it was directed at him. But he smiled and looked completely relaxed. "Because I live here."

I laughed. Balls. The man had balls.

"Can I get you something to drink, Rossi?" I asked. "I have some Pepsi in the fridge, tea, coffee?"

"Tea would be fine."

He wasn't smiling, but he didn't look quite as angry as he had just a minute before. Maybe he looked curious, like Ryder wasn't something he had expected to find.

I, for one, was going to take that as a good sign. I imagined living as long as Rossi had might mean that things could get pretty tedious. I hoped Ryder being interesting was better than Ryder looking like something bothersome that should be eaten.

I started heating the water for tea and put on a fresh pot of coffee. I could hear if there was conversation in the living room—small house—but so far, no one was saying anything.

"Ryder said his agency wants to talk to you about human-vamp relations," I said loud enough for my voice to carry into the other room. "He's the head of the welcome wagon."

"I know." Rossi did that vampire thing where his voice sounded like he was standing right beside me even though he wasn't. "I was here when he said it."

I pushed the coffee pot button and checked the tea kettle on the stove, then came back out into the room.

Ryder and Rossi were both still standing, the other three still sitting.

"So let's get down to it," I said. "First, there are a few rules."

"Rules?" Rossi asked.

"My house, my rules. One: no killing. Two: no harming. Three: no fighting. Four: no underhanded tricks that the other doesn't know about, which includes recording this session." That, I directed to Ryder, "or altering someone's mind or memories." That was for Rossi.

"I'm not wired," Ryder said. "I wasn't expecting this coffee and donut session to turn into introductions."

"There are donuts?" Crow asked. "Why didn't anyone tell me?"

"There are gonna be now." Jean tossed her keys to Crow. "Make mine maple."

"Apple," Myra said.

"I want a cupcake," I said.

"Oh, so now you're letting me out of your sight?" Crow asked. "So I can be your delivery boy? What if I just keep driving?"

"Please," Myra said. "We know you're not leaving town. Not without..." she caught herself just in time. "Not without our permission."

That brought us back to the second thing we really needed to discuss. The missing powers. It would have to wait until we settled this thing with Ryder and Rossi.

I didn't want Ryder here for the god power discussion. There was no way I was going to tell him gods vacationed in his hometown. Letting him know about vampires was enough of a security breach.

The kettle whistled and Crow held out his hand to Myra. "Credit card. I already pay for your wages with my taxes, I'm not paying for your donuts too."

She pulled a card out of the slim wallet in her pocket, and I went into the kitchen for tea for the vampire and coffee for the rest of us.

The only tea in my cupboard was Lipton black, a couple Earl Grey that I didn't remember buying, and a single licorice spice. I filled a cup with water and put one of each bag on a plate beneath it.

"All right. Let the fun begin. Tea." I handed it to Rossi, then returned to the kitchen for coffee, cream, and sugar. "Rossi, I didn't hear you promise not to use your tricks on Ryder," I said as I walked back in.

"You weren't in the room."

"He didn't agree," Myra said.

Ryder held his cup up over his shoulder and I refilled it. I sat, filled my cup, and handed the pot to Jean. She filled her cup and Myra's.

"So let's have that promise," I said.

The vampire was dangling three tea bags off his fingers. "We really need to talk about your lack of tea in this house. Lipton? Could you find nothing more...pedestrian? Doesn't Folgers put out a tea?"

"Still not a promise." I slurped coffee, which wasn't Folgers, thank you very much.

"Fine." Rossi chose the Lipton with a grimace. "I agree to your terms. Mr. Bailey?"

"Terms are good with me."

Rossi wasted no time. "Who is your boss?"

Ryder ground his teeth together for a moment and gave me a dirty look like I had coached Rossi or something. Finally he seemed to give in. "Jake Monroy."

"Your client?" I said before thinking. "Not your client," I corrected. Well, no wonder he'd been arguing with Ryder late at night on his doorstep. Now I wondered what they had been arguing about. "What about Frank?"

"He was a recruiter. He was my boss at the beginning."

"Did you or someone in your agency kill Sven?" Rossi went on like I didn't even exist.

"No."

"Did the hunters?"

"It's possible, but I have no proof."

"Give me their names."

It might not have been actual mental manipulation, but the way Rossi said it carried weight and pressure. As if the years of his life made each word come out heavier than it should.

"No."

"Bad move," Jean said. "Never piss off the fanger."

"He can say no," I said. "This is a discussion not an interrogation."

Rossi slipped his steady gaze over to me. From the corner of my eye I could see Ryder relax. I had sympathy for Ryder. Rossi's gaze could make a brick wall squirm.

"I didn't ask for your opinion, Delaney."

"That's okay, I'll give it to you for free. I want the names of the people in town hunting vampires too, but if Ryder gives them to you, then he's no longer useful to you. That isn't how you're going to behave. We've talked about you not killing him, haven't we?"

I didn't mean for it to come out in such a motherly sort of tone and felt my ears go hot with a blush as Rossi raised both eyebrows and gave me an incredulous smile.

"Did you just use a 'mom' voice on me?"

"No. That was my cop voice. And the statement stands. No killing Ryder."

"Did I say I was going to kill him? Delaney, I am a peaceful man. My soul is in balance. My Karma and conscience are clear. All chakras go."

None of that was actually a promise not to kill him.

"So why don't we make this easy." Rossi turned that molten gaze of his back on Ryder. "Who killed one of mine?"

That came with a flash of fang and that glowy-eye thing.

Ryder didn't move, but even I could tell his heart rate kicked up a notch. "I don't know. That's what I'm here to figure out. I only know one of those men, those vampire hunters. When I saw him in the bar, I knew they had to be in town looking for your kind. My job, Mr. Rossi, whether you believe it or not, is to make sure that your kind can live safely among the mortals of this world. I am not a vampire hunter. Not a vampire killer."

"Tell me why they had your blood, Ryder Bailey. Tell me why I should ignore that it was your blood that killed Sven."

"I wasn't a part of it. I donated to the Red Cross outside the hotel where I was staying. That's the only way I know someone could have gotten their hands on my blood."

"Who?"

"You tell me. I didn't even know my blood was a part of Sven's death until Delaney told me. While you're at it, maybe you can tell me who would have wanted Sven dead. If there are other vampires in Ordinary, and I'm assuming there are, why him? Was he just the most vulnerable? Was it bad luck? Did he do something that brought attention to himself?"

"He was new here."

"And? Was he new to being a vampire?"

"Time is such a relative thing."

"Was he relatively new?"

"Yes, from my perspective. But there are those who are younger than he is."

"So why did the hunters zero in on him now? Is there something else that brought attention to your town? That brought attention to the vampires here? You know why my agency came here—the capsized boat incident. But that was over a year ago. Why are the hunters here now? Did you do something?"

I was watching Rossi when Ryder asked that question and

I saw the slight tic of his jaw. No one who hadn't been staring right at him would have noticed it. It was such a tiny tell, even if someone noticed it, they probably wouldn't know what it meant.

But I knew what it meant. Rossi was hiding something. There *was* something that had brought the vampire hunters to town. I didn't know what it was, but I was keenly curious.

"No," Rossi lied smoothly.

"Is there something you did to bring attention to this place?"

"No." The lie was quicker this time.

"All right. Do you know enough about Sven's past for us to assume it could have been an old vendetta against him? Did he have any outstanding debts or alliances that would have caused this?"

Ryder was starting to sound an awful lot like a cop instead of a freelance monster negotiator or whatever his job description was. A bloom of pride warmed my chest. He really was trying to approach the murder with sympathy and problem solving.

He had good cop instincts, which in this case were also good survival instincts. For the first time since he'd been suspected in this killing, I got the feeling that he might actually be innocent and might get out of this alive.

I didn't know what I'd expected out of this confrontation. Well, yes, I knew. I expected a fight between Rossi and Ryder. But maybe Ryder had a chance of getting Rossi to listen to his side of the story.

Of course, Rossi had been known to "accidentally" drop people off cliffs after hearing them out. If he wanted Ryder dead, it would take a hell of a lot of interference on our part to keep that from happening.

Rossi did want Ryder dead, but Ryder was still here, breathing. This meeting was going a lot better than I'd expected.

"I am going to taste you, Ryder Bailey," Rossi's voice sent shivers down my neck. "And, when I do, I will know the truth of you."

Ryder was stock still. Finally his gaze drifted to mine. "Is that something that happens here?"

"No," I said, recovering my wits. "Of course not. No.

Rossi, what the hell? You know there is no feeding in Ordinary."

"I said taste, not feed."

"Whatever. No fang-on-vein. That's the rule. It's why we hold blood drives every other month, remember?"

"You...right, of course, you do." The words seemed to come out of Ryder without his permission and he firmly shut his mouth. He was probably wondering if Mr. Tudor, a sweet balding man who ran the community blood drives was a vampire.

He wasn't. He was a bloodthirsty little redcap.

"It only breaks the rules if the mortal is unwilling. If they are willing, well, it's a free country, baby."

"The country might be free but the blood isn't. No."

"What will it do if you taste me?" Ryder asked.

"It will break rules set in place long before you got here," I said. "No."

"I will know the truth of you," Rossi told him over my head.

Rude.

"You said that. What does it mean?"

"I will know your truths. I will know your deceptions. Perhaps I will know your soul."

That sounded like hippy-dippy stuff, or maybe vampy-wampy stuff. Or maybe it was the truth. Maybe a vampire, a very old prime vampire like Rossi could know the what and why of a person with one little sip.

Myra was scowling. She shrugged.

Jean's eyes were twice as wide as they should be. "Oh, shitballs. Are you going to do it, Ryder? Are you going to let a vampire bite you?"

"No. But I'll give him a taste if it means he'll believe I didn't kill Sven." He slipped two fingers into his front pocket and pulled out a pocket knife. He flicked open the short blade and held it over the tip of his ring finger.

"This really isn't necessary," I said.

"Oh, let the man make up his own mind. You're not his mom." Rossi strolled—no, more like glided—across the room to stand in front of Ryder.

I'd never seen Rossi drink blood. It just wasn't something

he ever did in public. As a matter of fact, all the vamps in town kept their blood habits quietly to themselves.

So I could admit there was a tiny bit of utter fascination on my part.

Would Rossi really know all those things about Ryder? Was drinking his blood like reading tea leaves? Would he know everything Ryder wanted to hide, all the good, all the bad?

Was I ready for the truth to come out, no matter what that truth might be?

No.

But then, this had never been my choice. I'd mostly been stalling this moment of truth, wanting to decide for myself on Ryder's innocence or guilt. Wanting a chance to stand between him and Rossi when the truth—Ryder's guilt—was confirmed.

I'd been harboring a very real fear of Ryder being guilty.

"I didn't kill Sven," Ryder said. "I don't know who did." He flicked the blade against his fingertip, just a tiny slice. Blood welled there in a rich, thick drop.

Rossi didn't even look down at Ryder's finger. He was watching Ryder's eyes. Then he bent just enough to lower his face so close, if either of them exhaled too far, Rossi's lips would touch Ryder's finger.

But neither of them exhaled. I didn't think they were breathing.

Which was normal for Rossi. But not for Ryder.

Rossi's hand moved so fast, I didn't even see the motion. One moment he was bent over Ryder's hand like a supplicant bowing to a king. Then his fingers were caught around Ryder's wrist, holding his hand tight. Hard.

Ryder's breathing went a little crooked before he evened it out.

Yeah, it was one thing to know Rossi was a vampire. It was quite another to see him display a tiny percentage of what being a vampire really entailed.

Rossi pressed the pinky of his free hand over Ryder's finger, just enough to hook the barest drop of blood off Ryder's finger. Then, staring straight into Ryder's eyes, he licked that drop into his mouth.

I had no idea what Rossi could actually discern from

Ryder's blood. I wanted to look over at Myra and see if she knew. But I couldn't tear my gaze away from the old west stare down going on in my living room.

"You disappoint me, Mr. Bailey." Rossi's words were cool, smooth and sent chills down my spine again.

I was starting to regret not having my gun on me. Not that a simple bullet wound would slow Rossi down.

"I had hoped you were a liar."

Then, just like that, Rossi let go of Ryder's wrist.

I could breathe again, and took in a huge lungful of air.

"He didn't kill Sven?" I asked.

Ryder threw me an exasperated look. "I've told you that," he muttered.

"He did not."

"It was his blood on Sven, though," I said.

"Yes." Rossi strolled back over to the chair and sat with his tea. He looked tired. I didn't think I'd ever seen him look tired. "Also, he doesn't know who killed him."

"Which is what I've also been saying." Ryder pulled a handkerchief out of his back pocket—seriously, who carries a handkerchief these days—and pressed his finger into it to stop the bleeding.

"It would have been easier if you were guilty," Rossi said. "Or if I could kill you. Both. Both would have been easier. We should do something about making this easier for me, Delaney."

That was the Rossi I knew. Annoying. Pain in the butt. Not above a little whining.

"I don't care about easy, I care about justice. You should want to catch the person who killed Sven, not go around randomly killing people hoping you hit pay dirt."

Rossi shrugged. "Potato, Potah-to."

Myra sighed. "Okay, so what we know is that Ryder is innocent in Sven's death. He is also a freelance agent for the Department of Paranormal Protection and wants to contact the vampires in town."

"You just bled for him," Jean said. "I think you can check 'Send fruit basket to the bloodsuckers' off your to-do list, Ryder."

"Good to know." He sat back down and took a drink of

209

his coffee. His hand was steady, and he had that easy sort of body language about him that might be a lie, but was also good enough I bet it would calm nervous dogs.

And apparently blood-hungry vampires.

"Did you join the police force to try to uncover the secrets of Ordinary?" Rossi asked.

"I joined the force because I was asked." He grinned. "But since I was there, I thought a little digging was in order."

"What did you find?" he asked.

"Nothing. Not really. The records are clean. The evidence room is so normal as to be boring. I was thinking I'd made a mistake. But then..."

"Sven died," I said.

"Are all the Rossis vampires?" Ryder asked.

We all looked over at Old Rossi. This was his call, his choice to out everyone in the town, to pull another agency into Ordinary and make some kind of tolerance deal with them.

"No," he lied smoothly.

I guess that was the answer as to how well Rossi trusted the agency Ryder worked for.

My front door swung open and Crow sauntered in with a box of donuts from the Puffin Muffin. "I'm back! What did I miss? Did we tell Ryder there are gods in town yet?"

Silence.

Then Jean burst out laughing.

Ryder didn't react to any of it. He just sipped coffee and watched each of us in turn. Finally, his gaze rested on me.

I could see the question there.

I rolled my eyes to tell him Crow was just joking. And crazy. Or both joking and crazy. And possibly dead after I got my hands on him. Crazy dead. No joke.

He narrowed his eyes, didn't believe me.

Holy crap.

I looked over at Myra since Jean's hooting was winding down.

Myra seemed to be weighing the consequences of telling Ryder the truth.

Mithra wanted Ryder there when I negotiated for the return of the god powers. Crow had just paved the way for me to tell him that yes, gods were real and he'd known dozens of them for most of his life and oh, hey, would he like to go with me to talk to one who had a beef with our town, and my family in particular, before those gods got really mad at me for letting their powers be burgled by a waitress?

"I can make him forget," Rossi said as if he were offering to order pizza without olives.

"No." Ryder didn't deserve to have a vampire messing with his memories. He was innocent in Sven's death and not the bad guy here. Sure, he'd lied about working for the secret government agency, but he claimed his agency was part of the good guys.

Right now all I wanted was to get rid of the bad guys. To do that, I'd have to find them.

Or let the old and very crafty vampire bend some of the town's laws so he could find them.

No. It was never a good idea to break Ordinary's rules.

"Ryder, would you do me a favor and step outside for a couple minutes? I need to discuss a few things with my sisters, Crow, and Rossi."

The man knew when he was outnumbered. "All right. Let me know when you've taken the vote on whether you should just tell me everything or not." He took his cup with him, palmed two donuts from the box Crow was holding open, then stepped outside.

"What. The. Hell. Crow?" I wanted to hit him, but he was wisely standing on the other side of the couch beyond my reach.

Jean hit him for me instead.

What were sisters for?

"You couldn't keep your mouth shut?" Myra rubbed at her temples. She didn't sound angry so much as just mildly disappointed. Yeah, we'd all grown up with Crow as more-or-less our uncle. If there was a pot to be stirred or trouble to start, Crow was for it one-billion percent. We expected that.

But, damn he had bad timing.

"Just because I'm Native I should be seen and not heard? Way to marginalize the Native voices." He tried to sound offended but the huge grin was sort of a give away.

"Why?" I asked. "Why did you do that?"

211

"If Ryder's going to know about the creatures in town, he might as well know about the gods. No one wants to have the Band-Aid ripped off twice. Donut?" He pushed the box out toward Jean who plucked up a maple bar.

"Really?" I asked her.

"What?" She took a huge bite. "All these secrets and sexual tension are making me hungry."

"Sexual tension?" My voice might have come out a little high.

Myra coughed over a chuckle, and Rossi sighed.

Only very old vampires could put that much suffering into a sigh. "It's not a secret how much you and Ryder want each other. Honestly, I thought the Reed pragmatism would have kicked in by now and you'd have realized that it will never work between you."

Both Jean and Myra stood and faced him.

I turned toward him too, so all three Reed girls had squared off, shoulder-to-shoulder.

"Want to try that again?" Myra asked.

"Don't be a dick, Rossi," Jean said.

And yes, it made my heart feel all glowy. I knew neither of my sisters were big fans of Ryder at the moment. Not since he'd broken up with me.

But they knew how I felt about him. Because apparently everyone knew how I felt about him. Even old vampires.

Okay, that part was a little weird, but knowing my sisters had my back still made me feel loved.

"Did they have cupcakes?" I asked Crow.

He held up a big, soft red velvet cupcake. "One." Then he took a huge bite out of it.

"Hey! That was my cupcake, you jerk."

"And it's delicious," he said.

Myra hit him again.

"Whatever I am or am not with Ryder isn't any of your business, Rossi." I thought I sounded rather calm. Relaxed. In charge.

But Rossi crossed his arms over his chest and made a rude sound.

"Right?" Crow pushed the rest of my cupcake into his big,

fat mouth. "There isn't any way to unknot those tangled life threads you two have going."

"What threads?"

"Ryder life threads with Reed life threads." Crow rubbed icing off his lips with his palm, then wiped his palm on the thigh of his jeans. Something on my face must have clued him in that I wasn't following his logic, and was also hating him for eating my cupcake.

"All the places where your paths have connected: his blood on the corpse you're investigating," he started around a bite of the donut he was now eating, "him part of a secret government creature outreach agency, *freelance* on top of it. You working for the government of your own free will. Monster hunters he knows who you might want to get rid of. And the fact that he probably loves you and you definitely love him. Childhood sweethearts."

"We were never sweethearts."

"You should have been," Crow said, not unkindly. Then he walked into the kitchen and put the box with the remaining donuts on the table. "So. How do we do this? Come clean, or wipe his brain clean?"

Everyone looked to me.

No pressure.

I opened my mouth.

There was the rap of knuckles on the unlocked front door. The door that pushed open, Ryder leaning into the wedge of space.

"Uh, Delaney?" he said.

"Yeah?"

He glanced over his shoulder. "You have a mob here to see you."

CHAPTER 14

"DELANEY," DEATH said as if we hadn't seen each other for months and months and were just now bumping into each other unexpectedly in the fresh flower aisle of the market over a bouquet of limp carnations.

"Than." I scanned the gods, all of them shoved into my living room, taking up so much space, we'd left the door open with the hope oxygen could squeeze in between us all.

I had ended up in the middle of the god mob, the coffee table pressed into the back of my calves. "What brings you all by?"

"You know why we're here." Odin leaned against the door frame, his untamed hair haloed by the grey light of our not-summer.

"Our powers?" Aaron, the god of war, said. "Our lost powers. That Crow lost. They are no longer in town as of yesterday afternoon. Outside of Ordinary, Delaney. You said you'd find them."

Ryder was half in and half out of the bathroom watching all of us. He seemed to be taking this pretty well. The influx of gods in my house. The idea of gods in our town. The reality of vampires.

His eyes, hazel, calm, caught me. That slight smile, like he couldn't believe any of this was real, but maybe he really wanted to, hooked deep in my chest and made me want to see it all the time. Want to see him smile. Want to be the one and only he shared these kinds of secrets with.

Maybe Rossi was right, maybe Crow was right. Ryder and I were tangled in knots, the threads of this town, of our days and years and lives, tied together in ways I'd never be able to untangle.

I could cut the threads, but that was the only way Ryder wouldn't be a part of this town, these creatures, deities, and my life.

Holy crap I was going to tell Ryder gods were real.

He was going to know Ordinary, the real Ordinary.

He was going to know these people, the real people.

He was going to know me.

Everything went hot and the rushing thrum of blood in my ears drowned out the argument Myra and Jean were having with the gods. It was something about giving us more time to secure the powers. It was about being calm and letting the professionals handle the case.

I thought someone, maybe Frigg touched my arm, maybe tried to ask me if I was okay, but I didn't answer.

I squeezed my way between bodies, my eyes on Ryder and only Ryder. He saw me coming, saw I wasn't stopping, and opened the bathroom door behind him without question, stepping backwards while I stepped in.

He shut the door behind us, my back to it, him leaning over me.

My house is small. My bathroom is tiny. The shower bathtub is tucked on one wall, the sink on the other wall and the toilet on the third. You could touch all three by standing in the middle of the room.

There is a window about the size of a cereal box on the shower wall, and through it the wooly grey light unraveled into the room.

"This isn't how it's supposed to happen," I whispered.

Ryder shifted closer, lowering his head beside mine so he could hear me.

I had pressed back up against the door, my hands on the doorknob as if my grip could keep anyone on the other side from opening it.

"Delaney," Ryder said, his voice barely above a whisper. "Tell me what you need. I'll do it. Anything."

A shiver ran uncontrolled down my body. Everything in me ached to reach out, to pull the heat of him, the strength of him, the weight of him against me until the world, the heat of it, the strength of it, the weight of it were erased by him.

"Don't think I'm crazy."

"Okay."

"All those people out there are gods. On vacation. But their powers were stolen. The god who stole them wants you to go with me to get them back."

"They're gods."

"Yes."

"All of them."

"Yes."

"But they don't have their powers. Someone stole them?"

"Yes."

He paused for ten heartbeats. I knew because I counted them.

"All right. Where do we need to go?"

"The casino."

"The casino. This is...okay, I can go with it. When?"

"Today. We have to be there today. I know you don't believe me. Just...don't think I'm crazy."

"Why would I think you're crazy? We're just going to go get the stolen god powers being held hostage by a god. At a casino. Do I have that right?"

He was so close I could see the lines at the edges of his eyes, smell his cologne, deep and a little sweet, and something that would always remind me of him. So close, I could see the freckles under the tan of his forehead and nose, could smell the coffee and sugar donuts on his breath.

I wanted him to kiss me. I thought he might want to kiss me too.

"Yes?" I said.

"What about all the gods in your living room?"

I swallowed and the tension drained away. He might not believe me, or maybe he did. But he was going to go with me. To see Mithra. So we could bring the powers back to Ordinary where they belonged.

"I've got it under control," I said.

I DIDN'T have it under control.

"You know who took the powers?" Aaron asked again. "And you're not going to tell us? They are *our* powers. You understand that, don't you, Delaney? Those powers belong to *us*." He waved in a circle to include all the gods. He included the vampire too, but I didn't point that out to him.

"You promised you'd get them back. You also promised they'd be safe."

I was beginning to think Aaron was being a jerk to start a fight.

Oh, right. Aaron was always looking to start a fight.

"Don't be an ass," Jean said. "We had nothing to do with the powers being stolen. Pick on Crow."

"Hey!" Crow yelped. All eyes in the room turned to him.

I felt the tension build.

Nope. There was not going to be a brawl in my living room.

"I know where the powers are and I'm going to get them back right now."

"Great!" Crow said too quickly. "I'll come with you."

"No. You stay here with Myra and Jean. I don't want you to screw this up."

"Hey, now," Crow said. "Uncalled for."

"Where are they, Delaney?" Zeus asked.

"I can't tell you."

"They are *our* powers," Aaron said again.

"I know they are. You know I don't want them. I just want to get them back to all of you without any other complications." I started toward the door, trying to look cool, hoping they didn't see the sweat rolling down the back of my neck. "As soon as I have them in my possession, you'll know. I'll bring them to you all, probably out at Odin's since it's his turn to watch over them."

"It's still my turn to look over them." Crow shrank back from the mob that glared daggers at him. "Fine. Jeeze."

"Who took them?" Odin asked.

I shook my head and moved past him. "That's not something I can share yet."

"Was it Ryder?" Aaron asked.

Ryder—who had been making his way through the throng of bodies toward the door as inconspicuously as a mortal among gods could—paused.

"No, it wasn't Ryder."

"Was it a mortal?" Zeus asked.

"That information is classified."

"We'll know," Zeus went on. "When we get them back. We'll know who or what touched what is rightfully ours. We could know now if we wanted to."

"Sure. If you wanted to leave Ordinary to go claim them. You know they're out of Ordinary, knew the moment they were taken outside Ordinary. Are any of you going to go get them, 'cause it would save me a trip." I waited. The gods didn't look like they were willing to give up their vacation time for chasing down their powers.

"No." Aaron sounded annoyed.

"Okay then. I'll go get the powers, bring them back, and we'll make sure they are held in a better place. A more secure place."

"It was secure," Crow muttered. "This shouldn't have happened. I had it locked against everything in Ordinary."

Odin made a little "hm" sound to that, and turned his single eye on me.

He wasn't the god of wisdom for nothing.

I gave him a big bright, and hopefully distracting smile. "So I'll be back soon, with the powers. Make sure you turn off the coffee pot before you leave."

That shouldn't have worked. With a house stuffed full of gods, I shouldn't have been able to just waltz out of there on a promise and a smile.

But Crow started bitching, Aaron started accusing, and Myra and Jean started crowd controlling.

Which was the perfect distraction for our exit.

We made it all the way to my Jeep before Death caught up with us.

Or rather, we caught up with him. He was standing next to my car, almost exactly where I'd been shot, his eyes at some distant point that I'd probably never see. I hadn't seen him leave the house.

"Hey, Than," I said.

"Delaney." Then with the slightest frown: "Mr. Bailey." Those cold eyes stared right into Ryder and I didn't blame Ryder for stopping mid-step. Even though Than wasn't currently in possession of his power, he was still Death.

It was the sort of thing one couldn't ignore. Especially

when one was being surveyed as if one were being fitted for a casket.

"Hello," Ryder said.

"You are not what I would have chosen." The comment was sonorous and creepy.

"Okay." Ryder looked to me. I shrugged.

"Chosen for what?" I asked.

Than folded his hands in front of his bright pink coat. The logo on the coat probably should have said HAPPY KITES, but because of a poor choice of fonts, it seemed to say HAPPY KILLS.

"You will bring the powers back to us, Delaney?" It wasn't the answer I wanted.

"That's the plan."

"Plans change," Death said.

"Sure."

"So do people."

"Right."

"But some can not change. They simply become what they are meant to be."

"Spooky," I said. "And really obscure."

His eyes flicked over to Ryder again. "Oh, I think I was very specific."

"Should I understand any of this?" Ryder asked.

"Probably not. I certainly don't. Nice jacket," I said to Than.

"Ah." Than brightened. "Thank you. I will be selling them at my shop."

"Happy Kills?" Ryder asked.

"Happy Kites," Death corrected.

"Right," Ryder lied. "I see that now. Happy Kites. The A-frame kite shop off the highway that looks like a haunted shack, named Happy Kites."

"It is authentic. Rustic. A place to bring children. Perhaps I will hire a clown to stand out front."

"No!" I cut in. Because, seriously, clowns? Could anything be creepier? "Maybe just put a sign on it so people know it's a kite shop."

"Oh, I'm having it installed today. Pink, with the name of

219

the shop."

"Just like your jacket?" I asked.

"Just so."

Oh dear gods. We were going to be the only beach town with a haunted house kite shop with a bloodthirsty pink sign.

"Great," I said, not wanting to stay and argue with Death over his graphic design choices. "Well, Ryder and I have a date."

Ryder choked on something.

My face flushed. "I mean a thing. An appointment to get to. So we can do that thing together. For. You know. Justice."

"Justice," Death repeated. "Is that what that thing is called now?"

"Yes. Justice."

"When on a date a man and a woman justice each other." Death blinked slowly at me. "Do I have that correct, Delaney?"

"Yes." My voice strangled and I was sure Ryder noticed, which just made me want to smack one of them. Both of them.

"I can only assume you will take the necessary protection with you," Death said.

"Don't worry," Ryder said. "I never leave home without it."

"You both suck," I mumbled.

"What was that you said?" Death asked.

I ignored him and climbed into the Jeep. Ryder slid into the passenger side. Death, wisely, stepped aside as I cranked the engine and started down the drive.

"Where are we going?" Ryder asked. "I mean since it's a date, and we're gonna justice each other, I want to know if I'm dressed appropriately."

"You are a jerk."

He grinned. "You're cute when you blush."

"Shut up. Never leave home without it? I'd rather not share that part of my personal life with Death."

"I was talking about my gun. For protection, remember? I'm a reserve officer, I always carry it. What did *you* think I was talking about?"

"Ha-ha-larious."

He grinned again. "So, gods, huh? The real all mighty fire and brimstoners own kite shops?"

"Yeah, in Ordinary they do. Believe it or not."

"Not. But then I didn't believe in vampires a few years ago. Rossi..." He squinted out at the scenery. "Yoga blood sucker. That's one I've never heard of."

"You don't think vampires should do yoga?"

"Seems a little out of their norm."

"There's a norm?"

"You know...darkness, goth, eyeliner."

"Wow. Racial profiling much? What kind of vampires have you met?"

Something flickered in his expression. I knew exactly the kind of vampires he'd met.

"The intense ones."

"Rossi's intense."

"I can see that. But he's also...human."

"Don't let him hear you say that."

"Why? Does he have something against humanity?"

That question carried a lot of undercurrents.

"I don't think he'd live here if he did."

"Which means?"

"You know why we have a monthly blood drive, right?"

"You mentioned it. It's not due to the small town sense of civic duty."

"Vampires are in charge of the blood collection in town. Well, vampires and one red cap."

He scrubbed at his forehead a moment. "Red cap. Is that like a...gnome?"

"Sort of a murderous goblin."

"So the blood collection is so the vampires, and red cap, can feed?"

"Yes. So they can feed. Though they only keep half for themselves."

"Delaney, that blood is donated to save lives."

"It is. And it does. Just some of those lives belong to vampires. You know what else? You'll never see an Ordinary citizen turned, you'll never see an Ordinary citizen bitten."

"You're telling me only nice vampires live in Ordinary?"

"Not at all. But I'm telling you they live by the rules here. A code. One that both protects their kind and human kind. It's a good thing. Something not found outside this town."

"And why is that? Why do the vampires followed those rules? Do you lock them up in garlic-lined cells if they don't? Kill them with kites?"

"No, Rossi kills them. Any way he wants to."

The conversation went silent while Ryder worked that out for himself. "He's the prime. This is his land, territory, law."

"Yep."

"And he teaches yoga."

"Yep."

"And does crystal cleanses and spiritual healing classes, and jogs the beach naked."

"Collects carved eggs, donates time to the suicide hotline, fills in at the Rhubarb Rally when my assistant dumps me with no warning."

He winced. "Sorry about that."

"You didn't leave just to go to my house, did you?"

He sighed. "I got a call. Had to check some things."

"Who called you?"

"Jake."

"What did you check?"

"A couple leads. He suspected the vampire hunters were headed this way."

It was still weird to hear him talk about vampires like it was no big deal. I had to admit, I liked it. Liked not having that secret between us.

"Still don't believe in gods?"

He stared out the window and was silent for long enough, I finally glanced over at him.

"All-powerful beings who have created universes? Created us? Beings that care for us, or care for the world?" The pause was long. Finally: "No. Not really."

"But if there was proof that gods were real? Something more convincing than those yahoos in my living room?"

His blunt fingers picked at the weather stripping on the inside of the window. "Not sure anything could prove that to me."

I thought that a god could do a heck of a lot to prove exactly what he or she was. I wondered if he'd believe in gods once we met Mithra. I wondered if he'd be able to see the powers in the water bottle. Understand that there were things, big things that none of us mortals would ever have a real grip on, and if he could come to terms with our incredible smallness in the big scheme of creation.

"Good," I said. "Good to know." Because, really, maybe it was better that he didn't believe.

CHAPTER 15

"THE CASINO?"

I looked over at Ryder. "Great powers of observation, Bailey."

"Someone stole god powers and hid them in a casino? I thought you were joking."

We walked toward the front doors. He strode along a little closer to me than was absolutely needed. The back of his hand brushed mine gently, perhaps by accident.

He turned to look down at me. Winked.

Okay, maybe not by accident.

"It's not a joke. Someone stole the...items and gave them to someone we're meeting here." We were in front of the sliding glass doors, and had to wait a minute for people to exit the casino before we entered.

I made a mental note to check and see if there was any mail for the gods while we were here.

"Who's the someone?"

"Mithra."

He frowned. "The giant moth that fought Godzilla?"

I laughed so hard, I almost tripped over my own feet. "That's Mothra. Hoo-boy. Hold on. I have to text that to my sisters." I pulled out my phone and tapped away at the screen.

"So happy I could be a source of amusement."

I grinned up at him. "Mithra is, uh...someone who is a real stickler for details." I hadn't really put a lot of thought into what I should tell Ryder to expect. "He's true to his word, but to the very letter of his word. He'll want us to be true to ours too. Don't promise anything, don't agree to anything. You know, maybe just stay quiet and let me do the talking."

"Is that why you wanted me to come with you? So I could be silent and watch you work?"

"No. I wasn't the one who asked you here. He was."

"He?"

"Mithra."

We were through the main hallway and headed to the coffee shop at the end. It was the place where I usually met with gods who wanted to enter Ordinary for vacation time.

"Why does Mithra know me? Why does he want me here?"

"I have no idea."

He lightly gripped my elbow, stopping me. I turned to face him.

"How dangerous is he?"

"Inside Ordinary? Not very. Here?" I shrugged. "He could probably kill us."

"What?"

"But he's more of an eye-for-an-eye type guy. Neither of us stole the power. I don't think he'll decide to off us without hearing our testimony."

"That's better?"

"Sure. He'll be looking to punish, not destroy. I think."

"You think."

"It's going to be fine," I lied.

"What are the chances that's actually true?"

"Ten, fifteen percent?" I grinned and patted his arm. "Good talk. To recap: Be quiet, don't agree to do anything, let me handle this, and don't lie."

"Why would I lie?"

I gave him a look. "I don't know, but I'm telling you not to. At all. Until we're back in Ordinary with the powers in our possession."

"God powers."

"That's right."

"Still don't believe in them."

"Probably doesn't matter if you do or don't, does it?"

He shook his head but gave me a flustered little grin. "I don't think that it does. Lead the way, Delaney."

I led. The coffee shop was full, the tables alongside the windows packed with people talking, laughing. One table near the back had only a single person sitting at it.

The guy certainly didn't look like a god. Short, scraggly salt and pepper hair about a week off from a good brushing, and a beard that was at odds with his look because it was neatly

225

trimmed. His eyes were overly round, deep set, his face gave the impression of a pug dog.

I was a little surprised he'd been allowed into the café since he was dressed in three or four layers of shirts—mostly T-shirts and flannel, and jeans that were ripped at the knees and thighs.

He was a god. He could look like anything he wanted to. I could only assume he had chosen this form because he thought it would blend in.

He looked homeless. For a being currently in control of a vast amount of power, he wasn't using much of it on his wardrobe.

He saw us coming. He had probably seen us coming since we left the boundary of Ordinary. Might have been spying on every inch of our travel via birds, weeds, clouds, or whatever else it was he used for eyes.

Still, his shaggy eyebrows rose upward at our approach as if he hadn't expected our arrival, as if we were a complete surprise.

Which, I knew, we were not.

"Hello, Mithra," I said. "Can we be seated?"

He was leaning back against the booth, his homeless gaze filled with an executioner's boredom. "Delaney Reed. You received my summons?"

"Piper told me you wanted to see me and Ryder. Ryder Bailey, this is Mithra. All-seeing Protector of Truth, Guardian of Cattle, Harvest and Waters, and Divinity of Contracts. Mithra, this is Ryder Bailey."

Ryder nodded, with just enough of a bend at his waist to make it a passable bow.

I was impressed. From the considering glint in Mithra's eye, he was too.

"Be seated."

I let Ryder slide in first, then I took the seat next to him.

"You have failed in your duties, Delaney Reed. How do you plead?"

Ryder tensed next to me. I guess he hadn't expected the god to be quite so straight-forward. Luckily for me, this wasn't my first tango.

"Not guilty. Also, I refute your claim to prosecute me or

my blood outside of the boundaries of Ordinary on a matter involving Ordinary and the deities and creatures within it, of which you have no standing authority over."

"I have every right to punish those who break contract, those who break law, those who break truth."

"You are a god. But I am not bound to worship you. None of my family is."

"The Reeds once chose to do right. Once chose to uphold oaths, defend the law." Mithra put some power behind those words. Enough that if I were only a mortal, I would probably be quaking from the intense need to bow to his will.

Good thing I was a Reed, and not so easily swayed by god power.

"We still do that. I have a shiny police badge to prove it." I gave him a smile.

He did not look amused.

Ryder was silent, but I could tell from the tension rolling off him that he might be rethinking his "there are no gods" thing. God power was a little hard to ignore even when the deity wasn't trying to prove a point.

"You have failed to uphold the contracts of Ordinary."

"When?"

"The god Raven took up his power and left Ordinary."

Shit. Yep. I knew where this was going.

"In doing so, no contract was broken. Do you agree?"

I knew that there would be no lying to Mithra. He had a keen eye for the truth. It was sort of his thing.

That and seeing that justice—his brand of justice—was done.

"Yes, I agree Raven taking up his power outside Ordinary was not a breach of contract."

"He was allowed to return to Ordinary. You allowed him."

I didn't say anything.

"Is that true, Delaney?"

"Yes," I grit out.

"He then relinquished his power into safe keeping. Yes?"

"Yes."

"He became once again the mortal Crow and resided within Ordinary. Is still there now."

227

"Yes."

"Must I repeat the contract of your land back to you, Delaney Reed? Must I remind you of the sacred covenant you have given to all gods, mortal, and creatures when you took up the mantle as the Eldest Reed and guardian of all those within Ordinary?"

"No."

"Then you admit to your guilt?"

"I admit to nothing of the kind. What you said is true. It happened. And yes, I know what the contract with Ordinary entails. I admit to no guilt."

He paused and those deep, watery eyes held the kind of edge that could cut through bone.

"Your father was wrong."

I clenched my hands under the table, but didn't show him how much those four words angered me. "About a lot of things, I'd guess."

"He was wrong about his ability. Wrong about his decisions. Wrong about you."

It took an effort to keep my mouth closed. Just because I was highly tolerant to god power didn't mean he couldn't undo every atom in my body with a snap of his fingers.

One did not live long if one pissed off a god.

"Maybe he was," I said, though it came out a little breathier than I wanted. "But what's done is done. He's gone now. Dead. Even you can't judge a soul beyond life."

He blinked once, slowly, then simply stared at me.

Waiting for me to break.

The weight of his power pressed down on my skull, pushed at my neck, shoulders. It stung like bees crawling over my skin. It hurt, but it wasn't anything I couldn't handle.

We Reeds were meant to face any storm that came our way.

Even if those storms were gods.

I squared my shoulders and leaned forward, toward him, toward that pain, toward that hatred he'd always carried for me, my father, my family line. The hatred he carried for Ordinary.

"I will not worship you."

I was pretty sure if someone threw gasoline at his reaction, we'd catch on fire.

"You can not continue holding the laws of Ordinary and the safety of powers in your hand without bending knee to a power larger than you."

"We Reeds are the guardians of Ordinary. Always have been, and we always will be. None of my ancestors worshiped you. I won't either."

"You are wrong. There was a time when your family was tied to me, very closely tied to me. It was a better time. One I suggest you return to immediately."

"No."

His nostrils flared and that crackling light in his eyes looked a little like lightning. He was in full-throttle smite. I was about to be smoted. Smitted. Smate. Whatever.

"How about we deal with the fact that you are currently in illegal possession of the god powers of Ordinary? Which makes you an accessory to a crime. A crime that breaks the rules and contracts of Ordinary."

"You hold no power over me."

"Ditto, Mithra. And you never will."

He went red, his buggy eyes somehow bugging out even more. "All contracts fall under my power. All contract breakers are mine to punish. Your father knew this. If you were the warden, you would know this too."

"No." My stomach went sour at the mention of it. Dad had spoken of the warden position off and on while I was growing up. There was a time, a long time ago, when Ordinary had the option of having a warden instead of guardians like the Reed family. It was back enough greats in my ancestral line that I hadn't paid it much attention. But Dad had.

Mithra had tried to force my dad to take that position. To become the warden of Ordinary, to worship only Mithra. Dad refused. Refused to be a god's sycophant, refused to be ruled by one god power.

Said it would be the kiss of death for our town. Said that it was better to be a police officer, someone who could enforce the mortal law of the land, the law of the town, and the laws put into place and agreement by all the gods who vacationed there.

One god calling the shots above all others was a very bad idea. As a matter of fact I was pretty sure that if we tried that,

Ordinary would be disbanded, the gods no longer vacationing, the creatures...well, I wasn't sure if the creatures would stay or not, but I was pretty sure some of them, like Rossi wouldn't want to have a god ruling them.

We might be a small town, but we were a hugely independent people.

"Ordinary must have a warden," Mithra said.

"Ordinary is just fine with a guardian—the Reeds. And a police force—also the Reeds. We have this under control. My sisters and I are more than enough to keep Ordinary safe."

"Objection." Mithra pulled something off the seat next to him and plunked it down on the table.

A bottle of water. What most people would think was an empty bottle of water.

It was not empty.

It was full, bursting, roaring. With song. With power.

My heartbeat thrumped up and up, faster, harder. The god powers sang to me, called to me, recognizing that I was their guardian, I was their path and bridge back to Ordinary, back to the deities to whom they belonged.

Mithra tapped his fingers on the table, a blunt counter-beat to my pulse.

"This can not happen, Delaney Reed. God powers. Bottled. Stolen. By a human."

"She's more than a human. You know that. You sent her to steal them."

He lifted two fingers, halting the tapping long enough to brush away my words. "She is still human. And these are still god powers. In a bottle."

Ryder exhaled a little shakily next to me. I hadn't forgotten he was there, but hadn't been paying him much attention either.

I could feel the nervousness rolling off him now.

Yeah, that was a lot of power sitting on the table in front of us, barely contained behind that thin plastic coating.

I wasn't even sure how Piper had managed to get the powers to fill the bottle, nor how they still remained there. But from the steady intensity Mithra was aiming my way, I decided he was probably behind it, behind all of it—Piper going after the power, Piper conveniently possessing a water bottle that could actually contain the powers, Piper giving him the powers in trade for that long-ago debt that he had tricked her mother into.

Mithra was a little bit of a dick.

"You have no right to hold those powers."

"Contracts have been broken. I am the judge here, not you. Bow to me, Delaney. Become my warden. You have twenty-four hours to tell me yes."

"Or suffer what consequences?"

"I will keep these powers for my own."

Ryder stiffened next to me, and he opened his mouth. I reached over and put my palm on his thigh to keep him quiet and let him know I could handle this. The sweat on my palm probably didn't help my case much.

"You don't have the power or right to claim those powers. They belong to the gods in Ordinary. All they have to do is step out of town, and the powers would be theirs again. If you're trying to threaten me, you're using the wrong leverage."

"I'm not threatening. I am upholding the justice for these powers, for these gods, for that town you were sworn to guard. I am giving you exactly twenty-four hours to accept the position of the warden."

There was an *or else* attached to that.

"Or?" I prompted.

"Or I will offer the position to someone else."

My stomach dropped, but anger quickly overran the sickness I felt. "You can't do that."

"I can." He leaned forward and the smile was smug. "And I will. When you refuse me. Because I know the truth of you, Delaney. You are too much like your father. You will never compromise your own sense of morals to follow me, not even if it would be the right thing to do."

"Ordinary doesn't need a warden. We've been doing just fine for years without a warden. It's not even written into the rules of Ordinary that a warden is allowed."

"A warden is not only allowed, it is necessary."

"Says you." I realized I was squeezing Ryder's thigh a little too hard, so I tried to relax my fingers and calm down before I relieved a little tension by punching Mithra in his face.

"Look. I understand there was a mistake made by allowing

Crow to put away his power before he had spent a year outside of Ordinary. I understand that is a breach in the laws. There were circumstances that lead us to believe his power had the flexibility to allow him to stay.

"It's clear now that we were wrong. Otherwise you never would have been able to pierce our boundaries and take the powers. But let's be clear here. You weren't doing it out of any sense of loyalty to Ordinary. You waited for your chance, found your loophole, and would just as soon seen this vacation town wiped off the map. You've been angling for this for years. Waiting for your chance to tear Ordinary apart. You can't stand anyone—mortals, creatures, or gods—to live somewhere where you can't boss them around."

"Don't assume you know me, Delaney."

Sure, he sounded aloof and bored, but I'd been around gods all my life. I knew when they were bluffing. He didn't like Ordinary and he never had. He'd do anything to take it apart.

"I'm going to counter your demands with a question, and I'd like you to answer with the truth."

He raised one eyebrow. I was pretty sure he was incapable of lying.

"Go on."

"Why haven't you ever vacationed in Ordinary? Maybe a little time off experiencing the world through mortal eyes would be a good thing. You know you're welcome—have always been welcome. No matter what you think of me or my family line, I swear to you I will do everything in my abilities to keep your power safe, and to make your vacation an enjoyable one."

"I would never willingly abandon my power. Never."

Yep. That's pretty much what I'd expected. Still, I had to give it a shot. One of the important things to remember was that while I was the bridge for powers to be stored in Ordinary, and the law the gods would have to follow while in Ordinary, I was also the human who had the most chance to ease the gods into the idea that taking a little time off could be a good thing. A great thing.

It was my job to let them know Ordinary was there, waiting and welcome.

"Twenty-four hours, Delaney, or I will offer the position

of warden to someone else."

"My sisters won't take it. I know them."

He nodded slightly. "I wouldn't offer it to them. I have some standards."

"Don't," I said. "You have no power over me, Mithra. Nor over my blood. But I won't sit here and let you insult my sisters. Don't think I won't punch you in the throat for that."

Something shifted on his face, and for a second, brief and fleeting and maybe mostly imaginary, I saw what looked like confusion or hurt. Then the flat stern judgmental face was back.

"Only a first born can become a warden," he said rather more quietly than he had before. Almost apologetically.

"Oh."

Well, this was awkward. Maybe he wasn't as bad a being as I'd thought. Maybe he was just misunderstood.

"I'd offer it to Ryder Bailey."

Nope. He was totally as bad a being as I'd thought. Worse.

"What?" Ryder choked out. "Me?"

"Him?" I said, just as startled. "Why?"

Mithra looked pleased as a cat in a box factory.

"He is first born. He is a son of the soil upon which he would lord over..."

"Lord over?" It came out a little loud. I didn't care if anyone was staring at us, but from the level of noise in the place, I was pretty sure no one heard us.

"*Lord* over?" Ryder sounded like he was trying to comprehend a new language. Yeah, well I suppose if one didn't believe in powers and gods, one might be having a hard time dealing with being hard-handed into a position of worship and lording over.

Was this how the dark side recruited? I was pretty sure this was how the dark side recruited.

"He is not going to serve the dark side," I said.

"I'm—I have no idea what you're talking about," Mithra said. "I am the god of justice. Contracts. Oaths. I am not a god of dark sides."

"Is that what this is?" Ryder asked. He had turned so he could see me, though I noticed his eyes kept shifting to Mithra. "Is he a Sith lord?"

God, I loved this man.

"No, not like that. But what he's offering you might just make you one."

"Not a chance. I don't give in to my hatred just because some wrinkly old man in a hoodie tells me to."

I grinned and he grinned back.

Mithra sighed and tapped his fingers on the table. "I believe we were having an important discussion? The fate of your town and these god powers depends on it?" He jiggled the water bottle.

"Hold your horses," I said to him. Then to Ryder: "Favorite Star Wars."

"Empire," Ryder said without hesitation.

"'I love you,'" I said.

"'I know.'"

Then it hit both of us what we'd just said. Ryder's eyes went wide, but his shoulders were set, ready to take the fall out for what he'd said, and not back down.

My mouth felt dry and my heart thrummed in triple time. I swallowed and my throat clicked. I'd just told Ryder I loved him.

But it was a movie quote. That didn't count did it? Did movie quotes count?

"Why are you so red?" Mithra asked.

Ryder's eyebrows were popped and he had this smug little smile on his face that I wanted to kiss off of him.

"Sunburn," I said.

"The sun hasn't broken through the clouds in two months," Mithra said.

"Rain-burn." I winced. "I have a rare condition. Allergic to rain. Get rain-rash."

"I don't think that's a thing," Ryder noted.

Was that laughter in his voice? That was definitely laughter.

"I don't even know what conversation we're having," Mithra grumbled. "But you will both return here, in twenty-four hours and one of you will bow to me."

That snapped me right back into the discussion at hand. The other discussion.

"No," Ryder said. "We won't."

I opened my mouth, but Ryder turned to Mithra. "I'll do it.

I'll be Ordinary's warden. Now give the powers back to Delaney."

The sheer hard delight that shone through Mithra's eyes was only equaled by the terror racing through me.

"No," I said. "He didn't mean that. You don't mean that. You can't. Don't do this, Ryder. Nothing comes without a price and you don't know what he'll make you pay."

"Done." That single word was filled with Mithra's power. I could feel the agreement finalize between them, like the hard crack of a jail door slamming shut.

"Shit," I said.

Ryder looked a little glossy-eyed. A little stunned.

Mithra handed me the bottle of powers. "Pleasure doing business with you, Delaney. Now leave. I have other things to attend."

One minute Mithra was there, apparently solid, real, breathing. Then...nothing. Ryder and I were sitting on one side of a booth and the seat on the other side was empty.

"Did I black out?" Ryder's words slurred. He blinked hard as if pulling up out of a dream. "Wasn't he just sitting there? Did he...disappear?"

I wanted to smack him for being such an idiot for accepting Mithra's offer. But he was looking at me with genuine confusion, and I just didn't have it in me to make him hurt.

Being the warden of Ordinary was going to do enough of that.

"Let's go home." I stashed the powers in the inside pocket of my jacket, the singing pulsing against my skin, vibrating through my bones with a delicious, familiar heat.

Ryder followed me out of the casino without a word.

CHAPTER 16

WE DROVE toward town, silent.

Finally, Ryder spoke. "Can we stop for a coffee?"

I wanted to tell him no. We were about fifteen minutes outside Ordinary. He could wait until we got back to the station to get something to drink. But I could use a little quiet without him next to me. A minute to catch my breath. Sending him to get coffee would work.

"We'll grab something at the Flying Tackle."

I slowed and turned on my blinker giving plenty of time for the cars behind us to brake so we could make the left into the Flying Tackle's pot-hole-riddled parking lot.

The bait shop sat between Highway 18 and the Salmon River and was a long skinny rectangle painted turquoise blue. A salmon mural covered some of the outer wall to the left, and the few windows it had clustered around the narrow door were filled with flyers about fishing trips, hunting licenses, and boats for sale. On the other side of the door and windows squatted a big old ice machine under a sign that declared "Ice Cold Beer."

To round out the decor was an American flag on a pole, and a few white plastic chairs around a patio table.

I parked in front of the shop and turned off the Jeep.

Even though Ryder had said he was thirsty, he wasn't moving.

"This is as fancy as it's gonna get," I said.

"Right." He rubbed his fingers over his face, as if shaking off a daydream. "Right. Think you can explain to me what really happened back there at the casino?"

"You met a god and he lured you to the dark side."

"Really. Is that what really happened?"

I looked over at him. His fingertips were kneading the muscle right above his knee, as if that would somehow keep him grounded in reality.

"You believe in vampires, Ryder. Why is the idea of deities

so difficult?"

"I'm an atheist?"

"Not any more you're not. You worship at the foot of Mithra."

"That's not even a real name. He's not even a real god."

"It is. He is. You can Wiki that up."

He drew one hand up to cup his mouth as he leaned an elbow on the window. "I didn't...I know I said I'd let you handle it..."

"You didn't let me handle it. You buckled in front of a god, and let him bully you into a decision that will change your life without knowing the consequences."

"I thought it was the right thing to do."

"You didn't trust me."

The rain drizzled around us, clouds parting enough to allow sunlight to turn it liquid gold.

"I was trying to help you." His words were small, uncertain in a way I hadn't heard since we were kids. "It was...a lot to process. I've had training. I know how to deal with creatures beyond the human. But that was.... Every word was painful. And he wasn't even talking to me. I can't imagine—how did you just sit there? How did you tell him no over and over again?"

"I'm meant for this, Ryder. My family's been doing this for generations. I know how to deal with gods, how to handle Mithra because that's not the first time I've ever had to deal with him. If you had listened to me, I would have kept you safe."

"Maybe I don't want you keeping me safe, Delaney. Maybe I want you to let me in."

"I let you in. You remember that one and only date we had? You pushed me away."

"It had taken me a year to get you to even look at me. A year of watching you be a cop, following in your father's footsteps because that's what he expected of you. You didn't see me as anything other than another person in town you had to protect. I didn't want to be your responsibility. And I didn't want you tangled up in the agency I work for."

"You could have told me that."

"You could have told me the secrets you were keeping."

We sat there for a moment. I didn't know what he was

thinking about, but I was thinking about missed chances and stupid decisions.

"So where does that leave us?" I asked.

The clouds shifted again, dulling the gold drizzle to silver and ash.

"I'd like...I'd like it to leave us at a beginning."

"A fresh start like nothing happened?"

"No. A fresh start like something did."

"Does that fresh start come with you buying me coffee?"

He smiled. "I might even toss in the cream and sugar for free."

I pushed out of the Jeep and so did he. We started toward the shop. Before I'd even reached the concrete sidewalk running in front of the building I heard the muffled growl.

It was a sound that reached in and plucked the primal chords of *fear* and *hunter* and *danger* inside me. I held perfectly still.

Ryder stopped. "Laney?" he whispered.

I held up a finger and tipped my head to my left, while shivers prickled across my skin.

The growl sounded again, low, angry, deadly.

I knew that sound, though I'd never heard it like that before.

There was a werewolf close by. A werewolf in pain.

"Easy," I said, keeping my voice soft. "I know you're hurt. I'm here to help you."

"What?" Ryder asked.

I held up another finger, waited for the answer. The wind pushed through the fir trees behind the bait shop. The cars shooting down the highway behind me were a steady hiss.

Werewolves ranged outside Ordinary all the time. It wasn't all that odd for one to be here at the bait shop. But the thing that was unusual was to hear one. Werewolves were shadow-silent unless they wanted to be heard.

Or were injured.

"You're going to be okay," I said to the wolf I could not see. "I'm Delaney Reed and if you're part of the Wolfe clan, you know I'm a friend. I'm going to make sure you're okay. So I'm going to turn now and come to you, all right?"

I waited, didn't hear anything else. I headed left toward the end of the building where I thought I'd heard the sound.

Ryder followed quietly behind me, his boots crunching in step with mine on the loose, wet gravel.

I saw the blood before I rounded the corner of the building.

Then I saw the werewolf. Not just any werewolf: Jame.

"Shit," Ryder whispered.

Jame was mid-shift, lying on his stomach, his body lengthened and nude and mostly human, but his face elongated, hands and feet sharp with claws, face fully fanged and dark fur covering most of his body.

"Is he a...is that a..."

I shot Ryder a look and he shut his mouth.

"Jame," I said soothingly, "it's Delaney. You're hurt. I need to see how badly you're hurt, okay?"

He was breathing too hard, his back rising and falling as he panted, growling as his ribs, lumpy and looking to be broken, shifted.

"Call 911," I said to Ryder as I eased my way forward. "Request Mykal Rossi and only him. We need an ambulance out here."

Jame growled, but it ended in a low whine, as if even that took too much effort.

Ryder hadn't moved, probably still trying to decide if werewolves were as easy to accept as vampires, or if they fell under the unbelievable like gods.

"Reserve Officer, Bailey," I said. "Now."

He snapped out of whatever trance he'd been in, and pulled his phone, quickly dialing and reporting the details.

I scanned the scrubby area and looked into the trees, wondering if Ben was anywhere near. I thought they'd told me they were going on a fact-finding mission.

Crap. They probably had done that.

This was the result.

"Jame, I'm going to touch your shoulder, then your head." I stopped beside him, then crouched down. He hadn't moved except for breathing.

The smell of mud and rain, motor oil and blood filled my

nose.

I reached out and put my fingertips on his shoulder.

An angry werewolf had reflexes like lightning and could tear a person's arm out of the socket with one swipe. Jame felt hot to the touch, his fur thinned so I could feel the flesh beneath. It was sticky with blood.

"You're okay. It's going to be okay." I touched the back of his head and winced at the give of his skull. Something had hit him hard enough that it was probably only his werewolf healing ability that was keeping him alive.

"Don't move, we got you."

"Ambulance is on the way," Ryder said. "Shouldn't we be applying pressure to his wounds?"

"Nothing big enough I can see to cause all this blood," I said.

We'd need to turn him over and make sure he wasn't gushing out of a gut or chest wound.

"Help me roll him over."

Ryder walked to the other side of Jame, who opened his eyes—gold and hot—and snarled at me.

"It's Ryder. He knows. He's safe. Trust me."

Jame's eyes clouded with pain and his mouth opened in a silent whine.

"This is gonna hurt. But we got you. Ready?" I glanced at Ryder.

It had started raining harder. Ryder was wet with it and I knew I was too even though I didn't feel it.

"It's me Jame," Ryder said. "You took a hell of a hit buddy, but we got you."

Ryder and I locked eyes, then moved Jame as easily as we could onto his back.

Jame whimpered, a soft almost child-like sound, and then went completely limp as he passed out.

"Holy fuck." Ryder pulled his hands away from Jame and shifted on the balls of his feet. "What the hell is that?"

It was blood.

A lot of blood.

Written in scrolling symbols across his skin. His fur.

But it was not his blood.

There were no gushing wounds.

I had seen these symbols before.

On Sven.

Ichor techne.

"Get some pictures," I told Ryder.

He paused.

"Before the rain washes it away. Photos. Of the symbols, his body, then the surrounding area."

Ryder got busy, while I gently pressed my fingers to the side of Jame's neck, looking for a pulse.

His heartbeat was thready and uneven. He hadn't shifted back into human form even though he was unconscious. His survival instinct had taken over, and his body was working hard to heal.

I pulled my fingers away from his neck. They were tacky with blood.

"Here." Ryder held out a kerchief.

I took it and pressed it against Jame's neck. That wound was the only one still leaking blood that I could find. I knew what had caused it. It was a bite. A puncture made by two fangs.

A vampire bite.

Jame's breathing changed and his eyes slitted open, amber burning through.

"Jame," I asked gently, "where's Ben?"

He snarled and showed teeth, but it was all he could manage. He lay there, staring at me, eyes like fire, chest rising and falling with shallow little jerks.

I scanned the area again. Didn't see any sign of Ben. "Check inside the shop." I told Ryder. "Be careful."

I had a moment to worry if I should have sent Ryder in there. I hoped he wasn't kidding about carrying his gun. Mine was in the Jeep, and there was every chance whoever had done this to Jame was still around.

There was also every chance that whoever had done this to Jame couldn't be stopped by a gun.

I shifted on my feet, reluctant to move out of Jame's line of vision. When I moved away, intending to check on Ryder, Jame whined and tried to reach out for me, which made him moan even more painfully.

"I'm right here," I said, holding the cloth to his neck. "I won't leave."

He worked his mouth. I knew he was trying to tell me something but with all his teeth and panting, it was impossible to sort out anything close to actual words.

The 911 call would go straight to Myra and Jean too, so they were on their way. But I needed someone else. I need Rossi.

I tugged my phone from my pocket and dialed Rossi one-handed.

"Delaney," he said, drawing out my name.

"Where's Ben?"

Silence. One heartbeat. Two.

"He's not in Ordinary," Rossi breathed. "I can't feel him in Ordinary."

"I just found Jame at the Flying Tackle. He's hurt. There's blood. I need you to tell me whose blood this belongs to."

The phone line went dead.

We were about fifteen minutes outside of Ordinary. Rossi lived toward the south end of town. In a car it might take him twenty minutes to reach us.

But he didn't need a car.

Less than a minute passed before Rossi came striding up through the trees, his dark hair loose around his face, eyes red with anger.

He paused, just the slightest hesitation, before he was within arm distance, his black boots not quite touching the puddle of blood and rainwater surrounding Jame.

"Whose blood is it?" I asked.

"Ben's."

The word was growled so low, I almost didn't hear it. But Jame heard it. He whined again, his hand spasming as he tried to move.

Rossi's head jerked once, eyes going wide, then narrow as he took in the symbols.

"It's the same as Sven, isn't it?" I asked.

He knelt next to me, long fingers surprisingly gentle as he removed my hand from the cloth at Jame's neck.

His nostrils flared as he stared at the bite there.

"Is that bite from Ben?" I was afraid of his answer but

needed to hear it.

"No."

Hell. "What happens when a vampire bites someone else's boyfriend?"

"War."

The thin wail of an approaching ambulance filled the air, and just behind it, around it, punching through it like needles through thick cloth, was the howling of wolves.

Jame's family, his clan, his pack, all the Wolfes in Ordinary were coming, calling, howling for their own.

CHAPTER 17

IT WAS controlled chaos. The Wolfes had arrived just before the ambulance, my sisters, and about a dozen of the Rossi clan.

Jean had quickly told Dave, the owner of the bait shop, that he needed to be closed for the day, promised an update as soon as she had it, and sent him home in his truck.

Dave hadn't had a chance to see Jame, since the ambulance, Jean's truck, and Myra's cruiser were strategically parked to block anyone's view.

Myra had cordoned off the scene of the crime, stringing yellow police tape like a particularly industrious spider.

My job was to try to keep the werewolves and vampires from killing each other.

Rossi and Granny both held tight to their human forms, so much so that I almost didn't notice Rossi's red or Granny's hot silver eyes.

When the wolves had arrived, in wolf form, a wall of gray and black and mottled brown, heavily furred, some big, some lean, but all of them killers, defenders, brothers/sisters/pack, I'd let them surround Jame.

Yes, it meant there was probably going to be a loss of evidence with the wolves walking through the blood and gravel.

But I'd dare anyone to stand in the way of a pack that wanted to get to their fallen brother.

I just hoped Ryder's pictures would give us what we needed to find the bastard who had done this.

Rossi had had the sense to back off a little ways while the wolves circled Jame, whining, growling, trying to lick, but wincing from the taste of the blood while snarling with ears flattened and tails tucked.

Granny Wolfe wasn't the biggest wolf of the pack, but there was no doubt she was the alpha. Her fur was black with streaks of gray, and she sniffed around Jame, bared her huge teeth, then paced over to Rossi and stopped in front of him.

She shifted from wolf to human so quickly, it looked fluid and painless, like her bones and body hadn't just gone from one state to another in a painfully fast three seconds.

Then she was standing there, naked, in front of Rossi, fury on her face, her hands at her sides in loose fists, like she was trying to keep her claws from popping out.

Short, naked, and petite, Granny's body didn't show her age. She radiated power. Her body was lean and lightly muscled beneath tanned skin that seemed painted on over sinew and bone.

Rossi's eyes never left her face. He pulled off the loose sweatshirt he was wearing, revealing the plain black tank top beneath. His muscled arms were swoon-worthy if one was into ancient ex-soldier vampires. He held the sweatshirt out to her.

She stared at him, never deviating her gaze to the proffered sweater.

She crossed her arms, making it loud and clear that she'd rather stand there naked in the rain, than accept a piece of clothing offered by a vampire.

Crap. The last thing I needed was the uncertain peace between the vamps and weres to turn into a certain war.

"Granny?" Myra walked up to the pile of wolves and around them, giving enough room so they only followed her with their eyes instead of lunging toward her. "I brought you a blanket."

Granny took the blanket from her, not looking away from Rossi.

"You dare think you can claim one of mine?" she snarled.

The blanket hung from her hand, and every muscle in her body was bunching up. Twitching, coiling with the need to attack.

"I have claimed no one."

A shift of shadows behind Rossi, and there were now twenty or so Rossis glaring at her and her pack with eyes that somehow managed to look hungry for blood, but bored that all they'd have to do to get it was kick werewolf butt.

Nope. This was not going to come down to a fight. Not on my shift.

"Ben's missing," I said.

Rossi didn't look away from Granny. "Yes," he said.

"And Jame's been bitten by someone or something that isn't Ben. Not one of yours. Not a Rossi."

"Yes."

Granny jerked at that, then finally broke the staring contest to glance at Jame. Her nostrils flared and she sniffed the air.

"We need to get Jame to the hospital so he can heal," I went on. "Tell a few of your pack to help us get him on the stretcher, Granny."

Mykal, an EMT and vampire, had wisely remained by the ambulance.

Granny dragged the blanket over her shoulders and lifted her chin.

Two of the wolves, a big grey and brown and a white and gray, moved slightly away from the dogpile and shifted.

It took them longer to change, and the painful sound of gristle and bone snapping and grinding filled the air. But if it was painful, they didn't show it once they were back in their human forms. They just looked angry.

The two wolves were Rudy, who I'd last seen driving Granny away from Joe Boy's gas station, and Fawn, who was one of Jame's sisters.

Naked, it was impossible to miss their hard bodies covered in muscles. I didn't think they'd need anyone else to help them get Jame on the stretcher. The wolves moved back as Ryder began maneuvering the stretcher closer. He was quickly relieved of that duty by a scowling Fawn.

Rudy and Fawn gently lifted Jame, who wasn't moving, but seemed to be breathing a little more evenly. The rain had washed away a lot of the blood, but Jame was still half-shifted, and there had to be a lot more blood soaked into his fur.

At least the bite on his neck had closed up.

"I'll need to ride with him," Mykal said, handing each of them a blanket to wrap up in. "Both of you can come with me, make sure I'm treating him the way you want. He's my friend. Not just because we work together."

I couldn't have thanked Mykal more for being so diplomatic with the Wolfes. Still, Rudy and Fawn glared at him as they rolled the stretcher to the back of the ambulance.

The Wolfes somehow wedged themselves into the ambulance along with Mykal, Fawn curling up beside her brother on the stretcher. The vehicle pulled out toward the hospital, lights flashing red, amber, white, siren screaming.

Now all I had to do was keep the remaining fangs and claws from getting into a rumble.

"We need to find Ben." It was probably unnecessary to state the obvious, but I thought putting the point on the situation might be for the best. "Can either of you or your people track him?"

"Yes," they both said.

It could have been taken as an agreement, but mostly it just sounded like a challenge.

"I want him back here alive," I shot that toward Granny. She gave a slight nod, though she still wasn't backing down from Rossi's glare.

Jean walked over to us.

"Trillium's on her way." Trillium was Ordinary's lone reporter, and kept the locals and tourists up-to-date on all the canned food drives, classes, and contests in town.

Also on the murders and assaults, though they were few and far between.

The Wolfes gathering at Granny's back, had hackles up, heads down, but were silent. I didn't know if silent was good.

"His blood's on your hands, *strigoi*," she said. "His pain, your debt now. We are not at peace."

Rossi's lips pulled back and I saw just the peak of fang. "He let my son be taken, bled, brutalized." It came out part growl, part hiss. His eyes flooded with red and black.

I unconsciously reached down for the gun that was not on my hip, my hand accidentally brushing the bottle of powers I had stashed in my coat like a second-rate bootlegger.

Wild thoughts shot through my head. They were going to fight. Rossi and Granny were going to kill each other, and drag all the vamps and weres into a battle that Ordinary hadn't seen since—no, had never seen.

Should I throw the god powers at his head? Would that stop a vampire? Or should I smash it on the ground like a smoke bomb between them?

"There are rules."

It took me a minute to recognize that voice. It was Ryder. I didn't recognize it because there was a timbre of power behind it. God power. But not really god power. More like weight or texture as if, along with his voice, something else was layered on top of it, or pushing through from behind it.

The alpha and prime turned to him.

It was...well, I don't think I could have broken their staring contest that quickly.

Ryder didn't look any different. He didn't even appear surprised that the head werewolf and head vampire were holding off on a serious smack down only because he'd said something.

He frowned though, like he was remembering something he'd read in a book once.

"You have agreed upon terms of peace, both individually and between your people. This attack, on Jame and Ben, does not negate the conditions you agreed upon. Unless it is proved that either a Wolfe or a Rossi not only threatened, but also carried through with potentially life-ending violence." His eyes focused, and he held Rossi's gaze then Granny's.

"There can be no war. Not until either Jame is able to testify to the events that led up to his injuries, or Ben is able to do the same."

Ryder nodded, as if satisfied that he'd settled that problem. "In accordance to your agreements, you will both give the other what support is needed and you are capable of providing to come to a resolution of this situation. That means finding Ben. Both of you."

I took a breath, held it.

No one told the prime vampire what to do. No one gave the alpha werewolf trotting orders.

Well, no one who wanted to keep their head attached to their spine.

"Warden," Rossi sneered.

"What?" Myra and Jean asked at the same time.

Granny sniffed the air, as if she could smell the position Mithra had bestowed upon Ryder, and didn't like the stink of it. "You let this go and happen?" she accused me.

"I told him not to. Said I'd take care of it. He didn't listen."

"Men," Granny said.

"Right?"

"Never gonna listen."

"Hey, now," Ryder protested. But when all of us, including Rossi, gave him a look, he just sort of slumped and stared at his boots. "It's not like there was another choice. You weren't going to say yes."

"No, I wasn't. And don't you think you should have taken that as a hint?"

"That you have authority issues?"

"That I'd refuse to tie myself to one deity's skewed vision of justice? That I'd ever let one god tell me who to be, how to live? That I'd ever let a god change me like that?"

"I'm not changed."

The silence said what we all thought about that.

Ryder scowled, then cussed softly. "I'm still myself, no matter what job or responsibilities I take on."

"But...warden?" Jean bit her lip, and looked from Ryder to me then back to Ryder. "Do you understand what that means? What it means between you and Delaney?"

"So," I said loudly, clapping my hands. "We need to find Ben. Now. Is there anything else we need to know before we pack this up and deal with the reporters and crime scene?"

"One thing," Myra said quietly.

From her tone of voice I knew I wasn't going to like it.

"The vampire hunters are dead."

CHAPTER 18

MYRA GAVE us the details that had come over the wire. Four men had rented a small boat up in Astoria. One of those men was the guy Ryder had known and spoken to at the bar. The four of them had seemed to think crossing the mouth of the Columbia River in rough swells would be a safe and good idea.

It wasn't. The mayday was called in, but even though the Coast Guard scrambled, by the time they got there, all they found was a capsized vessel and four dead bodies.

"Could be just an accident," Jean said.

Yeah, none of us thought that was true.

"Who's killing them, Rossi?" I asked. "Who has declared war on us?"

Rossi's eyes were still that terrifying red and black. "A dead man."

That might have been a threat or might have been the truth. I didn't have a chance for any follow up questions because the crunch of wheels on wet gravel filled the air, and between one blink and the next, Rossi was gone.

All the other vampires similarly disappeared, fading into mist that was lost to the rain and drizzle.

"He knows who it is, doesn't he?" Jean asked.

"I think so."

Myra was watching me. "You have an idea who it is too."

I nodded.

"How bad?" Jean asked.

"All the bad."

"Shit," Myra whispered. "Did you find the god powers?"

Car doors opened and slammed shut. Footsteps coming our way.

"Please tell me we have some kind of win in all this," she said.

"Yeah, I've got them. Jean, do you mind handling Trillium?"

"Sure. Are we going with mugging? Robbery? Drunken brawl?"

"Let's go with mugging. Nothing Dave would have seen or heard from inside the shop. Oh, and pull the video before she gets hold of it."

"I'll get the video," Ryder said.

I nodded. He might not know about everything that happened in Ordinary, but he knew enough now that I didn't think he'd do anything to compromise the video.

He jogged to the bait shop, and Myra fell into step next to me as I headed to the Jeep. "Are you okay?"

"Oh, sure. Just another boring day in Ordinary. I need coffee. With a side of coffee with coffee on top."

Trillium spotted us, but Jean cut her off with a quick greeting. "Trillium, glad you could make it out here. I'd be happy to answer any questions, but can't let you any closer to the scene of the crime until we're done gathering evidence. You know the drill...."

Trillium cast one more look over at Myra and me, then focused on Jean.

Myra walked over to my Jeep with me. Her cruiser was parked right next to it, light bar spinning a lazy pattern of reds and blues.

She pressed her hand against my arm, and squeezed tight enough I stopped.

"Why is Ryder the warden? Did Mithra force him to take it? Did he steal it from you? Did you give it to him? Didn't you warn him what it could do to him? This isn't good, Delaney. You realize it puts him in a higher position than us."

Everything—the standoff with Mithra, the deal to get the god powers back, Sven's death, Jame's broken body, Ben's kidnapping—twisted up inside me. I was tired, and tired of not getting ahead of what felt like one disaster after another.

"It doesn't make him our boss!" That might have come out a little louder than I intended. I toned it down a bit. "Just like none of the gods are our bosses, just like none of the creatures are our bosses. *We're* our bosses. We're still the law here. Both as police officers and as the Reed family. Ryder "the warden"," and yes, I did the ironic quote fingers, "can just suck it if he thinks he's going to boss us around."

"Feel strongly about this do you?"

"Terrifyingly so." That was so true we both gave each other the "me too" nod.

"So...coffee before the next disaster hits?" she asked.

I shook my head. "Have to get the powers back to the gods."

"Still haven't heard the story there."

"Mithra was just how we expected him to be: annoying and demanding. Made a lot of threats, reminded me who he was and how hard he wanted to tell us all what to do all the time."

"He threatened you?"

"Naturally. With the warden position. I said no. Ryder said yes."

"Yeah, I can see that. What I can't understand is why."

I shook my head, searching the front of the bait shop for Ryder. He was still inside looking for the video. "I don't think he understands what he just did. He doesn't even believe in gods."

"That doesn't matter when a god believes in you."

I sighed. "I tried to stop him."

She moved her hand to my shoulder and gave me a squeeze. "I know. Do you want me there when you hand back the powers?"

"Yeah, I think that would be good. Could you pick up Crow? We can meet at his shop."

"They're not going to let him store the powers."

"I know. Odin's up next, right?"

She nodded.

"Okay, so we should all just meet out at Odin's place."

"I'll gather the gods. You get some coffee on the way."

"That works. I think Piper should be there too."

"You really want to do that to her?"

"I'd rather she be revealed to all the gods when we're there to run interference than one-on-one when we're not."

"True."

Ryder strode out of the shop and headed toward us.

"Why don't you come with me," Myra said. "We'll drop the video off at the station and lock it up."

Ryder looked my way. "Okay with you, boss?"

It was so normal, so not like the last few hours, that I almost smiled with relief. "Yeah. Good. And come along with Myra to Odin's. You'll want to see that dog-and-pony show too."

He hesitated, his body language sort of bent my way as if he wanted to touch me, or hug me, and had decided halfway through that he probably shouldn't.

"Sure," he said. "See you there."

They got into the cruiser and I slipped into the Jeep. It might have been more comfortable to put the water bottle of god powers in the cup holder but I was feeling a little paranoid about letting it even that far out of my sight. So I kept it in the inner pocket of my coat, slid the seatbelt in a mostly-comfortable position over my chest, and headed toward the first drive-thru coffee shop in Ordinary.

HALFWAY THROUGH a quad-shot latte, I pulled onto Odin's property.

He wasn't out with his chainsaw, which surprised me a little since it wasn't raining. Not that everything wasn't still soggy as a broken wash machine's spin cycle, but there was a little bit of sunlight shouldering through the clouds just in time for the day to be slipping toward sunset.

Seemed like it'd be a perfect time to hack out a few more flat-face bears and one-winged owls.

The other gods weren't there yet, but I knew it wouldn't be long. I parked the Jeep and crossed to Odin's house, the cleansing perfume of green and wet and pine filling me.

Tucked beneath a small forest of tall Douglas fir trees, the house wasn't much bigger than mine. Cedar shakes painted brick red, shingled roof about three years past needing both new gutters and some moss control efforts, it didn't give off a welcoming feeling exactly.

Neither did the two headless wooden bunnies on the porch on either side of the door.

Or at least I thought they were bunnies. Beavers? I tipped my head. Nope. Ravens.

I knocked on the door. Didn't have to wait very long for it to open.

"Delaney." Odin glanced over my shoulder as if expecting someone to be there.

"Crow's with Myra," I said. "They're on their way over here with the rest of the gods."

He grunted and stepped aside so I could step in.

The outside might have looked like a graham cracker house that had been left out in the rain—a little soggy and soft around the edges—but the interior was quite the opposite.

The wood walls were polished to a soft gold glow. Furniture was mahogany, and the artwork leaned a bit Nordic and tribal, some from local artists, some from Odin's personal collection that either had never been seen by human eyes, or if it had, probably belonged in museums.

It was clean, uncluttered without giving up the impression of cozy, and something about the place made my shoulders drop.

Anyone in town might expect to find a bachelor's pad, maybe even expect unmatched socks to be balled up in the corners, or microwave dinners to be stacked on side tables. But it was nothing like that. It felt relaxing, refreshing. A retreat from the world.

Which, I supposed, was exactly why the gods had come to Ordinary. So it should be no surprise that Odin's house was a home, and a very comfortable one at that.

"Coffee?" He was already moving toward the kitchen.

"Yes, thanks." I drank down the rest of my latte and walked over to the stone fireplace on the opposite wall. It stacked up to the second floor which was basically a loft space that covered two sides of the upper story.

"You found the powers," he said. "Mithra have them?"

There was no reason not to tell him the truth. "Did you know all along that's where they were?"

He came back into the room with two huge ceramic mugs shaped like tree stumps and handed one to me.

"When they were taken outside Ordinary. There was a...sense of his disapproval I got through my power."

"Could have told me." I took a sip of the coffee, which was

so rich it almost tasted alcoholic.

"Not my job." He settled in the easy chair. "So Crow's leaving town?"

"He has to. And that means you're up next for storing the powers."

He nodded, like he didn't really care about that. "Never thought you'd let a warden in Ordinary."

I didn't ask him how he knew about that. He was a god. Just because he was on vacation didn't mean he had no lingering abilities. Or maybe he'd heard it from someone else. Didn't need god power if you were friendly with the town gossips.

"It wasn't my idea, trust me."

"Ryder?"

I nodded. "He's also a part of some kind of welcome committee for supernaturals in the world and Ordinary in particular. Government agency."

"Huh. That explains some things."

"Like what?"

"Like why he came back here."

"Couldn't it just be because he likes the town he grew up in and wanted to come back?"

"It's a big world, Delaney. Ordinary, in nature and design, isn't really a very interesting place, all things considered."

He was being awfully even-tempered about all this. "You told me Dad waited too long before he chose a side."

Odin drank coffee, his one good eye watching me over the rim of the mug. I noted the bottom of the mug said: "#1 Beaver Bait".

I lifted my cup to see what logging slang was painted there. It said: "Ask about my Butt Rigging."

"Really? No pecker pole jokes?"

"There are more mugs in the kitchen."

"My dad," I said. "What did he wait too long to choose?"

Odin put his cup down, and studied me in that way the very old gods do, especially the ones who have known me since I was a baby. It was sort of a mix of patience and concern, like they weren't sure I was old enough to handle what they were about to say.

"Immortality."

Okay. That was not what I expected. We Reeds lived a long life. Well, those of us who didn't drive off cliffs. There was one great-to-the-nth aunt who was said to have hit one-hundred and fifty years of age. I didn't know if that was true, but most of the Reeds were capable of rolling into the early one-hundreds at least.

It was either gift, curse, or by-product of being a part of keeping Ordinary vacation-ready for the gods.

But immortality? That had never been on offer.

"What's the catch?"

"Why do you think there's a catch?"

I wasn't used to Odin doing the wise-man thing. I was more used to him doing the gruff, crazy chainsaw artist thing.

"Because Dad didn't immediately say yes."

"True. But he had lost a wife. Had three young daughters to raise. Death changes every man's heart."

"Is that something I will be offered?"

"Immortality is generally only offered to a bridge. That's you, Delaney."

"So Myra and Jean?"

"Immortality isn't their destiny."

Already I was seeing the downside to this offer. Did I want to live long enough to see my sisters, maybe even everyone that I loved die? Would it be worth it to keep Ordinary safe?

"Who or what will give it to me? If I said yes. Not that I am. Saying yes."

"A god. Of your choice."

Something about those words felt ominous.

"And what do I owe to a god who would hypothetically offer me immortality?"

"That would be between you and the god in question."

"Would you give it to me if I asked for it?"

"You'd have to ask me."

"Did my father ask you for it?"

"Your father never asked anyone for it. Then that choice was taken from him, and it was too late."

"Was he killed? Was that accident not an accident?"

Odin picked up his coffee, took a drink. There was something else in his gaze this time. I thought it might be regret.

"That is a question I can't answer."

"You mean won't answer. You could know, could find out if you wanted to."

He turned the cup in his hand. Balanced it on the arm of his chair. "I'm a god. Well, not right now, but..." he shrugged. "There is very little that can be hidden from our kind."

"If I wanted to know if his death was an accident, would you tell me?"

"Maybe. Or not." He ran a hand over his bushy hair, causing it to spring up even higher. "Until you decide to ask me that when I am a god, the possibilities are fluid. Every second, every breath, every action and inaction affects the future. If you ask me, if I decide to tell you, when you ask, when I decide...it all muddles the outcome."

He'd have to pick up his god power to answer me. I wasn't sure I was ready for him to have to walk out of Ordinary for a year. After all, I'd come here to ask him to look after the powers for the next year.

"Okay, new question. If I accept immortality from a god, then I'd be bound to that god, wouldn't I? Just as if I had accepted the warden position, I'd be bound to Mithra."

"That's how it works, yes."

Poor Ryder had no idea what he'd just gotten himself into.

"I wouldn't have ever accepted the position as a warden."

"I know. Your father never said yes to Mithra either."

"He said it would change what we stood for as Reeds. What we did to help keep Ordinary ordinary."

"Your father was a wise man."

I was silent for a bit, drinking my coffee out of the tree stump not because I needed more caffeine, but because I needed a moment to swallow the emotions that rose with Odin's quiet assessment of my dad.

For all that Odin was mostly a cranky old chainsaw artist, he was also a god of wisdom. It meant something when he said things like that. Nice things.

"Was he right?" I asked, my voice a little smaller than I'd expected. "There's a cost to it, isn't there? Some huge horrible price to pay for being judge and jury over the town."

"Probably. But the warden isn't exactly judge and jury over

257

Ordinary."

"Devotee to Mithra, the god of contracts. How is that not a judge and jury position?"

"Warden is an overseer. A supervisor of contracts, deals, and agreements. Doesn't mean warden gets to lay the law down on everything. That's what that badge of yours is for. He just gets to point out who's cheating."

"Great. So I'm the strong arm and he's my boss?"

He gave me a brief scowl. "Why are you in my living room complaining about things I have absolutely nothing to do with? Another god's minion is of no matter to me."

Like I said, cranky.

"I need you to look after the powers for a year and a few months."

"Crow finally got himself kicked out of the place."

"He should have left three months ago. I'm correcting that mistake now."

"Mistake?" He *hrumphed*. "Might be just as well to have him out there for the year."

"So he's out of your hair?"

A clever edge slipped into his eyes. "He's a trickster. Don't you think this might be exactly what he wanted to happen?"

"No?"

"How many stories of tricksters have ended with the trickster not getting what they wanted?"

Exactly zero came to mind.

"This isn't a story," I said. "This is real life."

"And the tricksters of the stories are based on whom, exactly?"

"He probably wrote all those stories and just made sure he was always the winner. As a matter of fact, some stories say you're a devious, inscrutable trickster yourself."

"Your point is?"

That maybe I shouldn't really trust you either.

Yeah, well if I started thinking that about Odin, I might as well think that about all the gods. Stories were stories. What the gods did as gods wasn't necessarily what the gods did on vacation.

"My point is I need these powers hidden, locked away, and

safe. It's your turn to keep them."

The sound of cars arriving interrupted us.

"You invited all the gods out here to witness this, didn't you?"

"Only the ones who wanted to make sure their powers are going to be taken care of."

He sighed a particularly put-upon sigh. "Fine."

Engines quieted as cars parked, the creak and slam of doors opening and closing.

"Hera wasn't wrong," Odin said, his eye owl-bright, burning blue, watching me.

"That there's a war coming to Ordinary?"

"It's already begun."

It didn't exactly come as a shock to me, though it wasn't the cheeriest news I'd ever gotten.

"Sven murdered, four dead vampire hunters, Ben missing, and Jame left beaten and broken? Yeah, I didn't think it was the start of parade season. Rossi and Granny are about to throw down."

"The vampires and werewolves have never really been at peace. More like a cease-fire. That is not the war you should fear."

"What war should I fear?"

"The war for dark magic."

Okay. That was new.

"Dark magic? That's a thing?" As far as I knew whatever magic there was in the world was just that: magic. Not light, not dark, not good or bad, or any of the other defining characteristics we humans applied to such things.

"I want you to give me your word on something, Delaney."

So much for getting the confirmation on dark magic.

Outside, the sound of footsteps were coming closer to the house. I could hear conversation, some grumbling, some laughter. But I could not for the life of me look away from Odin's steady gaze.

"Promise me you will be very, very careful in the upcoming days."

It was such a weird request I just frowned. "I'm always careful."

"Be more careful."

"Why? How?"

"Because you are a target. And any way you can be, obviously."

Obviously. So helpful.

Then the door swung open—apparently none of the gods nor my sister and Ryder felt like knocking.

I, however, felt like someone had just thumped me hard in the chest.

Odin complained, loudly and at length that he didn't like his house being violated by everyone in town who didn't know how to wipe the mud off their boots, and why hadn't anyone knocked, and it wasn't like he was going to keep the powers inside, so get the hell out of his living room.

It all sort of washed over me like an ocean wave, while I sat there, his previous words a boulder trapping me flat to the ocean floor.

Myra caught my gaze over the crowd of quickly departing gods, and I gave her a wobbly smile. I pushed up to my feet, my hand falling to the bottle of powers still in my coat.

It was still there, one problem solved and almost off my to-do list. That was good, right? Something positive had come out of this day? I could deal with the war, with dark magic all in good time.

If I had time.

"Are you all right?" Myra asked as I headed toward the door. Piper was next to Jean, looking a little wide-eyed, but trying not to show it.

"Enough. I'll tell you after we're done. Let's get these powers put away."

Her light blue gaze shifted across my face as if looking for injury or lie there. Finding neither, she nodded. "Ten bucks if you can guess where he's going to keep them."

It was a thing we did. It was childish. We did it anyway.

"In a hollow log." I said.

"Gasoline can."

"Tool cabinet."

"Chainsaw."

We had followed the crowd of gods out to wherever Odin

had decided to stash the powers. Past a pile of discarded wood lumps that looked like they'd been mauled by a herd of mutant woodchuck termites, around his garbage can, burn barrel, and into the corner of his back yard that ended at the tree line of what seemed to be endless forest.

Right there, shining like a drop of molten silver between an old elm and older ash tree, was an Airstream travel trailer.

"Trailer," I said, even though our guesses were up. "Didn't even know he had one."

He not only had a trailer, he also had a big gray V-8 pickup parked in front of it with vanity plates spelling out SLEPNR.

Odin himself opened the door of the trailer and flicked on a light. The interior seemed to shine in gold, and in the falling light of day, it made the whole thing a lot more mystical than a travel trailer should be.

I'd never seen the inside of Odin's trailer, but what I could see from the door looked like all the wall space was taken up with shelves and shelves of books.

Huh. Not really what I'd expected.

"All right, all right." He came back out of the trailer, wiping his broad, nicked-up hands over the jug in his hand.

No, not a jug. A growler.

"Let's do this." He crooked one finger into the handle and sort of waved the growler toward me.

"A growler." That was, I think, Aaron.

"Old family heirloom. Got it in Norway."

It was earthenware, a nice brown and green glaze, the words WELL OF WISDOM were written across it.

"You can buy that at Bi-Mart," Zeus muttered.

"Doesn't matter, does it?" Odin said. "I'm keeping the powers. They stay where I say they'll be safe, and I say they'll be safe in this jug."

The gods shuffled a little as a slight mist started pushing down from the tree tops.

"That's correct," Ryder said.

Every head turned to him. He looked just as shocked as anyone else that those words had come out of his mouth.

Then all eyes shifted to me.

"Deities, meet Ordinary's new warden. Warden Bailey,

these are most of the gods of Ordinary."

"Ha!" Crow yelled, and pointed at Ryder's face. "And ha," he added, swinging a finger my way.

I was tempted to swing a finger at him too. The middle one.

"Piper, meet the gods in town."

She nodded and smiled like they were the best tippers she'd had all week.

"Piper is a demigod. Just thought you should all meet her. Mithra made her take the powers. She's sorry about it and promises it will never happen again."

She hadn't actually promised that, but I was pretty sure she would, if asked.

"Wait," Crow said. "Demigod. So who is her parent?"

No one moved. Someone chuckled uncomfortably.

I guess I had expected Poseidon to step forward, to recognize her. But this vessel who held Poseidon's power was at least four Poseidons past the one who had fathered her.

Then: "Oh." It was a soft, surprised sound. And Poseidon—the current Poseidon—stepped forward toward her.

He was a skinny guy, tall enough he had permanently hunched shoulders as if he needed to make himself shorter than he was. His hair was black and pulled back in a ponytail away from his long face. His eyes were wide and shifted between the colors of the sea.

"Piper?" He held his hands out, looking for recognition on her face. "I see you. I see you now."

She took his hands and smiled up at him.

"Oh," he said with soft wonder. "You're beautiful."

Piper blushed and that flush of interest in her eyes wasn't a look a daughter should give her father. Which, technically, he wasn't. Her father. That man, that vessel had died years ago. This man, this Poseidon was, well, he wasn't my type, and while he was much older than he looked, so was Piper.

Were they falling for each other? Was it incest if they were, technically not even related? Was this just another grand way Poseidon was screwing things up?

My head hurt. "So," I said to break up the insta-love going on because I could not deal with that right now. "Let's get these powers stowed."

I pulled the water bottle out of my coat and walked over to Odin. There wasn't a ceremony involved in moving the powers. Well, no more than what was happening today, which was that most of the deities liked to come out and watch the powers actually be transferred.

Not that gods were untrusting of their fellow deities.

No, it was *exactly* that the gods were untrusting of their fellow deities.

"All righty." I held up the water bottle that sang, hummed, thrummed with power. I still didn't know how Piper had shoved it into a water bottle, although if Mithra had given her the bottle, it might make more sense.

Odin uncorked his growler of wisdom.

"Odin, do you promise to guard and keep hidden the deity powers of Ordinary for the length of one year plus four months?"

"Yep."

"And you'll let any deity come to your trailer, and will allow them to see their power, or reclaim their power at any time, day or night?"

"Yes, but not unless I'm present."

"Right. Good. Everyone okay with that?" I looked around the group.

They looked...well, bored mostly, except for Poseidon who couldn't tear his gaze away from Piper. It wasn't like this was the first time we'd done this yearly hand-over.

"Crow, get in on this."

Crow walked over to me, looking like he expected the powers to bite. Which, maybe they would.

He took the bottle away from me, then tipped it into the spout of the growler.

Power isn't liquid. It doesn't really follow the rules of gravity. Power does, however, follow the will of the gods, and the rules and contracts of Ordinary.

My father said he saw the powers as bright flaming colors. I see light, yes, but it's soft and indistinct, more like a rainbow caught from the corner of my vision. What I do sense is the song.

Power, this much power, all mixing and colliding, created music that swooped down beneath my skin, pulling my pulse and breath and blood and bones to reach, to stretch, to feel the universe strumming through me.

My heart settled into the beat of the powers, my thoughts picked up and braided into the rising, falling, beauty of voice, chorus, song, song, song...until there was no time, no space, nothing but sound.

"Well, shit," Crow said.

I blinked. Blinked again. I'd lost some time. The gods were all gone, and foggy mist had descended on the forest floor. My mouth was dry and so were my eyes, as if I hadn't blinked or swallowed for an hour.

I did both, wincing at the pain and wiping away the tears at the corners of my eyes. Ryder and Myra were still there, Ryder looking like he was trying to decide if he had to burn his atheist badge, Myra looking steady and calm as she offered me a can of ginger ale.

"Thanks." I sipped the cool soda. "What's wrong?" I asked Crow.

"I have to pick it up." He was staring at the water bottle like a kicked puppy. "I don't want to go back to work."

Odin *humphed* and forcefully flipped the stopper back into the growler, locking it down with a little metal lever.

"You broke the contract with Ordinary," Ryder said. He walked over and stood next to me, staring at the water bottle with an inscrutable look on his face. "Your...power...uh, you have to take it back."

Crow raised his eyebrows and looked over at me. "Really? You gave him the warden job? What were you thinking?"

"It wasn't my idea, okay? I told him not to take it."

Crow shook his head. "You do realize this makes him your boss."

I grit my teeth and narrowed my eyes at Crow.

"Come again?" Ryder said. "Boss?"

"We'll talk about it later," Myra said.

"Take your power back, Crow," I said. "You like being a god, remember?"

He huffed an exaggerated sigh. "Fine. Whatever. It's not

264

like anything interesting is happening here anyway."

He tipped the water bottle over his left palm. A faint wash of black and silver twinkling with blue and green poured over his skin for what felt like forever, frozen outside of time. A brace of voices poured out with it in a joyous, devious blend of treble and bass, unexpectedly sweet, and funny.

And then Crow was no longer just my friend Crow. He was Raven, the trickster god.

"Well, it's been fun, my chickies." He tossed the water bottle to Odin and started walking.

"That's it?" I said. "I just saved your power from the clutches of another god, and I don't even get a decent good-bye?"

Raven turned back around, a grin on his handsome, godly face. "You know I love you, Delaney."

"I know you love to mess with me."

He held his arms wide. "Come to Uncle Raven, Boo-Boo."

"And here I thought you couldn't get more annoying."

"Come here." He made grabby signs with his hands. "Come here."

I closed the distance between us, totally not looking like a sullen toddler.

"Are you going to miss me?" He asked as he folded me into a big hug.

"No," I muttered against his shoulder.

"Liar face. You'll be crying in your cupcakes."

"From relief. That you're finally out of my hair. And my cupcakes."

He squeezed me a little around the shoulders. "About the war," he said, suddenly quiet and serious. "You know I have your back."

I opened my mouth to ask him what he knew about the war, what he could tell me, but he released me and took a quick step over to drop a hug on Myra, then slug Ryder in the shoulder.

"You dog, you," he said while Ryder rubbed at what I figured was going to be a spectacular bruise, if the sound of the impact was anything to gauge it by. "Getting tied up in things way beyond your understanding. Really, really stupid. Try not to die!"

And with that, Raven simply wasn't there anymore.

Ryder went absolutely still. "He disappeared."

"'People come and go so quickly here'," I quoted.

"I'm not in Kansas anymore, am I?"

"So very not, Toto."

He gave me a faint smile. On the one hand I felt a little sorry for him. He was running out of ways to cling to his old beliefs. That wasn't easy on anyone.

But watching him sort through the events and facts, even when they seemed impossible or were very clearly violent, in such a calm manner made me feel like maybe it hadn't been such a bad idea to let Ryder in on the town's secrets.

"Now get off my property," Odin said. He walked into his trailer and slammed the door leaving us in the fog and damp.

"So," Ryder said. "That was fun."

And even though I didn't expect it, it made me laugh.

CHAPTER 19

I SPENT several hours at the station, going over the evidence we had on Sven's death, and looking through the photos Ryder uploaded to the database. There wasn't a lot I could draw out of the photos of Jame that I hadn't already known by being there.

It was a vampire attack. The bite made that clear. The bloody ichor techne seemed to back it up. I didn't know how powerful a vampire had to be to take down Jame and kidnap Ben. Maybe it was more than one vampire. Maybe it had been vampires and other creatures working together.

Since it had happened outside of Ordinary, it could have even been a god who jumped them, though most gods saw our town and all those who lived within it as pretty much beneath their notice.

Until they went on vacation.

"Anything?" Myra asked from her desk. We'd sent Jean to the hospital to tell us when Jame was conscious enough to be able to speak. Hadn't heard from her yet.

I picked up my cup and made a face at the contents. When had I poured myself water?

"You've been drinking coffee like it's air," Myra said. "Hydrate before you get an ulcer or kidney stones."

I took a sip of the water, then drained half the cup because she wasn't wrong.

"I keep coming back to this ring." I gulped down more water, then shuffled through the pictures. "It looks square on top, right?"

Myra stood, and groaned as she stretched. I grinned at her. "You okay there?"

"Still sore from practice." The fanatic glow in her eyes meant she wasn't at all sorry about that. "Bertie cornered me earlier today."

"About the Cake and Skate?" I pushed the extra chair by my desk out with my foot, indicating she could sit.

She nodded and walked over. "I wasn't going to compete."

"Hold the hamburgers. She talked you into skating?"

Myra levered down into the chair. "You know how she is."

"Yes. I do. And you do too. You never fall for her Valkyrie ways."

"She was very convincing."

"Blackmail?"

"Worse. Revenge. Petty revenge. I am a sucker and fell for it."

I made clucking noises with my tongue. "You? Myra. It must be good if you're listening to the devil on your shoulder. It wouldn't involve a certain Rebecca Carver, would it?"

"I ran into her at Athena's tea shop."

"Picking up some of that fresh oolong from that tea farm outside Salem?"

"Yes. She was there complaining about the selection and the candles and the weather and the town."

"Did you have to stop Athena from breaking her nose?"

"No, she was reading a magazine and ignoring her. Which is what I should have done."

"What did Rebecca do? Tell you your tea sucks?" I was sort of fascinated to find out what had made Myra angry. Not that she didn't get mad, but out of all of us Reed girls, she was the best at keeping a level head.

"She told me she liked how my uniform made me look like I was in shape."

"You want revenge because she said you were fat?"

Myra was curvier than me or Jean, and tougher than both of us put together.

"No. I don't care if she thinks I'm fat. I'm in good shape for this job, and for myself. But then she went on about how sad it is that everyone from small, backward towns like ours are fat and uneducated. She said she had only agreed to compete in the fundraiser because she was sure that anyone from town who volunteered would have a heart attack, and how embarrassing that would be for them. A heart attack. Embarrassing! I sort of lost it."

"Did you yell at her?"

"No. I challenged her. Head-to-head. Skate off. Loser

matches the funds the winner raises."

I shook my head, but I was smiling. "You are going to own her and make rent doing it."

That got a small smile out of her. "Maybe. She's built like a marathon runner under her Gucci pantsuit. I haven't been back on skates all that long."

"When is the event?"

"Tomorrow."

"You should get some sleep."

"I'm fine. I'll be fine. I'd rather be working than wasting my energy on an old feud. Talk to me about the ring."

I handed her the picture and pulled it up on my screen too. "Man's hand. Not a wedding ring. Flat on top, maybe square? I think I've seen it somewhere."

"A lot of men's rings are square."

"I know."

"So where would you have been that you would take the time to note someone's ring?"

"Everywhere?"

"That's not exactly narrowing it down. Mithra? The casino?"

I thought back. "No. Maybe the diner?"

"Were Ben or Jame wearing a ring?"

"I don't think so."

"Lot of people at the Blue Owl."

I sighed. "I know."

"Maybe it will come to you."

"Yeah, like my luck's running hot right now." I glanced at the time on my computer. "It's getting late. I'll forward the phones to my cell. Let's both try to get some sleep."

"You don't want to talk about Ryder?"

I rubbed at one eye. "No. I can't believe he said yes to Mithra. He doesn't even believe in gods."

"That's probably why he said yes. I looked through the books. Dad's books."

"And?" I stood, took my coffee cup back to the small sink tucked into the hall and dumped out the water.

"There hasn't been a warden in Ordinary since mid-last century. Some woman named Duchess. Apparently, even with

Mithra's powers behind her, no one listened to her."

"Well, that sucks."

"It means Mithra has been dying to get a new warden in place ever since then."

"I wish he'd just take a vacation and loosen up. Did the books say we have to obey everything the warden says?"

"It's a little vague on the details, though there are some notes that suggest the warden should act as jury over the town, while the Reeds act as judge."

"That sounds better. I'd be his boss."

"There are also some notes that say the warden, being set into place under the power of a god outside Ordinary, doesn't have to follow any of Ordinary's rules and can be judge, jury, and executioner."

"Let's go back to the part where I don't want to throw Ryder out of town."

"That's the last thing."

I shrugged into my coat and glanced out the window while Myra set the security system. The night was cloudy and clear, no rain.

"What?" I asked.

"There's a question of whether or not any one god's power can directly affect Ordinary's laws set in place over the other gods."

Time worked in Ordinary. So did life, death, love, war, poetry, harvest, and all the many other aspects of life that gods ruled over. But gods generally did not like to be beholden to any other god. That was the whole reason why the Reed family had been set into place as guardians and law-keepers.

We were an unbiased party.

"Huh. So maybe Mithra is all noise, no substance?"

"It was pretty obvious that the gods at least noticed Ryder was the warden. Old Rossi and Granny Wolfe seemed to listen to him. Maybe it's one of those jobs that will be defined by the person who holds it."

I thought about that. Wondered what role Ryder would want to play in this town now that its secrets were being revealed. Wondered if it would get in the way of whatever welcome-wagon spy thing he was doing for the DoPP.

"We'll figure it out." We walked to the parking lot. "Get some sleep, My. You have a race to win."

"You too. Nice job with the powers, by the way. Can't believe Odin took them so easily, and Crow didn't argue about leaving town."

"Two tricksters behaving themselves? Maybe our luck is finally warming up."

She laughed as she got in the cruiser. Yeah, I didn't believe that, either.

I WOKE too quickly, sweat from restless dreams cold against my skin in the darkness. My cell phone rang again. I pulled it to me, not bothering to look at the caller before answering.

"Hey, Delaney," Jean's voice was thick with sleep, or the lack of it. "Jame's conscious. He can answer questions. Come on down?"

I rubbed at my eyes and shivered in the cool of my house. "I'll be right there."

I thumbed off the call, then glanced at the clock. Four a.m.

At least the roads would be quiet.

I dressed in jeans, flannel and boots, grabbing my official jacket on the way out. Just like I had since last May, I scanned the staircase and gravel dead end for shadows or people before I started down the stairs.

Someday I'd get over being jumped and shot in my own driveway. Today was not that day.

It took under three minutes to get to the hospital, the roads empty, the puddles having shrunk a bit from the break in rain.

Before I had a chance to ask where Jame was roomed, the receptionist pointed me down the hall and told me the number.

I was just now awake enough that I wished I'd taken some time to brew coffee before coming here.

Too late for that now. I knocked quietly, then let myself in.

There were five people in the room. Two of the Wolfe boys standing on either side of the door, twin columns of muscle and anger posted there as guards; Jean sitting in the chair at the right of his bed; and Granny Wolfe standing at the head of his bed on the left, her hand on Jame's shoulder.

271

Jame was more human than I'd last seen him, cleaned up, pale with a bandage on his neck. He was wearing a hospital gown, so I couldn't see any other wrappings or stitches, but there also didn't appear to be any other heavy-duty gizmos or equipment attached to him to indicate more serious wound care.

"Hey," I said quietly. "You're looking better."

Jame blinked slowly, his eyes going gold for a moment before returning to a more human shade.

I stopped beside Granny Wolfe who didn't take her eyes off Jame. "Can I ask you some questions?"

Jame swallowed. "Yes."

I winced at the gravel in his voice. He sounded like he'd been strangled or had screamed for hours on end. It made me angry that both things might actually be possible.

I wasn't going to go through the long and tedious line of questioning that would build a good court case, and tell me exactly every step of everything Jame and Ben had gone through. Not yet, anyway.

We needed to find Ben and catch a killer. The details could wait.

"Can you tell me what happened?"

"Contact. Jake Monroy. Government agency. Had information. On Sven. W-wanted info on vampires. R-rossi."

Everything inside me went cold and still. That was where I'd seen the ring. On Jake's hand. Holy shit. Ryder's boss had been the one holding up Sven.

Was he the murderer? A human? Vampires were so much stronger and faster, it was hard for me to accept one man could take them down. Was the Department of Paranormal Protection a front for killers?

Jame panted for a bit, as if those words had been pulled out by the root, exhausting him. But his gaze held mine, burning, angry.

I waited for him to catch his breath.

"The vampire...the vampire. Stank like death. Red eyes. Silver hair. Old. Old. He took...he took...Ben." The last word came out in a keening whine. Every muscle in Jame's body tightened, the cords of his neck popping, sweat covering his skin as he fought the wolf inside of him that was hurting for his mate.

Granny Wolfe squeezed his shoulder. "Jame. See me now. Only me."

His gaze lifted to hers and his muscles relaxed, his breathing evened out.

"Tell her the rest, but you stay here with me, now. I protect you. Protect my own. I protect your mate. Nothing else for you to worry about."

Jame lifted his chin, exposing the side of his neck, eyes sliding away from her.

"Good now. Good." Granny squeezed his shoulder again, gently.

"They wanted Old Rossi. Said they'd leave a path of blood to his d-door s-step. And Ben...he smelled Ben. He knew. Ben. He knew Rossi. Knew he made him. Made Ben."

Everything that was cold inside me flash hot. "Did they kill him?"

"He fought...we fought."

Silence filled the room, Jame swallowing and swallowing as he choked on memories.

"They took him. They took him. They took him, they took him, took him..." His voice broke into ragged whispers, a mantra of grief repeating pain.

Tears slipped hot down my face, and I wiped them angrily away with the heels of my palms. "We'll find him. We will. We'll bring him back. We'll bring him home to you."

I didn't know if he heard me, caught as he was in overwhelming pain and sorrow.

Granny Wolfe heard me. Finally turned my way, her hand shifting from Jame's shoulder to his head. She stroked his hair back off his forehead over and over, soothing as if he were a child.

"He's still not healed," she said. "They pumped him full of drugs. His sorrow's gonna be rage in the morning. We'll be hunting. We'll still be hunting."

"Has he said anything else?"

"Just that Ben's still alive. Old vampire has him. Don't know which way they went. Beat him black and blue to death's doorway. Used Ben's blood to leave that message. Message to the *strigoi*."

273

"We'll find him," I said again.

"Don't want him found," Granny turned her gaze back to Jame, who was staring blankly into the middle distance, unmoving as she stroked his hair. "Just want him dead."

I SENT Jean home to get some sleep, knowing the Wolfes would keep Jame safe in the hospital, as would all the other creatures and humans who worked there.

I was still trying to process what Jame had said. There was a vampire, an old vampire who wanted Rossi's attention. Ben was kidnapped, still alive, and Rossi had been given two blood messages, one on Sven's dead body, one on Jame's beaten body.

What did the messages say?

As dawn crept up over the eastern sky, pulling long shadows away from the town, I found myself sitting outside Rossi's house. He probably wasn't in. Probably was still hunting, just like the rest of the Wolfe family was out hunting.

Just like every vampire in Ordinary was out hunting.

But I needed to talk with him. Needed to know what those messages meant.

I got out of the Jeep, knocked on the door.

The house was dark.

No one answered. No one was home. Something about that felt oddly final, as if without Rossi, the old place went from home to mausoleum.

I drove. I wanted to stop for coffee, but it was early enough that even the drive-thrus were still closed.

I didn't know where Jake was staying, but Ryder would.

I knocked on his door, and the sound of footsteps reached me through the door. There was a pause, which I figured was him looking out through the peephole. Then the door opened.

"Hey, Delaney, come on in." Ryder looked like he hadn't slept all night, and from the spots of mud at his jeans' hem, was still wearing the same clothes from yesterday. "Coffee?"

"Gods, yes."

He headed into the kitchen and I followed him. "You get any sleep last night?"

He shook his head and reached into the cupboard to get

out a mug. "Jake's missing."

I sighed and sat on the barstool at the island. "How do you know?"

"His phone won't pick up. I drove over to the Nordic, and he wasn't there. Said he checked out yesterday morning."

"Why were you looking for Jake?"

He poured coffee into the mug, then into another mug that was already on the counter. Turned with both in his hands, offered me one.

"After finding Jame in all that blood. Seeing him shifted...He's a werewolf, right?"

I nodded, drank. The coffee was thick and hot. I wanted to crawl into the cup and pretend the world didn't exist.

"I needed to update him. Tell him about Jame. About werewolves being in town."

"Were you going to tell him about the gods?"

"I don't know. No?" He shrugged at my look. "I'm still not sure I believe that they're here, that they're real. Until I know, really know, I probably won't bring it up."

"Being fetch-boy to a god isn't enough?"

"That was...Yeah, that was weird. But what proof do I have that he's really a god? He could just be something else."

"Like what?"

"A wizard? A kobold? A siren?"

"That's...there's a lot of difference between those things."

"I wouldn't know. I haven't met any of them." He gave me a hopeful look. "Have I?"

"Probably. But that doesn't matter. Mithra is a god, and I'm sure he'll make that plain to you when you least want him to. Don't ever underestimate him, Ryder. Or Jake."

"Jake?"

"Jame said Jake was there when he and Ben were attacked."

Ryder paused with his mug halfway to his mouth, then placed it on the counter beside him. "Was he a prisoner?"

"No. Jame said he set up the meeting."

"With whom?"

"Ben and Jame and a very old vampire."

Ryder crossed his arms over his chest, his gaze shifted off to the wall behind me.

Spud, his mutt of a dog, trotted into the kitchen, then yawned and stretched as he wagged his tail. He gave me a sniff, I rubbed his head, then he nosed his way across the floor and folded down at Ryder's feet with a groan.

Looked like nobody in the house had gotten any sleep last night.

"Did you know about the meeting?" I asked.

"No."

"He's your boss in the DoPP, right?"

"Yes. But Ordinary is my territory. He shouldn't have done anything, made any agreements between citizens of Ordinary without contacting me."

"He's working with a killer, Ryder."

"Or he was trying to broker a conversation, a meeting that went horribly out of his control."

"I noticed his ring on his right hand. White gold or titanium?"

"Pure silver." His gaze ticked back to me, eyebrows dipping down. "Why?"

"That ring in the picture? The man who put his hand over Sven's mouth?"

Ryder exhaled. "You think it's him. You think he is strong enough to kill a vampire? To beat up a werewolf?"

"No. But I think he's working for a vampire, and maybe other creatures who are strong enough to do those things. Maybe they all wear matching rings. Maybe he's the leader of his own splinter group."

"Jake's not like that."

"Do you trust him? Trust him enough to bet Ben's life on it?" When he didn't answer, I went on. "I saw him on your porch a few nights ago. You were arguing. What were you fighting about?"

"He wanted me to get him inside Old Rossi's house. Wanted to meet Old Rossi. He thought he was a vampire. Thought he was the prime."

"Putting aside the question as to how he would have assumed that, why were you arguing with him? I thought it was your job to roll out the welcome wagon to the creatures in town."

"I didn't like his approach. I grew up here. I've known Rossi all my life. It just seemed...rude and unnecessary. Like he was some kind of criminal hiding something and we were banging down his door. Whether he was or wasn't a vampire didn't mean we shouldn't treat him with basic courtesy and respect. Just like anyone else in town."

My chest warmed and the rest of me went a little gooey. Thinking of Old Rossi as a vampire, but still a person with rights and feelings said a lot about what kind of man Ryder was.

"But you took him out there anyway."

"No. It was weird. Right after I'd told Jake to shove off because I wasn't going to rig up some false pretenses as to why we should get into Old Rossi's house, Old Rossi called. Had a remodel he wanted done for his studio. That's what he said, anyway. I'm not sure if that's the truth, or if he just wanted to put eyes on me and Jake because he suspected we were from the agency."

"He suspected. He might also want the remodel. Do you have any idea where Jake might be? Who he might check in with? A boss, a co-worker, family?"

"No. And if...if it turns out he was a part of Sven's death and the kidnapping. What they did to Jame..."

I waited. Wondered what he would do if, or more like when, we proved that Jake wasn't playing on the right side of justice.

"There are a couple people I could call," he said. "Agents he might get in touch with who might know where he is."

"Can you contact them?"

"Yeah. I can. How's Jame doing?"

"He'll heal. But if we don't find Ben...I don't know." I rubbed my eyes. "The vamps and weres have a pretty uncertain truce. If Ben dies, if Jame loses his mate, I just don't know how we're going to keep the situation under control."

Ryder walked pretty quietly for a big guy. His hands pressed gently on my arms and stroked upward. "What can I do?"

"For what?" I muttered behind my hands.

"For you."

I put my hands down and looked up at him. I was tired, broken-hearted over the visit with Jame. Worried. Very worried.

Whatever wasn't working between Ryder and me suddenly seemed inconsequential. "Just, maybe...hold me for a minute?"

He held his breath as if surprised at my answer, then shifted forward. I folded against his chest as his arms wrapped around my back, one wide hand cupping the back of my head.

And for a minute, maybe more, the world became only our heartbeats, our breathing, our warmth.

CHAPTER 20

TWO HOURS of phone calls, no new leads, no news from either vampires or werewolves. The case for finding Ben or Jake was getting nowhere.

I'd already drunk a week's worth of coffee and was on the way to the Cake and Skate. Yes, Ben was missing and we needed to find him. But the fundraiser was an immediate all-hands-on-deck situation. I had to be there for crowd control and general police presence, especially since Myra was participating instead of wearing a uniform.

The vampires and werewolves were some of the best hunters Ordinary had to offer and they were all out looking for Ben. If anyone could find him, it would be the Rossis or Wolfes.

The best thing I could do right now was get through the fundraiser, then get back to work.

An open lot next to the Puffin Muffin bakery was set up in bright Saturday Market style with tents and tables, streamers and balloons. The radio station was sheltered under a bright awning, playing tunes, giving out bumper stickers, and waiting for the big event.

For eight o'clock on a cloudy (but not rainy) morning, there were a lot of people gathered already, most of them walking, but a good portion were on bicycles too.

Dozens of umbrella hats bobbed along in the crowd, and I shook my head. I didn't know if people were wearing them because they were comfortable and (wrongly) thought they were fashionable, or if Crow was right and had blazed a new Northwest fashion craze to go with our flannel, craft brews, and mushroom hunting.

I parked my Jeep and strolled over toward the bakery. I scanned faces, looking for kidnappers, looking for enemies. While I saw strangers, I didn't see anyone who seemed out of place.

I also didn't see any vampires or werewolves, which felt

weird.

Death stood near the entrance to the open lot, wearing a bright yellow umbrella hat, a pink jacket with HAPPY KILLS scribbled across it, handing out balloons to children.

Okay, so that was weird plus one.

"You made it," Jean fell into step beside me and handed me a cup.

I lifted it and took a sniff my coffee-sour stomach clenching. Cocoa, not coffee. Perfect.

"How's Myra doing?"

"You have to see this for yourself." Even though Jean hadn't gotten much more sleep than I had, she was grinning, her pink and orange-streaked hair pulled back in two high ponytails over her ears, her step light.

I couldn't help but smile. I envied her ability to see the humor in the world, to always find something to smile about even when things looked grim. Not for the first time I was happy my parents had tried one more time for a boy, and instead given me a baby sister.

She led me around the crowd to the bakery parking lot.

Two pickup trucks were parked side-by-side at what appeared to be an impromptu starting line. In front of each truck five people stretched and waited. They all wore helmets, roller skates, elbow and knee pads. Myra was easy to spot by the blue truck, the swing of her hair curved a dark slash beneath her helmet. BLUE OWLS was boldly written in grease paint down both of her arms. The whole team wore blue tank tops, shorts, and high blue socks, with owls on the socks. Looked like the diner was sponsoring the team. Piper and the three Furies were among the skaters.

We hadn't brought Piper in on burglary charges. Since the powers being stolen was more a god-feud thing, it didn't fall squarely under mortal laws. Piper had not only admitted to her part in the theft, but she had also ratted out Mithra, which allowed us to recover the powers. Without Crow or any of the other gods wanting to press charges, Piper was going to get off with a warning. A stern warning, and we'd be keeping a close eye on her from now on, but not jail time.

Plus, I still needed to do some research on what place a

demigod had in this town. There was no reason to send her away, since she was following all the other rules of Ordinary that we require of the gods and creatures: mainly that she hold down a job and contribute to the community. And she didn't have a power that needed to be stashed with the other god powers.

Maybe I'd make her take the volunteer hours Jean had promised I'd serve for Bertie for the rest of the year. That would be stern penance.

The other truck was red, the team decked out in gear, all red, with RED WEEDS scrawled down their arms. Took me a minute, but I finally saw the logo for Aaron's garden center on the tank top.

Of course the god of war wanted a piece of this action.

Rebecca was on Team Red, slender and cool and sleek as a weasel. She sipped her designer water bottle without smudging her perfect scarlet lipstick, and stood just far enough apart from her team mates—a couple humans and two dryads—that it was clear they were not friends.

Myra had grease paint under her eyes, bruises on her arms, and corpse-blue lipstick that was probably borrowed from Jean's makeup stash. She looked focused and determined.

"She's going for blood," I said.

"Myra? Yeah, she's gonna to mop the street with Rebecca."

"All the money goes to charity?"

"Elementary school and children's hospital. Chunk goes to the food bank too."

I briefly wondered why Rebecca was involved in those charities, and had a shocking moment of thinking the woman might actually have a heart under her belittling, judgmental exterior.

Naw, she probably got roped into it like everyone else. Conscription-via-Valkyrie.

"Are there rules?" I'd never heard of Cake and Skate until Bertie had decided to throw one. I hadn't paid much attention to the details at the time. It was possible she had made this whole thing up.

"The teams load up the delivery orders into the backs of the trucks, then the truck takes them to the neighborhood drop points where skaters have to get the right breakfast bundles to the right people. Whoever delivers their bundles fastest and gets back to the bakery first, wins."

"So we follow along?"

"We can, although there will be a judge in the front and back of each truck. Even better, there's a live stream."

She pointed at two motorcycles near the trucks, each with a driver and camera person, then over at a screen set at the far end of the lot.

The radio station crew took over, introducing the teams, breakdown of rules, and threw in enough jokes and jabs to get the crowd laughing.

I fell into the familiar mode of friendly vigilance that these kinds of events required.

There was a countdown, then an air horn blast got the games going. The lot was part asphalt, part gravel, and all of it still wet from recent rains.

The crowd cheered as the skaters scrambled to get to the side of the bakery where tables were set up with crisp white bags and boxes, all carrying the Puffin's logo.

Shouting, shoving, laughing. One box tumbled to the ground, but landed without breaking open and was snatched up by Piper who seemed to know she'd need to catch it before a team mate accidentally ran it over.

A man on Red Weeds team stole a Blue Owl bag, and was hot-skating it back to the red truck. Myra dashed out after him and hip-checked him for his trouble. She took the blue bag quickly back to the correct truck while Red Weeds' driver gestured and pointed to get the judges to call a foul.

"Wow," I said. "That's...intense." This might be for charity, but it was no-holds-barred.

Jean hooted, then stuck her fingers in her mouth and whistled. "Go, Myra!"

Red Weeds got their truck loaded first and all the skaters hopped into the back of the bed. Two Blue Owls stood in front of the truck, blocking it and trying to keep it from pulling out of the lot. They got honked at, the engine revved, and the judge from the back of the Blue Owls's truck yelled out a foul, at which the crowd laughed and booed.

That delay gave the Blue Owls just enough time to finish

loading their deliveries. The two truck-blockers quickly got out of the way and hopped into the back of their own truck.

Red Weeds was the first out of the parking lot, with Team Blue right behind. One lane of the main road had been orange-coned off for the event, and both trucks rolled out at about five miles over speed limit, the motorcycles and bicycles following behind them like a school of bright, honking, bell-ringing fish.

"This is insane," I said with a laugh.

Jean bumped her shoulder into mine. "It's good to see you smile."

"I smile."

"Not since the Mithra thing you haven't."

We were walking with the crowd, watching for ordinary trouble in our ordinary town, and keeping an eye on the screen, which showed the trucks currently stopped at a red light. The skaters were either yelling insults, or laying down the most recent pop dance moves.

Bicyclists got into it, and it suddenly looked like the least coordinated flash mob in history, gyrating randomly and spastically throwing hands in the air.

Myra was laughing, her blue eyes curved in crescents. She waved at one of the cameras and curled her arm to show off seriously impressive biceps.

It was good to see her having fun.

"I guess we've all had a pretty hard go of it lately. We'll get through it." I said.

Jean shrugged.

"Hey. We will. There's nothing we Reeds can't do."

That made her smile. She sipped her cocoa. "Hogan wants to move in with me."

"That's great," I said. Then at her silence: "That's not great?"

"I'm not sure it makes sense. With my job."

"Because you work late and he works early? We can get someone in to handle the switchboard. Or just forward calls. I'd be happy to swap a few days with you so you had evenings with him."

"Thanks, but it's not the hours."

"Then what?" I didn't think Jean wanted to quit the force.

Though I hadn't asked her. Ever since she was small she'd been putting on Dad's shoes, wearing his hat and coat any time she got a chance. But maybe now that she was an officer, she had discovered she didn't like the work.

If she wanted to change careers, I would support her wholeheartedly. But selfishly, I hoped she wouldn't leave. One of the best things about my job was working with my sisters.

"I don't know if I want to lie to him all the time."

We stopped near the front of the line of tents where there was currently less traffic.

"About Ordinary?"

She nodded, the morning light softening her features so that for a moment, I could imagine she was painted in watercolor.

"You know if you want to tell him, that's your call. I'll back you up. Myra and I both will back you up."

"I know. Thanks." She fell silent for a minute. "Are you happy Ryder knows?"

"He doesn't know. Not all of it."

"But he will."

"He's on the force. He's serving a god. He's a part of a government agency that I've never heard of, which totally freaks me out. But yes. He will."

"Good." She bumped my shoulder again. "I've always thought he should know. I'm glad he's a part of all this now."

"Even the god thing?"

"Maybe not the god thing. He's not really going to start bossing us around about rules is he?"

"Not if I can help it."

"So where is the man?"

"Bertie has him doing something around here."

We walked down between tents, keeping one eye on the big screen and the skaters. The trucks had split up and stopped at their first neighborhoods. The split screen showed blues and reds skating up to front doors navigating stairs, grass lawns, dogs, kids, toys, and steep inclines.

The crowd cheered every time a delivery was successfully completed, and laughed when skaters tumbled or managed to miraculously get where they were going without falling down.

I held my breath as Myra worked her way up a rickety three-story stairway at one of the hotels to the crow's nest apartment at the top. She handed over the bag of goodies then methodically walked down the stairs, one hand tightly gripping the banister.

"Well done," I whispered as her teammates gave her high fives, then hopped into the truck for the run to the next delivery spot.

I glanced at the red team and they seemed to be making good progress too, most of their bags and boxes already delivered. It wouldn't be long before they were headed back to the finish line.

We'd made it to the end of the row of tents and turned the corner to walk up the next row.

I stopped short, and Jean let out an "Awww...."

Ryder sat bent forward, painting a little girl's face. Her back was toward us, but I had a good view of Ryder.

He'd brushed his hair back, and applied some kind of product that kept it out of his face but didn't look heavy with gel. He was talking with the girl, smiling, his hands steady as he delicately applied paint to her face with a brush that looked like it was something a professional artist would use for oil painting.

His face was caught in a shower of colors. Flowers, butterflies, and a little winged fairy with a sword created a mask across one side of his face. Frogs, superhero shields, and a robot created the other side of the mask. Lightning, storm clouds, and a flying saucer peeked out on the edges of the mask, as did ocean waves, a message in a bottle, and a listing pirate ship.

It was an amazing paint job, and should be overwhelming and cheesy. Instead, it looked like an homage to Ordinary, as if he knew all its secrets and had found the beauty in them.

He straightened, tipped his head slightly to consider the painting on the girl's face, then grinned and handed her a mirror.

She shrieked in delight. Her parents gave suitable "oohs" and "ahhs" when she turned to reveal the sparkling unicorn with a Supergirl cape painted across her chubby cheek and forehead.

The unicorn was wearing an umbrella hat.

Of course.

The girl and her parents ambled off. Ryder saw us and stood.

"Can I interest you in a new look?" he asked.

"I don't know. Think I'd make a good superhero?"

"Nope. I already know you would."

Jean stuck her fingers in her mouth and made gagging sounds. "Get a room you two. I don't want to watch while you draw her like one of your French girls."

He smiled, his eyes lit with glee. "Don't know that it's appropriate to talk the chief of police out of her uniform before noon."

I raised an eyebrow. "It's noon somewhere in the world."

"Well, then." His voice dropped into a sexy drawl, and he wiggled the paintbrush between his fingers. "Maybe you and I should go somewhere..."

A tumble of little kids ran toward us laughing and shouting. They washed up like a wave of chattering pebbles, all pointing at the designs sketched on poster board behind Ryder.

"...or maybe we should back burner that idea until later," he finished with a laugh.

"Later sounds good."

Jean elbowed me and coughed, though it sounded like "dinner."

I rolled my eyes. "Want to get dinner tonight?"

"Love to. Jump Off's?"

"Seven?"

"Seven."

That was all the time we had because the radio announcers and the crowd all went wild.

I glanced up at the screen.

The split screen was still split, one camera filming the back of a red and blue skater, one camera filming the front.

Myra and Rebecca.

The skaters were neck and neck, speeding down the middle of the highway, orange cones zooming past as they powered toward the bakery. Whoever made it to the bakery first, won.

Rebecca was lean and fast, her smooth strides eating up the distance.

Myra skated in a deeper crouch, arms pumping, legs digging into each stroke. If body language could make a sound, she'd be a snarl.

"Go, go, go," Jean whispered.

I crossed my fingers, my heart pounding in beat to Jean's chant.

Do this, I thought. *Take that woman down a notch and show her what Reed blood is made of.*

They were closing in fast, Myra catching up to Rebecca's lead inch by inch. The rumble of motorcycle engines was almost drowned out by the cheering crowd.

C'mon, c'mon, c'mon.

Myra pulled up beside Rebecca. For a moment that would have been captured in slow motion if this had been a movie instead of real life, they were in perfect rhythm, perfect stride, perfect unity.

They were on the last stretch.

This could be a tie.

Neck and neck. Step and step.

Then Myra winked at the camera.

Winked.

She dug in hard, put on a burst of speed, and left Rebecca in the dust.

If the crowd had been wild before, it went absolutely bonkers now.

Jean screamed, punched the air, and threw herself in my arms. I screamed, and patted Jean's back. Holding her tight.

"Nothing we can't do," she said fiercely.

"Damn straight," I said.

I looped my arm over her shoulder, and walked with her to gather up our sister for a proper celebration.

CHAPTER 21

OKAY. SO everything wasn't exactly going my way. But Myra winning the Cake and Skate for her team had done a heck of a lot to cheer me up.

There were no updates from the vampires or Wolfes, which worried me. I would have expected there to be enough of a trail to track down Ben, or at least Jake.

The doctor told me Jame was sleeping peacefully and healing well. Well enough Granny Wolfe had joined the hunt, leaving three pack members behind to guard Jame.

The dry morning had turned into a sunny afternoon. Tourists and locals took full advantage of it. Plenty of people walked and played on the beach. Plenty of people wandered into the shops, which were staying open late in hopes of making up some rain-delayed revenue. The town felt the most summer-like it had all year.

There were even kites in the sky.

I still had a few hours before dinner with Ryder at Jump Off Jack, but was too restless to sleep. I went home and changed into my shorts, tank, and running shoes.

A lot had happened in a very short time and I needed to clear my head, think through the details. A quick jog on the beach, alone with my thoughts sounded like heaven.

I stretched at the bottom of my stairs, then took off at a slow, easy pace down the road to the bottom of the hill, past a few houses to the narrow band of green that would take me to the hidden foot trail through bushes and down to the sand.

The late afternoon was warm, the wind just strong enough to cut the humidity. I headed north, into the wind, toward Road's End. I always ran into the wind so I could have it at my back on my way home.

The steady rhythm of my breath, the thump, thump, thump of my shoes hitting hard-packed wet sand, the shivering hiss of the ocean next to me soothed me, focused my thoughts. The muscles in my shoulders relaxed, my body warming, sweat prickling at my neck, under my breasts, down my back.

I felt like I could run forever.

Breathe, breathe, breathe.

Road's End had that name for a reason. An outcropping of land reached out to cup the beach and cut it off from continuing north. If the tide was low enough, I'd be able to pick my way over water and rocks, and around the bend to a procession of little pockets of stony coves. But the tide was coming in, and I didn't want to get stranded on the other side.

So I slowed, paced the curve of land, the rise of stone cliff at my back, and then stood just at the water's edge, staring out to sea.

Clouds gathered fast, moving ashore with an unnatural kind of speed. Lightning flashed. Thunder rolled. The sudden storm was urgent, as if warning of an even greater danger approaching.

"Thor?" I asked. Rain fell in hard, heavy drops. I felt like I should run. Thunder roared again, urging me to turn home.

I turned. I didn't even see the man before I was aware of his presence behind me.

But with that presence, I felt fear.

I tipped my head down so I could better see him out of the corner of my eyes as he stopped behind and slightly to the side of me.

"You are a sweet surprise." His voice was low, cultured, carrying an accent I could not place. But my brain wasn't trying to place his accent, it was screaming: *danger, death, predator.*

I had not brought my gun and carried no other weapon. My phone tucked into my back pocket wasn't going to bring anyone here fast enough to save me.

I suddenly knew I was very much in need of saving.

I had a moment to wish I was connected to someone in some sort of magical way that allowed them to see through my eyes or hear my thoughts to know that I was in trouble.

But I was just a Reed and those kinds of abilities were beyond me.

What does a Reed do? My father's words echoed in my mind. *We face the storm.*

Thunder crackled. Lightning shattered.

I anchored myself with the roots of my family that reached deep and strong in this land. Then I turned and faced the man.

Not man. Creature. Vampire, to be exact. Here in the daylight of Ordinary that doesn't make vampires burn. Here inside the boundaries of Ordinary unnoticed, because all the vampires were gone.

Ancient. He was built a lot like Old Rossi, his silver hair cut in a short, executive style. His eyes were black and shockingly devoid of humanity.

There was a nightmarish smoothness to him, as if all his edges were rubbed down to frictionless curves, as if he had been poured into shape instead of tailored by bones. Snake-like. Fluid.

Creepy as hell.

"Yes," he said as if I'd asked him a question. "I killed Sven. Sent him to my prideful brother. Still he didn't come to me. So I took his toy. The one he turned. Poor, breakable thing."

Ben.

"You will not do this," I said. "You will not hurt my people, my town." My words came out even, but my heart was pounding. Hard. I knew he could hear it, feel it.

He lifted his upper lip in a snarl. "Since he will not come to me, you will send him a message even he will understand."

I backed up and threw my hands in a block.

But vampires are fast. I didn't blink, but my eyes still couldn't track his movement. He wrapped one hand up in my hair, yanking my head to the side.

I kicked out, punched. He yanked my head harder, and shook me like a rag doll. I heard bones in my neck crack as my feet left the ground.

I yelled, fought, thunder echoing my anger, my fear.

Vampires are inhumanly strong. And even though I was tough, a Reed, I was still human.

He pulled me to him, wrapping me tight against the hard, cold, slippery length of his body, wrenched my neck bare.

I screamed as agony pierced my flesh, two hot, jagged fangs hooking down into my neck, seeking my pulse.

Every muscle in my body went lax as if I'd just been injected with Novocain.

Turns out being bitten by a vampire isn't as sexy as some of the movies might make one think. Although that might have something to do with the fact that this vampire hated me and would rather see me dead than show me a good time.

This was not good. Not good at all.

"Listen to me, Reed bitch," he said, teeth still buried in my flesh. "You are alive only because you are my final message to my brother." He slowly lifted his mouth from my skin. I was numb everywhere except for where his fangs pierced me.

There I only felt endless pain.

"He brings me the *Rauðskinna*. Or I take everything he has," his fangs slipped free of my flesh, and I almost blacked out from the agony, "and burn this world to the ground."

He shook me again. I would have screamed if my body were responding to my mind. But the world had become too heavy, folding down on me in layers and layers and layers. Everything was watery, fading, dark.

I wondered if I was drowning. If the ocean had risen up to swallow me whole.

Cold sand, concrete-hard slapped against my back...

...*had he thrown me?*

...someone was screaming in the distance.

Sirens.

And not the call-the-sailors-to-their-death kind of sirens.

Police cruiser sirens.

"Tell him," his whisper echoed in my head. *"Or I will tear each of you apart until I find the one who makes him scream."*

I heard voices. Myra, Ryder, Jean. I knew there wasn't sand under me anymore, knew I was wrapped in a warm, heavy quilt, a pillow under my cheek. I didn't know what time it was, didn't have the strength to open my eyes.

The wash of deep healing spread through me. I wasn't sure which creature or god they'd gotten to take care of me but it was wonderful. Marvelous.

"Sleep," Old Rossi said quietly in my mind.

At least I hoped it was Old Rossi. I'd had my fill of strange vampires touching me.

Before I could panic about that, I slipped back into

291

oblivion.

MORNING SUNLIGHT streamed in through my window. It was warm on my bare arm, warm on the side of my hip.

It wasn't burning me to a crisp, so I apparently hadn't turned into a vampire.

Go, me.

"Your sisters are in the other room, waiting for you to wake up."

I opened my eyes. Was surprised that I didn't feel too bad, all things considered.

The memory of healing washed through me again. I wondered who they'd ask to fix me.

Old Rossi sat in the chair at the foot of my bed, his elbows resting on his soft, worn-out blue jeans, his fingers linked, the first two pressed against his lips.

His ice blue eyes watched me. I didn't know why I'd ever thought they were cold or inhuman before. I'd stared straight into the devil's eyes, and Rossi was no devil.

Apparently he was related to one though, a brother, if what that devil said was true.

"He looked like you." I pushed up, so I was sitting. I pulled the blankets close, glad that someone had changed me into a dry T-shirt. "He was slicker, sort of smoother and had short silver hair, but he was old like you."

"Old?" Offended, he cocked one eyebrow.

"Very."

The eyebrow fell again. "I know."

"You can tell from the b-bite who did this right?"

"Yes."

"He told me to give you a message."

"Which is?"

"He wants you to give him the *Rauðskinna* or everyone dies, he burns Ordinary down, yada, yada, psycho-egomaniac, yada."

"He did not yada."

"He threatened. Death to all, make you scream, and all that jazz. There was probably some yada I didn't catch. I didn't have a chance to write down every word."

Old Rossi was silent. I waited. When he still hadn't spoken after a minute or so, I breached the quiet.

"He says he has Ben. Said he was your...toy. That he's...broken."

Flash of black in those eyes, glimmer of red. Still less evil than the vampire on the beach. "Did he?"

"Broken doesn't mean dead," I said, holding on to hope, no matter how faint it might seem to be.

"Broken means it would be better if he were." Old Rossi leaned back, the tension easing away just long enough for me to see he was tired. Very tired. Still, he made no move to leave the room.

"What is the *Rauðskinna*?"

For a minute, well, more like three, I didn't think he was going to answer me.

"It is a book. A book of dark magic."

Dark magic. Just like Odin had said.

"Do you have it?"

"Yes."

"Why do I have a feeling it's not the only dangerous thing you have hidden in town? No, don't answer that. I can't multi-task before coffee. Are you going to give it to him?"

Rossi didn't say anything. I changed tactics. "What happens if he gets his hands on it?"

"All the bad things you can imagine and twice as many you can't."

"So we don't give it to him."

Silence again. I was surprised Myra and Jean weren't in here by now, but we weren't really talking all that loudly. I wondered if either of them had gotten any sleep last night.

"What's his name?" I asked.

"That, you do not need to know."

"Like hell. He bit me. *Bit* me, Travail. I deserve to know which vampire permanently tagged me for his chew toy."

Black and red eyes again. Fury, barely contained. "I will break that tie to you. Erase his mark. Make him suffer."

"Tell me his name."

"Lavius."

Great. I'd been holding out hope he was dead, like Rossi

had told me before. I didn't want to have Rossi's ex-brother-in-arms declaring war on my town by killing people I cared for, people I'd sworn to protect.

"You told me he was dead. You lied to me."

"I had hoped. Foolishly hoped."

"He has Ben."

"Yes. But now we can find him."

"How?"

"Through the mark he branded into you."

I wasn't sure what I thought about that. Good? Maybe I was glad something positive could come out of me getting fanged on the beach.

The door to my room opened, and Myra walked in. "No we will not use that mark, or Delaney to do anything," she said. "You're going to erase his tie to her. I've waited until she was awake. You've had your chance to talk to her. Break his claim on her. Now."

Old Rossi's body tightened. "We have no other way to find him. Or Ben."

"We've only started looking," she said.

"*All* the vampires. *All* the werewolves, and not a scent of him in the wind. We will not find him before he's dead."

"And putting Delaney in danger would make anything better? Do you need more deaths on your hands, Rossi?"

"Wait," I said, holding up a hand, tired of the argument even though it had just gotten started. "Just. Wait. Both of you. Let me think."

They both shut up, though there was some glaring going on. The discussion had drawn Jean into the room, and like an angel from caffeine heaven, she handed me a mug of coffee.

"Hey," she said. She dropped a quick kiss on the top of my head, then sat down on the bed next to me, facing my angry sister and my angry vampire.

The coffee was warm between my palms and the fragrance made my shoulders drop and my pulse settle. It was just so...normal. With everything else going sideways, the scent of coffee felt normal, average, safe. I took a sip.

All right. I could do this.

"How would you use the mark to find him?" I finally asked.

"He left within you a trace of his life force."

Great. Now I wanted to vomit.

"You can track that?"

"Yes."

"Is he the one who bit Jame?"

"Yes."

Myra's voice was almost a yell. "Then why didn't we use that bite to track him before he found Delaney?"

"Werewolf." Rossi didn't look like he was going to add anything to that.

"And?" I asked.

"It is...harder to trace. A werewolf physiology fights such intrusion, such claim. But humans are more...pliable. Our natural prey. The link between you and him shines like silver."

Okay, I was starting to vote for team Myra. Just the idea of carrying anything that connected me to that creep was making my skin crawl.

Jean spoke up. "Didn't Ben bite Jame? They're living together, mated, right? Chose each other? I thought Ben would claim him like that. Couldn't we follow that link?"

"Lavius broke that link when he bit Jame."

"Is that the asshole's name?" Jean asked. "Creepy. How can he break a mated link?"

"He is very old, and very strong."

Well, hell. No wonder Jame was out of his mind in pain for Ben. Another question occurred to me. "Is...is one bite enough? Strong enough to track him? Will it fade?"

"Jesus, Delaney," Myra said. "You are not suggesting you put yourself out there to get bitten again."

Jean reached over and took my hand, squeezing it. "You aren't doing that," she said with absolute confidence.

"One bite is strong enough," Rossi said. "Because *he* is strong enough. And so are you, Delaney Reed."

"All right," I said. "Okay. Yes."

"Delaney," Myra turned to me. "Don't do this."

"I can't just let Ben die. And Jame...I can't do this to him. Not if we have a chance. Not if I have a chance to save them."

She closed her eyes and I noticed the dark circles beneath them. Then she squared her shoulders and, looking calm and composed, turned back to Rossi. "When?"

"In three days. When the moon is full and we have a plan."

I wasn't sure if I was happy about carrying around the bite and Lavius's life force tie that long. "How vulnerable am I?"

Rossi's eyebrows raised and for the first time, there was a ghost of a smile over his lips. It was not a warm one. "Other than the fact that he crossed into my territory and claimed you when I wasn't looking?"

"You were looking for Ben. I don't expect you to be everywhere at once."

"Neither did he, obviously."

I nodded. It was, I realized, a very well-executed plan. Ben as bait to pull all the vampires out of town, the Wolfes either hunting for Ben, or guarding Jame. According to the rules of Ordinary, all creatures were welcome. They didn't have to stow their powers like the gods, didn't have to go through me to live here.

That he had caught me alone on the beach wasn't all that surprising either. I loved to jog, and I lived alone. He could have found me at any number of places alone.

"You are less vulnerable that most humans. Much stronger than he might believe."

Images of him easily lifting me off the ground with one hand, shaking me like a wet towel, flashed through my mind. "I don't feel strong."

"Oh, but you are. It's your blood, Reed blood, chosen by the gods. You underestimate your strength. I am counting on him underestimating it too."

"So we have some time to plan. That's good." Look at me: Little Miss Bright-Side.

"Yes."

"Good," Myra said. "Then the plan starts with us letting Delaney take a shower and eat breakfast."

Rossi nodded. "It's a good start." He stood, and rocked his head from side to side as if stiff from holding still for so long. I wondered if he'd sat there all night.

"I'll come by later this evening. We can talk. Plan."

"Rossi?" I said.

He waited.

"Promise me we'll take care of Lavius before anyone else is hurt."

"You have my word." He left, and Myra followed him out and locked the door behind him.

Jean relaxed into me, laying her head on my shoulder and wrapping her arms around me.

When Myra came into the room she took one look at us then joined us on the bed, wrapping around both of us.

We held each other, silent, thankful, and whole.

"KETCHUP FOR your thoughts?" Ryder held the bottle out for me. I shook my head. He tipped the bottle over his plate, keeping his eye on the growing red puddle. "So how are you holding up? Really?"

We were sitting at my little breakfast nook. Ryder had brought us lunch from Jump Off Jack—burgers and fries since I'd sort of stood him up for dinner the previous night.

I'd used Ryder's arrival as an excuse to make my sisters go home and sleep. Roy was at the station covering the phones, and he would contact Myra or Jean if there was anything happening that needed police attention.

We still had no leads on Ryder's boss, Jake, and no other hints about where Ben might be.

"I'm..." I was going to say "fine," but couldn't force the lie out of my mouth. "It's been a weird week," I said with a laugh that sounded a little too hollow. "I'm sort of still processing it." I took a bite of fries, trying to enjoy the salt and heat and grease. "And you?"

"I'm good," he said with a grin. He took a drink of his beer, then dragged a few fries through the ketchup and Tabasco on his plate to mix it up. He shoved the fries in his mouth, chewed. "I mean, I've apparently given my life and soul over to a god I don't believe in, but hey—at least I didn't get bitten by a murderous vampire."

I made a face at him. "Oh, so now we're comparing war wounds?"

"If you want." His eyes flicked to the side of my neck and I felt my stomach churn—and not in a good way.

297

Some of that must have showed on his face, because his eyes, when he turned them back to me, were kind. "Have you looked at it yet?"

"I took a shower."

"Have you looked at the bite?"

I picked up my burger, set it down without taking a bite. "I...couldn't. I didn't want to see it. Didn't want it to be real. That's stupid, isn't it?"

"No, I'd say that's normal." He took a drink of beer again, then nodded toward my food. "Jean told me you didn't have breakfast. I know you missed dinner. You should eat."

"My sisters worry too much." I picked up the burger again and this time took a bite. It was good. Really good.

"Would it help if I was there when you look at it?" Ryder asked.

I knew he was still talking about the bite, the mark. "Maybe?"

He nodded. "I haven't sent a report to my superiors yet."

"About Jake missing?"

"About any of this. Vampires, werewolves, gods, and mermen."

"Mermen?"

"Chris Lagon?"

He was being all casual about guessing what creature was who in town, like it was no big deal. It was kind of cute.

"Gill-man. There's a difference. If you ask Chris, he'll tell you. At length."

He grinned and shook his head. "That's...it's just amazing."

"What?"

"This town. These people."

I liked that he still considered someone like Chris a "people" even though an awful lot of folks might consider him a monster.

"Have you figured out what Bertie is?" I said to tease him.

"Bertie's something?" He sounded like a kid who had just been given a present to unwrap.

"She's something else, that's for sure."

"I don't suppose you'd give me a hint?"

"Nope. You're going to have to earn your supernatural

bingo card."

"Sounds like that's going to take some time."

"It will."

"Maybe even years."

"Maybe."

"Or a life time."

"Yep."

"You'll be around while I try to figure it out?"

"That's the plan."

"Well then, I am looking forward to it."

Oh. I studied his face. He was done with his food, sitting back in the chair, nursing his beer. And yes, that look said he'd meant exactly what I'd thought he'd meant. He was staying here. And not just for the creatures. Not just for his job. Not just for the town.

He was staying here for me.

Something tight in my chest that had been knotted for months, finally, finally relaxed. I felt a little lightheaded from relief.

He might not know all of my secrets, but he knew enough. He'd accepted them, and still wanted to be with me. I knew Ryder still held secrets I hadn't uncovered. But wouldn't it be fun to try?

"There's a mirror in the bathroom," I said.

"I'd expect so."

"I'm going to go look at it now."

He waited as I stood. I held out my hand. "Coming?"

He stood, took my hand. "Anywhere you go."

We walked into my tiny bathroom to face the thing I didn't want to face. As I stood there, in front of the mirror, with Ryder's arms holding me tight, my back against his front, I finally looked at the mark.

Two black circles, each small as a freckle, but perfectly round, and perfectly placed.

It was strange that something that had hurt so much, something that had the power to change me so deeply, left so little a mark. I felt like I should be wearing a sign that said "damaged" or "failure" or, at least, "injured." But some wounds only scar on the inside.

Ryder was silent, his breathing steady, his warmth an anchoring necessity.

When I looked back up in the mirror at him, he was watching me.

"I'd like to forget this, for at least a little while," I said softly.

"Forget what?" His breath was warm against the opposite side of my neck, my cheek.

"Everything. Except us."

His arms tightened and his palm, resting on my stomach, shifted to drag upward so his fingers brushed the edges of my breasts.

"We can do that," he said. "But I still have one more question left."

"Question?"

"We agreed to ten. I've only asked you nine."

I nodded, my eyes never leaving his in the mirror. "Anything."

"Do you love me?"

My heart was pounding hard, my pulse fluttering. I could pass. I could say no. But we'd promised each other the truth, and I was so tired of secrets.

"Yes."

I think both of us stopped breathing, afraid to shatter this fragile thing between us. "Do you love me?" I whispered.

"Yes."

One exhaled word, heat against my skin, solace in my soul, and we were breathing again. But there was something new in the air. Something new in the world. Something new about us.

The truth.

"Good," I said.

And when I turned in his arms, when he kissed me as we stumbled to my bed, slowly peeling off each other's clothes, I knew that it was one extraordinary, ordinary truth that would never change between us.

MORE ORDINARY MAGIC?
YOU BET!

GODS AND ENDS:
ORDINARY MAGIC – BOOK THREE

Coming Spring 2017

ACKNOWLEDGMENT

THINGS IN this book which might be true: canoe jousting, doomsday gas station attendants, Cherry City Derby Girls, umbrella hats, eggshell carving. Things which might be not be true: umbrella hats ever catching on in the Pacific Northwest.

This book was a lot of fun to write and I have a lot of people to thank for making it so. Dean Woods and Dejsha Knight, you give me the kind of feedback that always makes my stories better. Thank you both for being so amazing. Sharon Elaine Thompson, thank you for not only being a talented woman, but also for being an excellent copy editor. Thank you to Lou Harper for this spectacular cover, and thank you to Skyla Dawn Cameron for your formatting genius.

To the Deadline Dames and all the indie published writers out there sharing information, stories and joy—thank you for being a part of my life!

All my love and gratitude to my husband Russ Monk, and my sons Kameron and Konner Monk. The three of you make the world a better place, and always make me laugh–often at myself.

To our sweet, nocturnal dog Opal, who gave me the experience of breaking a thumb while in the middle of writing a book. Good times, dog. Good times.

And most importantly, to you, dear readers. Thank you for spending a little of your time in the world of Ordinary, Oregon. I hope you enjoyed your stay and will come back soon to see what is next in store for our heroes, monsters, lovers, gods, and extraordinarily ordinary folk.

ABOUT THE AUTHOR

DEVON MONK is a national best selling writer of urban fantasy. Her series include Ordinary Magic, House Immortal, Allie Beckstrom, Broken Magic, and Shame and Terric. She also writes the Age of Steam steampunk series, and the occasional short story which can be found in her collection: A Cup of Normal, and in various anthologies. She has one husband, two sons, and lives in Oregon. When not writing, Devon is either drinking too much coffee or knitting silly things.

Want to read more from Devon?
Follow her online or sign up for her newsletter at:
http://www.devonmonk.com.

CPSIA information can be obtained
at www.ICGtesting.com
Printed in the USA
BVOW08s2135020217
475217BV00001B/39/P